PRAISE FOR
The Day I Left You

"An intriguing mystery, a moving love story, and a fascinating glimpse of life in Cold War East Germany, all wrapped up in Caroline Bishop's beautiful, evocative writing. I loved it."

FRANCES QUINN, author of
The Lost Passenger

"Caroline Bishop has woven an intricate and mysterious love story, spanning the Cold War, the fall of the Berlin Wall, and the present day. Exploring the importance and impact of memory, identity, and how far we'll go to protect those we love, *The Day I Left You* is a tense, moving, stunning piece of historical fiction."

ASHLEY TATE, bestselling author of
Twenty-Seven Minutes

"*The Day I Left You* is several books in one. A beautiful exploration of love, expectation, and all the complexities of building a life together. It's also . . . a fascinating tale of the messed-up world of the Cold War . . . Bishop manages all of this in effortless, beautiful, and evocative prose. I absolutely adored this book!"

LOUISE FEIN, bestselling author of
The Hidden Child

"Affecting, assured, and moving. I can't remember the last time I read a novel with such historical authenticity. An unflinching view of love in its many forms. It made me ask myself what it takes to be courageous."

AMANDA GEARD, author of
The Moon Gate

"Set against the dark and forbidding backdrop of the Iron Curtain, *The Day I Left You* is a heart-wrenching love story with a page-turning mystery at its centre, evoked in Bishop's charming prose. Fans of her previous works will be delighted—this is her best novel yet!"
HEATHER MARSHALL, #1 bestselling author of
Looking for Jane and *The Secret History of Audrey James*

"In *The Day I Left You*, author Caroline Bishop expertly juggles multiple storylines spanning two time periods as she peels back the complicated layers of the abrupt end to a seemingly loving marriage, set against the backdrop of the Cold War. When Greta is granted permission to leave communist East Germany to marry Henry, who is British, she thinks that the biggest challenges in her new life will be the separation from her family and the acclimation to living in Britain. Instead, much darker and more tangled complications soon arise, but she keeps them from Henry, who is utterly blindsided when one day Greta disappears, leaving only a brief note of apology. Thirty-five years later, he stumbles upon a clue that may finally lead him to answers. Not only is the story at the heart of *The Day I Left You* a fascinating one, filled with deception, Cold War intrigue, and the bittersweet hope of new beginnings, but the storytelling itself is enthralling. We find ourselves in the alternating perspectives of Greta and Henry in both the early 1980s and in 2018, as the truth slowly comes to light. And as searing as the Cold War storyline is, perhaps the storyline of love, loss, and regret hits the most deeply. An intricately carved puzzle box of a novel, *The Day I Left You* is spectacular."

KRISTIN HARMEL, *New York Times* bestselling author of
The Paris Daughter

"Caroline Bishop's page-turner delves into eternal questions: How far will we go to protect loved ones? Can we truly know the people who share our lives? Which choices will define our lives? I loved *The Day I Left You* both for its striking portrait of the Cold War years and for the nuanced depiction of a marriage."

JANET SKESLIEN CHARLES, *New York Times* bestselling author of
Miss Morgan's Book Brigade

"Amid the danger of the ever-present Stasi and the mystery of a decades-long disappearance, *The Day I Left You* deftly braids past and present together into a fast-paced Cold War tale of love and letting go."

STEPHANIE MARIE THORNTON, *USA Today* bestselling author of
Her Lost Words

"*The Day I Left You* tells the story of a man who's unable to give up on the love he lost and a brave but misguided woman searching for redemption without any belief she'll find it. Part exploration of love and loss and having the strength to start over despite risk, and part mystery, Bishop's writing is full of flawed characters who feel stuck in their circumstances with no clear path out. A captivating meditation on the weight of guilt and the even heavier burden of having the courage, and the grace, to forgive."

CHARLENE CARR, bestselling author of
We Rip the World Apart

"Bishop skillfully creates a decades-long love story within a mystery within a Cold War adventure—a glorious Russian doll of expert storytelling. I was hooked from the start."

JENNY LECOAT, *New York Times* bestselling author of
Beyond Summerland and *The Girl from the Channel Islands*

Also by Caroline Bishop

The Lost Chapter

The Other Daughter

The Day
I Left You

Caroline Bishop

PUBLISHED BY SIMON & SCHUSTER

New York   Amsterdam/Antwerp   London
Toronto   Sydney   New Delhi

SIMON &
SCHUSTER
CANADA

A Division of Simon & Schuster, LLC
166 King Street East, Suite 300
Toronto, Ontario M5A 1J3

This Simon & Schuster Canada edition February 2025

SIMON & SCHUSTER CANADA and colophon are trademarks of Simon & Schuster, LLC

For information about special discounts for bulk purchases, please contact Simon & Schuster Special Sales at 1-800-268-3216 or CustomerService@simonandschuster.ca.

Interior design by Wendy Blum

Manufactured in the United States of America

10 9 8 7 6 5 4 3 2 1

Library and Archives Canada Cataloguing in Publication

Title: The day I left you / Caroline Bishop.
Names: Bishop, Caroline (Caroline Helen), author.
Description: Simon & Schuster Canada edition.
Identifiers: Canadiana (print) 20230533353 | Canadiana (ebook) 20230533361 | ISBN 9781668047262 (softcover) | ISBN 9781668047279 (EPUB)
Subjects: LCGFT: Historical fiction. | LCGFT: Novels.
Classification: LCC PR6102.I84 D39 2025 | DDC 823/.92—dc23

ISBN 978-1-6680-4726-2
ISBN 978-1-6680-4727-9 (ebook)

For Matt

Prologue

1984

I will never forget the day I left you.

It started like any other: the low, steady whistle of your breathing as you lay next to me, your sleepy smile as you woke and reached for me, your reluctance to haul yourself from the bed after the thrice-snoozed alarm clock blared a fourth time.

"Just five more minutes," you mock-pleaded, as you usually did.

I gave you a gentle shove. "Come on, you'll be late." I had to say it, as I would have on any normal day, but the words broke me a little. *Yes, I wanted to say, let's have five more minutes. Just five more minutes of our life together before everything has to change.*

We both showered and dressed—me in jeans and an oversized jumper, my usual working-from-home attire; you in the trousers and shirt you always wore to your engineering firm. I drank the Italian roast coffee you made every morning, and took last night's leftovers out of the fridge and put them in a Tupperware box for you. Pretending everything was normal, pretending my hands weren't shaking.

"Shall we go to the flicks tonight?" you asked as you threw on your coat and tucked the Tupperware in a pocket. "The latest *James Bond* film is still on."

I nodded. "Sure." I had to force the word out.

"It starts at seven thirty. Might have to work late, so shall I see you at the Odeon? Popcorn for dinner?"

"*Genau.*" It felt less of a lie to agree in German.

You scooped up your keys, attached to the carved wooden key chain I knew so well, and came over and kissed me, as you always did, however late you were running. I thought I was smiling at you, but your face fell into a frown. "You all right?" you asked.

I turned away, busied myself tidying the kitchen. "I didn't sleep too well, that's all." It was nothing new, not lately.

"Right, well, I'd better go. See you later." You touched me on the arm. "I love you."

"I know," I said, struggling to keep my voice steady. "You too, *Schatz.*"

When your face broke into the widest of smiles, I held my breath and concentrated on a minor shaving nick on your cheek.

And then you were gone, the front door had clicked shut and the house was still. I let out my breath as my eyes filled, then blinked rapidly to clear them. There was no time for that.

In the bedroom, I rummaged deep in the wardrobe for the modest backpack I'd prepared the day before and took it to the kitchen, where I unfolded the note I'd written—the short, inadequate note I'd decided, after many, many drafts, was better than nothing—and tucked it half under an empty vase on the kitchen table. I touched my rings, gave them a half-hearted tug, but no, I couldn't do that to you, couldn't do that to myself, despite everything else I was about to do. I walked down the hall to the front door, put on my coat, slung my handbag across my body, and grabbed the backpack, each movement weighted with disbelief as I took a step closer to something I didn't want to do. Something I *had* to do—for both of us—however awful it felt.

The flat was quiet; empty already, before I'd even left. I stood for a second, looking around me, and my eyes landed on your scarf, the one you were wearing the day we met. I picked it up and wound it around my neck. *Now go*, I told myself. *Go, before it's too late.*

When I closed the door behind me, I couldn't bring myself to look back.

PART ONE

1

Henry

Henry is halfway through his fish pie when he feels a sudden but not unfamiliar urge to get up from the table and leave the house. It is Wednesday evening, and he's at his sister and brother-in-law's place for a quiet dinner and catch-up, as he often is on Wednesdays. The food is always good (Charlotte's sticky toffee pudding is legendary), the conversation is comfortingly familiar (even Ian's bad jokes), and the evening provides a welcome break from his usual routine of dinner for one and a film on the box back home. So he feels a surge of resentment that tonight has been infiltrated by a stranger. It's been a while since Charlotte and Ian have done this to him.

"And despite me telling him it was the best thing to do, he chose to ignore me and his business went belly up three months later." Victoria shakes her head and makes a *tsk* sound. "I mean, I offer the best advice I can, but what can you do if people don't listen to you?"

Henry utters a murmur of agreement, though he hasn't, in fact, been entirely listening to her—the stranger—his mind drifting to the tricky issue of how to fix the broken legs of the wooden rocking chair that arrived in his workshop earlier that day.

"Oh, that must be so frustrating!" Charlotte rolls her eyes in exaggerated solidarity with Victoria. "Don't you think so, Henry?"

Henry looks at his sister. Her eyes are slightly glazed from the wine, yet the message in them is clear, the silent sibling communication they have shared for six decades working as strongly as ever. *Make an effort, won't you? I invited her here for you.*

I didn't ask you to, Henry thinks. "Absolutely," he says, and he sees Charlotte's lips purse when he doesn't elaborate.

His brother-in-law snorts from across the table. "Man of few words, our Henry," Ian says as he tops up his wineglass.

Henry sighs and throws a tight smile at Victoria. It's not her fault she's been drawn into this oft-repeated family boxing match: in the red corner, Charlotte, determined to find her brother a romantic partner; in the blue corner, Henry, who is perfectly fine on his own, thank you very much. "If you really want my opinion," he says, "I think advice should be offered with no expectation of it being followed. People must live their lives the way they want to. You can take a horse to water, but you can't make it drink."

"That's very true," Victoria says with emphasis, as though he's uttered something devastatingly insightful.

Charlotte and Ian exchange a knowing glance, though thankfully neither says what they are no doubt thinking: *Well, you should know, Henry.*

He takes another bite of fish pie, swallowing his mild annoyance along with it. He doesn't want to have to make polite conversation with a stranger, not even a *go-getter* like Victoria, who runs her own business development consultant agency and is extremely successful and lives in a beautiful house in the leafy, middle-class Oxford suburb of Wolvercote, right next to Port Meadow. Charlotte told him all this in an introductory spiel when Victoria arrived at the door, half an hour after Henry. He smiled at her and said hello and asked questions and feigned polite interest, but underneath he bristled. There is a reason Charlotte and Ian didn't tell him their tennis club friend would be joining them tonight. They knew what his reaction would be.

"Anyway, I don't want to bore you by talking about my work." Victoria leans forward. "Tell me about *yours*, Henry—it sounds much more interesting."

What's worse, he thinks as he replies with his standard answer—"I repair and restore modern and antique objects, primarily wooden ones, in my workshop in Jericho"—is that his well-intentioned but exasperating matchmakers have clearly told this poor woman he is willing to be set up. Or not in so many words, perhaps, but he can just hear Charlotte implying as much. *I may be biased, but he's such a lovely man, my brother, and he's just never found the right woman for him, you know? It's such a shame.*

He's been steered into so many "dates" by well-meaning friends and relatives over the years that he knows their tactics, can sniff out their futile hope at a thousand paces. *Maybe this'll be the one.*

But he knows it won't be. He had his *one* more than thirty years ago.

He doesn't want to be rude, though, so he answers a few more questions from Victoria about his work, expresses interest in Charlotte's renovation plans for their kitchen, and offers his brother-in-law an eye roll of solidarity when Ian reminds his wife that he lives here, too, and wouldn't mind a say, and then when an acceptable length of time has followed their demolition of the fish pie, he pushes back from the table. "That was fantastic, sis, but I must be off."

"What?" Charlotte gasps. "But I've made sticky toffee pudding!"

"Oh, I don't know." He pats his stomach, which is rounder than he'd like it to be, but he supposes he looks a lot better than some sixty-two-year-olds he knows. "Trying to ease off the puddings."

"Since when?" Ian laughs, his face a picture of incredulity. "Come on, Henry, Charlotte made it specially."

Emotional blackmail—another tactic.

"Well, *I'll* certainly go for dessert," Victoria says with a broad smile. "Never been one to deny myself a pud."

"And nor should you," Henry mumbles, but his chest tightens a little as he sneaks a glance at his watch. It's quite a trek on the bus from here in Kidlington to his home in Cowley on the other side of Oxford, and he wants an early night so he can get to his workshop first thing tomorrow. He needs to finish waxing Mrs. Cleary's table before she comes to collect it—it needs another coat to make it shine in exactly the way he wants— and then he's got an old love spoon to repair and oil, before starting on that beautiful handmade rocking chair, all before the end of the week.

"Just a small portion?" Charlotte pleads.

"All right, then," he relents, and his sister beams before heading to the kitchen.

"That's the spirit," Ian says. "You don't have anywhere else to be tonight, do you?" He turns to Victoria without waiting for an answer and lowers his voice, mock-conspiratorially. "He's probably planning to get in a bit of work before bed. He could retire, but he's chained to that workshop of his. Anyone would think you've nothing better to do, right, Henry?"

Ian laughs as he says it, but the familiar jibe sounds stale and tired to Henry's ears. He is passionate about his work, that's all, and has no interest in joining his newly retired brother-in-law on the tennis court, or down the pub to watch the football, or whatever else Ian thinks Henry should be doing instead of sitting in his workshop with a coffee and some music as he loses himself in the soothing rhythm of sanding and polishing. None of Ian's pastimes are better than that.

"I think your work sounds wonderfully satisfying, Henry," Victoria says, "and extremely worthwhile."

"Thank you." Henry tosses a pointed glance at his brother-in-law and then smiles at Victoria. She isn't unattractive, this fiftysomething businesswoman with her glossy brown hair (clearly dyed) and petite figure (tennis twice a week), and she's certainly the sort of woman his sister would call "a catch," especially given the difficulties of meeting new people at his age. But he can't help but be irritated with how Victoria ends every sentence with an upwards inflection (she's Australian and still sounds it, though she left twenty-five years ago) or the way she laughs more than is strictly necessary when he makes a little joke (he's really not that funny) or the excess of mascara on her eyelashes, gathering in little clumps at the tips.

"Here we go!" Charlotte returns with the pudding and a jug of sauce, and Henry is grateful to escape Victoria's hopeful gaze.

It's another half an hour before he's scraped every last drop of toffee sauce from his plate and feels able to leave. He thanks Charlotte for the meal, ignoring her clear disappointment, and offers Victoria a polite kiss on the cheek.

"Great to meet you, Henry. This was fun," she says, the upwards inflection on *fun* making her sound more doubtful than perhaps she intends. Or not.

"Yes, it was." He tries to sound earnest. "Lovely to meet you, too."

Victoria cocks her head, analysing him perhaps, or waiting for him to say something else, something better, but he can't manage it. Silence hangs in the air a moment too long, before Ian breaks the tension. "See you soon, then, Henry. Don't work too hard."

Outside, Henry zips his jacket to his chin against the February chill and looks at the sky. It's impossibly dark—no moon, and the stars are covered with cloud—and the breeze is picking up. He sighs, expelling a white puff into the cold air. His life wasn't meant to turn out like this, going home on his own to an empty house after an awkward blind date. He was meant to be with Greta. His wife, his love, his *one*. "Face facts, Henry," Charlotte said after Greta disappeared on that awful day, leaving him only that bewildering, devastating note to come home to after she failed to show up at the cinema, "maybe she wasn't as perfect as you made her out to be. Maybe she wasn't your *one* after all." But he refused to countenance his sister's words. "Well then, why'd she up and leave?" Charlotte said, adding with a touch of cynicism, "Maybe you can't ever really know a person."

It was a depressing statement then, and it still depresses him now.

He puts his hands in his pockets and starts to walk away.

"Henry," Charlotte calls softly from the door, and he turns, expecting to see the usual questions in his sister's face: *Why didn't he like Victoria? Why can't he just give people a bloody chance for once in his life?* "Take care, won't you?" she says instead, a little sadly.

He nods and lifts a hand in a parting gesture, before turning back down the road. No, he *knew* Greta, and she knew him, he thinks for the umpteenth time as he walks towards the bus stop. And he knew that her abrupt departure was out of character, that it wasn't as simple as Charlotte made out. But that doesn't answer the question his sister asked thirty-four years ago, the question he has tried to suppress but which resurfaces every time someone attempts to set him up with another woman; the question to which he has never, to his anguish, received a definitive answer: Why did his loving wife wake up one day and choose to disappear from his life without a trace?

2

Greta

East Berlin, German Democratic Republic, February 1982

If I'm going to tell this story properly, Henry, then I should go back to the beginning: to the day I met you.

Did I fall in love with you at first sight? I don't know. I'm not sure I believe that's possible, but I did know, right from the moment I clapped eyes on you, that you would be a significant presence in my life.

It was a Thursday. I'd been at university that day, sitting through lectures, eating lunch with my classmates in the cafeteria, working on my latest assignments like the keen student I was. Lena, my best friend, had been at her dreary secretarial job, where she typed up correspondence and reports with efficiency if not enthusiasm, and we'd met up in the evening at the Alextreff in Mitte, as we often did, to drink martinis or vodka-cola and dance and let off steam.

13

We were two young women born and bred in the Hauptstadt der Deutschen Demokratischen Republik who were trying to live as fully as we could within the constraints of our homeland.

You were a twenty-six-year-old British machine engineer venturing behind the Iron Curtain for the first time.

When I think back now, it astounds me how that moment would change our lives forever.

It was Friedrich I saw first, winding his way along the edge of the crowded dance floor towards the tables at the back, where Lena and I had just sat down, sweaty and slightly drunk, after dancing to whatever the DJ had played. It was '82, so perhaps the Human League, or Michael Jackson, Duran Duran or David Bowie. The main reason we liked the Alextreff was because the DJs there seemed to play more Western music than Eastern, contrary to the government rule that it should be the reverse, and anything that pushed against our country's many, many rules was just fine by us.

Lena nudged my arm and rolled her eyes in Friedrich's direction. "Your boyfriend's here."

"Don't." I glared at her, and she laughed.

"*Hallo,* Greta, Lena." Friedrich held up a hand in greeting as he approached us, flashing his eager smile. It was a frigid February night outside, and his glasses were fogged up from the sudden heat in that humid, smoky bar.

"Fancy seeing you here," Lena said with a smirk, and promptly lit a cigarette, as though his presence required the relief of nicotine. "Did you pay to jump the queue?"

"*Nein,* my friend Günther is on the door tonight."

"How are you, Fred?" I smiled, trying, as always, to make up for Lena's hostility. She'd never liked my childhood friend and running partner—didn't trust him, she said, but then Lena didn't trust anyone since some unknown informer had shopped her uncle to the Stasi for attempting to organise a pro-democracy protest. I knew Friedrich was harmless, though.

His mother and mine were old friends; we'd grown up together, trained side by side for sports days and Spartakiaden. And although I knew he liked me more than I liked him, I'd never seen the need to keep my distance. The competitor in me enjoyed testing my legs against his on our regular early morning runs, and if I'm honest, my ego enjoyed his attentions, even though I had no interest in taking things beyond friendship. It irritated Lena that he often seemed to turn up where he knew we'd be, but I didn't really mind—and especially not that night, because, as it turned out, he brought me you.

"*Ja, alles gut,*" Fred replied, before turning and calling behind him in English, "Over here!" and it was then that I saw you.

Fairly tall, but ever-so-slightly stooped, as though uncomfortable with your own height. Shoulder-length light brown hair that skimmed the collar of a dark blue and red jacket with an Adidas logo, a green scarf looped around your neck. A kind, open face, cheeks flushed from the chill outside, and an uncertain smile that told me you weren't totally at ease in this place yet were determined to make a good impression.

Well, you did, Henry.

"Who are your friends, Fred?" I asked, smiling at you and another, older man standing behind you.

"Here is Henry and Mike, from England," Friedrich said in his badly accented English. "They come to install machinery from Britain at the factory." He grinned at both of you as you shrugged off your jackets. "I am being your supervisor, *ja*? And interpreter for the German. And friend!" He slapped you on the shoulder. "This is Lena, and here is my very good friend Greta. She speak English more better than me."

I stood up and put out my hand to Mike, and then to you, and it felt as though you had been sent to us, like the good coffee and Swiss chocolate my aunt Ilsa sometimes mailed from Westberlin.

"Hello, Henry," I said.

"Hi." Your smile broadened and caught in your eyes—vivid green-blue irises, I noticed. "Nice to meet you, Greta."

You didn't pronounce my name properly, but I didn't correct you right then. "*Grey-ta*," I would tell you later, when this initial encounter had morphed into something more, "not *Gretta*," but in those first moments your English pronunciation simply delighted me, like everything else about you.

Did you realise the effect you were having on me? Did you understand how incredibly thrilling it was for me to meet people like you and Mike? The Wall that had carved my city in two for almost all of my lifetime had physically divided us *Ostlers* from Westerners like you and attempted to block out your culture in the process—the books and music and television that our ruling Socialist Unity Party considered so ideologically corrupting. Although it was fighting a losing battle on that score by the time I met you, the physical barrier was still a tightly controlled divide, so it was rare I encountered Westerners. I'd mingled with foreign students at my university, but most of them were from other communist countries; I'd sometimes chatted to visiting West Germans right there in the Alextreff, as they sampled Eastern nightlife before their day visas expired at midnight; and I once got talking to some American tourists when they asked me for directions in the street. But I'd never met anyone from England. So yes, I was thrilled to meet you, Henry. Thrilled by your English accent, your Adidas jacket, your Levi's jeans, and everything else that indicated your delicious foreignness.

"You want something to drink?" Friedrich shouted to you and Mike over the music.

"Beer, please," you replied, but you were still looking at me, and I found I couldn't tear my eyes away from you, either.

"I get you a Moulin Rouge," Friedrich said. "Is better!"

"*Für mich bitte auch*," I said to him, and he wandered off in search of drinks as I stood rooted in front of you.

I wanted to reach out and touch you, but I didn't.

I wanted to say something, but my mouth was stopped by an uncharacteristic shyness.

And I knew, in that instant, that my reaction to you wasn't down to your Englishness at all, that it had nothing to do with politics and walls and the thrill of fraternising with someone from *the other side*. It was about you. It was a gut feeling. An instant attraction. An anticipation of good things to come if I stayed by your side.

I sensed Lena's knowing gaze on me as I beamed at you and my world shifted imperceptibly on its axis.

What happened next? As I remember it, Lena pulled Mike onto the dance floor and Friedrich got drawn into conversation with someone else he seemed to know, and suddenly the two of us were alone, as I felt sure we were meant to be, smiling at each other across the Formica tabletop.

"You don't like to dance?" I asked.

You shook your head. "Two left feet, I'm afraid."

I laughed. *Zwei linke Füße*. It tickled me that the same expression existed in both our languages. "I'm sure that's not true."

"Oh, it is. No rhythm at all, sadly. It's a lot safer for everyone if I just sit here with a drink." You gestured to your glass with raised eyebrows. "But what exactly is this thing Friedrich got for me?"

"A Moulin Rouge. Peach schnapps, orange juice, and red wine."

"Ah." You lifted your glass. "Well, when in Rome . . ."

"Pardon?"

"Oh, er, it just means when you're somewhere new you should try the local customs."

I grinned. "When in Berlin, you say *Prost*."

"*Prost*," you repeated in a delightfully terrible accent, and we clinked glasses, our eyes meeting for a few seconds until you took a sip and pulled a face. "It's . . . interesting."

I laughed, my eyes roving over your face. I couldn't get enough of you, this handsome *Engländer*, this fascinating slice of the West, sitting right here in front of me in my favourite disco. "Can I tell you something?" I said. "I study English at university, but you're the first English person I've ever met. Isn't that crazy?"

"You're a student?" There was a hint of surprise in your voice, as though you wouldn't have expected a girl from the DDR to go to university.

"Yes, at Humboldt. English language, translation, and interpretation, final year." And obligatory Russian, sport, and Marxism-Leninism, but I didn't mention that.

"You speak it very well."

Warmth bloomed in my chest. "Thank you."

"I'm sorry I don't speak any German."

"Don't be sorry. I feel like I've been waiting my whole life to speak English to an Englishman."

You smiled, and a faint blush rose to your cheeks. "I'd never met a German until arriving here on Monday—let alone an East German," you said, and I was struck by how little it mattered where either of us was from. We were strangers from opposite sides of a divide, but we were the same, really, weren't we? Two young people starting out in life, finding our way, looking for something that we couldn't really identify until we found it.

I leaned forward over the table, my heart skittering in my chest. "And what do you think of us?"

You glanced down at your drink and that blush deepened. "I think I want to get to know you a bit more." Then you looked up again, laughed self-consciously, and a heady rush ran through me as I understood that whatever I was feeling was mutual.

We couldn't stop talking after that. You told me you were from Oxford, a place that seemed as exotic to me as the Amazon jungle or the plains of Africa. You talked about your job as a junior machine engineer, which I didn't really understand but was grateful for, since it had brought you here. I told you a little about my parents and my teenage sister Angelika and my studies—all the usual things people talk about when meeting someone for the first time. But what I recall more than anything we said is how it felt to be sitting there with you that night, as though an invisible, visceral force was drawing us together. It was loud, busy, and hot in the Alextreff, yet that only served to push us towards each other. We leant close to speak, faces centimetres apart, and I felt the heat of you, caught the scent of you. I saw your hand curled around your glass and had to stop myself reaching for it and entwining my fingers with yours. I took in every detail of you as though I'd never seen such things before: the cold-chafed skin on your knuckles, the day-old stubble on your jaw, and the startling brightness of your eyes, which looked at me with the same budding hope I felt within myself.

One exchange I do remember clearly, however.

"Have you ever been to the West?" You asked it in the same gently inquisitive tone you'd used during the rest of our conversation, but the surprise of it jolted the smile from my face. Did you even have to ask? Or was it simply unfathomable to you that a country could prevent its citizens from travelling wherever they liked?

"Of course not," I said softly, but you must have seen my face fall.

"Sorry, I—"

"It's fine." I shook my head, revived my smile. "I'm determined I will, one day."

I meant it with a passion, though I was naive to think I'd ever achieve it as a young woman. Pensioners were allowed to visit the West, while people with first-degree relatives across the Wall could be granted permission for important occasions like births, weddings, and funerals, if the authorities deemed them unlikely to defect. The rest of us made the most of what other socialist countries could offer. I'd travelled to Bulgaria and Czechoslovakia with friends, and each year my family took a camping trip to the Ostsee or Lake Balaton in Hungary, places I liked well enough, yet it was the forbidden West I dreamed about: Paris and London and Venice and palm-fringed Californian beaches. I'd studied hard and played by the rules in order to get a coveted place on my university course, hoping that as a professional interpreter or translator there might be a slim chance of being sent beyond the Wall to work. After all, Friedrich's father knew someone who knew someone else who worked for an international organisation and occasionally got to travel to the West, so if *he* could do it, perhaps I could, too. But I was deluding myself, Lena said, if I thought the authorities would let me do that without demanding more from me than I was prepared to give them, and she was probably right. Sometimes I felt that my life was a balancing act, that I was constantly assessing which compromises I was willing to make to stay out of trouble and advance my dreams, and which ones I wouldn't be able to live with. So while I'd dutifully recited the Party line in the political exam I had to pass in order to be accepted on to my degree course, I'd sidestepped several attempts by officials to get me to actually join the Party. I was walking a tightrope, Henry, trying to play the good socialist citizen while dreaming of a different kind of life, but that night, when I met you, I fell right off that tightrope. Because good socialist citizens didn't associate with our capitalist, Western foe, and yet there I was, laughing and flirting with a British man in a place where there were bound to be *Horch und Guck*, as we called Berlin's many eyes and ears. And I realised in that moment there was one area of my life in which I wasn't willing to compromise, however much it could derail my dreams: love.

"Hey, *Freunde!*" We both looked up, startled, as Friedrich slid into a chair next to us. You threw me a little glance of regret or apology or sadness—whatever it was, I felt it, too—before turning to greet him, and the forcefield we'd created between the two of us dissolved.

My face must have betrayed me.

"What?" Fred said, nudging my arm in friendly jest, but he knew, he knew. How could he not?

I suppose when I think about it, that's what caused everything that came later. If only I'd better disguised how quickly and hard I fell for you, if only I'd given some thought to Fred's feelings, perhaps things would have gone differently. But what's done is done. I can't go back. I can't change any of this, much as I've wanted to over the years.

We didn't get the chance to resume our conversation that night. Friedrich made sure—intentionally or not—that we couldn't be alone again, and sometime later Mike said you both had to go, that you had to pick something up in Leipzig the next day and had an early start.

"I hope we'll see you again," Mike said to Lena and me. "We'll be here for eight weeks."

Eight weeks! "I hope so, too," I said, unable to stop myself glancing at you.

"Yes, I—" you started, but Fred cut you off.

"So much work to do at the factory! No time for drinks after this, I think."

I half laughed, but before I could object to this ridiculous excuse, Lena chimed in. "*Ja*, too bad. But it was nice to meet you. *Tschüß!*"

I turned to her, eyebrows raised. Her face was flushed and bright from dancing, but I felt the slight pull of her hand on my arm, the hint of a warning in her expression. *You've had fun tonight, but tell this cute Englishman goodbye and walk away*, it said. *He's not worth the hassle it could bring you.*

But I couldn't do that. It was already too late.

"Oh, that's a shame," you said. "I suppose this is goodbye, then." You gave me a rueful smile and started moving away from us, trailing Friedrich and Mike back through the tables towards the door. My chest lurched in panic, and I barely hesitated; I shrugged off Lena's hand and followed you, my pulse quickening in my throat, until I was close enough to reach out and touch your arm.

You turned.

"I want to see you again," I said, because it was the simple truth.

I watched as your eyes widened and a smile spread slowly across your face until every part of it lit up. "Just say when."

"Saturday. By the fountain in Alexanderplatz, ten a.m."

You nodded, and your hand brushed mine with the faintest of touches as you replied, "I'll be there."

3

Henry, 2018

Henry cycles through central Oxford to his Jericho workshop on Thursday morning: down the Cowley Road, over Magdalen Bridge and up the High, through St. Giles and down Little Clarendon Street, pedalling hard against a brisk wind. He locks his bike to a lamppost outside his workshop and fumbles in his coat pocket for the door key, his hand closing around the little wooden bear key chain he's used for so long. The door is stiff in the cold and he has to put his shoulder into it to push it open. Inside, he breathes in the familiar smell of wax, varnish, and wood shavings as he unwinds the scarf from his neck and hangs up his coat. Here he is again, in his safe haven, his happy place.

He runs his hand along Mrs. Cleary's table, feeling the smoothness of the surface, the result of hours of sanding. It's always worth it, the effort he takes. The objects he repairs have to be perfect before they leave his workshop. It pains him a little to think of the scars of life they will inevitably pick up once out of his care: the water ring from a vase of flowers placed on an oak table, the oily residue from a cat buffing its cheek against a teak chair leg, the dents and scratches left by an overzealous toddler driving his toy truck into a polished mahogany sideboard.

This table embodies the reason he set up this place, after years of repairing and servicing industrial machinery. He wanted to mend objects with stories behind them. Objects with a history, born out of love and human connection, objects with meaning, like that carved wooden key chain, which he's cherished ever since Greta gave it to him. So he took a woodworking course and learned about joinery and turning and marquetry; he discovered the way different woods react to different atmospheric conditions, and how to sand them and use oil, wax, or varnish to bring out the natural patterns in the wood grain. Then, because he could, because he had the time and nothing better to do with his evenings and weekends but sit in an empty house, he took metalworking classes, and a one-off workshop on watchmaking, and a Saturday morning ceramics course. Now, he can repair most things that come into his workshop (and if he can't, he usually knows someone who can), but he specialises in wood, his first love. No other material brings him quite the same joy.

The story behind this mahogany table has particularly touched him. It was a gift from Mrs. Cleary's late husband, she told him when she brought it in. Mr. Cleary had had it specially made on the birth of their son, who died in a traffic accident aged nineteen. The way she spoke about both of them—the son who died ten years ago, the husband who passed away last year—made his heart clench. The table was the embodiment of her love for them, and theirs for her. It was the most precious thing she owned. "Take good care of it, won't you?" she said as she inched out of the door. "You have my word," he told her, and he meant it. He would treat this table as though it were a gift for his own wife on the birth of their own son.

If his wife hadn't disappeared thirty-four years ago.

If they'd had children before she did.

Henry makes himself a coffee and turns on the radio, tuning out Radio 4's dreary prophecy of snowstorms in favour of an eighties music station. He picks up a soft cloth and dips it in the wax before applying it to the table's surface, watching it sink into the wood. He breathes out and the last of the tension left over from the previous night's dinner slips away.

It takes him a good hour to apply a coat, perhaps more, but he's so involved in the work that the time races past. When he's finished, he stands back and looks at it with a critical eye, but there's nothing to criticise. It is wonderful. He hopes Mrs. Cleary agrees. Actually, he knows she will. It's almost the part he loves best, giving the object back to the person who entrusted it to him, knowing he will have exceeded their expectations, will have given new life to something that is so special to them. *Almost*— because it's like a little death, too, parting with an object after he's put so much time and care into it.

He is writing Mrs. Cleary's name on a white envelope, his invoice tucked inside, when there's a knock on the door of his workshop. He sees a face through the glass, partly obscured by the classic gold lettering painted by a signwriter friend of his a few years back: HENRY HENDERSON REPAIRS. It's the face of a young woman: flushed cheeks, blond hair flying in the wind. When he opens the door for her (he usually keeps it locked, unless he knows he has appointments; he doesn't often get drop-ins), the wind seems to enter with her.

"Gosh, thank you, it's a bit breezy out, I thought I'd be blown right off the pavement! Am I in the right place?"

She is all noise; not only her words, which interrupt a track by the Cure that he's always loved ("Friday I'm in Love"), but the gasps of effort she expels, as though exhausted from an arduous journey, along with the crinkle of the large plastic bag in her hand and the swish of her leather handbag against her down jacket. Not to mention the whimpers coming from the baby strapped to her chest.

"Oh God, he chooses to wake up *now*? He's only been asleep for fifteen minutes, so I thought I'd get away with popping in here. Sorry."

Henry shakes his head. "Not a problem. How can I help?"

"Well." She walks over to Mrs. Cleary's table and, before he can stop her, sets down the plastic bag on its surface. "I've got this thing—"

"Not there, please!" He rushes over, removes the bag, and runs his hand over the table to check for marks.

"Oh, sorry." She smiles, as though it's nothing, what she did. "As I was saying, I've got this thing— Oh!" She points to the envelope on the tabletop. "Cleary? Janet Cleary, by any chance?"

"You know her?"

"Works part-time at Oscar's nursery." She pats her baby's back. "Lovely woman, and truly awful what happened to her son—but then if you will drink and drive. Thank God he only killed himself and not someone else as well. And then the poor woman had to deal with her husband all on her own."

Henry blinks. "Deal with?"

"Oh, you don't know?" She raises her eyebrows. "Another parent I know from the nursery told me he used to hit her. *He* liked the drink, too. Don't know why she stayed with him for so many years. Still, at least she's got a reprieve now he's gone. Apparently, she's like a new woman since he popped his clogs. Not that it's any of my business, but the mums at the nursery do like to gossip. Worse than schoolkids." She jiggles the baby, whose whimpers are growing more frequent. Henry is still digesting this new information, this brutally prosaic alternative to the story he'd considered so poignant, when she gestures to the plastic bag. "Anyway, so about this thing. It's a wooden vase, though I've never used it for real flowers since I assume wood doesn't hold water, but perhaps I'm wrong, I don't know." Henry opens his mouth to answer but she carries on. "Last week my eldest knocked it off the windowsill—she's just started ballet lessons, you see, and was attempting a pirouette—and it hit the tile floor and now it's got this great big crack all down it and I considered throwing it away but it seems a shame because I've always been quite fond of it."

"Does it have special significance to you then?" Henry takes the vase out of the bag.

She shrugs. "Only that Jack bought it for me, I suppose. That's my husband. We were in some French market years ago, I forget exactly when, and I just liked it. The guy who made it was very passionate about what he did, I seem to remember, so he probably talked us into it, even though I didn't exactly *need* it, but then Jack said treating yourself isn't about *need*, is it, so he bought it for me." She pauses a second, an expression Henry can't interpret flashing across her face. "Anyway, it's looked very lovely sitting on the windowsill, and I was quite sad when it got broken, so I asked my friend Sally and she recommended you and here I am! What do you think?"

Henry turns the vase in his hands. It's been carved from a single piece of beechwood, and done beautifully, he can see that. But there's a big ugly crack all down one side. An easy fix, though. "Yes, it shouldn't be too difficult," he says. "Leave it with me, and I should be able to do it by early next week."

"Oh good!" Her face lights up. "That would be wonderful."

Henry takes his order book from the shelf. "Your name and phone number?"

"Lucy Kenny."

He hands her a price and a holding receipt. "If you come back on Monday afternoon, I'll have it ready."

"Monday." She frowns. "I've got a sleep clinic appointment for this one at one o'clock—he's *still* not sleeping through the night, the little monkey—and then I have to pick my daughter up from preschool at three, but I should be able to come between the two, yes, if I'm organised, which isn't always guaranteed because these things are rarely under my control." She laughs. "You wouldn't believe how long it takes to get Oscar ready to go anywhere. Change him, feed him, put clothes on, pack at least one spare set, change him again if he soils his nappy right before we go out as he likes to do, pack snacks, toys, and Rab the rabbit. It's like preparing a military operation!"

Henry feels himself swaying backwards slightly, buffeted by her words

27

like a sapling in a gale. "Right, well, I'll see you on Monday, if you can make it."

But the woman—Lucy—has already turned from him and is looking around the workshop, unzipping her jacket as she does. She picks up the wooden love spoon from his workbench—the next object he must repair and re-oil, to give back to the woman who received it from her husband on their first anniversary twenty-five years ago. He recoils slightly to see it in Lucy's hands, but she puts it down again before he can say anything.

"It smells so good in here. Though I suppose you could get high breathing in varnish fumes all day." She laughs again. "And it's so calm and peaceful. Gosh, what I'd give to spend a day here all by myself. Want to swap?" She pats the back of her son's sling, and Henry utters a noncommittal mumble as the baby starts to cry properly then. "Here we go again. Well, I won't disturb your enviable peace any longer. Thank you, Henry Henderson. I will be back." She picks up her bags and walks to the door.

And it is then, just before she turns to go, that he sees it.

His stomach roils.

"Sorry," he says, "can you . . ."

She looks up at him, her face a question mark.

"Your necklace. Where did you get it?"

"This?" She extracts the pendant from her neck and holds it up, and he sees it more clearly, now: the way the metal is twisted into a three-dimensional heart, the intricacy of the design, like lace.

It can't be.

"My mum gave it to me ages ago," Lucy says. "I can't remember why—my birthday maybe? Or Christmas? Or some other time, because Mum's good like that; she often gives me little random presents whenever she feels like it. She'll say, 'Oh, I saw this thing and thought of you' and produce a table runner or a pair of earrings or a notebook with a cat on it or whatever—once she even gave me a spatula, just out of the blue, and I did laugh, but it's actually been pretty useful since. Anyway, I like this necklace very much—it's unusual, isn't it? I'd never seen anything like it."

Henry nods, prevented from speaking for a moment by the memories that rise up: arriving home to find Greta wearing a strangely beautiful bracelet she'd made by absently entwining paper clips in front of the telly; the smile she gave him when he presented her with some gardening wire and a pair of pliers the next day; the intricate, complex pieces she was making—obsessively almost, like a nervous tic—in the weeks before she left.

"Your mother?" he says to Lucy. "Do you know where she got it from?"

"No clue! A gift shop maybe? Or a craft market? I don't know. Not in Oxford in any case. She doesn't live here, my mum. She's up in Nottingham, where I'm from—as is Jack. We only moved here a year ago, just before Oscar was born, because Jack took a new job that he thought would be brilliant—although it's not turned out so great, to be honest—and I thought, well, I suppose I'm going to be on maternity leave anyway for a bit, so I guess for me it . . ."

Henry tunes out. He is mistaken. It couldn't possibly be one of Greta's creations. He is reading too much into things.

". . . and it was a good opportunity for him, so I said let's go for it, and hopefully I can pick up work again later. You have to make these sacrifices for each other in a relationship, don't you, and it was my turn; hopefully down the line it'll be his turn. *Shit!*—excuse my French—is that the time? I really have to stop blathering and get on. I'll see you on Monday."

And then she is gone.

His day's work is finished, after that. He tries and fails to keep his mind on the job, before throwing in the towel and cycling home as fast as the road conditions allow.

That necklace. He can almost picture Greta making it: the concentration etched on her forehead; the way her fingers worked so nimbly, twisting and bending the wire as her blond hair fell forward around her cheeks; the intense focus she gave it, so much so that she wouldn't hear if he asked her a question. "Hmm?" she'd say, looking up, fingers paused, "what was that, *Schatz*?"

Thirty-four years have passed since he last saw her lovely face. So long ago that the pain of the day she left him is no longer raw, but his body still remembers it, like an ankle that swells in hot weather years after being broken.

There he was, standing in the foyer of the cinema on George Street, two tickets to *Never Say Never Again* in his hand. He waited and waited, a little confused, then slightly annoyed, then worried, before hurrying home, hoping to find her there, to feel the relief of seeing she'd simply forgotten, or been distracted by her latest translation project.

But all he found was that note. That awful, unbelievable note.

> *I'm sorry, Schatz. I can't stay. Just forget about me.*
> *You can do so much better.*
> *All my love, G x*

He sat with that slip of paper for hours, analysing every word.

I can't stay—not *I don't want to stay.*

I'm sorry—as though she was regretful, as though she knew she was doing the wrong thing.

Schatz—that German term of endearment he so loved hearing from her: treasure, sweetie, darling; something you don't say unless you care about the person.

All my love—because she still loved him, she did; he knew it in his heart.

His wife had left him, and he had absolutely no idea why.

Other people were quick to offer their theories, however.

"What a cow! She clearly just used you to leave the GDR," was Charlotte's blunt verdict. "But look, Henry, you'll get over this—plenty more fish in the sea and all that."

"Sorry, sir," said the young policeman who came round to their flat, a patronising tone in his voice after he read Greta's note, "she's not missing, she's left you, that's all. Maybe she's run off with another bloke?"

"Ah, mate, I'm so sorry, she seemed so nice, too. Women, eh?" That from his colleague Mike, who'd met Greta the same day he did, and who might, Henry had thought, have had some useful interpretation of her disappearance.

"After all we did to help her fit in!" his mother commented, adding blithely, "But it's probably for the best, darling."

They all thought he should simply get over her and move on.

But he didn't want to. He *couldn't*. Not without an explanation that actually made sense to him, not without knowing why a happily married woman would so abruptly walk out on the husband who adored her.

He's gone thirty-four years without an answer. Thirty-four years without word of her whereabouts or even her very existence. Anything could have happened in that time. She could have died. He's almost managed to convince himself she must have done, that death is the only explanation for such prolonged silence, though he's never had any proof of it.

But now he wonders if the necklace worn by his garrulous young customer in the workshop today was actually a sign that she hasn't died after all.

Unless he's imagining the similarity.

When he gets to the house, he goes straight inside, neglecting to lock his bike in the shed, as he usually does, and heads directly to the attic. The cardboard packing box isn't hard to find, since Henry isn't one for mess. Each one is well marked, so although he hasn't touched some of them for many years, he has to read the labels on only two or three until he finds the one he wants: SUMMERTOWN STUFF.

Charlotte helped him take most of Greta's belongings to a charity shop when it became clear she wasn't coming back. Helped? No, practically forced—"Enough's enough, Henry, you can't live in this shrine"—but he surreptitiously saved a few things and brought them with him when, a few months after she left, he moved out of the Summertown flat he could no longer afford on his own and in with his sister and her then-boyfriend, Ian.

He takes out a jumper he always loved Greta in and holds it up to his nose, but there is nothing of her in it anymore. In an old biscuit tin are some letters covered in her familiar handwriting—letters of love and longing that she sent him before they were married, when they were living in different countries, a wall between them. And then there's her jewellery. She took a few bits with her when she left, and afterwards he spent hours trying to analyse her choices. Did the fact she took her wedding rings mean she still loved him? Did she leave behind the necklace he gave her for her twenty-fourth birthday as a sign she wasn't coming back—or a sign she would?

He delves deeper until he finds what he's looking for: a plastic Safeway bag containing several small items wrapped in tissue paper. Firstly, a bracelet. It's made of plain grey gardening wire, twisted and coiled and shaped into something with a unique kind of beauty. He puts it down and picks up a single earring, similar in design and just as unusual. And then there's a necklace: a long leather strap with a pendant hanging from it, the metal twisted and shaped into a three-dimensional heart.

His breath catches in his throat. No, he wasn't mistaken, back in the workshop; the necklace in his hand now is so like the one belonging to that woman—Lucy. Could someone else really have adopted such a similar style, or does this mean that Greta is still out there somewhere, still making her jewellery after all these years?

4

GRETA, 1982

For a few moments, I wondered if you hadn't come. The Brunnen der Völkerfreundschaft in Alexanderplatz was a popular meeting place, and despite the biting February chill and silvery sky, it was fairly busy that Saturday morning. As I walked towards the colourful fountain I scoured faces, but I couldn't see you. My chest tightened. Maybe I'd made a fool of myself in the Alextreff and you'd laughed to your colleague afterwards about the brazen East German girl who'd asked you out.

But I think I already knew that you weren't that type of man, and when I finally caught sight of you sitting on the low wall around the water, the tension inside me dissolved and I couldn't stop my mouth tugging into a grin.

You hadn't yet seen me, and as I walked towards you, I took you in: the slightly anxious expression on your beautiful face; that same green scarf you'd been wearing when I met you, pulled high around your neck in the cold; your hands deep in the pockets of your Western jacket. I glanced down at myself: my best Wranglers, a gift from Aunt Ilsa in Westberlin, which were thin and fraying now after so much wear; my old winter coat, the nicest I'd been able to find in the shops three years ago, which wasn't saying much; and my boots, cheap synthetic versions of the leather pixie boots worn by Western girls I'd seen on television. What would you think of me? Would I be enough? I inhaled deeply and held my head up as I walked on.

I was a few footsteps away when you saw me. Your face broke into a smile, and a fizzing sensation shot through my body.

"Hi," you said with a touch of surprise, as though you hadn't expected me to turn up.

"*Hallo*, Henry." Of course I was going to turn up; I'd thought of little but you since we'd met. "How was Leipzig?"

"Oh, it was . . . interesting." Later, when we knew each other better, you told me you'd found it grey, polluted, a bit depressing. "But I'm glad to be back in Berlin." Your eyes met mine, and my cheeks prickled as I understood the subtext. Glad to be here, with me.

"What do you want to do today?"

You shrugged. "Anything. Everything. Whatever you want to do, Greta."

"I thought I could show you some of the city?"

"I'd love that."

We walked back across the pedestrian square to the street where I'd parked my scooter—a little blue moped, do you remember?—and you climbed on behind me. You slipped your arms around my waist, and I turned to look at you, giddy with our proximity. Your face was so close I could see the white cloud of your breath mingling with mine in the air. "Ready?"

Those sea-blue eyes crinkled at the corners. "Ready."

I started the motor, and we set off around the city, joining Ladas and Trabants and Wartburgs on streets wet with winter slush. Past the imposing Dom and the redbrick Rathaus, down the wide avenues of Karl-Marx-Allee and Unter den Linden, past the twin towers of Frankfurter

Tor and the historic buildings of Humboldt University, and as close as was possible to the towering pillars of the Brandenburg Gate, that symbol of my divided city, where the Wall rose up as East met West.

We stopped from time to time and I played tour guide, pointing out cultural landmarks like the Staatsoper, the Berliner Ensemble, and the Kino International, showing you the *Kneipen* where Lena and I liked to go to drink if the unfriendly waiters deigned to give us a table, and taking you into the glossy, marble-floored Palast der Republik, the seat of our parliament and a popular nightspot for drinking, dancing, and bowling. Was I trying to impress you? Perhaps a little. Perhaps I wanted to show you the best of my city, but I wasn't so in thrall to it that I would avoid the rest, so I also pointed out the people queueing outside Centrum, the state department store, no doubt hoping to obtain whatever rarely available goods happened to be in stock that day; the visible bullet holes in Mitte's soot-stained prewar buildings, which sat in stark contrast to the rows and rows of new, identical prefab apartment blocks in the east of the city; and the vast, glass customs hall at Friedrichstraße S-Bahn station, where West German visitors tearfully left their *Ostler* relatives behind until next time—the reason we dubbed it the Tränenpalast, or Palace of Tears.

You seemed genuinely interested in it all, asking me thoughtful questions and never criticising the things that I now know must have seemed strange or hard to comprehend (even though I wouldn't have cared if you did), and I wished with my whole being that you could show me around your home city just as I was showing you around mine.

"Can you ice skate?" I asked when we stopped to eat *Ketwurst* at a snack bar, ketchup dripping down our fingers. It was still early in the afternoon, but the light was already fading, and steam from the boiled sausage spiralled into the cold air.

"I've never tried," you replied between bites.

"Do you want to?"

You raised your eyebrows. "What are your hospitals like?"

I laughed; I already loved your dry wit. "They're good."

You nodded, mock frowning. "Then I'll risk it."

So we finished eating, and I drove us to the new SEZ leisure centre in Friedrichshain, where we spent an hour tottering and laughing our way around the ice rink.

"*Ja*, I think your two left feet do not help you with this, either," I joked as you fell on the rink for the third time.

Your mouth dropped open. "Hey, how about a little sympathy here?!"

I held out my hand to pull you up. "Are you hurt?"

"Only my ego." You grinned and clutched me as you found your balance, your touch sending sparks skittering up my arms. "I think that's enough for me, though. I'll sit over there while you show me how it's done."

I guided you to the side and then took off around the rink, aware of your eyes following my body as I showed off as best I could, wanting to provoke the broad smile that often animated your shy, gentle face, and revelling in the way you looked at me, as though I was the best thing you'd ever seen.

"I've had a brilliant time, Greta," you said when I reluctantly dropped you off at your boarding house in the early evening. You'd agreed to meet Mike for dinner, and you didn't want to break your promise, which made me like you even more.

"So have I." I felt like crying that this magical day was over. That you would go into your approved accommodation, and I would drive home to my family's apartment, and we wouldn't spend the next hours or days together. I'd never felt like that before, Henry. That sense of yearning to be with a person and loss when I had to leave them.

"Can we do this again?"

The words sent a rush of warmth through my body, just as my eye was caught by a curtain twitching in a downstairs room. Your landlady, I supposed. A Stasi informer, no doubt, tasked with keeping tabs on the comings and goings of the foreigners in her building. It occurred to me then that throughout that whole day together I'd not once thought of the potential repercussions for me of being with you. And I wasn't about to start. "Yes, I'd love to," I said.

You moved towards me, as though you might kiss me, but then a door opened behind us, a figure silhouetted in the frame, and the moment was broken. You gave me a small wave instead, your eyes shining out of the darkness. "*Auf Wiedersehen*, Greta."

I beamed. "*Gute Nacht*, Henry."

"*Scheiße*, he's got you good," Lena said to me a few days after that outing, when my best friend and I were sitting in my family's Lichtenberg apartment watching a dubbed American TV show on a West German channel, the picture dropping every so often before Lena wiggled the aerial to adjust the signal. "Are you sure you know what you're doing?"

Lena liked you, Henry, and she was no stickler for the rules, but she also knew well enough what could happen in this city if you did something the authorities didn't like. Her uncle Jürgen's arrest and detention in Brandenburg Prison, and her father's subsequent application for him and Lena to emigrate to West Germany, had rained consequences down on the pair of them. It was why Lena was stuck in a job she hated and not with me at university, despite getting equally good grades at extended secondary school. It was the reason her father was regularly harassed by Stasi officers. It was why we hung out mostly at my family's apartment, since she was convinced her own was bugged—and if the earwigging Stasi heard us watching *Dallas*, it wouldn't exactly do us any favours.

"Doing what?" my mother asked, coming in from the kitchen, where she was making something for dinner, with begrudging help from my little sister Angelika.

"Nothing, Mutti." I shot a glance at Lena. I wasn't ready to tell my family about you because I knew what they'd say. My mother was a pragmatist. "*Wessen Brot ich ess, dessen Lied ich sing*," she'd often say. Play the game, it meant. Sing the right tune if you want an easy life. Don't bite the hand that feeds you. And then there was my wise, thoughtful, pro-reform communist father, who would remind me that we had plenty of good in our lives, plenty it wasn't worth risking in search of the things we didn't.

Mutti raised her eyebrows. "A likely story!" She smiled and leaned over to kiss me on the top of my head. "Can you set the table please, Greta? Lena, do you want to stay for dinner? There's enough."

"*Danke*, Frau Schneider, but I have to get going." She stood up from the sofa as the closing notes of *Dallas* played on the television, and my mother rushed to switch it off, ever nervous of the neighbours overhearing this Western theme tune. I rolled my eyes at Lena. At our age, we'd much rather have left home and lived together, but accommodation was tough to find in this city.

I followed my friend to the front door, where she turned and said in a low voice, "Just think about it, okay? Just know what you're getting into. I'm already screwed in this country, but you're not. Do you want to be able to finish your degree? Do you want your family to stay off the Stasi's watch list? I'm not saying don't do it—I mean, he seems like a lovely guy—but just make sure he's worth it, all right?"

"*Tschüß*, Lena," was all I said in reply. I couldn't bring myself to acknowledge her worries aloud. Because although she was right, although I knew my law-abiding, peacekeeping, quiet-life-loving parents would be anxious if I told them about you, and although I felt apprehensive about what might happen to me, or them, if I was seen too often with you, I just couldn't stop myself, because I was falling in love for the first time.

The day I knew for sure was the following weekend, when we went to the Fernsehturm.

The television tower dominated Berlin's skyline, and Lena and I sometimes went there to torture ourselves by staring at the view over the Wall into Westberlin, making up stories of what we would do if only we could get there. That Saturday afternoon you'd said you wanted to go, so we'd walked through Alexanderplatz, you'd paid the required ostmarks, and we'd taken the elevator all the way up to the observation deck.

"I didn't know all this existed in East Germany," you said, almost to yourself, as we stood there together, gazing at the streets and buildings and parks far below.

"What do you mean?"

"Everything you've shown me. The restaurants, the ice rink, the Alextreff and . . . is that a *Ferris wheel* down there?" You pointed towards the Kulturpark Plänterwald, which we visited as a family every summer, Mutti, Angelika, and I shrieking on the rides while Vati regarded us with an indulgent smile, pretending not to be scared.

"Yes, in the amusement park," I said, and you shook your head, as though you couldn't believe it.

"I didn't think you were allowed to be *amused*." You smiled, a little tentatively. We were still finding our way around each other's backgrounds and experiences, like dipping a toe in a hot bath and waiting to get used to the temperature.

"What *did* you think?"

"I don't know," you said. "That you were practically held under lock and key, I suppose. That you couldn't do anything without permission. That you couldn't have any fun."

I didn't reply at first. In hindsight, I can see exactly why you thought that. What a strange, illogical country I lived in! Did anyone understand it? Did *I*? Now, years later, I can see how the DDR had become what it was then. I can understand how, after the economic turmoil of the Weimar Republic in the early thirties, and the horrors of Hitler that followed, the prewar proponents of Marxism-Leninism were able to present it as an attractive alternative to capitalism and fascism when the war ended, despite its association with the Soviet soldiers who had just raped and rampaged their way through Berlin. It was meant to be about creating a better, fairer, classless society, where the state owned the means of production and in return provided everyone with life's necessities—a job and a home, free health care and education. A place where, unlike in capitalist countries, there wasn't a huge gap between rich and poor, and the former didn't exploit the latter; where everyone had enough, and no one was so dissatisfied that they'd look to another charismatic despot to solve their problems.

But not everyone saw it like that. My aunt Ilsa and uncle Wolfgang were two of the many thousands who left for Westberlin before '61 because they didn't consider the DDR to be better. Because they decided they'd rather be "exploited" in the Federal Republic and have more freedom of choice in their lives. Because they didn't want to live under the dictatorial rule of the Socialist Unity Party, which wouldn't allow free elections and a free press and the freedom to say and read and watch things that didn't proclaim state socialism as the only way to live.

So our leaders built a wall. An "anti-fascist protective barrier," as they called it, to keep us safe from the West. To protect us from the fascists and capitalists who wanted to destroy what they'd created. A wall that nevertheless required searchlights, trip wires, vehicle traps, gun-toting guards, and attack dogs to deter the many people who wanted to escape such "protection." Because everyone knew that it was actually to keep us in, to keep us from jumping the sinking ship like Ilsa and so many others had done.

And it *was* a sinking ship. By the time I met you, we had only to look around us to see that the government's planned economy could no longer afford to subsidise our rent and food and childcare and cultural activities, and the country was gradually going bankrupt. I didn't need to ask my friends and fellow students and their parents to know that many of them felt limited by their tightly controlled educational pathways and careers, angered by their lack of freedom to travel, and frustrated that although they had enough money, there was nothing of quality in the shops to spend it on—unlike in the West. Of course, the Party would have preferred us not to know how our Western counterparts lived, but we needed only to wiggle our television aerial or receive a *Westpaket* from a relative to find out, and so we all knew that people over the other side had better-quality food and consumer goods and opportunities than we did. Like East German cola, life here was cheap and mostly palatable, but we knew a tastier version existed elsewhere.

We couldn't say that, though. In the Party's warped logic, anyone who tried to leave, anyone who acknowledged aloud that the ship was sinking, the ideology didn't work, and the West was more appealing than our own country was considered an enemy of socialism, a dissenter, and faced the wrath of the all-seeing Ministry for State Security—the powerful, much-feared Stasi—whose arsenal of intimidation tactics and network of informers aimed to keep us in check. Want to progress in your career? Then join the Party, whether you agree with its politics or not. Don't want your children to attend the state-sanctioned youth movement, the Freie Deutsche Jugend? Then don't expect them to be accepted for higher education. Complain about our rigged elections and state-owned newspapers? Express a longing to visit France or America or even Frankfurt? Admit out loud that you prefer Western television, jeans, and chocolate (or, as Lena had warned me, men) to the DDR-made equivalents? Then be sure that whoever is listening will mark you out as a troublemaker and impose whatever consequences—surveillance, interrogation, even prison—they deemed necessary.

It was surely the opposite of what idealistic communists like my father and his parents had once dreamed of. It was a failed dream, one that our current leaders clung to more and more desperately, as young people like me muddled our way through the life we'd been born into while struggling to understand its logic.

Yet most of the time I thought of none of that, Henry. Most of the time I was simply a young woman wanting to enjoy myself and study hard and dance in discos and listen to the latest Bowie and Blondie hits on Western radio. The Wall, the watchtowers, the Stasi informants, and the vast Soviet embassy on Unter den Linden were as everyday to me as Coca-Cola and Nescafé were to you. There were many frustrations about the DDR, and I longed to have the chance to experience life elsewhere, but it was all I'd ever known. To me, these things were the background hum to a life that, in other ways, probably wasn't that different from yours: a life that involved study and sport and parties and holidays; a life that, yes, could be *fun*—at least for those who didn't step out of line.

"We have plenty of fun," I said to you, a little defensively.

"I can see that now," you replied, your voice soft. "It's not as different here as I thought it would be."

And yet. Down below I could see the Wall cutting through our city like an ugly scar. Two walls, in fact, separated by a bare, no-man's-land we called the *Todesstreifen*, the death strip, Westberlin's rooftops and streets visible on the other side. I imagined the people who must be occupying those buildings, the lives they must be leading. Aunt Ilsa, and my Oma—my mother's mother, who'd gone to the West on a visitor visa as soon as she became a pensioner and decided not to come back. How I longed to go and visit them! How unfair that I couldn't, that I had to wait for their occasional day trips to see us, when their hugs and laughter and gifts—coveted Western clothes, chocolate, and chewing gum for Angelika and me; good coffee, French cheese, and cosmetics for our parents—came with the bittersweet knowledge that we couldn't step into their lives like they'd stepped into ours.

I felt your eyes fixed on me, just as my own were fixed on the West, and I swallowed down a lump in my throat before I spoke. "The main difference," I said, "is that you've had the chance to find out."

I looked at you then and could see you struggling not to placate me with a *maybe you will, too, someday*, because we both knew that might not be true, however determined I was.

"I'm sorry you can't," you said, and then you reached for my hand and took it in yours. There was a moment—a millisecond—when you looked worried, as though I would object to the gesture and snatch my hand away, but of course I didn't. I held it firmly, and you responded with a smile that said everything—and that was the moment right there. That was the moment I knew.

Which is why, when we said goodbye later that day, when we stood close in the cold February air, the lights of the television tower a beacon in the dusk, I chose not to think about who might be watching; I chose not to consider the consequences of what I was doing.

"Is this okay?" you asked softly.

I smiled and took hold of the collar of your Western jacket, pulling you closer, and then your hand was in my hair and your lips met mine, and it didn't matter what might happen, what could happen, what had happened, it mattered only that I'd met you and had no intention of letting you go.

I didn't know that one day I would have to.

5

Henry, 2018

Henry hates shopping, yet here he is, trailing around after his sister on a cold, damp Saturday afternoon. At least they're in a DIY shop, albeit a posh independent one, which Charlotte thinks implies quality, but he knows usually means the same products as in B&Q but with better marketing and inflated prices.

"Don't you like this one?"

Henry shrugs. "It's veneer. I really think you want solid wood if you're looking for something that will last."

"But I like the colour."

He shrugs again. It's not his kitchen. No skin off his nose. "Fine."

Charlotte frowns. "Don't say *fine*; I asked you to come with me today because I want your opinion."

"I gave it. I told you to go for solid wood instead of veneer, but it's up to you." She doesn't really want his opinion. She wants to buy the one she likes the look of and have Henry agree with her.

"Okay, you win," she says, though he hadn't known it was a competition. "I'll go for this oak set instead. It's lovely, too, if a bit pricey. Come on, let's find a salesperson."

"Doesn't Ian get a say?"

"He doesn't care; he'll go with whatever."

Henry isn't so sure about that, recalling his brother-in-law's grumble last week, but he knows better than to get involved in the dynamics of his sister's tumultuous marriage to Ian.

She drags him to the counter, where they spend the next half hour signing up to a kitchen refit at a price that makes Henry's eyes water, particularly since there's nothing wrong with the kitchen units Charlotte and Ian currently have; they are old and could use a lick of paint and some new handles, is all. And that won't be the half of it. His big sister—still, at sixty-four, like a kid in a sweet shop with her credit card in hand—also wants to buy a new carpet for the hallway and get someone in to repaint the walls, and then she'll spend weeks buying new things to deck out the kitchen. She doesn't need any more *things*, but Charlotte will undoubtedly find something: a new coffee machine, perhaps, to replace the perfectly decent one they have, but which Charlotte has told him clogs up occasionally ("Clean it then," he has said, but she only huffs and rolls her eyes—"I can't be bothered"); a fancy blender she will use to make smoothies for approximately three weeks before forgetting about it; a new lamp to create mood lighting when actually you need to be able to see what you're chopping.

Greta was never bothered about *things*. Though she loved clothes and records and books, a childhood in East Berlin hadn't instilled a love of superfluous stuff; in fact, she'd been a bit overwhelmed by choice when she first came to Britain. It was one of the many examples of the cultural divide that existed between Greta and his family, as much as he tried to erase it. He'd encourage his wife to join Charlotte and their mother on one of their regular shopping trips, but she'd return home afterwards with no purchases and a slightly dazed look. "There's too much; I can't decide on anything," she'd say, adding, "I'd rather save for a trip somewhere anyway." He'd take her to his parents' house for Sunday lunch and play conversation facilitator, desperate for his wife and his family to love one another as much as he loved them all, but somehow the cultural gap always got in the way.

"What, you didn't even have a *phone*?" Charlotte screeched during one such lunch when Greta was relating details of her childhood.

"We've been on the wait list for years, like most people," Greta answered with a shrug. If anyone wanted to get hold of them, she added, they could call Frau Weber on the ground floor, who acted as message taker, neighbourhood gossip—and probable Stasi informant—for the whole apartment block.

His sister's face was a picture. "Thank God Henry saved you from all that," she said, in a tone that made Henry think another meaning lingered underneath, but Greta didn't reply.

How did it make her feel that Charlotte considered her "saved"? he wonders now. How did it make her feel when his *Daily Mail*–reading father referred to "bloody commies" and his mother indulged her Stalinesque vision of the GDR, fretting that Greta hadn't had enough to eat as a child, or should go to the doctor to check she didn't have any unusual diseases?

"Right," Charlotte says when they finally leave the shop, "can I buy you tea and cake to say thanks?"

He pulls his coat collar up against the cold air as they walk down Summertown high street. It's full of artisanal coffeehouses and upmarket bakeries these days, quite a change from when he lived here with Greta in the mid-eighties. After he moved out of their flat, it was years before he could bear to come back to the area. Couldn't walk past the building they lived in, the butcher's where he'd buy those sausages she always liked, the library she'd go to at least once a month, returning with armfuls of books she'd devour in the weeks that followed.

"I really shouldn't," Charlotte says, as they stand by the counter in her favourite café, looking at the cakes, "but I'm going to. Chocolate slice?"

"Go on, then." Henry takes a seat at a table for two while his sister orders. They come here often and always have the same exchange prior to tucking into whatever takes their fancy that day. The familiarity of it comforts him. As much as Charlotte frustrates him sometimes, he is glad they have reached this stage of their lives as friends. Long gone are the days when Charlotte would dismiss her little brother as an annoying nerd she wouldn't be seen dead with, or flounce out to some party with her latest boyfriend while teenage Henry stayed at home with his parents, wondering if he'd ever have the confidence to ask a girl out. The body blows that the years have thrown at them both since then—Greta's departure, Charlotte's up-and-down relationship with Ian, their parents' deaths—have gradually drawn them closer, and now there is a solid bond between them that he is sure no amount of bickering can destroy. He doesn't know what he'd have done without her all these years.

"Listen," Charlotte says, after she's settled herself at the table with a tray of tea and cake, "there's something I wanted to ask you, and please don't say no straightaway."

Henry frowns. "If this is about Victoria . . ."

Charlotte waves her hand in the air. "No, no. You made your feelings perfectly clear on that score. But there is someone else I'd like you to meet."

He raises his eyebrows and takes a forkful of chocolate cake.

"Just hear me out. She's a colleague of a friend of Ian's, a teacher at Oxford High, in her late fifties, I think. I met her once at a party, when she was married. Nice woman—and I liked her husband, too, but then some time ago he keeled over of a heart attack during a game of squash, quite unexpectedly. Poor woman was devastated, of course. But it's been a few years now, and Ian's friend says she's started online dating, so she's clearly ready to meet someone again, and I seem to remember she's very attractive and fun and has lots of friends; she's not a sad old lonely person." *Like you*, Henry hears, though she doesn't say it. "So what do you think? Just one date? See how it goes?"

He sighs. He could. He could go on a date with this woman—this Samira—and have a perfectly pleasant time. But there's bound to be something about her that'll annoy him, something he won't be able to overlook, something Greta never would have done. Anyway, he's sick of Charlotte meddling in his love life, however well meant it may be. Which is perhaps why, despite knowing what her reaction will be, he says what he says next.

"Actually, I have something to tell you, too."

"Oh?" Charlotte frowns and takes a bite of cake.

"Do you remember the jewellery Greta used to make?"

"What, that weird, twisted metal stuff? Sure."

Ah, yes. He had forgotten Charlotte's snobbishness about Greta's jewellery ("It's just ugly grey metal, Henry. Why can't she use silver, and add some gemstones or something?"). "Well, a woman came into the shop the other day wearing a pendant that looked exactly like one of hers. I couldn't believe it. I went home and compared it with the stuff I still have of Greta's, and I'm sure it's the same style. The woman said her mother bought it for her, so I thought if I ask her to find out where she got it, then there's a chance—a slim chance, I admit—that it might lead me to Greta, after all these years."

Charlotte puts her fork down and gives him the Look. "And if it does? You're going to beg her to take you back after she hurt you so badly all those years ago?"

He shrugs but says nothing.

Charlotte scrapes the last bit of chocolate cake from her plate and gives a small sigh. "Henry, I can't believe you're doing this again, after so bloody long."

"Doing what?"

"Pining after that woman. For God's sake, it makes me so mad. If I saw her again, I'd ruddy well throttle her for what she's done to you. You've spent thirty years self-harming because of her. You've hobbled your chances of happiness, and now you're an old man on your own, and you're going to continue to be an old man on your own because you won't give anyone else a chance, and it makes me so mad, Henry—and sad. It makes me *sad*."

She sits back in her chair, and Henry is surprised to see tears in her eyes. Charlotte—his confident, forthright, some might say *scary*, sister—never cries.

"I'm not self-harming," he says quietly. "I just haven't met anyone else I want to be with like I did with her. It's not like I haven't tried." Yes, he's tried; he's been with other women, though, in truth, not for a long time. After Greta left him, he wasn't himself for a while; he'd go to bars and take women home, hoping to find comfort but only feeling empty afterwards. A few years later he met Francesca and they dated for more than a year, but he danced around any further commitment, unwilling to give her the marriage and babies she wanted. It would have felt like accepting that Greta wasn't coming back. And anyway, he was still married and couldn't bring himself to start divorce proceedings, despite his sister's urging ("You *can* divorce a missing person, I checked").

Since then, there's been no one, really, bar a few dates here and there, usually engineered by his sister or a friend. No one who has ever matched up, in any case.

"But that's my point, Henry. You're not going to meet anyone else who is like her, because everyone is different, every relationship is different. But you won't give anyone else a chance because you think your relationship with Greta was perfect. You're stuck back there because it ended when you were still in the honeymoon period, before you had a chance to see it for the flawed, imperfect, *normal* relationship it was. And ever since then, you've put her on a pedestal so high no one else can ever reach it."

He snorts. "What are you, a pot psychologist?"

"No, just someone who's watched her little brother spend three decades ruining his own life."

He bristles. Sometimes he enjoys their verbal sparring, but that was harsh, even for Charlotte. "I haven't ruined my life."

"No, you're right—*she* has."

"You never liked her anyway. You wrote her off because you couldn't accept that she was a bit different from you. And you couldn't understand that I loved her wholeheartedly, because you've never felt that way about Ian, have you? You don't think that kind of love even exists. You're a cynic." How many times has Charlotte stayed at his after she and Ian have had blazing rows? How long did it take them to reconcile after Ian had an affair years ago?

"No, I'm a realist, Henry. Ian isn't perfect; I know that, but I love him anyway, despite his flaws. But Greta? She wasn't perfect, either, but the difference is, you pretend she was. You've glossed over all the bad bits like you varnish one of your sodding tables. You make out she's the love of your life, your soulmate, your *one*, as an excuse for never giving anyone else a look-in."

Henry raises his eyebrows. "Well, she *was* my one. What's wrong with that?"

"What's wrong with that is that there's no such thing." Charlotte shakes her head. "And you're living in a Richard Curtis film if you think there is."

"Richard who?"

"Makes those soppy films with floppy-haired Englishmen, the ones Mum always loved watching." Charlotte waves her hand dismissively. "My point is, you are allowed a second *one*, Henry. You can give yourself that happiness—it is *allowed*—and it makes me furious that you've sacrificed yourself over a woman you think is perfect but who isn't at all; she's just as flawed and human and normal as the rest of us."

"There was nothing flawed about Greta." He recalls her beautiful smile, her lovely thick hair, and the long limbs that were toned and lean from running. Her adorable accent. The delight in her eyes when she teased him about something. He even loved the frown line between her eyes as she'd arrive home tired and taciturn after a shift at the café she worked in when she first arrived in Oxford, and the way she'd cajole him into driving somewhere on a Sunday, when he actually wanted to stay home and read the paper.

He blinks away the memories. "Really, she *was* perfect—for me, anyway."

Charlotte scoffs. "I can point you towards a big thing that was wrong with her, Henry—a whopper, in fact. She used you and then left you. I'd say that makes her pretty bloody *im*perfect, wouldn't you?" She shakes her head and looks at him with a gaze that makes him want to turn away. "You know, Henry, I think you actually enjoy living in the rose-tinted past because it's easier than trying to fix your rather monochrome present."

Henry flushes. "Don't be ridiculous! What a mean-spirited thing to say."

"So prove it, then. Go on a date with Samira."

Henry doesn't sleep well that night, his sister's words circling in his head. *You enjoy living in the past . . . your rather monochrome present.*

Charlotte has always been blunt, has never beaten around the bush when she's got something to say, and while he often admires that about her, that particular sentiment cut him hard. He does not have a monochrome present—he likes his work, his home, his routines; he's happy enough, most of the time—and he does not live in the past, though of course it preoccupies him. Why wouldn't it? Who else has experienced their loving spouse walk out with no explanation, never to contact them again, not even for a divorce? Isn't that strange enough to warrant preoccupation?

As he lies awake at night, his thoughts fly back to the hours and days after she left. After the shock waves had subsided, the first thing he did was try to contact Greta's family. Perhaps they would know where she'd gone; perhaps they could tell him that this was nothing more than a practical joke, a mistake, a bad dream.

So he called their neighbour Frau Weber, asking in his rudimentary German to fetch Greta's father. But neither of her parents were there, and her younger sister knew nothing. "She leaves? What do you mean?" Angelika asked in her halting English, and he understood that Greta hadn't contacted them. There was anger, too, in the teenager's voice—anger and worry for the sister Henry had not only taken away from her, but now lost. "What did you do to make her leave, Henry?"

Those words were a sucker punch. *Had* he done something? Had he not been a good-enough husband for her? Part of him—the part that had been too shy to ask women out when he was younger, that had almost expected the rejection that had usually come after a first date—believed it. Her words took him right back to those awkward years of early adult-hood: to his first, short-lived girlfriend, who'd left him after a few weeks with the damning indictment that he was too boring and too quiet; to the date he'd taken out for pizza, followed by *Alien* at the cinema (the cost of which left him broke for weeks), who dumped him the very next day for a friend of his.

And yet, his relationship with Greta had changed him. Right from the moment he met her in that strangely unsophisticated disco, it was as though an invisible, unbreakable string was pulling them together. Their attraction was physical, absolutely, but it was more than that, too. It was as though they'd always been together; as though they fit together. His shyness, his inability to think of anything interesting to say, disappeared when he was with this vibrant, passionate, impulsive woman. He was funnier, more relaxed, more himself than he'd ever been with anyone else. She made him feel as though he was worthy of being loved.

In the weeks following her disappearance, drinking too much and sleeping too little, he wrote regularly to her family in Berlin, imploring them to tell him if they heard from her, but he never got a reply. He called the apartment block over and over, until a stream of German diatribe from Frau Weber made it clear he shouldn't call again. He scoured the flat for Greta's address book and railed with frustration when he realised she must have taken it with her, and with it any chance of his contacting Lena or Greta's aunt or anyone else who might know where she'd gone.

He wasn't ready to give up, so he summoned back the police, and the same officer as before came to his house, sat on the sofa, cocked his head, and offered a sympathetic smile, as though humouring a child.

"She didn't take her passport," Henry implored, a detail that had been bugging him, since she'd considered it such a precious document. "She hasn't used our joint bank account since she left. She took only a few clothes, a small bag."

"But she took *some* things, didn't she?" The police officer sighed. "There's no evidence of a crime, sir, that's the thing. She told you she was taking off, so she isn't really *missing*, is she? She just doesn't want to be found. Maybe she'd stashed a load of money away for a rainy day. Maybe she's gone back to her family. Whereabouts are they?"

Henry sighed. "East Berlin."

"Ah. Well, there you go then," the policeman said. "Funny lot, over there."

As the weeks turned into months, as Charlotte moved him out of the flat and encouraged him to move on emotionally, as well as physically, to accept that his wife had simply used him and discarded him, he couldn't let go of his instinct that there was more to it than that. Why were her family not replying to him? Had she told them not to say where she was? Or had she disappeared from their lives as well as his? But she loved her family, he was certain of that. He could try to convince himself that she'd duped him, that she didn't love him at all and had simply used him to get to Britain, but he would never believe that she didn't love *them*.

No, something else was going on back then. Something he's never been able to explain. And now here comes Lucy Kenny with her necklace, this potential clue to Greta's whereabouts. Perhaps if he follows its trail, he'll be able to track her down and finally get the answers he needs.

Whatever his sister says, it is worth a shot.

6

GRETA, 1982

By your fourth week in Berlin it was clear to me that our fledgling romance was the real deal. We spent as much time together as we could, meeting a couple of evenings a week for a beer and some food in a *Kneipe*. And when we weren't together, I thought of little but you, so much so that I wasn't sleeping properly as I relived the way you kissed me, the feel of your hand on mine, the things you said in the English voice I loved. I'd turn up to my morning runs with Friedrich either late or not at all, provoking a scowl on his face that sat in stark contrast to the distracted smile on mine. "You're late again; we'll have to do a shorter route," he snapped at me one day, when I dragged myself to meet him the morning after another evening with you. I mumbled an apology, but he looked at me with a mixture of hurt and disgust. "Actions have consequences, Greta," he said, but I only laughed and told him not to be so pompous.

In hindsight, I should have taken that for the warning I now see it was.

But I was blind to anything but you during those early days, Henry. Unlike Friedrich, you never showed an ounce of pomposity. You were always so humble, so down-to-earth, as though you couldn't see what a good guy you were, and it only made me want you even more.

"There are no lights on," I said one night, when we arrived back at your boarding house on my scooter after another evening together. I nodded to the front room, belonging to your landlady.

"Maybe she's gone away," you said.

I grinned. "So . . . I could come in?"

Your face lit up like you'd hit the jackpot in a game you didn't know you'd entered. "Wait there," you whispered, and I stood in the shadows as you darted to the front door and unlocked it.

A minute later you beckoned me into the dark corridor and we ran up the stairs, trying to suppress our laughter, and tumbled into your room. You switched on the light, illuminating plain beige walls, a brown rug, and a metal-framed bed, and our laughter tailed off in the sudden stark glare. We stood facing each other for a moment, the air between us thick and heady.

"Are you sure?" you asked.

I nodded, my heart thudding so hard I felt certain it was audible. It seemed strange that something so alive was about to happen in such a tired, drab room. "Completely."

You stepped forward, laced your hand with mine, and kissed me. And then the ache that had built up between us over the past few weeks gave way to a frenzy of discarded clothes and desperate kisses and tangled limbs. You weren't my first, but you were the first I'd loved, and there was something so different—so right—about the way our bodies fit together compared to the clunky, awkward encounters I'd experienced with my short-lived university boyfriend. That night, I, too, felt like I'd won some competition to know that you—this gentle, caring, quietly funny man— should want to be with me.

Afterwards, we lay wrapped in each other, my head on your chest, your hand resting on my back.

"I love your hair," you said sleepily. "It's so thick and beautiful, and it smells like . . ."

"Sulphur?" I joked. According to you, my city smelled strongly of the brown coal briquettes burned in many homes and factories, but if it did, I was so used to it that I didn't notice.

"No, like apples or something. A juicy Granny Smith."

I laughed. "I don't know what that is."

"The queen of apples."

"Then I accept the compliment." I pushed myself up on one arm and ran my finger over the dark birthmark on your right bicep. "And I love this. It's almost the shape of the DDR."

"Ha, I think you need glasses."

"But then I might not only have eyes for you."

"You're right. Forget it, then."

I laughed, kissed the birthmark, and lay my head back on your chest. I was so happy in that moment, Henry. The scent of you, the warmth of your skin, the rise and fall of your breathing—it all filled me with a contented calm, with the simple knowledge that this was where I was meant to be.

"What would you do, if you could do anything you wanted in life?" I asked then. Was I assessing our compatibility? Was I dreaming there could be a chance we could spend our lives together?

"This?" You ran your hand up the curve of my body, and I heard the grin in your voice.

I laughed. "Apart from that."

"Oh, I don't know. I don't have any grand ambitions, really. But I suppose I'd like to make things, or repair things, or do something with my hands that doesn't involve industrial machinery."

I liked that answer. You would fit in perfectly in Berlin, then, where the lack of available goods meant people were careful to look after what they already had: mending things that had broken, fine-tuning their precious cars, growing fruit and vegetables that were scarce in the shops, making the type of fashionable Western clothes that our department stores didn't stock. Before I met you, before I wanted to spend every free minute with you, I spent most Sundays at home with my mother and Angelika, poring over the patterns in Aunt Ilsa's much-thumbed editions of West Germany's *Brigitte* magazine, planning the next creations we'd whip up on Mutti's sewing machine.

Yes, you'd fit in well. But you would never move to my city. It would make no sense at all, so I wasn't going to ask.

"I approve, Herr Henderson, because I can tell you're very good at doing things with your hands," I said in a mock-serious voice.

"Glad you think so." You laughed. "And what about you? What would you do, if you could do anything?"

I sighed and rolled onto my back, staring up at the ceiling. "Travel," I said, "anywhere and everywhere." I looked at you. "Tell me where you've been? Tell me what you've seen, in the West?"

So you told me about family camping trips to northern France as a child: raucous games of Frisbee with your sister on the beach, barbecues in the campsite, and *steak frites* in the restaurants. The festival you once visited in Spain, where real live bulls rampaged through the city streets, chasing men in white T-shirts and red neckerchiefs. And the post-exams trip you took with schoolfriends to Italy, where you'd eaten the best ice cream you'd ever had, and swum off the coast in turquoise waters teeming with marine life. "It was so beautiful," you said, "I'd take you there if I could. You'd love it." *Ach*, how I wanted to do that, how I wanted to be there with you!

But as it was, I wasn't even allowed to visit my aunt and grandmother in Westberlin, while those who tried to leave the DDR were rarely successful. Did I tell you those stories? Not right then, lying together in a Stasi-monitored building, but later, walking on frost-white paths through the Volkspark Friedrichshain on a fine but cold early spring day, yes, I think I told you—

About my childhood friend Sigrid who hadn't seen her parents for two years, after they applied to leave the DDR and were summoned to the Ministry of the Interior as a result.

About Stefan, a guy Lena and I went to school with, who last year stood outside the Tränenpalast customs building protesting against the strict travel rules, only to be arrested and jailed, much to the distress of his fiancé and parents.

About Hanne, a girl a few years older than me in school, who, as a young child, had tried to flee with her father over the border to Czechoslovakia before being caught and sent to an orphanage while her father went to jail.

"I can't imagine . . ." you said, but the sentence dried in your mouth. We were walking side by side, and I looked across at you, took in the worry lines on your forehead.

"What?"

You stopped and turned to me, brushing a strand of hair off my face. "I don't know how I'll be able to leave you behind, Greta."

I smiled and kissed your hand. *Then don't*, I wanted to say. "We still have a few weeks," I said instead.

Oh, what a mess I had got myself into. But I wouldn't have changed it for the world, Henry.

Were the authorities observing us as our romance progressed? Did they see me leave your boarding house with a stupid smile on my face? Did they notice how perfectly your body melded into mine as we rode around on my scooter? Were they writing notes, taking photographs, putting it all in a file somewhere, for future use?

Of course they were—and they made sure I knew it. The two shadowy figures sitting in a dark-coloured Lada outside my apartment block. The unsmiling *VoPo* who twice stopped us in the street during those early weeks.

"*Ausweis*," the policeman said that first time, holding his gloved hand out.

I handed over my identity card and told you to give him your visa and passport.

"*Engländer*," the *VoPo* said with a whiff of disdain. He looked you up and down, then flicked his eyes to me. I held his gaze, kept my chin up, refused to look away.

"Yes, over here for work," you said, offering him a smile, but he didn't return it; he only stared at you again and then handed back our documents, to your obvious relief.

"Am I making things hard for you?" you asked me after he'd left us. "I really don't want to do that."

I shook my head, dismissing the echo of Lena's words in my ears. *Just know what you're getting yourself into.* "It's simply what they do," I said with a nonchalance I didn't entirely feel. "We'll ignore it."

My mother felt differently, however, when I finally told her about you.

"*Schatzi*, what are you *thinking*?" she asked when I broached the subject one day. I was drying the dishes next to her at the sink in our apartment when I told her I was in love with an Englishman. She nearly dropped a pan on the floor. "But you'll ruin everything you've worked for!"

I shook my head. "I won't," I said, though I wasn't sure I meant it.

"Oh, Greta, you might be prevented from graduating, or arrested and interrogated, or worse! Remember Herr Fischer?" My mother was obsessed with that story. My former English teacher at high school had been arrested last year after giving a forbidden Western book to a student; he'd lost his job and served time in prison, while his colleague was unexpectedly promoted to *Schulleiter*—a reward, we suspected, for informing on his friend.

"This isn't about books, Mutti," I said. "He's just a person, and I love him. How can they object to that?"

She was silent then, but I saw her eyes fill with tears before she turned back to the dishes.

Don't misunderstand me, Henry. My parents liked you right away when they met you. They saw you for who you were, just as I did; never mind politics and walls and Iron Curtains, they saw you were a good person, and the right person for me in many ways—calm and considered to my flighty and impulsive; steady and reliable where I was prone to flashes of fire and ice—apart from one huge, unignorable flaw: your Britishness.

You tried to understand their worries, but I don't think you really did. No one could properly understand if they hadn't lived lives like ours. After all, you hadn't had your parents and siblings taken away from you during the war and sent to the Nazi camps, like my father had, leaving him with a lifelong mistrust of the "fascist" West and a natural allegiance with socialism—if not the Party's dictatorial way of imposing it, which he grumbled about daily, behind closed doors. You hadn't spent decades living in a parallel universe to your sister, like my mother had since Ilsa fled to the other side before the Wall went up in '61; it would be eleven years before she was allowed back to visit us. You hadn't lived life keeping your head down for fear of the consequences: warning your children not to tell anyone you watched Western television at home, even though everyone knew that everyone did; dutifully casting your vote come Election Day, despite there being no real choice to make; and never criticising the government in public, lest the wrong person be listening. This *double-talk* was an everyday survival strategy: say what you like in private, but bite your tongue in public.

My parents weren't unhappy with their lives: they worked hard, my mother as a nurse at the Charité hospital, my father as a typesetter at a state-run printing press. They saved up and waited patiently for years to get us what they could, like our pastel blue Trabant, beloved and meticulously cared for by Vati, in which we took annual camping trips to Lake Balaton or the Ostsee. They enjoyed those holidays, liked their jobs well enough, appreciated their friends and colleagues and social lives, loved their daughters, were grateful for what they had. But living a decent life in our Berlin meant not rocking the boat, and you—gentle, kind, unassuming you—threw a grenade into that boat, whether you realised it or not. The worst that could happen would be that you'd ruin our lives, raining consequences down upon us that you could never have imagined. The best that could happen . . . well, I couldn't contemplate that yet, because despite the strength of my feelings for you, I hadn't decided if I could actually do it.

"You really love him?" my mother said a few minutes later, breaking the silence that had settled over us as she washed and I dried.

I nodded.

She sighed and gave me a sad smile. "Then you'd better invite him for dinner."

We lived on the fifth floor of a six-storey *Plattenbau* in Lichtenberg. It was a small, two-bedroom apartment, newly built when we moved into it seven years previously. We had our own toilet, hot water on tap, and central heating, things we hadn't had before when we lived in Prenzlauer Berg. Thinking about it now, I imagine it looked pretty modest to you, but you didn't say so.

I pulled you quickly and quietly past Frau Weber's flat on the ground floor, hoping her eye wasn't pressed against her peephole, and led you up five sets of stairs to our front door. It was already open, my family lined up as though waiting to greet royalty: Mutti's face torn between apprehension and excitement; my sister feigning disinterest; Vati at the back, arms folded across his chest.

Who was more nervous, I couldn't say. I think we all held our breath in that moment.

"*Guten Abend*," you said in that charming accent of yours. You stepped forward and held out a bottle to my father.

Vati hesitated for what felt like an age, before his habitual frown softened and he took the bad Hungarian wine (it wasn't your fault; there was little choice in the shops) and held out his hand for you to shake. "*Willkommen*, Henry."

You charmed my little sister immediately, thanks to the bar of Cadbury's Dairy Milk you brought her. Our chocolate wasn't a patch on the Western stuff Aunt Ilsa sent over in her *Westpakete*, so when you presented Angelika with a bar of precious British chocolate—the last of the stash you'd brought with you, you told me later, which made me fall in love with you a little bit more—her face lit up like it was caught in a searchlight. She was yours.

My parents? They weren't so easily bought, but it didn't take them long to like you. My heart soared to see the effort they'd made. Asparagus to start, which my sister later told me she'd queued for forty minutes to get; then melt-in-the-mouth steak, which the butcher had kept behind the counter for my mother, one of his favourite customers; along with green beans I knew she'd got from our neighbour in exchange for a bottle of ketchup; and a potato gratin rich in cream. I suspected this menu aimed to show you we weren't the unsophisticated, deprived people Western propaganda made us out to be, but I also took it as a sign that Mutti was willing to give my choice of boyfriend a chance, however worried it made her.

It was an exhausting evening for me—not only because of my nervous energy, but because I was playing interpreter between you and my parents, whose English was rudimentary at best—though Angelika, thankfully, spoke a little. But at least that meant I could steer the conversation in the way I wanted, playing down my father's criticism of the West and batting away your interest in my sister's Freie Deutsche Jugend uniform, which, to my embarrassment, she was still wearing after some kind of activity earlier that evening.

What did you think of my sister that first time, I wonder? If I lived my life in constant restlessness, always dreaming of what I'd do and where I'd go if only I could, Angelika was the flipside of the coin. She was sixteen then, six years younger than me, and it was almost as though the age gap had put different filters on our eyes. Unlike me, my little sis enjoyed the organised fun of the FDJ: the summer camps, sports days, outdoor activities, and big parades, all of which came with a heavy dollop of socialist ideology. She liked wearing the regulation blue shirt that most of us found distinctly uncool, and she didn't care that every young person was basically forced to join first the Young Pioneers and then the Free German Youth if we didn't want to deny ourselves opportunities in life. She accepted everything she was taught at school about the West (full of drugs, homeless people, striking workers, and warmongering fascists), and the state's justifications for throwing peaceful protestors like Lena's uncle Jürgen in jail (they had broken the law; they were criminals). The only things Angelika coveted about the West were Levi's jeans, Michael Jackson records, and good chocolate; the only thing she yearned to see was the Eiffel Tower. "Don't you question anything, ever?" I asked her once, but my sister only shrugged and replied, "What's wrong with being happy with what you've got?" I had to admit, I admired her a little for that. Not that I was *un*happy, but I certainly had questions, the biggest being: wasn't there something wrong with a country that had to ban its citizens from leaving for fear none of them would ever want to come back?

Whatever you thought of my sister—of all my family—you were the picture of English politeness that night, Henry. The evening passed in a blur of curious smiles, nervous laughter, and compliments about the food. I remember only one awkward moment.

"Did you know Greta is the first in our family to go to university? We are very proud of her," my father said after we'd finished our steaks, and I flushed to translate his words for you. "Of both of our girls. You young people are the future—I hope you can do a better job of bringing peace to the world than our generation has."

"I think everyone wants lasting peace," you said in that mild, even-handed way of yours. "The alternative is unthinkable."

But Vati shook his head. "Not Reagan. He only wants to escalate tensions with the Soviets. He'll end up destroying us in the crossfire."

I stayed silent, but Vati looked at me pointedly. "Translate that, please?"

I turned to you and relayed his words.

"I don't think that's—" you began, but before you could contradict my father—something that never went down too well, especially on such sensitive matters—my mother and sister saved the day.

"Dessert?" Mutti stood up, interrupting your reply.

"*Genau*," Angelika said. "Pudding is much more appetising than politics."

I translated, and you laughed. "It certainly is."

"Vati?" I nudged my father's foot under the table, and when he smiled, the tension that had hovered over the table during that brief exchange dissipated.

"On that we can *all* agree," he said. "And I hear Katharina has something special for us."

I felt a rush of love for my mother when she stepped into the room carrying her homemade *Schaumtorte*: a meringue, whipped cream, and fruit dessert she made only on special occasions. But instead of berries grown in Vati's allotment and preserved in jars each summer, this extra special version was decorated with tinned pineapple from the Intershop, that treasure trove of expensive Western goods, a place that smelled so delicious, with its heady mix of Western cosmetics and washing powder and candy, that even if I had no West marks to buy anything, I would go there just to breathe it in. You wouldn't have understood the significance of this precious tin of pineapple slices, but to me it confirmed that this dinner was a big deal to my family.

I looked over as you ate, wondering if you had this sort of thing all the time, if pineapple was as common as brown bread where you were from, but if that was true, you—lovely, thoughtful man that you were—didn't say so, you only complimented my mother on how delicious it was and went back for seconds when asked.

When our plates were scraped clean, I put down my fork and looked up, locking eyes with my mother over the dinner table. She held my gaze for a second and then gave the slightest, almost imperceptible nod of her head. And it was then, over *Schaumtorte* in my family home, in the city I'd grown up in, that I fully acknowledged the best thing that could happen as a result of meeting you—the *only* thing, if I wanted to see you again: that it might be possible you could take me away from here, to be with you, to pursue the life I wanted, to seek the freedom I craved.

Even if it meant leaving my family behind.

7

Henry, 2018

The minute he hears the tap on the door and sees her expectant face through the glass, his chest lurches with a mixture of apprehension and excitement. He turns the key in the lock, the carved wooden bear swinging from the key chain, and Lucy Kenny bustles in on a gust of cold air.

"It's practically Arctic out! God, hurry up, spring!"

"Hello there." His gaze goes straight to her neck when she unzips her jacket in the warmth of the workshop, but the necklace is not there; the only thing it reveals is the baby, snuggled against her chest in a sling. Perhaps he imagined it. Conjured it.

"I can't stay long, got to rush home before picking up Millie from school, but I made it more or less when I said I would, and believe you me, that's an achievement these days, so count yourself lucky!" She laughs, and he smiles back tentatively. He is unsure how to respond to this woman, but she doesn't seem to need much response, given how easily she fills the air with words herself.

"Well," he says, "it's all ready for you."

He goes to his workbench, where the vase now sits, repaired and re-oiled. It didn't take him long, but he enjoyed doing it, carefully reglueing the wood and clamping it together, lightly sanding the surface and re-oiling it to bring out the beauty of the grain. It may have no backstory for her, it may be simply a vase she quite likes and chose not to put in the recycling bin, but he knows it will have been important to the person who made it, and Henry respects the craftsmanship, the time and skill it took to produce.

"Wow." Lucy takes it from him, turns it around in her hands. "That's amazing, I can't even see where the break was. How on earth did you do that?"

Henry shrugs, but he feels a flush of pride. The baby is awake, and he, too, is staring at the vase, at the patterns in the wood, as his mother turns it. "I'm glad you like it."

She shakes her head, and, to his astonishment, tears spring to her eyes. "God," she says, jabbing at her face. "How embarrassing. I'm so sorry, ignore me, I'm probably just tired. I mean, I'm always tired, but sometimes I just . . . I mean, look at it, it's so beautiful! I can't thank you enough."

"You're very welcome. I hope it survives your daughter's pirouettes."

"Oh, I'll put it out of pirouetting distance from now on," she says. "It's more likely to be struck by an edible missile or projectile vomit, but I'll do my best to keep it out of harm's way. We have so few nice things in the house these days—everything seems to be soiled by sticky fingers or stained by puke or poo—so I'm going to do my best to protect this beautiful vase." Her words make Henry wince a little, and he wants to snatch the vase back. "Oh God, too much information! I'm so sorry, I shouldn't be let out!" She laughs, then her face falls and her whole body seems to sag.

"Do you want to sit for a minute?" Part of him wants to usher this oversharing woman out the door right now, but the other part—the part that glanced at her neck the moment she walked in—wants to keep her here.

"Oh gosh, yes, thank you."

He directs her to his old leather armchair, and she collapses into it with a long sigh, like a balloon deflating. "I can't stay long, though," she says, her eyes closed. "Just five minutes."

Henry hovers in front of her and opens his mouth to speak, to bring up the necklace, but no words emerge. Instead, he returns to his workbench, where he's been oiling a decorative wooden box containing a set of dominoes. It was brought in the other day by a man of about his own age who used to play the game with his father as a child. "He always won," the man said, "and I remember thinking how mean it was that he didn't let me win occasionally, but now I really appreciate it. It made me better, you see, made me want to push myself to beat him." He looked away then, but not before Henry saw the emotion in his eyes. The man's father had died recently, at the age of ninety-five. Having the dominoes box repaired was part of his grieving process.

"You live nearby?" he asks Lucy, for something to say.

She opens her eyes and shakes her head. "Cowley, the other side of town. So I drove, but I had to park a few streets away because it's always so jam-packed round here, isn't it, and there are only so many slots anyway, what with all the residents' parking and all the out-of-towners stalking the streets waiting for someone to leave, and then this one"—she pats the baby—"was asleep, so I waited in the car for ten minutes because he gets so grumpy if I wake him early so it's just not worth it, and I need him to sleep, otherwise he'll be cranky later, so that's why I was a few minutes late."

Henry wonders if she'd be less tired if she didn't talk so much. "I live in Cowley, too," he says.

"You *do*?" she says, as though this is the biggest coincidence. "Which street?"

He tells her, and she laughs. "I'm only two streets over, 43 Leopold Street! I expect we'll bump into each other then. Though I suppose you're down here in Jericho every day of the week, and I usually don't go far, just to the park and the shops and shuttling back and forth to the school for drop-off and pickup. Such is life, these days! You wouldn't know I was a full-time vet before, would you?"

"A vet?"

"Yes! Well, veterinary nurse. I was training to be a vet when I got pregnant with Oscar. I will go back to it, some time, when I can." Her bottom lip quivers, the tears from earlier not far away, before she continues with forced brightness. "You repair objects; I repair animals! We're not so dissimilar after all, are we, Henry?" She says his name as though they've known each other for years, and he smiles, despite himself. "Only my office smelled of disinfectant while yours smells like a . . . Scandinavian pine forest at dawn."

"I like that," he says. A flash of poetry among all her prose.

She laughs, and then suddenly seems to look at him properly. "What are you doing?"

Henry explains that he has fixed the broken hinge on the dominoes box, lightly sanded away the scratches, and glued together a crack on the bottom, and now he is carefully re-oiling the box and each domino, one at a time.

"You must be a very patient person. To spend all that time on something, to put in the hours to do it well, to make it perfect . . ." She shakes her head. "I run around like a headless chicken most of the time, never doing anything properly at all."

"You have a busy life. A family, two young children . . ." He picks up the next domino and dips his cloth in oil.

"You can say that again. Have you got kids? All grown up now, I imagine."

He doesn't look up, but he feels her eyes on him. "No."

"Oh well . . . a much quieter life then." She sighs. "Oh, for a quiet life! Do you know, sometimes when Oscar is crying and Millie is asking me something and I've got a million and one things to do in the house, I can't hear myself think, literally, and then I remember my mother saying exactly the same, and how I used to roll my eyes and say I don't think that's physically possible, Mum, but now I understand that it really is, because I'd say it happens to me on a daily basis."

He looks up from the bench. He's always had time to think—too much time, his sister used to say. *Stop dwelling, Henry, and move on.*

As Lucy continues talking, his mind wanders back to when he was a young man, when he always presumed he'd have a family of his own one day. After he met Greta, when he already knew he wanted to spend his life with her, he would imagine coming home from work to a house filled with children's laughter; he would imagine doing bath time and reading them bedtime stories and then settling on the couch with Greta, sharing a bottle of wine in front of a video he'd picked up from the rental shop on the way home. And it could have happened. They were married. They had a nice flat. He had a decent job with promotion on the horizon. A child was the obvious next step. Everyone said so.

Except Greta.

He shakes his head, dislodging the thought.

". . . and Jack has been working so hard lately that when he comes home, all he wants to do is crash, and I understand that, I really do, but I don't think he always understands that I need to crash, too, that I work just as hard as him but it's different work, that's all."

"Jack's your husband?" Henry says, vaguely aware she might have told him that already.

She nods. "Total whirlwind romance!" she says, and Henry knows he's done it now, she's going to tell him their whole relationship history. "We met on Tinder when I was twenty-five. He's a few years older than me. Anyway, first date, we were meant to be meeting in a bar in Nottingham, but neither of us clicked that there were two bars of the same name—well, not quite the same, one is Giraffe and the other is the Giraffe's Neck, but close enough, I guess, and that's what he said anyway, when he got the wrong one, because of course we'd said Giraffe and not the Giraffe's Neck, which is where he ended up, whereas *I* went to the right one. So I thought he'd stood me up, and I was so mad, because I'd had a series of bad online dates, and one guy who hadn't shown up at all, and it's so rude, don't you think? So I was about to go home and swear off men forever when he texted me and asked where was I and I said where are *you*? And then we realised what had happened, so then he came to find me, and honestly, we laughed the whole night, it was brilliant."

"Brilliant," Henry says.

"And then six months later we got engaged in Paris! The wedding took *so* much work, but it was perfect in the end—just us and about a hundred of our closest friends and family. Thing is, I must have been a bit lax, you know, because I got pregnant with Millie straightaway, which wasn't exactly planned. Honeymoon baby! But I wouldn't have it any other way."

He smiles, but her words make him a little sad. Internet dating. Texting. How the world has changed since he and Greta met in East Berlin. How things have moved on, whether he wanted them to or not.

"What about you?" Lucy asks. "Married?"

The question takes him by surprise. "Was," he says, but the word catches in his throat and emerges in a strangled tone.

"Divorced?"

He shakes his head.

"Oh," she says, and he almost sees the false assumption land in her head. "I'm so sorry. I'm so sorry you lost your wife."

Lost. As though he's misplaced her—and sometimes that's exactly how it's felt, especially at the beginning, though of course that's not what Lucy meant. He shakes his head again but doesn't correct her. He isn't like Lucy, he isn't used to talking about something so personal with a near stranger.

"Was it recent?" Lucy leans forward in the chair, her brows knotted together in sympathy.

"No," he mutters.

She cocks her head. "Still, these things can take a long time, can't they? My friend's aunt lost her husband ten years ago, and honestly I don't think she's ever got over it. Her house is plastered with photos of him, like a shrine, and recently my friend told me she broke this mug he gave her once and totally flipped out, like, practically had a breakdown over it, and I wonder if—"

"She's not dead," Henry interrupts, his face flushing. "At least, she could be, but she didn't die back then, as far as I know. She left me, more than thirty years ago." He says it with a shrug, as though he doesn't care one bit.

"Oh, right." Lucy's eyebrows fly up, and he sees her eagerness for a story, for gossip, and though part of him is annoyed by that, at least it makes a change. At least she won't roll her eyes and get cross if he brings up Greta's name, like Charlotte does. So when Lucy says, "What happened, if you don't mind me asking?" he realises that although a part of him finds it incomprehensibly brazen and actually quite rude that she should ask a near-total stranger such a personal question, another part of him wants to tell her everything.

So he does.

"And you haven't seen her since?" Lucy has been left open-mouthed by his description of that day—the cinema, the note, the aftermath.

He shakes his head. "She never contacted me—not even to ask for a divorce—and I never knew how to contact her. She just vanished. I'm only grateful she left a note or I might have thought she'd been abducted." He laughs a little, as though it's a joke, as though it doesn't matter, as though he hasn't blamed himself all these years for a reason he has never been able to pin down. *What did you do to make her leave, Henry?*

"You're still *married*? God, this is awful, how could she do that to you?"

He wants to take the words back, to erase the horrible picture he's created of his wonderful Greta. "I'm sure there was a very good reason, because she wasn't a cruel person." He glances at Lucy, but embarrassment prickles his face and he looks away again. "I'm sorry, you don't want to hear all this."

"No," Lucy almost shouts, "I do! It's absolutely fascinating—I mean, sorry, I know it's your life and all, but I have to know what happened. I mean, what possible reason could she have to disappear?"

He shrugs. "You tell me." And he sees, in that moment, that this is his opportunity to say the thing he's wanted to ever since Lucy arrived here today. "The thing is, I . . ." He thinks of Charlotte, of her anger at his desire to revive this quest after so many years, but he can't stop himself; it's his only chance, albeit a slim one, to get an answer, and it literally walked into his life.

"What?" Lucy leans forward, gripped by the soap opera of his life like a rubbernecker at a car crash.

"The necklace you were wearing the other day, the one made of twisted metal. I know it sounds silly but . . . I think it could have been made by Greta, my wife. She used to make jewellery like that, you see; it's very distinctive, and when I saw it on you, I recognised it—that's why I asked you about it."

"No way!" she almost shouts, eyes impossibly wide. "You're kidding!"

"I suppose there's a chance I'm mistaken, but I wondered if perhaps you might be able to tell me where your mother got it from, because maybe if I can trace its origins, I might be able to find out if it's hers, and if so, it might give me some clue as to where Greta went, or where she is now."

"Oh my goodness, *really*?" Lucy rummages in her handbag. "This is amazing!" She pulls out her mobile. "I love it. I mean"—she has the grace to look sheepish—"sorry, I don't love what she did to you or anything but I do love a mystery, and I am *totally* up for helping you with this. I just *knew* there was something about this place that was drawing me to it, and now I know it wasn't only because it's like a Scandinavian pine forest; it was because of this, because you have this mystery to solve and I'm meant to solve it! Mum?" she speaks into the phone. "It's me. So listen, I'm here with Henry Henderson, that's the woodworker guy I told you about, who was fixing that vase Millie broke, you know? And it turns out that a necklace I was wearing when I brought it in was made by his wife who disappeared on him all mysteriously thirty years ago and he has no idea why she left or where she went, because she only left him some rubbish note that didn't even say anything, and so he wants to know where you got the necklace from because perhaps it's a clue . . ." She pauses. "Yes! The pendant with the metal heart, the one you gave me. Yes, in Oxford. Yes, I know you didn't buy it here, but . . . Right. Uh-huh. Yes. Okay, great! Well, maybe he can contact them and ask. Brilliant! Thanks, Mum, see you in a fortnight if you're still coming down? Love you, bye."

Henry wonders if she took a single breath the whole time she was blurting out his personal life to someone he has never met.

Lucy puts her mobile down. There's an actual sparkle in her eyes. What does she think this is, an episode of *Inspector Morse*? "So Mum said she got it on holiday in a shop in Spain, would you believe it, somewhere near Barcelona. She's going to try to remember the name and will let me know. I mean, perhaps the owner won't recognise the necklace since it was quite a few years ago now, but you could email them with a picture of it and ask if they know who made it. What do you think? I could even help you; I'd be happy to. You could come round for tea or dinner or something, and we can plan it, or I can come to the Scandinavian pine forest again. So how about it, what do you think?"

There is a momentary silence while Henry catches up with all her many words.

There is only one he needs to say in return.

"Yes."

8

GRETA, 1982

The day I'd been dreading had arrived. Your eight-week working adventure this side of the Iron Curtain had come to an end. Later that evening you and Mike would be driving across the DDR, slipping through to the West and back to your lives in England, where I couldn't follow.

"How long will it take you?" I tried to keep my voice steady as we walked through Volkspark Friedrichshain. We were talking about the mundane details so we didn't have to address the bigger picture.

"Oh, about three hours to the border checkpoint at Marienborn," you said. "But Mike wants to allow four, to make sure we're there by midnight, when our visas expire, so we're leaving around eight."

Just five hours' time.

I couldn't help it, I stopped on the path by the lake and started to cry, a small child stamping her feet and refusing to walk any farther.

"Hey, *mein Schatz*," you said, and your use of the German term of endearment, uttered in a strong English accent, made me laugh and sob at the same time. "I'll come back; you know that."

"You'd better. If only so I can teach you to speak German properly."

"*Genau*." You grinned and kissed me, and the gesture loosened a knot of rage inside me—at the Wall, at the Party, at this stupid division.

"*Ach, Mann!* Maybe I'll sneak out in the trunk of your van after all!"

You smiled nervously. "I'll be double-checking, just in case."

I punched you lightly on the arm and then slipped my hand into yours as we walked on. I hadn't really meant it, and you knew that. In recent days we'd discussed the various possibilities for me to commit *Republikflucht*—the crime of fleeing the country. Always with a light touch, as though we wouldn't really contemplate something so dangerous, though I knew underneath we were both considering it more seriously than we made out. I could attempt to cross the Hungarian border into Austria whilst on holiday, I told you. I could try to find an escape helper and pay them to smuggle me out. I could build my own hot air balloon and fly myself over the German-German border (hardly, but Lena and I loved it that one resourceful family successfully escaped that way a few years previously). It would have been thrilling to flee like that, to put a finger up to the *Grenztruppen* in the watchtowers and the *VoPo* on the street corners and the Russian soldiers every woman knew to avoid and the Soviet officials who visited each Republic Day to watch our Nationale Volksarmee recruits march down Karl-Marx-Allee. The impulsive side of me loved the idea, and I could see, despite your clear anxiety at the prospect, that you would have risked something like that for me if I'd asked for your help. But I wasn't going to. I didn't want to get shot in the process or be arrested, or—if I actually succeeded—risk anything happening to my parents and sister as punishment for my actions. I'd heard too many stories of escape attempts gone wrong to try it myself; too many tales of those left behind being sacked from their jobs, subjected to constant intimidation by the Stasi, or even imprisoned after being charged with the crime of helping their loved one defect. So I'd told you, when we talked about it, that my only option was to try to leave legally—but even that came with risks. Applying to leave was technically allowed, but it was usually considered a political act, a betrayal of socialism. As Lena and her father had discovered to their cost, those who applied suffered in any number of covert and overt ways, with no guarantee of eventual success. And if you *were* successful, you had to give up your citizenship and right to return, along with any chance of ever seeing the loved ones you'd left behind.

"Listen," you said when we reached the lookout at the park's highest point, Mont Klamott. "I mean it, Greta. I have to go now, but I'll come back, I promise." It was mid-April, and the air was full of spring, new leaves budding on the trees, birds chattering in the branches, sun shining on the rooftops of Prenzlauer Berg down below—an oddly lighthearted backdrop for such a painful moment. But this was Berlin, where so much lurked beneath the surface, just like the remains of wartime bunkers under our feet on this grassy, artificial hill. "I'm not giving you up. Not if you don't want me to. I love you, Greta."

I felt the beat of my heart as your words hung in the air. Despite the speed of our relationship, we hadn't said it before. I put my arms around your neck and looked in those lovely eyes. "*Ich habe mich in dich verliebt.*"

You laughed and cocked your head—"I hope that means you love me, too?"—and I nodded and kissed you.

"Well, good, because . . ." You blew out a breath, as though preparing yourself for something, and reached into your pocket. "I'm sorry it's not a fancy one, I didn't know where to go to buy one, but I'll get you a better one later, when I can, and if you want it—I mean, if you want this one."

I looked at the plain band you were presenting to me, and joy bloomed in my chest. I had entertained the possibility, I had wondered what I would say, but I never thought you'd ask. We'd known each other just eight weeks. We were from opposite sides of the Iron Curtain. I knew you to be a cautious, sensible man, not an impulsive dreamer like me.

"I want to help you leave, but that's not why I'm doing this," you continued. "I've never found this stuff easy, Greta, but then I've never been out with a girl who makes being with her feel so easy." You cleared your throat, that familiar blush rising to your cheeks. "I love how determined and passionate you are. I love that you're a talented runner yet can match me drink for drink in a bar. I love that you'll queue for an hour to buy your mother a cucumber but have no patience for a slow Trabant on the road in front of you. I love that you mock me for my terrible ice skating, but I know it doesn't really matter to you one bit. I love how I can be myself around you and not feel that I have to be something else, something more or better." You took a breath. "I want to spend the rest of my life with you, Greta."

"*Henry*." How had this happened? How had I fallen in love with an Englishman right here in Berlin? It was the stuff of dreams. Actually, my dreams hadn't even gone there; it was too unrealistic, too unlikely.

"I mean, if you want to spend it with me, too, and if they let us," you went on. "And they might, right? They might let you leave to be with me, if we were married, if they can see that politics has nothing to do with it. So will you? Will you marry me?"

A breeze picked up then, the warm breeze of spring, rustling the new leaves on the trees around us. It filled me with optimism. It made me think that you could be right: for love, a genuine love that was clear for even the most hardened Party officials to see, perhaps, perhaps, they'd let me go.

And it *was* genuine, Henry; I hope you've never doubted that. I loved that blush on your face and those sea-blue eyes. I loved the way you spoke about your family with the same affection I had for my own. I loved your dry humour and your thoughtful questions about this crazy country. I loved it that I knew you'd consider living in Berlin for me, though I would never have asked you to. And so, there was only one answer inside me. I didn't care that the ring wasn't *a fancy one*, that it wasn't the sort of diamond or ruby-encrusted creation the women wore in the dubbed American romance movies I'd seen on West German television. I cared only that you were giving it to me.

"Yes, Henry," I said, holding out my hand. "Yes, I will."

It was ironic that the first person I should see after you proposed was Friedrich. Thinking back now, I wonder if he'd been following me, or if someone else had told him where I was. In any case, while it was clear he was giving you and me a great deal of thought, I really hadn't given him much thought at all in recent weeks. Our morning runs had fallen by the wayside, and I hadn't seen a lot of him, given I was spending most of my free time alone with you. He knew we were a couple, but I didn't imagine he was really that bothered by it. Fred and I were never going to be anything but friends. He knew that. Surely he wasn't still hoping for more?

But he was—I can see that now.

It was a form of masochism, then, for him to "bump into" me on Artur-Becker-Straße as I was rushing to Lena's place, full of my news and eager to share it with my best friend, the one person I knew who would be truly happy for me.

"*Hallo*, Greta." Fred stopped when he saw me and smiled, but it didn't reach his eyes. "I haven't seen you for ages."

"No, I . . . I've been busy."

"With him, I guess. The Englishman?" He'd been working with you for weeks, but he couldn't even say your name—which should have told me our relationship bothered him more than I thought.

"Yes." I smiled. "I suppose so." I never wanted to rub it in, but right then, newly engaged and brimming with love for you, I couldn't help it.

He shook his head, pursed his lips. "Not for much longer, though. They've finished at the factory; they leave today."

"I know." I didn't do it on purpose, I swear. But just then a gust of wind caught my hair and blew it in front of my face. I put my left hand up to brush it away, and as I did, I realised what Friedrich had seen at the exact moment he understood what it meant.

"What's that?" He grabbed my hand.

"My wedding ring," I replied—because that's what it was to me. We didn't really do engagement rings in the DDR. As per tradition, this would be my wedding ring; it would move from my left hand to my right when we married.

"You're not . . . ?" Friedrich dropped my hand and closed his eyes for a second, as though enduring some inner pain, and I was sorry then. I never wanted to hurt him. I'd known him most of my life. We'd had fun training together and watching each other compete at track meets. He was a nice person, a friend; I simply didn't love him, that's all.

"I am," I said softly.

He came close to me then. His eyes seemed to scour my face, though I don't know what he was looking for.

"A *Westler*?" He spat the word.

I half laughed, bewildered. Fred and I had never talked politics together. I knew his father was in the Party, though I'd assumed it was simply to further his career rather than because he was an ardent supporter. And it was clear Fred was more content with his life than I was, that he didn't share my restlessness, my desire for freedom from the control our country imposed on us. However, I didn't think he believed everything negative we were told about the West.

"A good person," I said simply.

"You hardly know the guy!" He lowered his voice. "If you're just doing this to leave, they'll know."

"But I'm not." I shrugged. "I'm sorry, Fred, you know I'm not. I love him. It's real."

He looked thrown for a moment, and then he composed himself, shook his head. "You don't know what you're doing, Greta," he said, his voice hard, and his comment from weeks ago came back to me then: *actions have consequences.* I'd thought it pompous, condescending, but now it felt ominous.

I held my head up and looked him straight in the eyes when I replied, "I'm doing what I want."

Happily, Fred's reaction was quickly shaken out of my head by Lena's.

"I decided he was worth it," I said, a huge grin on my face when I turned up at her place brandishing my ring.

Lena screamed and grabbed my hand. "I'm so happy for you!" She flung her arms around me, and I beamed over her shoulder until she pushed back and looked at me, eyes glassy. "This means you're going to try and go to England?"

I nodded, and she expelled a short, sharp breath. "Of course you are. *I* would. *Scheiße*, Greta, can you smuggle me out in your suitcase, if you go?" she joked, as tears leaked down her cheeks.

It was a big "if." But I didn't want to think about that right then; I simply wanted to revel in the knowledge that I was engaged to a man I loved. "I wish with all my heart I could," I said, knowing how much it would hurt to leave my best friend behind, and how much worse it would feel to be the one who was left. I wiped my eyes. "Come home with me?" I asked. "I need the backup."

We rode the U-Bahn back to Lichtenberg, walked up the stairs in my apartment block, and broke the news to my family.

I doubt I ever told you about that in full, Henry, because it wouldn't have been nice to hear. Mutti burst into tears and hugged me so fiercely, it momentarily squeezed the breath of out me. My father hung his head and wiped his hands over his eyes, a gesture of resignation, as though he'd known this would happen from the moment I first mentioned you. But it was my sister's reaction that broke me. She looked at me with such hurt in her face, such fierce indignation, that I felt sure I'd cut her so deep she would never forgive me.

"But why would you do that?" Angelika said. "Why would you want to go and live in a place we can't visit?"

I extricated myself from my mother and stepped forward to pull Angelika into a hug, but she moved away from me and crossed her arms over her body. *My little sister. My lovely parents.* I may have decided that I was strong enough to leave them, that your love made it worth it, but I hadn't considered they might not be strong enough to see me leave.

"I can come back and visit you," I said softly. "If they let me leave to be with Henry, it's not political, so I shouldn't have to give up my citizenship and I can come back to visit—with all the Dairy Milk I can carry." I smiled, but Angelika didn't return it.

"*If* they do, Greta," Vati said.

I didn't reply. I would go to the British embassy and ask them what to do. I'd get them to help me. This was love. Surely no one could stop me marrying whomever I pleased?

"But you could have stayed here and had Friedrich!" my sister wailed. "I know he likes you. He told me."

"*Schatzi*, I can't help who I love." My eyes flicked to my mother, who stood dabbing her cheeks. She gave me a sad smile but said nothing. My parents had always liked Fred, and it would have been easier for them if I *had* wanted to be with him. His family dutifully attended all the parades and took the subsidised holidays with his father's colleagues and often offered us vegetables from their allotment in exchange for my mother's sewing skills. Unlike you, he didn't rock the boat. He pretty much *was* the boat. But I knew you were the one for me, and my mother's silence told me that, despite her tears, she knew I'd have a brighter future with you than I ever would with Fred.

"Friedrich wouldn't make her happy, you know that," Lena said gently to my sister, and I threw her a grateful glance.

"And Friedrich couldn't help her leave," my father said.

It's ironic, really. Little did Vati know what he was saying. Little did he know exactly how Friedrich could "help" me. And neither did I, right then. Fred's *favour*, the deed that would set in motion a sequence of events I still, now, struggle to compute, was yet to come. I shook my head at my father's words. That wasn't the reason I was choosing you over Friedrich. I wasn't attracted to you because of your potential to fulfil my dream of leaving. I just happened to fall in love with someone who could.

"I can understand you wanting to explore the world," Vati continued, his voice gruff. "You've grown up here; you haven't seen the West, and it's only natural to be curious. But *I* have, Greta, and I can tell you it isn't as glorious as you think it is. They don't do everything right, just as this country doesn't do everything wrong. And when I think what that system did to your grandparents, what those fascists deprived us of . . ."

"I know that, Vati," I said softly. "I know." And I did, to an extent. While I was intelligent enough to realise that my teachers' criticism of the terrible West—an exploited workforce, an unequal society, a capitalist system on its last legs—was exaggerated, I also watched enough West German television to know it wasn't perfect, either.

But regardless, it didn't matter what it was like over there. It didn't matter if it was the worst place in the world or the best place for me, I simply wanted the right to discover its failures and triumphs for myself, to escape a country I felt trapped by, to be free to live where I liked with the man I loved.

Later that day, as I stood with you outside your boarding house, I took my keys out of my pocket and worked off the little wooden bear key chain I'd treasured since my father pressed it into my hands on my eighteenth birthday. Carved by my grandfather for his true love, my grandmother, years before they would both perish at the hands of the Nazis. A promise to my own true love, in exchange for the ring you'd given me.

You shook your head when I placed it in your hand and explained its significance. "That's too special, I can't."

I closed your fingers over it. "Yes, you can." I spoke carefully to overcome the catch in my throat. "But lose it and I'll never forgive you," I joked.

You put it in your pocket and looked at me solemnly. "I promise I won't lose it."

I kissed you, and we stood there, arms around each other, until Mike cleared his throat and said the van was all packed and it was time to go.

Remember this feeling, I told myself. *Remember this, in case he changes his mind and doesn't come back.*

And then you were gone.

9

Henry, 2018

He tries not to obsess about the necklace, and what it might mean, for the rest of the week following Lucy's return to the workshop. He gave her his number before she left, and she promised to phone him if her mother remembered anything about the shop in Spain, but he recalls the encounter with increasing embarrassment. He has never spilled his emotional guts to a stranger like that. Has never spoken to anyone other than Charlotte about the devastation he felt after the abrupt end to his time with Greta. When it happened, he couldn't bear to talk to his parents, who only offered up half-hearted sympathy and unbearable platitudes. Some of his friends drifted away after he shut himself off in the flat for weeks, watching bad films, eating poorly, and drinking too much. And those who remained didn't ask him much about what happened, preferring—as emotionally stunted British men in the 1980s tended to do—to take him to the pub and talk about the relative merits of the Ford Fiesta over the Vauxhall Astra, which was absolutely fine by him. It was only Charlotte he really opened up to, Charlotte who saw him in real pain.

He knows that's why she doesn't want him looking for Greta again, why she spoke so harshly to him the other day. But still, there are only so many digs about his *monochrome present* that he can handle, so he doesn't go round to his sister and brother-in-law's place on Wednesday like usual, and he doesn't tell her he ignored her advice and asked Lucy to investigate the necklace's origins.

But as it turns out, she knows anyway.

He is settling down to an episode of Attenborough's latest wildlife programme on Thursday evening, three days after Lucy's visit, when his sister calls him.

"Yes?" He bristles—at being interrupted, or at Charlotte herself, he isn't sure.

"I wanted to call and apologise," she says briskly.

"Wonders never cease," Henry replies, watching a leopard stalking an antelope.

"But then I changed my mind because a certain young woman got in touch."

"Oh?"

"Lucy Kenny, your necklace woman. She messaged me on Facebook, out of the blue. Got to hand it to her, she's good at finding people. Said some friend Susie or Sally or something had told her you had a sister called Charlotte who worked for Oxford University Press, and she did some online stalking and voilà. Anyway, she said she wanted to know if her instincts were right."

"Instincts?" he blurts, his brain still computing the fact that Lucy has talked to Charlotte.

"That you were a good guy and hadn't given Greta a valid reason to leave you back then, like knocking her about, or that other modern thing, what did she say? Coercive control, that's it."

"*What?*"

"I have to say, she's right to ask. For all she knows you could have been Ted Bundy."

"*Charlotte!*" He hardly knows what to say. Lucy, that exhaustingly garrulous, faintly absurd young woman, has had the foresight to check that Henry isn't a nasty piece of work before potentially giving him information about the whereabouts of his lost love. His cheeks flush at his misjudgement of the harried young mother, and her very sensible concern about him, a man she knows next to nothing about.

"What did you say to her?" It occurs to him briefly that Charlotte might have sullied his character in some way, just to put Lucy off, but surely she wouldn't be that mean, whatever her reservations about his mission.

"Don't worry, I said you were a lovesick puppy back then and wouldn't have hurt a fly. She said that's exactly what she thought, but she wanted to double-check. Sounded very happy. Said she had news."

"What news?"

"I asked her to do you a favour and not pursue this, but she was most insistent you had a right to know."

"Know what?!" He is sitting on the edge of the sofa.

"I don't know. She'll call."

He rolls his eyes. *Damn you, Charlotte.*

"And Henry?"

"Yes?"

"I *am* sorry," she says softly.

"Thank you." He sighs; he needed that.

"But that doesn't mean I think you should go ahead with this."

"I know."

"And I still think you should go on a date with Samira."

He nods into the phone. "Perhaps."

"Here," Lucy hands him her necklace, "take it."

They are standing in South Park as though it is a balmy spring day, when in fact it's hovering around zero and the grass and paths are dusted with a film of frost. Henry has his warmest jacket on, a woolly hat, thick gloves, and a scarf, yet still he is cold. It would help if they were walking, but instead, they are standing by a children's adventure playground, watching Lucy's daughter as she climbs a wooden structure, no sign of the cold in her flushed cheeks and delighted expression. "She's like a dog," Lucy said when he asked her why Millie wanted to play outside on a day like today. "She needs to run around a bit, use up some energy."

"But it's yours," Henry says now, though the twisted metal of the pendant heart draws him to touch it. Could Greta have touched it, made it? And if so, how long ago, and where was she when she did? The stories it could tell, this necklace.

Lucy shakes her head and smiles. "Keep it until you find her—then I'll have it back." Strapped to her chest, the baby gurgles, and she looks down and kisses him.

Henry hesitates and then takes the necklace from her and slips it into his pocket.

"And this—CAREFUL, MILLIE!" Lucy shouts and Henry turns to see the child sticking her head inside a hollow in the trunk of a large oak tree near the playground, "is the name and web address of the shop." Lucy fishes in her pocket and holds out a slip of paper. "Mum racked her brains for the name but couldn't remember—I mean, who would? It was years ago—but then she had the genius idea of searching on Google Maps because she thought she could vaguely remember where it was—some village north of Barcelona apparently—and she came across a familiar-sounding shop name, so she used the street view function to see the front of the shop and she recognised it! Isn't that amazing? And of course they have a website now, so anyway, there it is!"

He'd checked his phone as frequently as a teenager after Charlotte told him Lucy had news, and when she messaged him this morning asking if he would come to meet her in South Park, he dropped everything and dashed out the door. But now he's here, his face prickles with embarrassment—at his desperate need for whatever information she can give him, at her "background check" that hasn't yet been acknowledged.

"Thank you. Really, thank you—and your mother." Henry takes the slip of paper. Carina, the shop is called, in a place called Calella. He has never been there—never heard of it, and he tries hard to remember if Greta had ever mentioned it, if it was one of the places she dreamed of visiting. But no, he doesn't think so. Then again, if she wanted to disappear, wanted him never to find her, then she'd go somewhere she'd never talked about with him, wouldn't she?

Over the years, he's never stopped wondering where she went—or *how*, without her passport. Maybe she'd obtained a West German passport from the embassy in London, something she once mentioned would make travelling easier for her, but if so, she never told him. Perhaps, with that precious document in hand, she went to Hamburg or Munich or somewhere else in the Federal Republic. But he doubts it. She was always so eager to suck up new experiences; she was more likely to be living in Brazil, or Australia, or the Faroe Islands. He pictures her on the sofa in their old flat, flicking through brochures picked up from the travel agency in town. The Italian lakes. Paris. The Greek islands. New York. Places she'd wanted to go but had never been allowed. "We'll go on holiday soon," he would say to her. "But we need to save a bit first." He was so skint back then, after all those trips to Berlin. But to be honest, it wasn't only that. He'd travelled a bit after leaving school and he'd enjoyed it, but he wasn't the adventurous type, really. A week in the Algarve once a year was enough for him. Beyond that, he'd rather have spent his money on a decent home for them, somewhere big enough to house the family he hoped they'd start soon. Perhaps he should have admitted all that when they first met, but he could tell how much she yearned to travel and he worried she'd be disappointed he wasn't the avid explorer she'd assumed he was.

"I think you should email the shop, or call them." Lucy's voice snaps him back to the present. "But writing might be easier since you can use Google Translate to prepare a message in Spanish. I can help you if you like. Unless you don't want me to, of course, which is perfectly fine, I completely understand, I mean, it's your history, your life, and you probably don't want some random stranger dipping her oar in, do you? But if you *do* want help, I'm totally up for it."

Henry hesitates, hearing his sister's voice. *You're self-harming, Henry.* Perhaps he is. This stranger with her necklace is prodding an open wound that's been left to fester for far too long, and it hurts, it really does.

"You need to know, though, don't you?" Lucy asks when he doesn't reply. She puts a hand on his arm, squeezes it gently, and he startles at her touch, at the kindness in it. The kindness of a stranger. Then the moment is broken as she yells "MILLIE! DON'T GO DOWN THE SLIDE HEADFIRST!" and rushes over to the climbing frame, where her child is lying on her belly at the top of the slide, laughing at her blatant disregard for her mother's rules.

As Henry watches them, another life slides into view, a life filled with cheeky smiles on flushed young faces, with playgrounds on weekends, a sleeping baby strapped to his chest, and the mother of his children—Greta, because he only ever wanted to do that with Greta—by his side.

Yes, he needs to know.

"If it weren't for caffeine and sugar, I don't think I'd get through my days without falling asleep on my feet!" Lucy says as they sit in a café near the park. Oscar is merrily banging a spoon on the table, Millie is occupied by an enormous piece of chocolate cake and a babycino, and it occurs to Henry that it is Saturday and yet Lucy has the kids by herself, like she does all week, and her husband is nowhere to be seen.

She opens her phone. "Right, what do you want to say to the shop?"

"Er, I don't know."

"Let's start by asking them if they remember the necklace, and, if so, do they know who made it and whether she lives locally. Okay?"

"Okay."

She starts typing. "I'm writing it in Google Translate, and then we'll take a picture of the necklace and put it all in an email. Shall I do it from my account or do you want to send it from yours? I don't mind which. Maybe yours? I mean, it's your business, I don't want you to think I'm prying, or trying to take over or anything."

"No, it's fine," Henry says. "We can do it from yours." He likes the idea of having a gatekeeper, someone to shield him from what could be momentous news. He doesn't know if he could handle opening an email with news of Greta, after all these years.

He watches as Lucy types, muttering to herself as she does. "What was your wife's name? I'll include that, in case they remember her."

"Greta Henderson," he says, ignoring the use of the past tense. "Or Greta Schneider, I suppose, if she went back to using her maiden name."

"Schneider? What was she—German?"

"East German, actually."

Lucy looks up. "Wow! Then how on earth did you meet her? *Marry* her?"

"With some difficulty." He smiles, and tells her about his trip to East Berlin all those years ago, about meeting Greta in the Alextreff, about getting to know her over the weeks that followed, a relationship that was all the more intense for the short period of time they knew they would have together. He never could have imagined how that trip would change his life. How he would find love in a place so alien to him; how something so beautiful could come out of such an odd, grey, polluted city, where toylike Trabants trundled down the streets and a portrait of GDR leader Honecker hung in every public space, where the clubs felt like school discos and the restaurants were ridiculously cheap and an acrid smog hung over rows upon rows of identikit apartment blocks promising a dull but secure future under communism. If he'd known what would happen, would he have stopped himself falling in love with her, knowing how badly she would eventually hurt him? Charlotte asked him that once, and he hadn't needed to consider his answer. Of course he wouldn't.

"That's incredible," Lucy says. "What an amazing meet-cute."

"A what?"

"The way you met—it's like something out of a romance film. A Cold War romance film. Lovers on opposites sides of the Wall, drawn together against the odds." She moves a hand through the air as though painting a picture, and he smiles. She's a romantic. Like him. "I loved the Cold War module in history class at school. So fascinating," she adds.

History class. My God. He's so old. He doesn't know Lucy's age, but he imagines she wasn't even born when he met Greta. She's probably too young even to remember the Berlin Wall coming down, while he'd been on his own five years by then and watched it on the telly by himself in his new house, imagining Greta watching it on another television screen in another place. Where? In Britain? Farther afield? Or perhaps she was actually there—had she gone back to Berlin to be reunited with her family, to chip chunks off the Wall and celebrate their new freedoms? He scanned the crowd, knowing it was futile to do so but hoping to see her face, to know, for the first time in five years, where she was.

"A bit different to the way Jack and I met!" Lucy turns her phone screen to him, where the background image is a picture of herself and a tall, red-haired man. "This is us on our wedding day. It was the *best* day. We hired an old barn in Hampshire and got a wedding planner. I was a total bridezilla, but it was so worth it to get everything just so."

Henry takes the phone from her. It's a posed photo of the two of them standing in a field on a sunny day: Lucy in a floor-length dress with a train puddling on the grass, her hair in a complicated arrangement adorned with a floral headband; Jack in a tailcoat, a silvery waistcoat and a tie the same colour as the flowers in Lucy's hair. *The whole shebang*, as Charlotte would have said. Not the small, understated affair he and Greta had—she in a handmade gown, him in his best interview suit as he couldn't afford a new one. But the expression on Lucy's and Jack's faces is the same as theirs was. Happiness. Love. Certainty.

"What a lovely picture."

"It is." She smiles, and then rolls her eyes. "And now look at us! From young and carefree to nappies and babycinos," she says with a laugh, but there's sadness in it.

"Where's your husband today?" Henry asks, as nonchalantly as he can.

"Oh." She looks momentarily flustered. "He went to watch football with a friend. Work's manic at the moment, and he needs the downtime, you know?"

Henry nods. He wonders when Lucy gets any downtime.

"Anyway, what do you think?"

He reads what she's written on her phone and hands it back. "Perfect."

"Brilliant, I'll send it now. How exciting! I hope they reply."

"Thank you," he says, suddenly unsure about all this. A few days ago, he didn't know this woman, and now here she is promising to help him solve the mystery that has tormented him for more than thirty years. It is as though they are moving swiftly from strangers to almost friends, and he doesn't know why this young woman with a family would want this old man twice her age as an almost-friend, why she is helping him at all. Does she feel sorry for him? Does she need a "project" to distract her from the stresses of motherhood? He doesn't want to be anyone's pet project, doesn't want to be pitied. And yet she is the only person for many years who has taken any interest in what happened to him, who wants to help him instead of telling him to give up and move on.

"Lucy," he says, before he changes his mind. "Can I ask—why are you helping me?"

She looks at him but, for once, doesn't say anything straightaway. A flush rises to her cheeks, and he wishes he could take the words back. He has embarrassed her, though he doesn't quite understand why.

"I suppose I . . . well, I . . . You deserve to know what happened to your wife, Henry. *I'd* want to know, if it were me. If Jack had walked out on me with no decent explanation, I couldn't leave it, either." Her eyes fly back to the wedding photo on her phone screen. "It's not right. And I suppose I want to *make* things right. I mean," she pauses and turns to him, adding in a small voice, "is that okay with you?"

He nods, but he can't stop his eyes filling. *It's not right.* Yes—exactly. Something went wrong, the day Greta left him, and rather than writing off her love for him as some kind of deception or falsehood, like Charlotte did, Lucy believes in their love—he can see it on her face—and she wants to know, like him, why a loving wife would do what she did.

"My sister wouldn't approve," he says with a wry smile, an acknowledgement of her contact with Charlotte.

Lucy blushes a little. "Well, big sisters don't always know best." She smiles and nudges him with her shoulder. And although it should feel strange to receive that small but weighted gesture of familiarity, of understanding, from a person he didn't know a few days ago, this person whom he has only just considered an almost-friend, not even an *actual* friend, in fact it doesn't feel strange in the slightest; it feels a lot like he imagines it would to have a daughter or granddaughter, and for there to be no *almost* about them at all.

10

GRETA, 1982

Things went back to normal for everyone else after you left Berlin, Henry. No one really thought I would actually marry you and leave, you see. For most of my friends and family, our romance was a flash in the pan, a misjudged rebellion on my part that hopefully would be quickly forgotten. Though I sometimes caught my mother staring at me with a sad look in her eyes, she never asked me about you. Vati threw himself into organising our annual family holiday to our favour-ite campsite at Lake Balaton like it was a trip to New York. "How lucky we are to be able to go to Hungary!" he'd say with a loaded glance in my direction. "What a beautiful place it is!" Even Angelika seemed to forget the hurt I'd caused her with our engagement. You were gone, somewhere on the other side of an impenetrable wall, somewhere so alien to Angelika that I suppose it was as though you'd stepped off the planet entirely.

As for Friedrich, he was frosty with me initially, but he gradually thawed and resumed asking me to join him on a morning run, which I did to smooth things over, despite the way he'd spoken to me. He never mentioned my engagement again.

Clearly, no one thought you would come back for me.

I did, though. I wore that precious, imperfect ring every day: in my lectures at university, when I gazed out the window and wondered what you were doing; on my runs with Friedrich along the river Spree, pounding the pavement until the Wall rose up and we turned back; when we went on that camping holiday to Hungary and I swam in the lake with Angelika while Vati barbecued freshly caught fish on shore. My grandmother, Aunt Ilsa, and Uncle Wolfgang joined us there, as they did most summers—a chance for our divided family to meet up away from the city that had cut us in two—and I went on several long walks with my aunt, who asked me all about you and stoked my excitement about our future life together in the West.

"I'm over the moon for you, Greta," she said as I strolled along the lakeshore with her one day. "It's the best thing that could have happened. You'll have so many more opportunities in the West—you'll see."

A lump rose in my throat to see the genuine delight on her face. "You're the only one of my family who's happy for me."

"Oh, don't be so sure." She squeezed my hand. "Your mother would have tried to leave herself before the Wall went up if your father had wanted to. They'll miss you, that's all."

Her words surprised me. I knew Mutti wasn't a dedicated socialist, that she kept her head down for an easy life, rather than because she agreed with the politics, but she'd never told me she'd stayed here only for Vati.

"Have you put in your marriage application yet?" Ilsa continued.

I shook my head. "I went to the British embassy, and they told me to wait until I've graduated," I said, recalling the strange mix of excitement and fear that ran through me as I'd stepped into that building. Excited to take my first steps towards marrying you. Scared that the Stasi were almost certainly noting down my visit in the file they undoubtedly now kept on me. "They said I risked being kicked out of university if I did it sooner."

My aunt blew out a breath. "Probably so. Do it right after you get your results, then."

"But what if . . . what if I make things worse for them?" I nodded in the direction of my family, back at the campsite. The repercussions worried me. Maybe the Stasi would cause problems for Vati at work. Maybe they'd haul Mutti in for questioning and force her to say my relationship with you wasn't genuine and I was a political dissenter wanting to escape by any means possible.

My aunt stopped on the path and took my hands in hers. "*Schatzi,* sometimes you have to be a little bit selfish. Hopefully, nothing will happen. But if it does, they will cope. They will be okay. This is an opportunity for you to get out of that awful country and you should do everything you can to make it happen. And I'll be right there waiting with a welcome banner when you come through that bloody wall!"

I hugged her, relieved by her enthusiasm, which gave me hope this could all work out. Because at times it still felt like an impossible dream. If it wasn't for your letters, I'd have almost been able to convince myself our love affair had been a figment of my imagination. Thankfully, you wrote to me regularly, reminding me that I hadn't conjured our brief time together, that you still loved me and wanted to marry me. *I miss your laugh and your sexy accent,* you wrote. *I miss your Granny Smith hair. I even miss drinking terrible cocktails with you in the Alextreff.*

Sometimes those letters would turn up opened and resealed, with DAMAGED IN TRANSIT stamped across them, which told me the authorities were reading them, too, but I tried not to think about that. Instead, I devoured your words, drinking down everything you told me about your life in Britain: your work; your weekly pub quiz evenings with Mike and your other colleagues; and your day trips to Brighton and Bournemouth with friends, where you'd swim in the waves and barbecue on the beach, exactly like we did in Hungary. You'd never been to Lake Balaton, just as I'd never been to Brighton. Were we really any different, then? Were my freedoms actually more curbed than yours? My father would have said not; he would have urged me to appreciate everything I did have, rather than dwelling on what I didn't. *The grass isn't always greener, Greta.* But Vati was still clinging to an ideal about the DDR that I couldn't share. He still hoped that with the right leadership and the right reforms it could be the place his persecuted parents had dreamed of: a safe, peaceful haven where everyone had a fair chance at a good life and the evils of the past could never rise up again. It was a hope that made him willing to put up with the travel restrictions, the Stasi surveillance, and the control the state had over our lives, because he thought it would be worth it in the end.

But I didn't. I failed to believe that the only way to maintain peace and prevent evil was to live in such a constrained way. I was a racehorse champing at the bit, desperate to gallop, and this country was holding me back—something that was only confirmed to me when I got my exam results and the details of the job I would be ushered into.

Despite my top grades, I'd been turned down for the position I wanted—an interpreting role with a foreign trade organisation—and lumbered with a boring desk job translating technical manuals for imported agricultural machinery, with no chance of business travel to the West. I was obliged to accept it, or some equally unlovely role, as per the agreement every student signed in order to study at university, so that was that. It felt like a jail sentence, and I knew that in a sense it was—that I was being forced to endure this three-year contract as punishment for my relationship with you. But the authorities were sorely deluded if they thought this petty act of retribution would bring me into line. Because all it did was make me even more determined to leave. I saw my life stretch out before me, controlled and manipulated by the state for the next thirty years, working day in, day out in a dreary job I hated, and I knew I didn't want the dried-up brown grass of Berlin, that I had to hope for something greener—with you—or I'd go mad.

So I put my fears for my family aside and wore that ring when I filled in my application to marry you and sent it to the Ministry of the Interior.

The next few months were an exercise in patience that I struggled to endure. I felt I was holding my breath the whole time—as I continued my morning runs with Friedrich, as I struggled to focus on the technical instructions I was meant to be translating in the job I had now started, as I waited in queues to buy whatever sought-after produce might exist at the end of them, as I met up with Lena at a *Kneipe* and drank too much beer, testing her own patience as I moaned about my boring job and lamented how much I missed you.

"Maybe you have to accept it won't happen," my friend said, lighting a cigarette. Her father's application for them to emigrate had just been denied, no explanation given.

"No." I was vehement. "No, I won't accept that. It *will* happen; it has to. I love him."

"At least I won't lose you, if it doesn't," she said softly. "I love you, too, you know."

I reached for her hand across the table, heat prickling my cheeks. Here I was, moaning about my situation, when at least I still had a shadow of a chance. "I don't want to go without you."

"But you will. You want to leave with him more than you want to stay with me."

I hesitated, then nodded. I couldn't lie to my best friend, and she'd see through it anyway. "You would do the same, though, wouldn't you?"

She smiled with shining eyes. "In a heartbeat."

What was it, I've often wondered, that meant they said yes? They could have rejected my marriage application and doled out whatever repercussions they felt necessary. But perhaps I was right, back when you proposed, to think there could be some sliver of humanity in the hearts of those who made these decisions. Perhaps all the letters between us that they'd opened and read had convinced them we were truly in love and this wasn't just a ruse to help me leave. Perhaps my downstairs neighbour Frau Weber understood that the emotion in my voice when I spoke to you on her telephone was heartfelt. Perhaps, even, those faceless bureaucrats in the Ministry of the Interior and Stasi headquarters begrudgingly respected the fact that we were clearly continuing our relationship regardless of the barriers between us.

Whatever it was, on 3 November 1982, I received permission to marry you.

"You'll be needing a dress," my mother said quietly one Sunday afternoon, when only the two of us were home. "Shall I help you make one?"

My sister wasn't speaking to me, and my father was busying himself in his allotment, suddenly awfully keen to harvest his turnips. Only my mother seemed to accept the situation. I nodded, fighting back tears, and sat next to her on the sofa as we browsed *Brigitte* magazine for ideas.

"Have you ever regretted staying here for Vati, instead of going to the West with Ilsa when you had the chance?" I asked her as we flicked the pages.

Her hand stilled. "I wish I could have had both," she answered. "But no, never."

It was early December when you arrived back in Berlin with your best suit and your sister, and I will never forget how it felt to see you again. You were actually here—you hadn't changed your mind, or heeded whatever warnings your own friends and family may have given you about marrying me. And your face when you saw me again reflected the joy and excitement in my own.

"Greta, this is Charlotte, my sister and best woman. Charlotte, meet Greta, the love of my life," you said with a wide smile, when we'd disentangled ourselves from each other and acknowledged the woman standing beside you, whose eyebrows went up just a notch at your guileless declaration.

"So you're real," she said to me. She was slim, wearing stonewashed jeans and a fleece-lined bomber jacket, with a mass of brown curls framing her face. "I was beginning to wonder if he'd made you up." She held out her hand, with a smile as sharp as her fashion sense.

"It's so great to meet you finally." I stepped forward and pulled her into a hug, but she held me so lightly it was as if she didn't want to touch me. "I've heard so much about you," I added, ignoring the coldness I perceived in her greeting. Your face, looking on, was proud, eager, and I knew how important it was for the two of us to get along.

"Well, don't believe everything you hear," she said, a glimmer of warmth in her face.

I laughed, thinking she'd already thawed, but as I reached out for your hand—a hand I hadn't been able to touch for so many months—I saw her lips slightly purse.

In the days to come, I tried hard with your sister, but she never seemed completely at ease—with me or with Berlin, or perhaps both. *We're no different from you; we're all human*, I wanted to say to her, but I didn't. I only smiled, ignored her frostiness, and included her in the wedding preparations. I hoped she would eventually accept me as her sister-in-law, though I'm not sure she ever did. Sometimes I feel Charlotte knew me better than you did. Or, at least, she saw my flaws and weaknesses clearly, whereas you never seemed to. "He's sensitive, my brother," she said to me the day before our wedding in a rare moment when she and I were alone together. "Don't use him and discard him." I denied the possibility with a vehemence I truly felt, yet her words worried me; they made me feel I had a great responsibility, that your heart was a delicate, fragile thing I could crush if I wasn't careful.

All the time and money it took to obtain decent dress material, and all the hours I spent sewing under my mother's careful supervision, were worth it for the look in your eyes when you saw me in that homemade wedding dress. I wore it with a white, embroidered jacket Aunt Ilsa had brought me from the KaDeWe department store in Westberlin, better quality and more fashionable than anything I could find here. East and West, my past and my future; it was the perfect outfit in which to marry you.

I wonder what you remember about that day, Henry; what memories, if any, you still have of the moment our marriage began in a short civil ceremony at the *Standesamt*. I hope you have some happy ones. I hope you haven't blocked it all out because of everything that happened after that very promising start. As for me, here's what I remember: firstly, you, looking so anxious yet hopeful in your smart suit as I walked towards you in that drab administration room, and my own nervousness mixed with delight that you had come back for me, that you still looked at me with that same sense of disbelief and amazement.

"Hello, beautiful," you whispered, taking my hand and entwining your fingers with mine. There was such certainty in your touch, and it filled me with joy.

"*Hallo, Schatz.*"

"We're actually doing this."

"We really are." I searched your lovely face and saw nothing but genuine delight, but perhaps I wanted to give you a get-out clause, a final chance to change your mind about this marriage across the divide and choose a less-complicated English girl instead. I leant towards you, catching the familiar scent of you as I whispered in your ear, "No regrets?"

You looked me right in the eyes. "Not a single one," you mouthed.

And then I remember Charlotte passing us the rings during the ceremony. Lena urging me on, a bittersweet smile on her face. Ilsa beaming widely. My mother dabbing at her cheeks. Angelika sullen and distracted. My father stoic, resigned.

"Are you sure you want to do this, Greta?" Vati had asked me the day before, and I'd heard the unspoken questions echoing after the one he'd said aloud.

How can you want to leave us?

When will we see you again, once you've gone?

Do you really want to abandon everything you've ever known for something that may not be better?

But I simply hugged him tight, the day before our wedding, the day before the start of the rest of my life, and said the only thing I wanted to: "I do."

11

HENRY, 2018

She seems nice, Samira. Recently turned sixty. Widowed five years ago, with two grown-up children who live in Edinburgh and Southampton (she rarely sees them at the same time). Teaches history part-time at Oxford High but hopes to retire soon. Petite, casually but stylishly dressed in a dark denim skirt and a pale blue mohair jumper, with short dark hair, the roots showing just a little.

"Okay, then," Henry said to his sister, the day after Lucy sent the email to the Spanish shop. "I'll go for lunch with that woman."

He didn't really want to, but he was willing to do it to appease Charlotte's misgivings about Lucy helping him trace the necklace. Perhaps it will also demonstrate to his sister that this mission to solve the mystery of Greta's disappearance isn't about rekindling his marriage but about finding answers. (He doesn't know if he believes that himself, but it's what he's told Charlotte.)

"I must say, you're not quite what I expected, Henry," Samira says over her crab salad. It is Saturday, and they are in Browns, surrounded by groups of thirtysomething women with buggies, lunching middle-aged friends, and young people curing hangovers with a posh full English. He would much rather be in one of Oxford's cosy old pubs, but Browns was Samira's idea, and he is making an effort, after all.

"Oh?" Henry squirms a little under her gaze, though she is smiling.

"Don't get me wrong: it's a very pleasant surprise." She swallows and continues talking. "Only, your brother-in-law is quite a character, isn't he? And I expected, given we're meeting through him and his wife, your sister, that you might be somewhat similar."

Henry harrumphs as he cuts into his steak. "Not exactly. Ian and I tolerate each other in small doses, but each of us finds the other an acquired taste."

Samira laughs and takes another bite of her salad. "Well, I can understand that, and if I may say so, I find you very tolerable indeed."

"Oh." Henry shifts in his seat. "Thank you." He scrambles for some compliment to give her in return. "And I'm tolerating you just fine, too."

There is a brief silence and his stomach plummets, but to his relief Samira breaks out in raucous laughter.

"Sorry," Henry adds. "I meant to say, you seem very nice, and I'm enjoying your company."

Samira waves her hand as her hilarity subsides. "It's okay, I know what you meant. And you make me laugh, so that's even better." She pauses and sips her wine, then cocks her head as she looks at him. "It's not easy, is it, dating again after so long?"

"No. Sometimes I feel I've lost the ability to socialise altogether." If he ever even had it in the first place. "I'm sorry about your husband. That must have been hard."

"Extremely. But it's been five years, and my friends say it's time to *move on*," she waggles her fingers in air quotes, "so I'm trying. How about you, Henry? Ian said you were married once—how long has it been since you divorced?"

Henry puts down his fork and fixes his eyes on his near-empty wine-glass. "Oh, a while now."

"Well, these things take time. There's no manual for loss, is there?" Samira smiles. "Shall we order more wine?"

Their "date"—if that's what Henry is meant to call it—progresses pleasantly enough through to midafternoon. The restaurant empties out until there are only a few lunchtime stragglers like them, lingering over coffee. Samira is witty and entertaining, the wine is relaxing, and Henry feels no huge urge to flee, this time. Yes, she's wearing a little too much perfume, which overpowered the aroma of his steak; yes, she talks with her mouth full on occasion; no, she's not one bit like Greta. Yet he has to admit he's quite enjoying himself. He can almost hear Charlotte, congratulating him on this semi-successful foray into dating, urging him on, encouraging him to pay Samira compliments—decent ones, this time—to lean over the table, look her in the eye, *flirt*.

Nevertheless, he can't help but feel it's all a charade. He thinks of those exotic birds in Attenborough documentaries who waggle their colourful tail feathers and strut about in an awkward dance while the object of their desire pretends not to notice them. It is a game, a game he has never been particularly good at. A game he never had to play with Greta, because it was all so natural right from the beginning. He didn't need any tail feathers with her.

He thinks of Lucy's quest, of the email she has sent the shop, and the reply they are both hoping will arrive soon. Is it crazy to think it could lead to something?

"I'm really enjoying it, and it's so refreshing to do something different," Samira is saying.

"I'm sorry?"

"The salsa class I'm doing," she says gently, and he flushes to realise she knows he wasn't listening. "It keeps me fit, gets me out and about, but more than that, it's just joyful. I laugh the whole time, and that's really important, don't you think?"

"Yes, it is," he says, wondering when he last really laughed—a proper belly laugh. He used to laugh like that with Greta, didn't he? At least, in the beginning. But as time went on, perhaps they laughed a little less, as work and money worries and life got in the way.

"At first, I felt a bit guilty, going out and having fun, dancing and laughing, without Andy. But then I remembered he'd have hated salsa dancing; he'd never have gone with me anyway." She smiles. "It's so easy to romanticise those who have left us, isn't it? Easy to forget they'd drive you crazy squeezing the toothpaste tube from the middle and never being on time for anything and thinking Boris Johnson is a good chap, really."

Henry snorts.

"So I decided not to feel guilty and to just enjoy it," she continues with a shrug. "Because it makes me feel good—makes me feel young, too. That's what dancing with a thirty-year-old Venezuelan does for you, I suppose! Not that we're old, are we, Henry? But sometimes I can't quite believe how quickly time passes. But they say sixty's the new forty, and we potentially have another thirty or so years of life left, so there's no point letting ourselves stagnate, is there?"

Henry shakes his head. "You're quite right." Thirty years? The thought is terrifying. Is he going to be on his own all that time? Is he going to let himself just peter out, like an electric toothbrush running out of juice? And would anyone really notice if he did?

It is gone three by the time they step out into the late February air, the cold a slap in the face after the warmth of the restaurant. *The beast from the east*, the radio dubbed the tumultuous conditions this morning, and though he dislikes the British obsession with weather, he has to admit that this does feel different from the usual grey but uneventful UK winters. The air feels ominous, a harbinger of some great drama.

Samira slips her arm through his as they walk briskly to the bus stop.

"Thank you for lunch, Henry; it's been lovely. Perhaps we could do it again some time." To his surprise, she smiles at him with undisguised expectation, and it humbles him. He has not been the perfect lunch companion, yet despite his awkwardness, and his obvious dips in focus, she wants to see him again.

A bitter wind howls around them, whipping the bare branches into a frenzy and sending an empty crisp packet tumbling along the pavement. It occurs to him that he could be hit by a falling tree tomorrow. He could slip on icy pavement and smash his head. Or he could peter out unnoticed as he sits at home alone, still dreaming of being twenty-six and falling head over heels for his perfect woman.

"Yes," he finds himself saying, "we really should."

When he arrives in his workshop on Tuesday, after an arduous cycle on treacherous roads, he makes himself a coffee and examines the rocking chair in the corner. It came in with a broken leg and several deep scratches, derived from a shoddy moving company and several years abandoned in a shed, according to its owner, a fortysomething dentist called Jenny. She rescued it from said shed after her grandfather died; he made it himself as a young man, she told Henry, and she remembers sitting in it as a child. Now she wants it repaired so her own kids and eventual grandkids can use it.

He settles down to sand back the old varnish on the chair, and the morning passes quickly, as it usually does, with music on and a task to immerse himself in, so he is startled when there's a knock on the door. He turns to see Lucy's familiar messy blond hair and flushed cheeks through the glass.

"Do you mind if I make myself a coffee?" are her first words upon entering the shop. "I need coffee. Strong coffee."

When the kettle's boiled, she brings him a mug and takes her own to the armchair, where she sits, breathing deeply, eyes shut. Henry's heart is pounding, but he fights the urge to ask if she's found out anything about the necklace, if that's why she's battled the so-called *beast from the east* to be here. There is a film of ice and snow over the streets, felled trees blocking roads, schools closed due to broken boilers, yet still she has come.

"Bad day?" he asks instead.

She opens her eyes and smiles, a little sadly. "Bad *night*. I reckon I got two hours' sleep, max." She shakes her head. "Maybe it's the weird weather, I don't know, but I couldn't *get* to sleep for some reason, even though I was completely knackered, and then when I finally did, Oscar woke up three times in the night, and each time I really struggled to fall back to sleep afterwards, but eventually I did, only for Millie to wake up at six a.m., and that was it really." She sighs. "Honestly, I reckon you live a lot longer if you don't have kids." She laughs and looks at him. "I mean, I bet you sleep well, don't you?"

He shrugs. "Not every night." Certainly not the last couple of nights, when his thoughts have flitted between Greta and Samira, between the past and the present, between nostalgia for what could have been—*should* have been—and the glimmer of a chance offered by the here and now, a chance he doesn't know if he's brave enough to take. *You are allowed a second* one, *Henry*.

"At least this is Oscar's one afternoon in nursery, so I get a minibreak." Lucy laughs. "A minibreak in your Scandinavian pine forest."

"At dawn?"

"Precisely. Better than Prozac."

He doesn't ask. Instead, he watches as she sips her coffee and a line forms between her eyes. Stress? Fatigue? Preoccupation? It reminds him of Greta towards the end, the times he'd catch her sitting at her desk frowning out the window, or staring into her coffee as though the answer to life's big questions could be found within. *What's wrong, love?* he'd ask, but she'd only throw him a forced smile, enigmatic and indecipherable. *Nothing. I'm fine*, and he chose to believe her.

He stops sanding and looks at Lucy. "What is it?" He suddenly sees she is reluctant to tell him something; that she, who could talk for Britain, doesn't want to say aloud what she really came here for.

She sighs, her eyebrows knotting together. "I finally heard back from the shop in Spain."

He puts down his sandpaper. "Oh? They didn't recognise the neck-lace?"

"Actually, they did. They knew it well—said the woman who made it used to bring them lots of different pieces, and they were really popular. Then one day she moved away and didn't even tell them, and they were pretty sad about it, actually. They even owed her money from recent sales, but she never came to claim it or contacted them to send it on."

"Okay . . ." Was Greta in Spain? Did she live there for a while and then disappear again? He hears Charlotte's words, pictures her disapproving face, hears Samira saying, *It's so easy to romanticise those who have left us, isn't it?*, but he can't help it, can't stop himself. "And did they say it was her?" he asks. "Did they know her name?"

Lucy sighs again. "That's the thing." She pauses and looks at him, sadness all over her face. "I'm so sorry, Henry, but it wasn't her. It wasn't Greta. They said the jewellery maker was someone called Marianne Kerber."

12

GRETA, 1983

I think the ease with which I was allowed to marry you lured me into a false sense of optimism about my ability to leave Berlin. We were *married*. Yes, your visa expired after two wonderful days and nights together in the huge Interhotel Stadt Berlin on Alexanderplatz, forcing you to leave without me. No, I didn't know how long it would take for my exit visa to be processed. Yes, I had to remain in my tedious job, remain living with my family, remain behind the Wall until some official in a dark office somewhere in the Ministry of the Interior allowed me to go and be with my new husband. I assumed it would happen, however. I assumed, for the first few weeks after our wedding, that I would soon be granted permission to leave. Why would they have let us marry, otherwise?

But Christmas came and went, 1982 rolled into 1983, Berlin froze through another glacial winter, and I heard nothing. I'd filled in the endless forms. I'd jumped through all the hoops the authorities had asked of me. But all I got in return was silence. A great, oppressive silence, which I could fill only with the same old stuff: morning runs in the arctic air,

Sundays sewing with Mutti and Angelika, Fridays in a bar or disco with Lena, though I avoided the Alextreff, since it was too painful to think back to the moment when everything changed for me while right then it felt like nothing had.

I knew from your letters that you were as desperate as I was to have me with you in Britain. You couldn't wait to see me again, you wrote, to introduce me to a new life in Oxford, to show me off to your friends and family, the people you felt sure would become *my* friends and family, in the absence of my own. To be honest, I wasn't sure about that; despite my yearning to be with you, there remained within me a sharp stab of pain at the thought of leaving my family and friends behind, but I was grateful for your enthusiasm, your wide-eyed excitement. *I can't wait to meet them all, and to get to know Charlotte a little better*, I wrote back. *I'm so excited to create a life together—if they ever let us. I miss you so much, Henry. I feel like our marriage is in stasis, like my life is on hold, and it's not fair. Is it too much to ask to be able to live with my husband?*

It was a plea to whoever was reading our letters. A demonstration of the agony they were causing. *Look!* I was saying. *This is love. This isn't political.* It was only later that I understood they were using that agony to get me to do what I eventually, unwittingly, would agree to.

Then, one day in early April, as spring was finally showing signs of life, I bumped into Friedrich. I hadn't seen him for ages—not since I invited him to our wedding and he declined. He hadn't turned up at any of our usual haunts, or invited me to go running, and I'd accepted the demise of our friendship as collateral damage for marrying you. But one afternoon as I walked down Charlottenstraße towards the U-Bahn after work, there he was, unable to avoid my presence any longer.

"I thought you'd left," he said, though I was sure he knew perfectly well that I hadn't. My hometown was a tight-knit place, where something as momentous as a departure didn't go unremarked.

"Not yet," I said, as brightly as I could. "Soon, I hope."

He looked down at his feet, couldn't look me in the eye, so I was taken aback when he said what he did next.

"I could help you, if you like. I know some people. Maybe I could move things along."

He looked at me then, and his face was how it used to be: warm, open, friendly, like the old Fred, the one who would tease me about being a sore loser and challenge me to sprints.

"You'd do that for me?" I didn't think—or chose not to think—about *how* he could do that for me, or what type of people he must have known to make such a thing happen. You might think that naive or stupid, Henry, but what you have to understand is that in this Berlin in 1983, life ran smoothly only if you had what we called "vitamin B"—the *B* meaning *Beziehungen*, or connections: being friendly with the local shop-keeper who would save you some fleetingly stocked item in return for a favour; having contacts in the West who could send you good coffee, quality fruit, and Lux soap; keeping on good terms with the neighbours so they'd exchange what they had too much of for what you could offer them. Though it surprised me a little that Fred should have connections in high places, it didn't surprise me as much as you might expect.

Oh, who am I trying to kid? If I'm honest—because that's what writing this is all about, Henry—I *did* think it odd that my old friend would be able to pull strings at such a high level. Odd. Unexpected. Disconcerting. But I told myself it didn't matter; I told myself not to ask.

"*Natürlich*," he said with a shrug. "If you'll promise to do something for me when you get to Britain.

My heart sank a little, but his request was nothing onerous. I only had to promise to visit an old family friend, that's all. A man who left Germany years ago, before the war.

"We haven't heard from him lately, and Vati is a bit worried. We'd love for you to go and see him in London, to make sure he's okay."

"Of course." I wanted to laugh with the relief of it. "I'll visit as soon as I get there."

So, because of Friedrich and his *Beziehungen* in places I didn't like to ask about, I was granted permission to leave. I didn't tell you about all that, Henry, because I didn't deem it important. It was a modest request, in exchange for a huge favour he'd done for us. A favour that I, in my desperation to leave my country and start a new life in Britain with you, didn't think nearly enough about. I closed my mind to it, refused to ask myself the obvious questions, failed to compute the consequences.

But in the end, it changed everything.

"Henry?" I was waiting outside my apartment building when you finally reappeared in my life in late May, nearly six months after our wedding.

"Have you forgotten what I look like already, Mrs. Henderson?!" You stepped out of your car—a battered but spacious blue Ford, so incongruous in this city of Trabants and Ladas—like a mirage in the desert.

Your hair was a little longer, your skin slightly tanned, but it was still you, the same face I'd fallen in love with, the same man I'd married. I flung myself at you and kissed you fiercely, ignoring Frau Weber's disapproving face at the window of her apartment. This was legal. This was rubber-stamped. Informants like her could go to hell. "I can't believe this is finally happening!"

"Are you ready?"

I thought of everything I'd been through, all the bureaucracy and the waiting, the tension in my chest, the ache of missing you. My exit visa had finally been granted; I'd received approval from the authorities for everything I wanted to take with me; and I'd been to police headquarters in Alexanderplatz to collect my brand-new passport, an almost mythical document, since only those travelling to the West required one.

"I couldn't be more ready," I said.

Ahead of us was the short but momentous drive into Westberlin, where we'd visit my aunt and grandmother. A few days later we'd drive back into the DDR and transit the country to cross the border proper into the Federal Republic, then onwards through Belgium, France, and on to the UK, a journey I anticipated with so much excitement I could barely contain myself. But I tried hard, because before all that, I had to say goodbye to my friends and family.

You packed my belongings into the trunk while I hugged them, promising I'd come back when I could, and that I'd write, send photos and Dairy Milk and Nescafé. "*Scheiße*, you're actually going," Lena said, her voice wavering. "I can't believe it." I held her tight, a sob catching in my throat, before moving on to run the gauntlet of my family: the hurt in my sister's face, the shine in the eyes of my normally unemotional father, the fierceness of my mother's embrace. "Make the most of it, *mein Schatz*," Mutti whispered out of Vati's hearing. "Seize this opportunity with both hands." I knew I was hurting them, but I thought it was worth it, thought I was leaving them to pursue a long, happy life in Britain with someone I loved. I didn't know I was putting them through all this only to later touch a match to my opportunity and see it go up in flames.

Friedrich showed up to say goodbye, too.

"Here." He handed me a postcard depicting the bulbous, silvery television tower, the pride of the Hauptstadt, set against a bright blue sky. I flipped it over. An address was scribbled on the back. "Don't forget."

"I won't." I tucked the postcard safely in my handbag. "I really appreciate what you did, Fred." I stepped forward and pulled him into a hug as you waited by the now-packed car. "Really. Thank you."

And I have never forgotten what he said in response, his eyes cast down in what I thought was sadness at my leaving or dented pride at his failure to win me for himself. "You deserve it."

I waved at them all as we set off, my vision blurred with tears, but when we rounded the corner and I could no longer see them standing on the curb, my eyes dried and my stomach flipped. You looked at me and smiled, and I put out my hand and squeezed your leg. This was it.

My whole body trembled as you rolled the Ford up to the checkpoint on Heinrich-Heine-Straße. I handed over our paperwork to the border guards. We waited for what felt like hours as they checked and rechecked it and finally stamped it and handed it back. I tried hard not to think about the people who had attempted to cross the Wall without paperwork over the years, those who had become ensnared by the searchlights and the wire and the gun-toting guards on the *Todesstreifen*. I was one of the lucky ones. I was being granted the freedom those other people had been imprisoned for, or even died for, because you loved me. What had I done to deserve that?

We passed through the checkpoint as though it was nothing, and you stopped the car on the other side.

"Okay?"

I nodded and opened the door, placing one foot and then the other out of the car until I was standing on Western soil for the first time in my life. When I was able, I took a deep breath and looked up at the side of the Wall I had never seen. *Die Mauer*. Above it, back on the other side, the television tower rose up, so near and familiar yet suddenly so, so far away. My knees buckled, and I sank to the ground. It was nothing to you, this sight, yet to me it was everything.

You came around to my side of the car and crouched down before me, concern all over your lovely face. "Are you all right?"

I nodded. I couldn't speak.

"We made it," you said softly. "*You* made it."

"We did," I said finally, laughing and crying at the same time. "We really did."

I stood up and you pulled me into your arms, and as I hugged you, I stared at the Wall over your shoulder and saw my future spreading out before me.

I was in the West, where everything would be different.

PART TWO

13

Greta

Tofino, Vancouver Island, Canada, 2018

Greta shuts her laptop as the low sun streams through the window of her camper van. She has been typing a little each morning: waking early, making herself a coffee, and wrapping herself in her duvet to fend off the late February chill as she writes.

Though she is writing to Henry, she doesn't intend for him to read it, of course. She knows where he is—these days, most people are easy to find if they aren't trying to hide, and when she googled him several years ago, his website told her he works as a furniture restorer in Oxford, where she left him back in '84. It doesn't surprise her. In a way it makes her feel she did the right thing. He is where he was meant to be, where he always wanted to be, doing the thing she always hoped he would. Not out here, far away from family and friends, accompanying her on this strange nomadic life she leads.

Sure, you tell yourself that if it makes you feel better.

At first, she didn't understand why she was writing this—what? A letter, a confession?—but now she has come to realise that it's because of Tomas. Because, more than thirty years after she fell in love for the first time, she's fallen once again. And she can't make sense of her feelings this time around until she comes to terms with what went wrong back then.

She remains in bed for a minute, listening to the caw of the gulls and the crash of the waves on the beach, then reaches for her phone and turns it on to read the message she knows will be there.

Morning, sweetcheeks x

Tomas will have sent it hours ago, up early, as usual, to get to the restaurant. She imagines him taking delivery of the day's orders, plying his staff with coffee and croissants when they arrive, before ushering them to their workstations to begin the long, detailed prep for lunch service.

Morning, Schatz, she texts back. He likes her using the German term of endearment. Treasure. Darling. Sweetie. It's been nice to use it again, to have someone to use it *on*, once she got used to the idea. The first time she said it to him, a few months ago, it was accidental—it came out of her mouth unbidden, and though it felt natural, it scared her a little that it did. "What does that mean?" he asked, and she explained, and he looked at her with such softness in his eyes that she had to look away. Ever since then, each time he's messaged her he's greeted her with a different English synonym of the word: Pumpkin. Honeybun. Sweetcheeks. Snookums. It makes her laugh.

Sometimes, it makes her want to run away.

She throws back the duvet, goes to the sink, and splashes water on her face, drying it on the towel in the small shower room an arm's length away. She can walk the length of her home in three strides, but she loves this camper van despite its small size. It is simple, uncluttered. "I don't know how you stand it," Tomas has said on more than one occasion, "it's so cramped." But she just shrugs. She doesn't know what she'd do with the kind of space he has in his beautiful wooden house farther up the peninsula. Her camper contains all she needs. And if there's one thing she's learned over the past few decades of moving and stopping and then moving again, it's that she doesn't need much.

Nevertheless, a few precious possessions are important enough to have earned their spot in her life, accompanying her as she's moved from place to place, country to country. Hanging over her bed is her grandmother's embroidery sampler, which takes her right back to late-sixties Berlin, before Oma reached pensionable age and left to live with Aunt Ilsa in the West. In the drawer under the fold-down bed is a battered tin that once held East German chocolates—not nearly as good as the Western stuff Ilsa would send in her *Westpakete*, but they ate them nonetheless—which she now uses as a jewellery box for the rings she doesn't have the right to wear and the silver bracelet she does. Among the few paperbacks she keeps on a shelf below her bed is a copy of Orwell's *Nineteen Eighty-Four*, given to her in Oxford by someone she shouldn't have been meeting, a book she's kept all these years as a sort of masochistic reminder of her bad decisions. And hanging on the coat hook is Henry's old scarf, a little moth-eaten now, but as precious to her as everything else.

She pulls on leggings, a long-sleeved T-shirt, and sneakers, and scrapes her shoulder-length grey-blond bob into a ponytail. She steps out of her van, locking it behind her, and starts to run along the path through the woods, breathing in the scent of pine needles mixed with salt from the sea, which lies just through the trees. Tomas always worries about her doing this alone—there might be bears in these woods, or even a Sasquatch, if legend is to be believed—but Greta has run alone for years, and she isn't about to stop now. In any case, it's not animals or mythical creatures that pose a threat to her.

She runs every morning. It has kept her fit, and at fifty-eight she is lean and toned, a little too much, according to Tomas, who cooks for her or takes her out for dinner at every available opportunity. She doesn't object. The food here is glorious, especially his, and she never seems to put on weight, however much of it she eats, a consequence not only of the running but of the wariness and hypervigilance that have become her constant companions over the years.

She knows he just wants to take care of her. She understands that with each dinner, each date, they are moving ever closer to a shared life, a shared home. And perhaps she should let it happen. Is she really going to keep living in her van when she's eighty? Does she really want to shut out this second chance at love? But the thought of it is as unnerving as it is compelling.

She does her usual ten-kilometre loop until the woods part and she sees the sea. She warms down on the beach, going through her stretching routine, before returning to her van, where she'll shower and maybe write for a while before she's due to meet Tomas at the taco place. It's their regular Saturday lunch date, a commitment that never changes, and she lets him have this, lets him pin her down for that hour or so. It's her way of showing him that their relationship is important to her. But if she's honest with herself she knows it's not much of a commitment, not when she continues to live in her van, by herself, knowing she could take off and leave him behind at any moment.

The taco place is another van, a silver bullet parked up in the car park of a surf shop, from where cheery young chefs whip up the best fish tacos on the island. There is always a queue, even in February. But Tomas is always invited to jump it—he knows one of the chefs, Matteo, just as he knows everyone involved in food on the island. Thirty years he's been here, ever since arriving from the mainland after a decade learning his trade in other people's kitchens, ready and able to set up his own right here.

Thirty years! Greta can't imagine staying in one place for so long, now. After the first twenty-three years of her life in Berlin, she's lived in so many places she's lost count. In fact, it's unusual she's stayed here in Tofino, Vancouver Island, for more than two years, her nomadic lifestyle temporarily paused by a man who looks at her in much the same way that Henry did, a long time ago, in another life entirely. A man she loves, just like she loved her husband, though she almost wishes she'd never met either of them.

As she approaches the taco van, she sees Tomas sitting on one of the wooden picnic benches strewn around the car park. He is playing idly with his phone, looking up occasionally to wave hello to someone or take a sip of beer from the bottle in front of him. Most chefs are wedded to their kitchens every Saturday, but after directing the prep, Tomas likes to leave the lunch service to his sous-chef, a young guy called Danny Wong with a bright future ahead of him. It's a chance for Danny to shine, Tomas says, and a chance for him to spend quality time with her.

He's a good person, Tomas. A kind person, an open, friendly person who is fiercely loyal and would never let anyone down. What he's doing with someone like her, who is guarded and fiercely independent and has let down more people than she can say, she doesn't know. They are like chalk and cheese, and she's told him so—if not all the reasons why. "Yeah, but I love cheese," he said. "I think I'm the chalk," she replied.

She walks closer to the silver bullet, skirting the queue, until she's nearly in front of him. He catches sight of her and puts his phone down, his face lighting up.

"Hey." He leans forward to kiss her as she sits down opposite him. "I already ordered—your favourites, naturally."

"I'd have expected nothing less." She smiles and takes the bottle of beer he pushes towards her. "You okay?"

"Better for seeing you." He squeezes her hand across the table. "I feel like it's been a while."

"It's been three days." She laughs.

"I guess I just miss you. But at least you leave me some loving reminders. Your hair in my plughole, a mug of half-drunk coffee on my windowsill . . ."

"I did? Sorry." She pulls a face. "It's only so you won't forget about me."

"Not possible." He laughs and takes a swig of beer. "You know I'm joking—I love your hair clogging up my plughole."

"Is that a euphemism?"

"You're the translator; you can take it as you wish . . ."

"I'm still trying to get my head around your weird sense of humour, *mein Schatz*."

"Weird?" He looks askance. "Coming from a German? Is there even a German word for 'sense of humour'?"

She swats him on the arm. "Not fair! I don't know Latvian culture well enough to tease you back."

"*Canadian*-Latvian: we're a breed unto ourselves."

"Peculiar, you mean?"

"Touché." He laughs, before his expression changes into one of uncertainty, a little boy about to ask for more. "You know," he says, "there's a way we could both get used to our funny little habits a lot more quickly." He looks away and then back again, as though steeling himself for her reaction, and she sees what's coming and she wants to stop the words in his mouth, to push them back down his throat where they can't ruin everything, where they can't change the status quo. She likes the status quo. It is enough for her. More than she's allowed herself for a long time.

She is saved, briefly, by their food arriving, delivered with a smile and an "Enjoy, folks" by Matteo. She reaches for a taco, but Tomas stills her hand.

"Listen, this isn't me messing around. I've been wanting to ask you for a while." He hesitates. "I know you said you want to take it slow, and you're stupidly attached to that shitty camper van of yours, but we're not getting any younger, and I want us to be a proper couple. I want you to move in with me. Can't you take a chance on us, Marianne? Can't you take a punt on a stupid chef who loves you something crazy?"

Greta's stomach churns with the contradiction in his words. *She's* the stupid one. She's the one who's managed to mess up her life to the extent that the man who loves her doesn't even know her real name. She's the one who's spent decades running and is still too scared to stop.

He is looking at her. She must say something, must respond to this perfectly reasonable question before her lack of response says everything and she loses him. Her hand goes to her necklace, feels the twisted metal of the flower-shaped pendant she is wearing. "You know you'd have to put up with my stinky running shoes in your hallway," she says, trying to revert to the lighthearted banter they shared before his big question.

"I'd embrace that stale sweaty odour like it was my very own."

She laughs, hoping that's the end of it, that she has wriggled out of the question, but he is still looking at her, waiting for more. She owes him more.

"Let me think about it," she says, the only thing she can say, the only thing that is honest, but it spears her heart to see a smile broadening across his face at what he takes as halfway to something she isn't sure she should give him, a brief glimmer of a future she's never let herself see before.

14

GRETA, 1983

It was thrilling, moving in with you, Henry. I can hardly express how exciting it was to finally be able to start our marriage properly in a country I'd never thought I'd see. I was Alice in Wonderland, Dorothy in Oz.

I didn't have a job now, of course, so in those first few weeks, when you were at work, I'd go exploring. I wandered through Oxford city centre, gazing up at the gargoyles and dreaming spires I'd only ever read about, pottered through the covered market, and glimpsed manicured college quads through tiny, old wooden doors. I went to the supermarket and stood open-mouthed in front of the vast range of products: a kaleido-scopic array of fresh fruit and vegetables; dozens of different cheeses from all over Europe; so many brands of biscuits and orange juice and chocolate that I'd spend hours choosing; and proper Coca-Cola, such an intense shot of flavour compared to the version I was used to in the DDR. The clothes shops were eye-popping, too: well-fitting jeans in quality denim; blouses and jumpers and dresses in wool, silk, and cotton, a world away from the unfashionable polyester clothing in the shops back home. Then there was the library, from where I'd borrow books I'd heard of but never been able to get hold of freely—Orwell's *Animal Farm* was my first pick—which I devoured with relish in the park or on the sofa, and the travel agent where I'd pick up brochures about Greek islands and Californian beaches, places I now had the freedom to visit.

Best of all was being with you after so long apart. When we were together, you made so much effort. On the weekends we'd get in your Ford—"the old banger," you called it, a phrase I added to my growing mental dictionary of English colloquialisms—and go somewhere I hadn't yet been. To a Cotswold village where we'd walk through the picture-perfect lanes and picnic in the fields. To beautiful Stonehenge and nearby Salisbury, or down to Brighton or Bournemouth, where we'd eat ice cream on the beach and swim in the waves (with our swimsuits firmly on—unlike back home, naked bathing was not the done thing, you told me). In the evenings we'd go to the cinema to watch a new release I knew wouldn't make it to Berlin for several years, if at all, or rent the latest Hollywood action movie from the video shop and snuggle up on the sofa with no concern about who might judge our viewing habits.

"I'm sorry this house isn't up to much," you said to me one night soon after I'd arrived, when your housemates John and Ant were out and the two of us were sharing a bottle of wine and a pizza in front of the television, which required a thump in the right place to make work. "We'll get our own place as soon as I can afford it."

I kissed your cheek and smiled. "It doesn't matter. I don't care where we live as long as I'm with you." I meant it, though it was true that the house we shared was pretty bad. The sitting room was constantly messy and contained only a sagging sofa, that temperamental television, and a tatty old striped rug. The bathroom had mould growing between the tiles, and your room—*our* room, now—smelled musty and dank, however much I tried to air it. I'd been surprised at first, having assumed that British homes would be so much better than those in the DDR, and I admit my heart sank a little as I pictured the modest but clean and comfortable family apartment I'd left behind, but I brushed the feeling away. This was just the start of our life together; the point was that we now had the time and the opportunity to do whatever we wanted with it.

"I got you something," you said later that night, when the film was over and we were kissing on the sofa like the newlyweds we still were. "I wish I could have given it to you before but, well . . . Anyway, I hope you like it."

You handed me a small box, which I opened to see a ring nestled in the velvet lining—a single cut diamond set in a band of pure gold.

"Henry, I . . ."

"I wanted to do things properly, to get you the engagement ring you deserved."

"You really didn't need to," I said, thinking of how much it must have cost, money we could have put towards a home of our own, but I smiled as you took my hand and removed that old ring, the one you'd given me back in Berlin, and put the sparkling new one on my finger in its place.

"It's beautiful." It really was, Henry, and when I looked into your face, I saw how much love there was in it, and how much pride that you'd been able to do this for me, to *do things properly*, as you put it. I saw, suddenly, that you were that sort of man; that falling in love with a girl you'd met on a work trip beyond the Iron Curtain had been way outside your comfort zone, but putting a traditional diamond engagement ring on her finger wasn't.

I never told you—because I felt sure you wouldn't understand—that I didn't much care for that perfect ring with its perfect diamond. I liked the plain, unfussy one you gave me in Berlin, when we were heady with each other, revelling in the newness of our love and the anguish of your impending departure. I didn't mind that it had no diamond, or that the join in the metal was clearly visible. I loved it anyway, because it embodied the moment you gave it to me, and it represented us in a far more realistic way than a sparkling diamond ever did.

"I can't believe you're here," you said that night on the sagging sofa in Oxford, and I dismissed my burgeoning realisation about the difference between us. I dismissed it and let myself be enveloped in your delight and enthusiasm for our fledgling marriage.

"I'm here and I'm not going anywhere," I said.

Something else I did in those first couple of weeks in Britain was pay a visit to the address written on Friedrich's card. I wasn't desperate to meet this old man—though I always intended to, because I'd promised I would—but the fact he lived in London made me keener than I otherwise would have been. Until now, this famous city could have been on the moon for how easily I could get there, but now it was a short train ride away, and I had ample reason to go. I would fulfil my obligation to register at the East German embassy, spend some time exploring the city—Big Ben! Buckingham Palace! Trafalgar Square!—and then go to see Fred's family friend.

I took the train to Paddington and spent the morning wandering the capital, your battered old A–Z in hand. I took pictures with your automatic camera and imagined how I would describe it all in letters to Lena or Angelika, wishing they were there with me to see for themselves— because only other *Ostlers*, I realised then, could truly understand what this freedom felt like.

In the afternoon I took London's U-Bahn—the Tube, as I later learned to call it—to Stockwell and walked down a busy road before turning right into a quiet residential street. Number 5, top flat, according to the address on Friedrich's card. The home of the man who called himself Olaf Lang.

He had an abundance of hair. That was the first thing I noticed when he ushered me into his apartment after answering the intercom. He was a large man, probably in his sixties, but age had not challenged his follicles. The hair on his head was thick and bouffant, silver streaking through what must once have been a rich brown. It spread down the sides of his face until it merged into a beard, which was greyer than his head hair but just as copious. His eyebrows sat in dense, dark half-moons above vivid blue eyes. Even the backs of his hands were covered in wiry, silver hair. I wondered what he would look like after a haircut and shave and had absolutely no idea—and that, I realised much later, was probably the point.

He welcomed me in, and I followed him into his flat, the small hallway leading into a sitting room that had the air of a sepia photograph. The carpet was a faded green, the wallpaper an off-beige with an unappealing flocked pattern. There was a brown sofa and a matching armchair, which was clearly Olaf's favourite seat since it faced the television, while an adjacent side table held a book, a pair of reading glasses, and a copy of the *Radio Times*, open at that day's listings, with several programmes circled. The radio was on. *The Archers*, he told me. "Do you know it?" I shook my head. "Soap operas are the best way to get to know a country," he said with a smile, before leaning towards me in a conspiratorial manner and adding, "Just make sure you don't get addicted, like I did."

He made us coffee and cut slices of pink-and-yellow Battenberg cake with—rather oddly, I thought—a penknife, which he produced from one trouser pocket and wiped on a handkerchief of dubious cleanliness from the other.

"It's kind of you to visit. Here, please take a seat," he said in his clipped English voice, to which I replied in German, thinking he might appreciate a rare opportunity to speak his native language, but he didn't take it.

"I do not speak German in this country," he told me. "In any case, you must continue to practise, to eliminate that small accent of yours. It is the only way to properly assimilate."

I shrugged, bristling slightly at his acknowledgement of my accent, but I was happy to speak English. And he was right—I'd noticed the sometimes curious, sometimes hostile reception I'd had on opening my mouth in this country, and I didn't like it. I wanted to fit in, like he clearly had.

"So, my dear, how did you come to be in Britain?"

I related my story, told him about meeting you and our wedding and departure, and he listened attentively, a kindly old uncle humouring his favourite niece's breathy enthusiasm. In turn, I asked him about his own circumstances, how this German sixtysomething had come to be addicted to *The Archers* in a small top-floor flat in London.

"I came here because of the evil that took over our country"—he said, and for a minute I thought he was referring to the Soviets—"the Nazis."

His father saw the evil in Hitler from the beginning, Olaf continued. He understood how economic depression, poverty, and high unemployment following the crash of 1929 had caused unhappiness and unrest among ordinary Germans. But Olaf's father was never taken in by the new chancellor's supposed answers. He embraced a different alternative, a way he saw to truly make the world a fairer place—communism. He passed his Marxist views on to his son, and as Olaf grew up in the thirties, he became an outspoken student member of the German Communist Party, and therefore a target, along with the Jews and the Romani people and anyone else Hitler despised, for Nazi persecution.

It was Friedrich's grandfather, Kurt, a family friend and fellow communist, who helped Olaf and his brother get out of Germany and flee to England not long before Hitler invaded Poland.

"We came here with hardly anything in our pockets—apart from this knife." He waved the penknife in front of me, and I understood, then, his attachment to it. "And here we have remained. Well, *I* have remained. My poor brother died in the fifties, hit by a tram during thick smog. Can you believe it, Greta? Thwarted Hitler, only to be felled by the number twenty-two." He laughed, and I smiled tentatively back. "Of course, many others didn't get out at all. Our parents perished in the camps for their communist views."

"My father lost his family, too—all of them," I said.

"Then you understand." Olaf looked at me with no hint of surprise in those blue eyes. I wondered, later, if he already knew my family history, if Friedrich had told him, and if that's what made me vulnerable. "That's why we must do all we can to uphold the communist state. It's the only way to protect ourselves from the ongoing threat of fascism." He leaned forward. "And it's more critical than ever now, with that warmonger Reagan poised to unleash his Pershing missiles on us all." His voice trembled on the final word, a flash of anger, before he sat back in his chair and his benign smile returned.

I tried to supress my surprise. Here was a man who had lived in the UK for more than forty years, who enjoyed British soap operas and Mr Kipling cakes, who spoke near-unaccented English and refused to converse in his native language. I had assumed that he would be fully assimilated in the capitalist West, that he wouldn't be on the same side as the DDR in this Cold War. And yet there was an echo of my father's words in his own.

"If you're still a dedicated communist," I ventured, "then can I ask why you never moved to the DDR, after the war?"

He regarded me with those clear eyes, but I couldn't interpret his expression.

"Because life is more complicated than you know, my dear." He smiled, and I knew I'd get no more answer than that. "Now, would you like more cake?"

Later, back home with you, I told you all about the hirsute old man who refused to speak German and had lived in England most of his life yet seemed fervently devoted to the DDR.

"Eccentric old duffer," was your judgement, but I couldn't dismiss him like that. I couldn't dismiss someone who had grown up under the rise of Hitler, who had lost his family and watched his city be nearly destroyed before being divided by foreign powers. It would be like dismissing my own father.

Instead, I vowed to go back soon, to give this—yes, slightly eccentric, but welcoming and friendly—old man a bit of company from time to time, to talk to him about my country in a way I couldn't with anyone else here, and to see a little more of London in the process.

You'll be glad to hear he's well and in good form, I wrote to Friedrich. *I'll visit him again.*

It was the start of something, Henry, but I didn't see it then. I was Alice. I was Dorothy. I was at the start of a colourful new journey, and I didn't know what darkness awaited me as a result of meeting Olaf Lang.

15

HENRY, 2018

Henry doesn't expect to see Lucy again. There is no reason, after the disappointment of the necklace, for her to remain in his life. This knowledge stokes the maudlin mood that descends on him in the days following the revelation that *Marianne Kerber*, whoever she may be, made Lucy's twisted metal pendant. It's for the best, he tells himself. He tried—*Lucy* tried—but Charlotte is right, he should drop this search now, it isn't good for him. Nevertheless, he can't seem to lift himself out of the funk he's fallen into. He loses himself in his work, spending long days at the workshop sanding and polishing and oiling. He goes to bed early, not wanting to endure his solo evenings any longer than necessary. He avoids Charlotte's calls and messages—*Why haven't you rung Samira? Won't you ask her out again?*—and doesn't reply. He enjoyed himself on their date. He felt inspired by Samira's talk of salsa classes, her desire to laugh, her unwillingness to *stagnate*, as she put it. He was going to call her. He *should* call her. Especially now. Yet more than a week has passed, and somehow he can't bring himself to pick up the phone.

So it lifts his spirits considerably to see Lucy's face in the window of his workshop door the following Tuesday afternoon. She bustles in with her usual flurry of noise and curls up in the armchair, like a stray cat making herself right at home in a stranger's house.

"What are you doing here?" he asks.

"It's Oscar's afternoon at nursery, isn't it?" she replies, as though he should have been expecting her, as though this is where she always is now, at two p.m. on a Tuesday afternoon.

He smiles, realising with a jolt that it's the first time he's done so in days.

"What are you working on today?"

"It's a jewellery box." He holds it up so she can see. It's made of walnut, with an intricate rhombus pattern on the top. The woman who brought it in said it was her grandmother's, given to her by *her* grandmother sometime in the 1930s, but it's become a little battered and dirty over the years, so could Henry please give it a clean and a polish, and fix the broken hinge?

"Wow, that's beautiful. How do you make a pattern like that? I've never seen anything like it."

"It's marquetry." Henry traces his fingers over the lid. "You use a scalpel to cut out the shapes you want from different types of wood veneer, and then carefully glue it all in place. It's a real art."

"Can *you* do that?"

He nods. "In a basic way, yes, but I'm better at repairing it than actually creating it in the first place. I think you need an artistic vision to do work like this, and I don't have that really. I prefer preserving what other people have done."

"Well, that's pretty important, too. Like, maybe I'll pass on that vase to my grandkids one day, and I wouldn't be able to do that if it was all cracked and broken." A pause. "Have you ever had anything in here you couldn't repair?"

"Nothing wooden. But sometimes people bring in ceramics and other things, and I might have to pass them on to a friend if I can't fix them myself."

"But everything's fixable by *someone*, right?" Her expression is almost worried, as though the answer he gives will be very important to her.

He shrugs. "I can't think of much that would be completely beyond repair."

"Right." Her features relax—the correct answer, then?—and she's quiet for a moment, before adding, "Speaking of handmade things"—and he somehow feels that they aren't—"I've been thinking."

"Oh no."

Lucy laughs. "Just because that necklace turned out not to be made by your wife doesn't mean we can't find her another way."

Henry sets down the box. "No, I've decided there's no point. I shouldn't have started digging up the past again."

"What?!" Lucy almost shouts. "You can't mean that. Don't you want to know what happened?"

"Of course I do. But it's not good for me. It's far beyond time I put it all behind me, where it belongs." He tries to sound decisive, tries to channel his sister's conviction, but it sounds false, even to his ears. If he was putting it behind him, he would call Samira.

Lucy sits forward in the chair. "I can understand that, really I can, but why don't you give me one shot at it?"

He sighs and regards her levelly. Charlotte would be furious; she would boot this woman out right now. He probably should, too. "Where would you start?" he asks instead.

Lucy smiles. "I think you mentioned she had a sister, right? And she must have had friends. Do you have any addresses or emails for them? No, I suppose you won't have current ones, but if you give me their full names, I'll do a bit of googling and see what I can find. Everyone's on the internet in some shape or form. Facebook, LinkedIn, or what have you. And then we'll see what they say, but you know what, I bet we can find her because no one can really disappear these days; the world's too connected—did you watch that Will Smith film from years ago, the one where Gene Hackman has to blow up his secret home because Will Smith left his phone on or something and the baddies tracked him there? So I think we have to keep looking and asking people, and someone's bound to know someone who knows where she is, don't you think?"

"Yes, no, yes, and maybe," Henry says.

"What's that?"

"I was just answering your questions. It was hard to get a word in after you asked them."

"Oh, sorry, I talk too much sometimes, don't I?" Lucy smiles, but there's hurt behind her eyes and he wishes he could take it back. She's only trying to help him, only spending her scant child-free time trying to figure out the answer to the mystery of his marriage.

But why? The question comes to him once again. Why is she so intent on doing this when she could be spending her one free afternoon a week seeing friends, or doing whatever hobbies she must have, or treating herself to whatever it is that women like to treat themselves to?

"No, *I'm* sorry. I appreciate you trying to help, I really do." He writes down the names he remembers: Lena Hoffmann, Angelika Schneider. "I just don't think you'll get anywhere by contacting them. If you can even find them."

"You could be right. I'll give it some thought this weekend. Jack's taking the kids to Legoland on Saturday, so I've actually got time to breathe, so as well as sleeping—because I really need to dedicate some serious time to that—I'll see what I can find out. You leave it with me, Henry, okay?"

"Okay. You aren't going with them? To Legoland?"

Lucy reaches down and reties the laces on one of her boots. "Not this time. It's good for Jack to have some time with the kids without me, and anyway, like I said, I'll welcome the chance to chill out and sleep a bit. Not often I get to do that! I can't wait!" She laughs, but it sounds as false to Henry as his earlier feeble claim that he is putting it all behind him.

"You know," Henry says, "it would be nice to meet Jack some time."

"Oh yes, of course! He's just so busy with work during the week and then weekends we spend child-wrangling most of the time, but yes, you absolutely will meet him some time, for sure." She looks at her watch. "Oh God, I'd better go, it's not long till I have to pick up Oscar and I really must nip to the supermarket first, get something in for dinner. But thank you for the time in your pine forest, Henry, and I hope I'll have some news for you after this weekend. I'll come again next week, shall I? Excellent, I'll see you then. Bye."

His eyes follow her out of the door before it slams shut.

The stillness of his house greets him when he gets home that evening, as it always does. He puts on the television to fill the quiet, places a pan of water on the hob, and starts to chop an onion, eyes streaming. As he cooks, he thinks of Lucy, of the hope and excitement in her face as she rabbited on about that silly Gene Hackman film and tracking down Greta's friends, and how mean he was to her, how dismissive. He is so quick to notice other people's faults—Victoria, Samira, Lucy—when he is hardly perfect himself.

Dinner is well underway when Charlotte calls. He sighs, considers ignoring it, but no, here is another person trying to help him, however misplaced her tactics may be.

"Why haven't you phoned Samira?" she asks when he picks up.

"Hello to you, too." Henry puts his mobile on speaker as he drains a saucepan of pasta—three modest handfuls of penne, the perfect quantity for one.

Charlotte expels a short, sharp sigh down the line. "It's been ages, Henry. It's rude."

"I don't know why I haven't." He spoons Bolognese onto his pasta, then takes the bowl and his phone to the kitchen table, where he's placed a single fork. "She was nice, I'm just not sure she's . . . for me." He avoids, just in time, saying "*the one* for me."

"If you got on well and neither of you found the other physically repulsive, then why on earth not?"

"It's a low bar you've set there, sis."

"Well, it's not like you've had much precedent in the past thirty years."

He pours himself a glass of wine. "No, I suppose not."

"Come on, Henry, stop thinking about it and call her. What's the worst that can happen?"

He doesn't answer. He takes a sip of wine, and his eyes catch on the necklace, which is lying on the kitchen counter by the fridge. *You can keep it until you've found her.* Lucy seems so determined that she will. Maybe he's being defeatist not to help.

"Henry? Seriously, remember what I said. Give yourself a chance to be happy. Focus on the present, not the past."

But he isn't really listening. His mind is musing over the name Marianne Kerber. Kerber sounds German. Is that simply a coincidence? Could two entirely different German women make such distinctively similar jewellery? Maybe Greta copied something she'd seen. Maybe this Marianne woman was already established, and Greta came across her work and thought she'd try and do the same. But he knows that isn't how it happened. He remembers her playing with those paper clips, remembers how that idle habit grew into something more, on his encouragement. It was organic. She didn't copy anyone.

"Henry? Are you even listening?"

"I'm sorry, Charlotte, something's come up. I have to go. I'll speak to you soon."

"And you'll call Samira?"

"All right," he says without thinking, "I will."

When he hangs up, he opens a browser and types a name into the search bar.

Marianne Kerber.

He may as well see what he can find out.

16

GRETA, 1983

I'd been in Britain about two months when I started making jewellery.

It started with a tin of paper clips that your housemate Ant had left lying around in the sitting room. The three of you were all out on a boys' night, and I was slightly bored, unsure what to do or where to go without any friends to do anything with, yet unwilling to linger in a house that still didn't feel like home. I switched the television on, thumping the set in the right spot until *Coronation Street* sprang to life—after all, soap operas are the best way to get to know a country, Olaf had said—but I couldn't concentrate, could barely understand the characters' northern accents anyway, at times, and so my hands reached for the tub of paper clips on the coffee table and began idly twisting and breaking the metal, linking them together, bending and manipulating these humble bits of metal until I'd created a bracelet with a certain odd appeal. It was scratchy on my wrist, the sharp bits of broken metal grazing my skin, but I liked it nonetheless, and I'd enjoyed making it; the act of twisting and breaking and bending had calmed my mind a little, had soothed the worries that had begun to gather in my head in recent days.

"How is my favourite wife?" you said when you got home later that evening, your smile as wide as ever, your eyes a little bleary.

I laughed, though I suddenly found myself blinking back tears. "Fine."

You flopped down on the sofa and kissed me with beery breath. "God, I love coming home to you." Your hand grazed the bracelet on my wrist. "What's that?"

"Oh." I shrugged, a little embarrassed. "Nothing. I was just messing around."

"You made it? Wow, it's really good."

"You're drunk."

"I am, but it's also really good." You picked up my hand and looked at the bracelet more closely. "You should do this, Greta!" you said with a sudden rush of childlike enthusiasm. "You should create amazing things. Because you're amazing, and amazing people can do amazing things."

"I think you need to go to bed."

You grinned. "Only if you're coming with me."

I lay awake that night, unable to sleep as you lay snoring next to me, my bracelet discarded on the bedside table. In the morning, you'd see it for what it was—a load of broken paper clips. But the next day you came home after work and gave me a present—a roll of garden wire and a pair of pliers. "It should be easier to make stuff with this," you said, "and it won't scratch your skin."

Oh, Henry, how I loved you for that.

When I think about it now, knowing how this craft has been a constant therapy ever since, I can see that my jewellery making was born out of anxiety. Of my sadness at being far from my family, of the culture shock I was feeling, of the strange way I was missing a country I'd been so excited to leave. Twisting and bending the metal, creating something unique from not a lot, reminded me of those Sundays at home with

Mutti and Angelika, cutting and sewing material to create a new dress or top. This was a sort of substitute, a way to try to feel at home in a place that still wasn't.

Because by that point, my new life in Britain was beginning to lose its sheen a little. Without a job, I rattled around that damp, messy house far too much. While you, John, and Ant went to work, I'd clear up after you all in an attempt to pay my way, given I was effectively staying for free. I think that was appreciated—when any of you actually noticed—but being your live-in housekeeper wasn't what I'd dreamed of.

You encouraged me to go out, giving me money to explore and sight-see, but I felt guilty about that, knowing you didn't have much cash to spare, something that was challenging my assumptions about life over here. Back home, our school citizenship teacher had crowed frequently about the exploitation of workers in the West, the huge divide between rich and poor, and the massive failings of capitalism. But he'd also told us the DDR was an economic success, and since I could see around me that the latter wasn't true, I hadn't wholly believed the former, either. But now I could see there was at least some truth in it. You, John, and Ant were constantly short of money—or "skint," as Ant would say, another Brit-ishism I soon adopted—often racking up overdue bills and going over-drawn to pay your rent, which seemed extortionate to me in proportion to your modest salary. I once found a credit card statement you'd left lying around, and I saw how much it cost you to make all those trips to see me in Berlin, and to buy that second ring I didn't need, and it made my heart swell with both love and concern.

Other assumptions I'd made were slowly being skewered, too. I'd thought everything would be beautiful and well-kept in Britain, unlike the often dilapidated or uninspiring buildings of the DDR, and while Ox-ford was, indeed, beautiful in many ways, I soon learned to avoid certain insalubrious areas, and was shocked by the gaunt-cheeked homeless people begging by day and curling up under cardboard at night. You told me most of them were probably unemployed drug addicts. Back home, everyone had a home, a job, and enough to eat, and no one took drugs. And yet *this* was meant to be the glorious West? My father's words were never far from my mind in those moments. *The grass isn't always greener, Greta.*

I'd also been struggling to find a suitable job. I was university-educated, a trained translator with nine months' experience in that dull yet professional office environment, but I wasn't used to job hunting— to competition—and the few appropriate roles I applied for came to nothing. Instead, I got a part-time waitressing job in a café in town, and the irony of coming to this supposed land of opportunity only to waitress in a café wasn't lost on me. At least I could drink all the coffee I wanted for free—and it was actually *good* coffee. But the pay was meagre, and everything was so expensive here. I couldn't afford the big-brand jeans and fashionable dresses in the shops, though the abundance of choice on the rails overwhelmed me in any case. Neither could we afford a trip to Venice or Paris or California, as I'd long dreamed of, since every penny we were able to save was to put towards a deposit that would get us away from our messy housemates and into a place of our own. Even our weekend trips became less frequent as the weeks went on, my requests to see Liverpool or Lyme Regis met with decreasing levels of enthusiasm. "Petrol's so expensive," you'd say in a gentle voice. "How about we stay home this weekend?" The brochures I'd picked up from the travel agent soon became almost as torturous to look at as they would have been in Berlin. In the West, I now realised, you were only as free as your wallet allowed.

I told all this to no one. Not to you, who'd done so much for me— married me, brought me over here, given me a new beginning free from the restraints of my homeland, offered me prospective opportunities I never could have hoped for before, even if some of them were yet to materialise. Not to my family back home, who surely wouldn't want to know that I wasn't completely happy in the life I'd hurt them so badly to have. And not to Lena, who so desperately wanted what I had, to whom it would have felt churlish and ungrateful to complain.

It's certainly different! I wrote. *You'd love the clothes, Lena, I can't believe how much stuff there is to buy, how much choice. I'm enclosing some pages from a fashion magazine—ask my mother to help you copy the styles!*

Nor did I have any friends in Britain I could talk to. The only people I'd met were through you, and once their initial fascination with me had waned, their everyday lives continued as they always had. They wouldn't have understood the disconnect I felt.

And then there was your family.

Each Sunday, unless we were off on a day trip somewhere, we'd go to your parents' house in Botley for a roast lunch, prepared by your mother in such a bewildering way that the meat was usually dry and overcooked, and the vegetables soggy and flavourless. It always made me yearn for my own mother, knowing how delicious all that produce would have been in her hands. But I wouldn't have minded the bad cooking if they hadn't made me feel like an alien in their home.

One particular Sunday stands out.

"You got a job?" your mother asked, as she served us sherry on the sofa before the meal. "That's wonderful, Greta, I'm so pleased for you."

"Thank you." I was surprised. Given Susan was a happy *Hausfrau*—a strange concept to me, coming from a country where most women had a job—I hadn't been sure what she'd think of me working. "It's only waitressing, though. I'm still looking for a translation role. It's frustrating I can't find anything."

Your mother cocked her head and smiled. "Oh well, that's not a surprise, is it?"

"What isn't?"

"I mean, your qualifications"—air quotes were definitely implied—"won't necessarily be valid here."

"But why not? I have a degree in translation and interpretation."

"Yes, dear, but . . . Don't you agree, Barry?" She glanced at your father, who took the prompt.

"You can hardly expect them to think it's the same thing, a degree

149

from a commie country." He threw me a shrug and a smile. "Who knows what they teach you over there!"

I bristled. "I had a good education," I replied. "Humboldt is a respected university."

"But you could be writing anything!" your father said, laughter lines animating his round, red face. "You could be inserting commie propaganda into everything you translate, for all they know!" He snorted and slapped his leg, as though it was all a big joke.

"Dad, as if," you said with an indulgent smile.

"I'm not a communist," I muttered.

Barry laughed. "Thank goodness for that; I don't have to worry my son's going to be interrogated if he doesn't bring you breakfast in bed! *Vy did you not make ze toast.*" This last in a silly German accent that made me cringe. He couldn't even pronounce my name properly, and yet he would mock us for our English?

"For God's sake, Dad . . ." you said, glancing at me.

"It was a *joke*, son. Greta can take a bit of friendly ribbing, can't you, love?"

Thankfully, your sister saved me from replying.

"What *are* you, then?" Charlotte and her new boyfriend, Ian, had joined us in the living room after smoking in the garden, much to your mother's disapproval.

"I don't know, I'm . . . not political." It felt the easiest thing to say.

"Everything's political," your sister shot back.

"Yes, I suppose you're right." I always felt a little nervous around Charlotte—I never knew what kind of mood I'd find her in—but I admired her, too. "Well, I certainly don't agree with a lot of what my country's government does, but that doesn't mean everything there is bad," I continued, realising as I said it that I meant it, that the weeks I'd spent here had highlighted not only the UK's flaws but the DDR's virtues.

"Sounds familiar," Charlotte raised an eyebrow, making Ian laugh.

"Sweetheart, you really can't compare here to over there," your father said, aghast. "This is a democratic country, with an elected government."

"Yeah, and we go and vote for a shit like Mrs. Thatcher, so we've only got ourselves to blame."

"Charlotte, language!" Susan cried, but your sister only rolled her eyes.

"That woman has done more for our country than—"

"Oh, Dad, don't start," Charlotte cut him off. "Heard it all before. I want to know what Greta thinks."

"I obviously want democracy in the DDR," I said. "There's so much I want for my country. But there's plenty we already have that I'd vote to keep."

"Really, dear?" Your mother leaned forward, as though she couldn't believe it. "I thought everyone was miserable and desperate over there."

"Desperate to get out, you mean!" your father added.

I shook my head. I recalled what you said when I was showing you around Berlin. *I thought you were all held under lock and key. I didn't think you were allowed to be amused.* Is that what everyone in Britain thought of us? I had a sudden urge to tell your family about the good things, about our subsidised rent and food and transport and childcare, about the free health care, the study money I received for being at university and the holidays I took to Czechoslovakia and Hungary: all the things that meant many people, like my father, were generally content with their lives and didn't want to leave at all. But the words stuck in my throat. I *had* been desperate to leave, hadn't I?

"Anyway, I'm sure you'll enjoy working at the café, Greta, it's such a sweet little place," your mother said when I didn't respond. "Lunch is nearly ready, shall we all head to the table?"

Later, after we'd forced down your mother's floppy carrots and limp cabbage, after we'd left the house and walked slowly through town towards home, you apologised.

"They're not always like that. It's just a lot for them to get their heads around. You're not the sort of person they expected I'd marry."

My eyebrows shot up. "What does that mean?"

You shrugged. "A foreigner."

I stopped in the street and turned to you. "Are they unhappy that you did?"

"Oh God, no! They love you, Greta," you gushed, but I didn't believe it.

"And are you?" I don't know why I asked. You hadn't ever given me any reason to doubt your feelings for me. But I suppose I understood how it felt to have divided loyalties, to love your family and your partner while knowing they didn't quite fit together in the way you'd hoped.

"How can you ask me that?" You looked at me as though I'd slapped you. "Of course not! I'm happier than I've ever been, Greta. I know things aren't perfect, but they will be, I know it, because we're perfect together, and that's all that matters, isn't it?"

I felt my muscles relax, the strange hardness in my throat dissolve. *Perfect*. No, I didn't think so. But good enough, yes—and that was enough for me.

Still, in the following days I found there was only one person I wanted to talk to about all this: Olaf. He was the only person in my new life who understood what it was like to move to a new country, to feel like an alien, to love your homeland while lamenting what it had become.

The café gave me one midweek day off, so on the next available Tuesday, while you were at work, I went back to London.

"Greta, dear, how wonderful to see you." He welcomed me in as before, a wide smile parting that bushy beard, and offered me the same incredible coffee. I sat on his sofa while he made it. The blinds were up, and the sun was streaming through the window. I thought of how much I loved summer in Berlin, of running by the river Spree under a canopy of trees in Treptower Park, of meeting university friends at the Pratergarten in Prenzlauer Berg to drink cheap beer and listen to folk music, of riding the Ferris wheel with Angelika in the Kulturpark Plänterwald.

"It's hard, leaving behind everything you've known." Olaf's words jolted me out of my thoughts, which had clearly been plastered all over my face. "Give yourself time, dear."

"It's what I wanted," I replied, taking the coffee mug he held out to me, a picture of Princess Diana and Prince Charles on its ceramic surface above a scroll with the words *Royal Wedding, 1981.*

"That doesn't always mean it's easy." He sat in the armchair opposite me, his bulk filling the space from arm to arm. "But you'll meet people in time, make friends. They're not all capitalist *Arschlöcher* over here." He winked and I laughed, feeling brighter already. It was the first German word I'd heard him say, and he'd chosen that one.

"I knew it would be different, but I suppose I thought I'd fit right in," I said. "My father warned me it might not be as wonderful as I'd hoped."

"He sounds like a wise fellow, your Vati."

I nodded. I missed him. Missed them all. "But we don't always see eye to eye, me and him."

Olaf gave a short laugh. "Whoever does? Family is complicated. Life is complicated."

"You said that last time. What do you mean, exactly?"

He cocked his head. "When you came here, what did you want?"

I shrugged. "The freedom to make my own choices, I suppose. To travel where I liked, to read and watch and say what I wanted, to be with the man I love." I heard how small those wishes sounded, compared to his own reason for coming here, but they weren't small to me.

"And here you are, free as a bird." He smiled, and I felt his meaning: I wasn't as free as I'd thought I'd be; it wasn't perfect, here. I thought I'd always known that, but perhaps I didn't, not really.

"Freer than I was back home," I said, hearing the defiance in my tone.

He sighed. "Do you know what I see when I look at you, my dear?"

I shook my head.

"I see a beautiful, intelligent, well-educated, well-brought-up young woman who knows more about life than the silly youths I see on the

153

streets around me here. You're a credit to the country that produced you, the result of a system that *will* work, if only its citizens would believe in it properly, if only so many hadn't left when the going got a little tough. You came here seeking freedom, and that's only natural, Greta, yet in doing so you undermine the country that gave you so much." He spoke gently, without malice or reprimand, yet I felt myself recoil a little.

"You haven't lived there; you're only seeing the best in it."

"I'm not a fool, dear, I know the GDR has its faults, but it's like a relationship—you must work at it, to make things better, but that can only happen if you fully commit, not run away." He paused. "Do you think the system they have here is faultless?"

"Of course not."

"Then why is it wrong to try for something better? The GDR is a young country, an experiment, still growing and learning, like a rebellious teen finding his way. We tried the capitalist system and it didn't work—it led to exploitation and hardship; to fascism, war, and genocide. And so we're trying to do things differently, and we need the anti-fascist protection barrier to keep what we're creating safe from outside influence. But people over here can't tolerate that; they feel threatened by it, and so they try to destroy what the GDR has created through fascist rhetoric and outright lies."

"Like what?"

"My dear, there are propaganda organisations here who think nothing of spreading malicious falsehoods about our country." He heaved himself up from his chair and walked over to a cabinet in the corner, from where he pulled out a flyer that he then handed to me. *Amnesty International, East Oxford chapter*, it read. *A global movement for human rights.* "Left-wing extremist organisations like this have a lot to answer for," Olaf said as he sat back in his armchair with a little *ouf* of relief. "If the neo-Nazis succeed in obtaining power in Europe, it will be their fault."

"What do you mean?" I knew of Amnesty, had heard of their campaigns by watching the West German nightly news programmes with Mutti, but I didn't really know what they did in concrete terms.

"They're putting so much focus on the things we perhaps haven't yet got right that they're undermining all the good of it. They play right into the hands of the capitalists and neo-Nazis who want to crush communism completely, entirely for their own gain, of course." He leaned forward in his chair. "You go and see for yourself what lies they are spreading about our homeland, Greta."

I looked at the flyer. The next meeting of Amnesty International's East Oxford chapter was next week. If nothing else, it would give me something to do of an evening. If nothing else, I might meet some new people.

"Huh." I looked up from the flyer into that hirsute face, those watchful eyes. "I might just do that."

17

GRETA, 2018

Tomas's restaurant boasts one of the best locations in Tofino. The terrace faces west, perfect for watching the sun burn orange as it dips below the horizon, turning the sky to fire. The sunsets—and sunrises—are epic out here on the West Coast.

But Greta doesn't sit outside; she's stationed with her laptop at her favourite table near the bar, from where she can see Tomas, a tea towel over one shoulder, commanding the open kitchen. Unlike some chefs, he doesn't harangue his staff like an army sergeant; he's firm but fair, expecting a lot but offering them the support they need to achieve it. He wants them to succeed, to learn, to flourish enough to one day leave him and set up on their own.

"Hey." He comes over with a coffee and a trio of handmade chocolate truffles on a plate. "For you."

She smiles. "Thanks."

"I've got to get back to the kitchen." He leans over and kisses her. "But can you hang around? See you in an hour or so?"

She nods, gesturing to her laptop, where she's been continuing her letter, her confession, under the guise of working. "I have plenty to occupy me."

"Good." He grins and winks at her before heading back behind the counter.

She watches him as he calls out the latest dessert orders to Ciara, the pastry chef, receiving a "Yes, chef!" in return, and her heart clenches. She never intended to love him. She told herself it wasn't a good idea to get involved, and yet here she is, considering moving in with him, this friendly bear of a man, who cooks like a dream, laughs louder than anyone she's ever met, and, for some reason she can't fathom, seems to love her back.

They met right here in the restaurant, some eighteen months ago now, when she'd come in by herself one night with a book to read between courses. It was by a German author she loved, and she'd been so totally absorbed that she didn't notice time passing until the restaurant was near-empty and the tables were being cleared around her.

"New in town?" She looked up from her book to see him wiping down the table next to her. A broad, dark-haired man wearing a striped apron over a white chef's jacket. She was surprised he wasn't leaving the cleaning to the waitstaff. It was only later she realised he was simply the sort of person to muck in and help clear up if help was needed.

"A few months." She closed her book and smiled. "How can you tell? Because I'm a billy-no-mates?" It was an expression she picked up years ago, back when she lived in England. Probably one of those things she got from Ant or John, Henry's housemates.

He laughed. "We don't get many solo diners in here, that's all," he said as he straightened a chair. "Nothing wrong with it, of course. You look pretty content there."

She shrugged. "Yeah, a good book, a glass of wine, and some delicious food, and I'm happy."

He smiled, stood up. "I never get time to read, running this place."

"You're the manager?"

"Chef-patron." He came over to her table and held out his hand. "Tomas. I'm glad you enjoyed the food."

"Marianne. It was amazing. Particularly the dessert. I've never had anything like that before."

"It's kind of my take on a Latvian classic," he said. "That's my family's heritage, and I like to keep the old dishes going. Though I think my grandfather might have had something to say about me messing with the traditional recipe." He adopted a grouchy voice. " 'You can't improve perfection, Tomas.' "

Greta laughed. "Perfection's a little dull, isn't it?"

He pointed a finger at her. "Exactly." And then he rushed into the kitchen and returned with a plate, which he put down in front of her with a flourish. "Have you got room for a second dessert? Pineapple upside down cake with lime cream. If you like it, it's going on the menu."

She smiled. "I'll force myself, if it helps you out."

He came back a short while later, when her plate was scraped clean, and she told him his new dessert was excellent. "I think you could increase the quantity of cream, though."

He looked mock-askance. "What you trying to do, obliterate my profit margins?" And then he laughed, flopped down at the adjacent table, and asked her everything about herself.

She lied, of course, like she's lied to everyone new she's met over the years, concocting a different story each time. She told him she's from Hamburg, in the former West Germany. She told him she doesn't have any family, that her parents are no longer alive (which is true) and that she doesn't have any siblings (which isn't). She hasn't told him she was married—could still be married, technically, though the name on the marriage certificate isn't the one he knows her by. She hasn't told him how and why she left her husband.

So many lies. How can she move in with a man she is lying to? How can she let him love someone he doesn't even know? It can only end in pain, all this lying. She knows that from experience. Perhaps she should tell him, then. Perhaps she should let him read what she's writing now, trust him enough to make him the first person in her life as Marianne to know about her life as Greta. But the thought gives her chills, because lying is her protective shell; mistrust her armour. It's her own personal wall guarding the soft part inside her that she's worked hard to keep safe for so long.

"Hey," Tomas says, "you waited."

"I did." Greta turns her head to look up at him, memories slipping away in the darkness. She stopped writing a while ago and now sits outside on the restaurant terrace, her parka zipped up to her chin and her woollen hat pulled down over her ears against the night chill. It may be cold, but it's worth it to sit there and listen to the waves of the Pacific hitting the shore.

Tomas slips into the seat next to her. He rubs his eyes with his hand and tips his head back, breathes deeply.

"Tough night?" she asks.

"Just busy—and Adam couldn't keep up with orders in the fish section so I ended up doing a lot of it myself." He sighs. "But he'll get there."

"He will with you as his teacher." She leans in to him. "He's lucky to have you."

He picks up her hand and kisses it. "And *I'm* lucky to have *you*."

"Aw, shucks," she jokes, but she kisses his neck, breathes him in. She didn't feel an instant attraction to Tomas, the night they met. She didn't experience the instinctive, heady rush she had with Henry. Their relationship has grown slowly, cautiously, as she imagines it always would with two people who have been burned before, but now, more than a year on, loving him—having his love—feels like slipping into a hot bath after a long day out in the cold.

And yet, and yet . . .

"I mean it," he says, and from his tone she knows he's going to ask

160

her if she's decided, if she has an answer to the question he asked her on Saturday.

Her chest flutters in anticipation of what she's about to say. It is likely the wrong decision—for her, and for him. It will probably only end badly. But isn't it time, after all these years, that she relax a little, that she allow herself to love and be loved, to have some semblance of family life again? Even if it means standing still for once.

"Yes," she says.

He shifts to look at her, and she lifts her head from his shoulder. His face is a burnished gold in the red light of the patio heater.

"Are you saying . . . ?"

She nods.

"God, Marianne, you've made me the happiest man alive." He laughs and kisses her and she ignores the jolt of guilt she feels to hear the name that isn't really hers, and the tightening in her chest at the thought of moving out of her van, her home on wheels, her escape vehicle.

Home. She's moved around so much over the decades that nowhere has truly felt like home, but this little Canadian town at the tip of an island peninsula has come closer than anywhere else—and a lot of that is to do with Tomas.

"I love you," he says then, and again later, after they've made love in his bed in the house they will soon share.

"You, too," she whispers back, and she means it, she does, even though it scares the life out of her, because she loved Henry, too, but look what she did to him.

When morning comes, she lies in bed and watches Tomas dress for his shift. He kisses her goodbye, a silly grin on his face, and when he's gone, she lies in silence for a while, gazing through the French doors of the bedroom, though the double glazing means she can't hear the hush-suck of the waves as she can when she's in her van. She gets up, pulls on one of Tomas's jumpers, throws open the doors, and breathes in the salty air. Nearly the same view, though; the same air, the same water. The difference is that here, when she moves in, she will share living space with another human for the first time in three decades.

She puts a coffee on to brew in the kitchen and wanders into the living room. It's spacious but cosy, with a well-loved red sofa, a brown velvet beanbag, a battered old wooden coffee table, a large television, and an uplighter they mock-argue over every time she spends an evening here—she likes its soft glow, while he prefers the stark yellow of the main light. In one corner stands a fishing rod, evidence of the hobby Tomas loves but rarely finds time for, while a shelving unit holds biographies of chefs and sports stars, and cookbooks by Elizabeth David and Alain Ducasse. On the walls are several framed photos: Tomas as a twentysomething chef de partie standing in a group of six men in chef's whites; as a young boy with his little brother next to their parents and late grandfather—the Latvian one, as she recalls; and a recent picture of Tomas with his adult son from his long-defunct marriage.

What meagre possessions does she have to add to this home? Not much. "I want you to make it ours, not just mine," Tomas said last night. "We can redecorate if you like. We can make the snug into your office so you've got space to work. We can do whatever you like—just say." But the thought of entwining her stuff with his, of buying things together—new curtains, a desk, a picture for the wall—feels like a net closing in around her, cutting off her escape route.

Nausea rolls in her stomach, and she sits down, puts her head on her knees. *Stop it*, she tells herself. *You don't need an escape route. You don't have to run. You're safe here.*

For about half an hour, she believes it. She believes she might be able to commit properly to this man. To see her toothbrush next to his on the sink, her running shoes alongside his winter boots on the front porch; to leave each other notes on the fridge; to wake up next to him every day. Yes, she can nearly believe it.

Until she idly scrolls to a news website while she's drinking her coffee at the kitchen island.

Former Russian spy critically ill in UK after suspected poisoning

And she knows that this morning was a different day, and now everything has changed.

18

GRETA, 1983

When I look back, there wasn't a single day, a single action, that precipitated the crisis to come. It was gradual, a series of events so seemingly innocuous that it's hard to pinpoint when it became too late. When I met you? When I received my exit visa? When I visited Olaf? Or was it when I went to my first meeting of the East Oxford chapter of Amnesty International?

That July evening, I was welcomed into the drab, musty-smelling community centre in Headington by a long-haired man in his mid-thirties who introduced himself as Rod Kendall, the leader of the group. He took my name, welcomed me enthusiastically, made a joke about biscuits that I didn't understand, and ushered me towards a table of refreshments, where I stood slightly awkwardly, the new girl in class. I wasn't sure what to expect from the meeting. I nearly hadn't come at all, but I'd shown you the flyer and you'd encouraged me. "Maybe you can help campaign from here to change things over there," you'd said, and I'd agreed. I didn't really know *how* Amnesty campaigned for change, but I was keen to find out.

Perhaps I could make a difference. Perhaps moving to Britain would give me the chance to do something for those I'd left behind.

"First time at a meeting?" I turned to see a young woman about my own age with short dark hair styled in a spiky crop, wearing a pink blouse tied at the waist and stonewashed jeans.

"Oh yes, hi, I'm Greta." I held out my hand.

"Sarah." She shook it and smiled. "Biscuit?"

"He said they were nice," I replied, nodding my head in Rod's direction, and Sarah laughed and rolled her eyes.

"Prefer a custard cream myself," she said, and I couldn't help feel I'd missed some sort of British in-joke. "Greta—is that a German name?"

"Yes . . ." I hesitated. If I admitted I was from the DDR—an insider, an Easterner—they'd want to know all about my life behind the Wall. But I didn't want to be an object of fascination, I wanted to blend in, to sit quietly and listen. So I lied. "Hamburg," I said. "I'm from Hamburg."

Sarah's eyes widened, anyway. "As a boring old Brit, I can't imagine how it feels to have half your country cut off by an evil regime. Do you know anyone in the East?"

Evil regime? I was still digesting the starkness of that phrase as I shook my head in another lie. "But my best friend does. Her uncle Jürgen was arrested a few years ago for trying to organise a pro-democracy protest. He's still in prison now."

"Bloody hell!" Sarah leaned forward and put her hand on my arm. "You should share that with the group. We might be able to help campaign for his release."

"Really?"

"If he was involved in nonviolent protest, then yes, absolutely. How much do you know about what Amnesty does?"

"Not a great deal. I came to find out."

"Well, a big part of it involves trying to help people who've been thrown in jail simply for expressing their views or trying to exercise their human rights. Prisoners of conscience, we call them. We write to their governments, and sometimes to the prisoners themselves. We campaign for their release and publicly highlight the human rights abuses many of them suffer, like not being given a lawyer or the right to appeal, or being treated terribly in custody while awaiting trial. We hear awful stories from former political prisoners in the GDR who were eventually bought out by West Germany. Psychological abuse, sleep deprivation, forced confessions, their families threatened . . . It's horrific."

I nodded, absorbing her words. *Prisoners of conscience. Human rights abuses. Bought out by the West.* I knew enough stories and had heard enough rumours for these phrases to ring true. Jürgen wrote noticeably little about conditions in Brandenburg Prison in the rare letters he sent to his brother, but Lena's father knew him well enough to read between the censored lines. A young colleague of my father's had been jailed for circulating the records of a dissenting songwriter, and later ended up in the Federal Republic, phoning his distraught fiancé to say that he'd been bought out by the West, stripped of his East German citizenship by the GDR authorities, and banned from returning. And my mother had told me my old schoolteacher Herr Fischer, the one who'd been arrested for giving a forbidden book to a student, was so traumatised after his spell in prison that he refused to speak about it—or perhaps felt he couldn't, for fear of being arrested again. I felt lucky, once more, that I'd managed to leave without being interrogated or detained or denied my citizenship, that my love for you had given me a nonpolitical exit strategy, one that hadn't endangered myself or my family. But, of course, I couldn't say any of that to Sarah.

"Right, shall we get started?" Rod said to the room, with a clap of his hands.

"Here, sit next to me." Sarah gestured to two grey plastic chairs at a table facing the front, and I felt the warmth of a budding friendship as I slid into my chair.

"First of all, welcome to our newest member, Greta Henderson," Rod said. "Thank you for coming, Greta. If you're not sure about anything, please ask—we don't bite." He pulled a jocular face, provoking some titters from the others, and I saw that this tall, gangly thirtysomething liked this role, liked standing in front of an audience, liked leading. He'd been an ardent socialist at university, Sarah told me later—"but not a commie, obviously"—and I remembered Olaf's claim that this was a *left-wing extremist group*. How complicated the world was! How many different opinions existed on how to live life, when surely all most of us wanted was to live in peace and harmony, safety and comfort.

I listened intently as Rod introduced the business of the day and then handed over to various members of the group tasked with updating us on certain prisoners this chapter of AI had been supporting. Jan, a middle-aged woman in purple tie-dyed trousers, stood up to report back on the health of a man held for years in a psychiatric institution in the USSR, where he'd been drugged and kept in appalling conditions, all because he refused to accept Soviet restrictions on practising his religion. Next, a youngish, kind-faced man who turned out to be Sarah's husband, Kevin, told us about the welcome release of a man in Cameroon jailed for seven years without charge after being involved in the distribution of leaflets criticising the government.

Nausea built inside me as I took in all the terrible things that happened to these people, and when Rod stood up and started speaking about the DDR, my stomach clenched.

"A contact in Berlin has been able to confirm the incarceration of two men whose whereabouts after their arrest last year had been concerning us," Rod said. "One's a scientist who had repeatedly requested and been denied permission to leave the GDR, and the other is a university professor who criticised the regime in his lectures. Now we know they've been remanded in Hohenschönhausen Prison awaiting trial, we're going to take up both of their cases, so I'd like you all to write to the GDR authorities about them." He nodded to Sarah. "Can you pass around the paper and pens, please?"

My head reeled. Alt-Hohenschönhausen was a neighbourhood not far from my own, and rumour had it there was a prison there, given the restrictions on the surrounding streets and the blanked-out area shown on city maps. Lena's father had always assumed that's where his brother was held before trial, though he was never told. A chill bloomed in my chest to receive confirmation that this secret prison actually existed. But who was Amnesty's mysterious contact in Berlin?

"We're never told that, at group level," Sarah said when I asked. "The names of sources are always protected. It could be an escape helper in the West, or possibly a friend or relative of a prisoner. They supply AI with information, when they can, and we use that to campaign from here. For example, if they know someone's been remanded without charge, or denied a lawyer. We don't often receive such information, though, because it's so difficult and dangerous for these people to get it to us."

I nodded but said nothing. In the back of my mind, I heard Olaf: *You go and see for yourself what lies they are spreading about our homeland.* But I shook his voice away. They weren't lies, I knew that, and the thought of this person in my home city risking their own safety to help sleep-deprived and psychologically abused prisoners in a secret Stasi prison gave me chills.

"So what do we write?" I asked Sarah, looking at the names of the prisoners concerned. Erich Nagel, Martin Biermann. I imagined the frantic worry of their relatives, the bone-shaking fear of the unknown. Nagel could have been one of my own university professors. Biermann could have been a friendly neighbour. Doing what they thought was right. Voicing their opinions aloud, acting according to their principles—and being locked up for it.

"Here are the guidelines." Sarah passed me a piece of paper. "But the general aims are to ensure the GDR government is aware we know what they're doing to these people, and to lobby for their release. East Germany needs the West, after all. They don't want to be seen in a bad light—they want to be legitimised. But their actions go against international human rights obligations, so we're doing all we can to make sure everyone knows it, and to pressurise them to stop it."

"Right."

"It's brilliant you've joined us, Greta; it's always best to write in German, and now we've got a native on tap to help us!"

I nodded, happy to put my nationality and translation training to good use, but I couldn't still my brain enough to write. I thought of Sarah's description of my government as an *evil regime*, of Olaf's belief Amnesty was undermining all the good that existed in the DDR, of your mother's assumption we were all living desperate lives. Of Lena's cynicism, and Angelika's contentedness, and my mother's simple desire to make the best of things.

There was no one truth about my country, I realised. It wasn't *only* the horrors relayed in this meeting by people who had never been there. It wasn't *only* the relative security and basic comfort that underpinned the lives of most people back home. It was a complex mix of the two and so much more.

And there was no one truth about myself, either. I wasn't a fully fledged *commie*, as your parents seemed to think I was, nor a fierce opponent of the place I grew up in and still thought of as home. I was somewhere in the middle: a woman who simply wanted to see the world for herself and make up her own mind about how life should be lived. A woman who didn't believe that a place should be defined only by the things it was doing wrong, nor that its people should be dictated to by a government that thought it was always right. A woman who couldn't deal in black and white, when there were so many shades of grey.

But that didn't feel like enough for all the people who met me. Not for your parents, not for the members of Amnesty, not for Olaf. I didn't feel like I was allowed to linger in the grey. I felt like I had to choose a side.

"My dear, you look tired," Olaf said when I turned up at his doorstep one Tuesday afternoon a week or so after that meeting; I gratefully accepted the sofa, the cake and the coffee, as always. There was something about coming to his dingy, tired flat that soothed me, that made me feel like I was visiting the grandfather I didn't have.

"I've been doing some long shifts at the café," I said. "We're saving for a deposit on a flat."

"So expensive here, isn't it?" Olaf eased himself into his favourite arm-chair. "And be careful when you move out of where you are now—these money-grabbing landlords will do anything to charge you for the slightest wear and tear." He cocked his head and smiled at me in that kindly but knowing way he had. "Now, what else have you been up to lately?"

"I met a new friend. Sarah—she's in the Amnesty group, and we've already been out for a drink together." I smiled, a little self-consciously. It felt good to have the beginnings of a friendship, to go some way to finding a little of what I'd had with Lena back home. *I think you'd really like her*, I'd written to my best friend. *She's got this punk-style haircut and a real flair for makeup.*

But Olaf didn't want to hear about my fledgling friendship. "Ah, you went to the Amnesty meeting?" he said, and from then on that was all he asked about. Who was the leader? How many people were there? What did they ask me to do? What did they say about the DDR?"

I answered all his questions—I saw no reason not to, and anyway I was curious about this old communist's response to Rod, the student socialist, and the others in the group who all seemed motivated by doing the right thing, by standing up to the Party's human rights abuses.

"Did you hear evidence of these so-called abuses?" he asked, when I told him this.

"I didn't have to. I know that some people back home are arrested for no good reason."

Olaf raised his impressive eyebrows at me. "There's always a good rea-son, my dear—whether you think so or not."

I sighed. I was fond of Olaf, by then. I didn't want to argue with him. But I knew what I'd heard and experienced back home, and the claims by Amnesty's contact in Berlin rang truer than this weak defence from someone who'd never lived in the DDR. "So why is it that Amnesty is in contact with someone in Berlin who's told them about two political prisoners incarcerated in Hohenschönhausen Prison, where they're probably being abused and threatened, simply for speaking their minds?"

Olaf scoffed at my tone. "It's a prison, Greta, do they expect a red carpet? Political prisoners indeed! They must have acted illegally, whatever you think. They'll have broken the rules—rules the capitalist fascists don't agree with. Well, too bad. I don't agree with many of the rules over here, but if I broke them, I'd accept my punishment. Everyone is equal under the law." He sat forward in his chair and eyed me. "Who is this so-called *contact*?"

Oh, that question.

You have to believe me, Henry, I really didn't know what I was doing. All I did was tell Olaf what the Amnesty group had told me, and that wasn't very much. I didn't know the name of their contact, but I didn't think twice about telling him the names of the two prisoners. Why would I? I was in Britain now, far away from the country where I had to watch what I said, and Olaf was simply a harmless, slightly deluded and exasperating old man who hadn't been to Berlin for decades. I had no idea, at that point, who he really was and what he was making me do.

So maybe that was the moment right there, the moment it became too late.

Too late to extricate myself from a situation that would affect the rest of my life.

19

HENRY, 2018

Sleet speckles Henry's glasses as he cycles up the Cowley Road at about six thirty in the evening. *The beast from the east* has quelled, its frigid fury giving way to a mild grumble, and the icy storm now seems as much of a crazy dream as the extraordinary events that have occurred in Salisbury, and yet both are real. He thinks of the Russian and his daughter as he pedals, feeling how fragile life is, and how delicate human beings are, should someone want to hurt them.

Perhaps that's why, when he approaches the turnoff for Lucy's road, just two from his own, he abandons his usual rule never to show up at someone's home uninvited and makes the turn. It is Tuesday, yet Lucy didn't appear in his workshop today, as she promised she would, and he finds he misses her abundance of words and her easy laughter, not to mention her enthusiasm for finding Greta. He also has things he wants to tell her.

He leans his bicycle against the fence and rings the doorbell. Footsteps sound inside, and then the door opens a crack, a face appearing around it at about waist height.

"Hello, Millie," Henry says. "Is your mother home?"

The girl smiles and nods, clearly unbothered by the orange smear around her mouth. "She's on the phone."

"No, no, I said I wouldn't, didn't I?" Lucy's voice floats towards him from somewhere inside. "Look, can we talk about this another time, please? There's someone at the door—I've got to go." The volume of her voice increases, and then the door opens wider and Lucy is standing there, mobile phone against one ear. She smiles at Henry and beckons him in, but he can't help but be shocked by her face. Her eyes are red-rimmed and puffy, her cheeks pale and drawn.

"I've finished my Lego treehouse," Millie says as he follows her down the hall. "Do you want to see?"

"Oh yes, I do," he replies, but he stops in the doorway when he en-counters the hectic scene in front of him.

The sitting room is probably the same size as his own, but it immedi-ately feels much smaller, due to the many things packed into it. On the wall opposite the sofa is an enormous telly, which feels too big for the room. On either side of the fireplace are bookshelves haphazardly stuffed with paperbacks, board games, and photo albums. The carpeted floor and most of the sofa are scattered with toys—pieces of Lego; cards featuring cartoonish animals; assorted wooden building blocks; and a couple of picture books flung open, as though abruptly discarded mid-read. When Henry imagines what his own home might have looked like with Greta and a couple of children inside it, he pictures a neat wooden Wendy house in the garden (made by himself, of course), some C. S. Lewis and Roald Dahl in the bookcase, and a yellow rubber duck in the bathtub, but he doesn't imagine this . . . mess.

"Get off, Socks, that's not for you, it's for Oscar!" Millie shouts at a black cat sitting on a quilted mat on the carpet. It flees, tail high, and Henry sees the reason for its name—three white paws.

Millie sits cross-legged on the floor and beckons Henry to follow suit, so he does, his tendons twinging in response to the position he probably hasn't adopted since primary school assemblies. "Look!" She presents the treehouse to him, eyes wide, a smile of pride lighting up her face.

"Beautiful—very well done," he says, fighting his urge to rearrange the leaves on the tree canopy, which look a bit haphazard, and redo the staircase so the steps are evenly spaced.

"Yes. No. Yes. Tomorrow, okay?" Lucy is saying, and then more softly, "Okay, then. Bye." She comes into the room. "You're meant to be finishing your dinner, little miss. Back to the kitchen, please, before it gets cold."

"Ohhhh, but I'm not hungry anymore."

"Too bad. Skedaddle."

Millie groans as she picks herself up from the floor like every limb weighs a ton, and then leaves the room.

"I'm so sorry to intrude." Henry heaves himself up, and it really does feel as though every limb weighs a ton. "I was just passing and I . . . I thought you might have come to the workshop today but you didn't, and so I . . . er, thought I'd stop by to see if everything was okay." He tries not to show he's noticed her blotchy face, her red eyes. Should he say something?

"Not intruding at all!" Lucy says with her usual brightness. "I'm sorry I didn't make it today—it's been such a crazy day and I had a million and one things to do when Oscar was at nursery, but I did them all, so that's quite something really! And now he's in bed without too much persuasion and Millie's eating, so it's actually the perfect moment, and I'm so glad you stopped by because I have all sorts to tell you, but would you like a drink first? Tea or coffee? Or a glass of wine? Or we might have some beer kicking around somewhere. Or water? Juice? Squash?"

"A glass of wine would be lovely. If it's open."

"It's not, but it most certainly will be—much needed tonight, I think." She smiles and he opens his mouth to say *Are you okay?*, but she has already turned to leave the room and the moment is gone.

He removes a grubby cloth from an armchair and sits, taking in the room properly. There's a video games console under the television, which he somehow doubts is Lucy's. There's a wedding photograph—the happy couple sandwiched between five bridesmaids and five groomsmen, all in perfectly coordinated outfits—and another photo on the wall of the family somewhere by the sea, Jack's arm around Lucy, Oscar in a backpack on his father's back, and Millie standing in front of them, pulling a silly face. There are books on the shelves that point to eclectic—or separate—tastes: Marian Keyes next to George R. R. Martin; Patricia Cornwell next to Nick Hornby. There's a chess trophy on a shelf, but he somehow doesn't see Lucy as a chess player (she wouldn't keep quiet for long enough), and a child's drawing of a family of four blu-tacked to the front of the living room door.

This is a shared home. There is a father, somewhere.

He shakes his head. What had he been thinking, that she made him up? Of course there is a father—there are children, after all, though he supposes these days a father isn't always necessary for that.

"Here we go." Lucy comes back into the room carrying a bottle and two glasses. She pours the wine and hands him a glass, before sitting on the sofa. "Cheers."

"Cheers," he says, and then, as nonchalantly as he can, "Jack not around tonight?"

She frowns a little. "No." She takes a large gulp of her wine. "You've missed him, sadly. He's gone to the pub with a friend."

"Ah, I always seem to miss him." He sips his wine, hoping the alcohol will sedate his rising anger at this man he has never met. Why isn't he here, with this family he has been lucky enough to have? Why isn't he putting his son to bed and sitting with his daughter while she eats? Why is he always in the pub, or working, or taking the children away without his wife? Why isn't he holding them all together, as close as can be? *You are so lucky, and you don't even know it*, he wants to say to him.

"Oh, you'll meet him soon, I'm sure," Lucy says in a tone that sounds false to his ears. "Anyway, listen, I'm glad you came over because I did want to tell you something, actually; I just hadn't had a chance to do it this past week because of . . . well, stuff. But now here you are, so I can!"

She pauses for effect, and he sees her eyes are brighter now, less bloodshot. "Guess what?"

"I don't know—what?"

"I found Lena!"

Henry sits forward. "*What?*"

"Yeah, I know! I put her name in Google and loads of Lena Hoffmanns came up, so I emailed all those I could find an address for, and one who worked at a university replied almost immediately."

"Wow, and it was her?"

"No!"

"What?"

Lucy laughs. "She said she sometimes gets emails meant for another Lena Hoffman who works for the UN in Geneva—their email addresses are similar. So I emailed that one, too—and *that* was her."

"Gosh." When did the internet become a thing? Fifteen years after Greta left, perhaps? Maybe twenty until he had his own computer (he was a late adopter). So much time had passed. So much pressure from Charlotte and Ian to *move on*.

"I said I was a friend of yours and was helping you look for Greta, and she wants to help!"

"Does she know where Greta is?"

Lucy shakes her head. "No. But she wants to talk to you. Here, put this number in your phone." Lucy reads it out, and he taps it in. Lena Hoffmann. Just like that he is able to dial the past.

"I'll do it tomorrow. Thanks, Lucy—really."

"You're very welcome. I hope she knows something. Maybe she'll still be in touch with Greta's sister. I haven't found her yet—there are way too many Angelika Schneiders in the world—but I'll keep trying."

"I know you will." He smiles. "And I've been trying, too. I followed your example and googled the jewellery maker, Marianne Kerber. Turns out her work is sold by a shop in Canada. I thought I might email them and ask a few details about her."

Lucy's eyebrows shoot up. "What, you think she's somehow linked to Greta?"

He shrugs. "No. I don't know. It's probably nothing." But for some reason he can't quite pinpoint, he has a feeling it means *something*.

"Well, you've nothing to lose, right? Go for it!" she says as a wail floats down from upstairs. "Oh, here we go. He's only been asleep an hour. I should go up. He won't settle unless I do."

"Yes, of course. I'll leave—unless I can help in any way?"

"No, no, there's nothing."

"Jack will be back later, I presume?"

Lucy hesitates, just half a second, but he notices. "Yes," she says. "He'll be back."

The next day, in his workshop, Henry finds he can't concentrate on work until he's completed the two tasks in his mission: to email the Canadian shop and to call Lena.

He dials the number Lucy gave him and waits, imagining Lena sitting in some office in the United Nations building. Though he didn't spend much time with her back then, he remembers her clearly. Clever. Shrewd. Too cynical for someone so young. He recalls Greta telling him they thought she'd been denied a university place because her uncle was in trouble with the authorities. And now she works at the UN? How hard she must have worked to achieve that.

"Lena Hoffmann." Her voice whips his heart into a canter.

"Lena, it's Henry Henderson."

There is a pause, and he feels the weight of the past between them down the line. And then: "Henry, I'm so glad you called." Her accent is soft, the words neat and confident. So different from the basic, heavily accented English she spoke back then.

"It's been so long."

"A lifetime." There is warmth in her voice. "Are you well?"

"I am." He pauses. "If a little preoccupied right now."

"I hear you're looking for Greta, after all these years?"

"Yes. I'm not sure I ever really stopped, in my head at least."

A soft laugh. "I know what you mean."

"So you haven't seen her, either, since then?" He remembers how much Greta missed her friend when she was in Oxford.

A sigh. "No. But maybe that's not such a surprise. Things got . . . complicated for me." And then she tells him what's she been through, a story so brave, so incomprehensible that he has trouble digesting it. "I was so depressed after Greta left Berlin," she says. "I just wanted to leave, too, but there was no prospect of that for me. I hated my job. Hated my life. Hated the government for harassing my father and limiting our lives. We'd applied to emigrate but got nothing but hassle in return. And then we received a letter from Jürgen, my uncle. He'd been released from prison and deported to the West. That gave us the idea—we'd get ourselves arrested on purpose in the hope we would eventually be deported, too, or maybe bought out of prison by the Federal Republic."

"*What?*"

"Everyone knew about the *Freikauf*—the buying-out of political prisoners—although our government tried to keep it quiet. We didn't know how it worked, but we knew it was possible, and right then, in the mid-eighties, East Germany's economy was in such terrible trouble that they needed the money. So one day my father and I stood outside the Tränenpalast with signs protesting against the strict travel rules. We were arrested for impeding public and social activity and jailed for ten months."

"My God. That must have been horrific."

"Those first few weeks are a blur. I slept so little I couldn't think straight. They kept the lights on in my cell all night and checked on me—noisily—every twenty minutes. They'd haul me in for questioning at all hours, trying to get me to inform on other people. At one point they asked me about Greta's family, actually. Tried to get me to say they'd done all sorts of things. And they asked me if I knew where Greta was, which made no sense to me because I thought she was in England with you."

"They did?" Henry's chest leaps.

"It may not have meant anything. They asked me about lots of people I knew. I tried to find out, later. After reunification you could apply to see your Stasi file, if it hadn't been destroyed in the last days when those *Arschlöcher* ripped up as many as they could. Unfortunately, mine was one of them, and I'm still waiting for the puzzlers in the Stasi Records Archive to piece it back together."

"Puzzlers?"

"The researchers employed to reconstruct the files from all the scraps. They still have a long way to go." She laughs.

"Right, I heard about that. So would Greta have had a Stasi file?"

"Almost certainly, given she got involved with a Westerner. But only she can request to see it—if it still exists."

Henry blows out a breath, thoughts jostling for space in his head. "Please carry on. What happened to you and your father?"

"Well, I endured six months of my sentence, and then they told me I was being deported to West Germany. They could see I hadn't changed my views, that I was only going to cause more trouble for them. And who knows, maybe they got some money for me." She pauses. "As for my father, he wasn't so lucky. He got very ill in prison. When he came out, they wouldn't let him emigrate. He stayed in Berlin and had health problems until he died a couple of years later."

"I'm so sorry."

"Yes. Well." Another pause, pregnant with the unspoken feelings within it, then she continues. "When I got myself established in Hamburg, I wrote to Greta many times but never got a reply."

"I suppose that would have been well after she disappeared. I'd moved out of the flat by then, so maybe the new occupants didn't forward your letters." Such a wrench, it was, leaving the rented flat they'd shared, but it was necessary—and not just financially. He might still be back there, an unwashed, unshaven figure watching telly in the dark, whisky in hand, if Charlotte hadn't shepherded him to her place like a lost sheep.

"That makes sense. Then I wrote to Greta's family, and they told me she'd left you and gone off somewhere but they didn't know where, and I found that very strange because I always thought Greta was head over heels for you."

A jolt shoots through his body. She was? She really was? All this time he's been told to accept that his wife used him to leave the GDR, that she was only pretending to love him, and now, here, finally, is another person—Greta's closest friend—saying what he's always been unable to let go of: she loved him.

"I asked them to let me know if they ever heard from her, but they never did. They were quite . . . curt, actually, though I didn't take it personally. I was an enemy of the state with a criminal record; it wouldn't have done them any good to correspond with me. I moved around a lot in those early years, and in the end I stopped passing on my address to her family. There just didn't seem any point."

"So that was that."

"Not quite."

"Oh?"

"Years later, well after reunification, I bumped into Friedrich. Do you remember him?"

Friedrich. He knows that name. His translator and supervisor during those weeks at the factory. A tall, lanky guy with a patchy beard. It is thanks to Friedrich that he met Greta. "Yes, of course. He never liked me because he had designs on Greta."

"And I never liked him," Lena says. "Anyway, when I mentioned I'd lost touch with Greta, he said something like 'I'm not surprised she disappeared, given what she did.'"

Henry's eyebrows shoot up. "What she *did*?" he echoes. "What did she do?"

"He wouldn't tell me. But he was really angry at her. Said if he ever saw her again, he wouldn't be responsible for his actions."

There's a momentary silence on the line as he digests Lena's words. *Given what she did.* It's rubbish. Sour grapes because Greta chose Henry over Friedrich, surely.

"What do you think he meant?"

Lena sighs. "I don't know. From her letters to me, Greta was happy in England, happy with you. She talked about the clothes and the food and the films you saw. I couldn't tell you any more than that. But I always thought Friedrich was an *informeller Mitarbeiter* . . ."

"A Stasi informer."

"Yes. So if he believed Greta had done something bad, maybe . . . I don't know, Henry, it's all conjecture."

"Do you know where Friedrich is now?"

"I have no idea."

They talk a little longer, Henry finding comfort in this link to the past and—to his slight shame—in the fact that it wasn't only him who was deserted by Greta, but Lena, too. The thought lingers when they say their goodbyes and he hangs up. Right from the start he thought something else must have been happening for Greta to leave him like that, but for lack of an explanation, he'd let himself be half convinced by the theories of others. She'd used him to leave the GDR, said Charlotte. She'd run off with another man, said the police. Henry must have done something, implied Angelika. *What did you do to make her leave, Henry?* But what if something darker was happening? Something to do with Friedrich? With the Stasi?

He's sanding the legs of an oak chair a while later when another, more unexpected, question strikes him. *What did you do to make her think she couldn't tell you about it, Henry?*

20

GRETA, 2018

Her favourite café in Tofino is a relaxed, bohemian little place near the water, with big French windows through which she can watch the sea as she works. Greta often comes here with her laptop to send her completed translations to her clients. She doesn't have Wi-Fi in her camper, and her pay-as-you-go phone has only limited data, since she doesn't like to use it much, anyway. The world is so connected these days it scares her. She isn't on social media, doesn't have a phone contract, yet it would probably be easy for someone to find her, should they somehow know the name she uses now.

Perhaps that should be reassuring, since it must mean no one does.

And yet, the news about the poisoned spy in Salisbury, back in England, has reminded her that she should never be complacent, never let her guard down, just in case. There's always the possibility someone could come after her, even after all this time. Look at the Russian! Sixty-seven years old and fighting for his life in hospital. And then there's his daughter, poisoned alongside him, an innocent caught up the crossfire. Collateral damage. Greta couldn't bear the thought of that happening to Henry all those years ago—and she can't bear the thought of it happening to Tomas now.

All because of her.

"Bring round your stuff whenever," Tomas said the day after she'd agreed to live with him. "I can come between shifts and help you, if you like."

"I will," she replied, "but there's no rush, and I've got quite a bit of work to do, so maybe I'll stay in my van and put my head down until it's finished."

It is true, she currently has a glut of translations to get through—it's feast or famine, being a freelance translator—but that's not why she's still living in her camper instead of at Tomas's house. The news has thrown her right back there, has made her cling to the mobility of her van like a security blanket. It's also made her neglect her work in favour of scrolling through the BBC News website.

Nerve agent confirmed in Salisbury poisonings: police treat case as attempted murder

"Crazy, right?"

Greta looks up as Kelly, the café's manager, sets a muffin and cappuccino down on her table, nodding to the laptop screen as she does.

"It really is," she says, though it doesn't actually surprise her at all.

"It's like something out of a sixties spy film! A Russian double agent holed up in some two-bit town in England. Salisbury." She pronounces it Sal-is-berry.

"Sols-bree," Greta corrects her. It took her a while to get her head around English town names when she lived in the country. Bicester (*biss-ter*), Worcester (*wuss-ter*), Reading ("Not *reading* as in reading a book, *red-ding* like the colour red," Henry explained).

"You know it? You're German, aren't you, Marianne?"

"Yes, but I . . ." She stops herself saying *lived in England for a few years.*

She hasn't told anyone here that. "I have a friend who used to live not too far from there, actually." She thinks of the day trip she and Henry took to that part of the world, wandering around the strange, unfathomable structure of Stonehenge and then going into nearby Salisbury to find a cheap lunch. "It's a pretty place."

Not the sort of place you'd think would be home to Russian spies–turned–British intelligence agents. No, it's the sort of place you'd raise a family and live a comfortable, happy, regular life. Where you'd go for dinner in a pizza restaurant for your child's birthday, where your children would walk to school on their own with no fear for their safety. The sort of place that's pleasant, uneventful, unremarkable.

"Lovely cathedral, I hear," Kelly says brightly. "But this can't have done much for its tourist industry!"

Greta musters a smile in response, and Kelly laughs, moving away from her table. When she's back behind the counter, Greta googles the victim—the target, as he'd have been considered by those who poisoned him. Sergei Skripal, a former Russian military intelligence officer who fed secrets to the Brits in the 1990s. Arrested, tried, and convicted in Russia. Released four years into his thirteen-year sentence as part of a spy swap with Britain and the United States. Settled in Salisbury in 2010.

Her mind absorbs the facts. He'd already been caught and punished. Already served time in a Russian prison. Released and pardoned. And yet clearly he hadn't actually been pardoned at all. Clearly the Russians used him to get their own people back, but they hadn't forgotten what he did; they'd held a grudge all those years, waited for the right moment, and then . . .

She feels sick. *She* hasn't been caught and punished. And while she has often hoped they'd have forgotten, it could be fatal to assume that.

She closes her laptop and looks out the window at the sea. She's been happy here, in this comfortable, pleasant, pretty place. But she has run from many such places before. As she thinks about the Russian and his daughter, she can no longer fend off the thought that's been brewing in her head ever since she first heard the news: perhaps it's time to run again.

Later, her mind heavy, she walks through town, past Tomas's restaurant, past the studio where she sometimes takes yoga classes, past Ashley's gift shop on Main Street where her jewellery is on sale, an extra, much-needed income stream on top of her translation work. It is a small, friendly community here: a smattering of streets and houses clustered on the north of the peninsula, sandwiched between a sheltered inside passage, where bears forage along the shoreline and orcas patrol the waters, and the wild Pacific Coast, where surfers ride the waves that crash onto long sandy beaches. She's been here more than two years now, and it's been good to her, it really has—especially since she met Tomas.

At the far end of town, she sits on the wooden boards of the dock and looks out to sea, where the last whale-watching boats of the day are visible in the distance, heading back to shore. She did that with Tomas once, in their early days. She told him she'd never seen a whale, so he called in a favour with a friend who ran a tour company, and they went out on his rib on a private trip. For three quarters of an hour they saw nothing but seabirds and the occasional leaping fish, and they were about to turn back when a humpback breeched in the distance. A plume of water shot upwards like a geyser, and then its distinctive tail made a slow, graceful arc in the air before thwacking down on the sea's surface. "Did you see it?" Tomas asked, an excitable puppy beside her, and she could only nod, tears springing to her eyes at the majesty of it, this creature swimming free in the endless ocean. "I saw it," she said.

Freedom: that's always been her aim, during this strange, restless life she's led. It was what she craved when she was growing up in a country that said she couldn't travel where she liked, read what she liked, think what she liked. What she still wanted when she got to Britain and quickly came to realise she wasn't as free as she thought she'd be. And it's remained her chief desire through all these years, through every move, every new start.

At first, in those early days after she left Britain, she stayed for only a few weeks in each place, hopping from Singapore to Thailand to Malaysia to India with just a backpack. She was reeling from the trauma of leaving Henry behind in Britain, and the knowledge she might never see her family again. But it was also excitingly liberating. With the money she'd been given—her payment for services rendered—she was free to lose herself in the bustling markets, overwhelming cities, and remote islands; to soak up everything she'd daydreamed about; to absorb the colours, sounds, and smells of a world she'd once thought she wouldn't ever get to see. She couldn't forget what she'd done to obtain her precious freedom, couldn't forget she was alone now, but it made her all the more determined to make the most of it, to lap up every experience, since it had cost her so much.

As the years progressed, however, it became harder to move on. She was kept in Norway for five years by a friendly coastal community, a decent amount of work, and a local man she had no-strings fun with for a while, until a new friend, Solveig, started asking too many personal questions and she got spooked and left. Later, a spell in Greece ended abruptly when—to her horror—she thought she saw Friedrich on a beach one day. She decamped to Ireland, where she met Sean, a man she could have loved, if she'd let herself, but then the Russian defector Litvinenko was poisoned in a London hotel in 2006, and she felt too close and her fear rose up again. She fled to Spain, then South America, then Canada . . .

Throughout it all, she's always tried to keep her freedom, to outrun those who wanted to take it from her. And she's still running now, at the age of fifty-eight.

What she didn't know, all those years ago, was how exhausting it would be.

How lonely it would be.

As she sits on the dock in Tofino, Tomas's restaurant visible along the shore, she realises she doesn't want to run anymore; she really doesn't.

21

GRETA, 1983

The irony is, Henry, things were looking up for us by the time I realised what I'd got myself into.

In the same week as I started freelancing for a translation agency that had decided to give me a trial run (much to the surprise of your parents), you came home one day with fantastic news.

"We're going to have our own place!" you said, taking me into your arms and swinging me around the kitchen.

I smiled at the happiness in your face. "What do you mean?"

"My old schoolfriend Rob's parents own a flat in Summertown, and their tenants are moving out. They're unhappy with the letting agency they've been using, so they want to find their own tenants now, and they're willing to give us mate's rates."

"Sorry?" I didn't know that phrase.

"I mean, they'll reduce the rent for people they know and trust. Plus, the deposit's halved, so we can totally afford it, especially with your new job." You put your hands on my arms and grinned. "So it's ours, Greta, if we want it!"

I laughed and kissed you fiercely. "Thank you, *mein Schatz*."

"It's just luck, Greta." You shrugged, but I saw the pride in your face, pride and perhaps a little relief that you'd been able to do this for us, and I knew my slight culture shock and homesickness must have been showing, despite having tried to hide it from you, and that you were glad to do something to make me happier.

"It's amazing, that's what it is." I felt a surge of optimism. If the translation agency liked my work, perhaps I'd be able to reduce my hours at the café. Maybe, once we'd settled in and my new income started landing in our bank account, we'd even be able to take a short holiday to Italy, the first place on my travel wish list, or go back home to visit my family—or even both.

"What's the flat like? Not that it really matters—anything will be better than putting up with Ant's toilet habits."

You laughed. "It's a garden flat, two bedrooms. The kitchen and bathroom are small, but they're pretty nice. There's a lovely bay window in the living room—I thought maybe you'd want a desk there."

"Or I could work in the spare bedroom."

"Yeah, until we need that as a nursery."

I almost did a double-take, and I'm sure it must have shown on my face. A nursery? I was twenty-four; I was only just starting my career, only just settling into life in the West. I wanted to travel and enjoy my new freedom and spend time with you, the husband I'd been living with for only a few months.

"Well, maybe eventually . . ." We'd never discussed children, before we married. Perhaps I should have asked. Perhaps you shouldn't have assumed.

"Let's not wait *too* long, though." Your beautiful eyes were excited, your face animated by laughter lines. "It'd be amazing to have a mini-person about the place, don't you think?"

"But we don't have the money."

"I'm hoping to get a promotion soon, and if I do, then we'd be okay."

I hesitated. I wouldn't sour what had been such a great moment. "Well, we can talk about that later. For now, how about we celebrate?"

You held up a finger—*wait*—and picked up an Oddbins carrier bag you'd put on the kitchen counter. You rustled around inside it for dramatic effect, and then pulled out a bottle. "Ta-dah!"

We spent the next hour or so in bed, drinking that cheap sparkling wine, making slightly tipsy love, and talking about how we'd decorate and furnish our new home, if our finances allowed. I put thoughts of children to the back of my mind and focused on the here and now. All that mattered was that we loved each other and we finally had our own home, a place to properly start our future together. Everything else would work out in time.

It was all going so well, then, until the day I attended my next Amnesty meeting.

"*Guten Tag*, Greta!" Rod greeted me in that jovial way he had. "Everything all right with you?"

I chatted with him and the others, telling them about my new job and the flat we were soon to move into.

"Will you have a housewarming party?" Sarah asked. "I want to meet Henry."

"Yeah, maybe." I hadn't explained to you that I'd told them I was from West Germany, but you'd understand the lie. Nevertheless, I was reluctant to introduce you to my new friends. I'm not sure why. Perhaps I wanted to keep this part of my new life to myself, since I was so reliant on you for everything else. Perhaps I didn't want talk of secret sources and prison conditions and psychological torture to sully the wonderful life we were trying to build. Or perhaps I already knew, deep down, that I'd got myself into something I wouldn't be able to fix.

No, no, that's not right. I'm overlaying the knowledge I have now onto what happened back then. I didn't know a thing, Henry. Because I remember, with startling clarity, the growing realisation that crept over me during that meeting. I remember the sour taste in my mouth and the sickening feeling in my stomach as Rod told us the terrible news: the person who had been Amnesty's source in Berlin had been arrested.

"He's likely in Hohenschönhausen, though we can't confirm this," Rod said over tea and Bourbon biscuits. "Nor do we know what charges are laid against him. There's little we can do for him personally at the moment, so all we can do is continue to put pressure on the GDR government about their human rights record."

"That's awful—the poor man." Sarah echoed the dismay of the others in the group, and I murmured my agreement, but an unwelcome thought fluttered in my head. It had nothing to do with me, surely. But my chest tightened when I thought of my visits to Olaf, his devotion to the DDR, the Amnesty flyer he'd so casually handed me. And why had I been eating Battenberg and drinking coffee in the home of some aging communist? Because of Friedrich and his *vitamin B*; because he'd helped me leave the DDR by calling in a favour with friends in high places, an act I hadn't thought deeply about because I wanted the end result so badly. Well, now I did. Who were these friends of Friedrich? In exactly what position would you have to be to expedite an exit visa? And why would Fred arrange that for me, someone who had spurned his long-term devotion in favour of another man? *You deserve it.* His words came back to me then, and my stomach turned over.

"How did this happen?" I asked, the words catching in my throat.

"We don't really know, but I expect some informer in Berlin found out what he was doing and ratted on him." Rod looked at me with sympathy. "It's a shock, I know, but these things happen all the time, Greta, as I'm sure you're aware. These contacts of ours, they risk their freedom in order to help others because they know it's the right thing to do, so we must keep on doing what we're doing. It's the best way to help them. Right?"

I forced myself to nod, but I couldn't speak. I fled the meeting quickly at the end, declining an invite to join them in the pub afterwards. Instead, I rushed home, told you I had a headache, and went straight to bed, where I lay awake all night, one painful question pulsing in my head.

Was this all my fault?

I returned to London because I wanted to see Olaf's reaction. I hoped desperately that my hunch, which had induced a constant low-level nausea in the days following the AI meeting, was simply a nightmarish fantasy.

But I knew, as soon as I mentioned the arrest, that it wasn't.

"It's treason to pass on information to foreign powers," he said in a calm, slightly patronising tone. "He would have known that. He'd have understood the risks."

"Someone informed on him."

Olaf shrugged. "Quite right, too. It's a crime not to report something like that. You know as well as I do, Greta, dear, that the Firm must make it their business to know everything about everyone, since one never knows where traitors may be hiding in plain sight."

The Firm. The Ministry for State Security. The Stasi. He held my gaze until I looked away, down at my trembling hands. It was true: this was on him. On me.

I hadn't told Olaf who the Amnesty source was because I didn't know. But I *had* given him the names of the two prisoners involved, and perhaps that was enough for someone back home to put two and two together. And now this brave Berliner was probably in some cell somewhere, suffering who knows what at the hand of the Stasi interrogators. *Psychological abuse. Sleep deprivation. Forced confessions.* All because Olaf was—what? Some kind of Stasi officer in Britain? Because Friedrich had sent me to him like a lamb to slaughter. Because I'd been so single-minded in my quest to obtain freedom for myself that I hadn't seen what was right in front of me.

I forced myself to look up, to meet those sharp eyes once again, to say as defiantly as I could, "I don't think I'll go to Amnesty meetings anymore."

He regarded me a moment, and then his bushy eyebrows twitched. "That's a pity," he said evenly. "I enjoy our discussions about it, I must say."

I bet you do, I thought, fury building in my chest. I'd been fond of this man, despite his delusions that the DDR could still be the utopia he'd always dreamed of. He'd been a friend of sorts, the grandfather I'd never had, a kindly father figure to stand in for the one who wasn't here. But he'd betrayed me.

I rose from the sofa. "I need to leave."

Olaf gave me that familiar smile, an expression I'd once thought so benign, but it was nothing of the sort. "Are you sure, Greta? Why not stay awhile, and we can talk some more about this. We could help each other, you know. You continue to visit Amnesty meetings; I give you a little money to help you and Henry in your newly married life."

I stood stock-still, this deal, so brazenly stated, reverberating in my head. "No," I blurted, unable to keep indignation from my tone. "No, absolutely not."

I ran hard through the streets of Oxford that evening. I ran until my legs shook and my chest heaved and I threw up what little I'd eaten in a muddy corner of Port Meadow, splattering my trainers.

I'd had them forever, those running shoes, and they'd felt so special to me because they contained so many memories from my youth. I'd worn them when I won my age category in the 1500m at a sports festival in Leipzig as a teenager, and when I'd run regularly with Friedrich, each of us trying to outpace the other. They were plain white—a grubby, off-white now, after years of use. Nothing flash. No coveted Western brand name. But it had felt right to bring them with me to Britain, to wear

194

them as I ran through Port Meadow or South Park or along the streets of Cowley and Summertown. They'd earned it, this freedom to pound different pavements.

But now, bent double, chest heaving, looking at the vomit splattered on the toes of those trainers, I saw how naive I'd been, how I'd allowed my nostalgia to colour the reality of life in my country, during these first few months of settling into a new one. I'd been homesick and frustrated and defensive about criticism of my homeland from those who'd never been there. I'd yearned for an evening with Lena, drinking and dancing in the Alextreff, or watching *Dallas* and dreaming of the West. I'd missed Sundays sewing with Mutti and Angelika in our neat, clean, familiar apartment. I'd reflected on the holidays I'd taken, the university studies I'd enjoyed, the parties and track meets and summer outings to the amusement park, and I'd allowed myself to occupy the grey, to sit between the opposing viewpoints of Olaf and Amnesty, understanding both yet never fully agreeing with either. But now my ambivalence was gone. Olaf's actions had sullied all the good memories I had. It had made me realise that everything in the DDR—the good as well as the bad—was propped up by people like him: people coercing and betraying and threatening and spying on others. Our free education, our cheap rent and food, our subsidised theatre and cinema tickets—everything the state gave us—was all infected by the ideology we rejected at our peril.

I thought of the miners here in Britain, the tabloid newspapers, the countless people in this country who openly spoke their minds, or went on strike, or chained themselves to oak trees, or wrote highly critical opinion pieces about Mrs. Thatcher's polices. Amnesty's unfortunate contact wasn't allowed to do any of that in his country, so he'd done what he could instead—highlighted the plight of others who had been arrested for speaking their minds, for breaking unfair rules they'd had no say in putting in place, or for trying to leave a country that had no right to keep them there. Britain was far from perfect, that was true, but it was free in the way that mattered most.

"I don't feel well," I said to you when I got home that night. "I just threw up."

"You run too hard and don't eat enough, that's why." You said it kindly, but I snapped back.

"Don't tell me what I do."

"Hey, hey, love." You got up from the sofa and pulled me into a hug. "What's wrong?"

"Nothing, nothing. I'm sorry. I'm just tired."

"Shall I run you a bath?"

I shook my head, forced a smile. "I can do it."

You shrugged. "All right."

I could have told you. I could have said I'd accidentally become involved with someone I now thought was working with the Stasi, and a Berliner had been arrested because of me. But shame stopped me. You thought the DDR was behind me and we were free to lead the life we wanted here in Britain. You thought I was this wonderful person, the perfect woman for you, who deserved all your efforts to create an amazing life for us both. You were such a good person, Henry, and now I felt like the very worst.

Thankfully, you didn't need to know. I'd made a big mistake, but it was over. I wouldn't return to AI, and I would refuse to see Olaf. It was awful, what I'd done, but it wouldn't happen again now I knew who—what—Olaf was. I would put it behind me and move on.

Before I got into bed that night, I went out to the rubbish bin by the front porch and threw my old trainers away.

22

HENRY, 2018

Henry sits in the workshop's armchair—Lucy's armchair, as he now thinks of it—on his lunch break, tucking into the ham and cheese sandwiches he makes for himself each morning at home. Two slices of granary loaf, the nice ham from the butcher's (fat carefully removed), mature cheddar cheese, and an evenly spread dollop of Branston Pickle. He should go and eat them down by the river and stretch his legs at the same time, but it's still distinctly chilly outside, so instead he's here in the warm, reading the news on his phone as he eats.

He's been glued to the latest from Salisbury: Britain's military science laboratory Porton Down identifying the nerve agent, the UK prime minister accusing Russia of being responsible for the poisoning, calls for Russian diplomats to be expelled from Britain in retaliation. It's like a Cold War spy novel, and the whole affair has reminded him of his trips to East Berlin, of the latent threat that hung over everyday life, of the ways and means the Stasi had to control and intimidate—and even kill. Never could he have imagined such darkness could occur in the UK in

2018, but there you go, he thinks, sometimes the truth is stranger than fiction.

His phone bleeps in his hand—a new email. He puts the sandwich down on his workbench and opens it.

His chest leaps to see it's from the Canadian shop.

Dear Mr. Henderson,

Greetings from windy Tofino! Thanks for your email and your enquiry about Marianne Kerber's jewellery. Yes, she is a German designer-maker, though she's lived over here in BC for several years now. You are welcome to place your order through our website, or if you prefer, please let me know which pieces you would like, and I will send you a payment link. We post to the UK.

Have a nice day!
Ashley Tremblay

Henry puts down the phone and takes another bite of his sandwich. It means nothing. So what if this jewellery maker is German? There might be millions of Germans in Canada—couldn't there be others making jewellery in a similar style?

He swallows, the bread heavy in his throat.

Or maybe Marianne Kerber is actually Greta Henderson.

Don't be ridiculous, he thinks. *Why on earth would she change her name?*

But then Friedrich's words to Lena come back to him, mingling with his thoughts of East Berlin, of the Stasi, and producing an answer he's never considered before. *Because you didn't know her as well as you thought you did.*

He throws the rest of his sandwich in the bin and goes back to varnishing two armchairs brought in by a woman who wanted them repaired as a surprise for her husband on his sixtieth birthday. They were his grandparents' chairs, she told him, but they'd sat in a state of disrepair in their garage for years. "If you could get them back to how they looked when he remembers them in his nan and grandpop's house," she said, "he'd really love it." Henry switches the radio on and dips a brush in the pot of varnish before applying it in long, even strokes.

He spent his own sixtieth in the pub, dragged there reluctantly by Ian and Charlotte, who'd demanded he celebrate his big birthday even though he'd have been perfectly content at home alone with a film and a good bottle of red. They ordered steak, but the chef had overcooked it, and Henry didn't want to kick up a fuss, so he chewed it slowly while Ian talked about a tennis tournament at their local club and Charlotte asked Henry about his goals for the next decade of his life, a question that made him feel somewhat maudlin. "I don't really know," he shrugged, "do I have to have goals?," and Charlotte pursed her lips and told him he only had one life and their father had died at sixty-five after all, and then Henry wished he *had* stayed at home alone with a bottle of red and a steak from the butcher that he would have cooked a lot better than the one in front of him.

He puts down the brush. Sixty-two, he is now. Greta would be fifty-eight. So much time has passed since they were young. Would she look the same, or similar enough for him to recognise a description?

He picks up his phone and types a reply to Ashley Tremblay in Canada. *I'd like to place an order for that twisted metal heart pendant*, he writes, thinking on the hoof. *And by the way, sorry if this sounds strange, but I think I might have met Marianne once, but I'm not sure if it's the same woman. Is she in her late fifties with blond hair? Is she a keen runner?*

He presses Send, feeling faintly ridiculous, but before he can carry on varnishing, the phone buzzes in his hand.

He smiles and answers. "Hi, Lucy, I'm glad you called, actually, because I had something to—"

"Er, sorry," a man's voice says. "This isn't her. I'm Pete." His voice is faint and hard to hear with all the background noise—traffic on tarmac, strained voices, the bluster of the wind. "You were in her recent calls list. I was first on the scene; it happened right in front of me. The ambulance guys are here now, but I thought I should call some people who know her."

"What?" Henry says. "What are you talking about?"

"Lucy—the woman whose phone this is? I'm sorry, mate, but she's been in a car crash."

Henry hates hospitals, especially this one. It doesn't seem to have changed much since he visited his father here all those years ago, following his first heart attack. The same smell of disinfectant, the same off-white walls, peeling and scuffed at the edges, the same generic pictures of flowers and landscapes in the waiting rooms, the same uncomfortable plastic chairs.

He asks for Lucy at the nurses' station and is directed to a room down the corridor. He hesitates outside. Perhaps he shouldn't be here. He's not a relative, not even a close friend, just some old man she seems to want to help. But he can't ignore the information given to him by that stranger over the phone: Lucy's had a car crash; Lucy is hurt.

He holds the bunch of daffodils in front of him, knocks, and pushes open the door.

"Look, what's done is done," a weary male voice is saying. "But I really don't know if I can deal with all your shit, Luce."

Henry turns to leave, but it's too late.

"Henry?" Lucy says.

She is lying in bed, gauze taped to her right temple and a brace around her neck. Next to her, sitting by the side of the bed, is a young man with red hair, a pale, lightly freckled face, and long limbs. He is leaning forward, looking at her through black-rimmed glasses, brows knotted. Henry's mind flits back to a similar scene twenty-five years ago: his father in the bed, his mother by his side.

"I'm sorry to interrupt, I'll leave you be."

"No, come on in." Lucy shifts a little in the bed and waves him over. "It's really nice of you to come. I heard that guy Pete phoned practically everyone on my recent calls list, which I guess was good of him, but seriously, I didn't need Millie's teacher or the receptionist at Oscar's sleep clinic to know about my silly prang."

Henry laughs, but his insides curl up a little. Is he no more to her than them? "These are for you," he says, stepping forward. "To add to the greenhouse." He gestures around the room, where several bunches of flowers sit in vases of various shapes and sizes. He is reminded of the first time he met Lucy, of the vase she brought in, and the necklace she wore, which seemed to connect them, which seemed to imply she was meant to walk into his workshop that day.

"They're gorgeous, thanks so much, Henry. Come and take a seat—and look, you can finally meet Jack, my husband." Her eyes turn to the man by the bed. "Henry's been asking about you ever since we met."

Jack stands up and stretches out his hand to Henry, who shakes it and tries—but fails—to smile. He does exist, then: the husband who never seems to be around, who doesn't do anything to help his wife with the kids, who hasn't shouldered the load that has stopped Lucy sleeping, that has drawn lines on her face and rimmed her eyes with red, and potentially, he suspects, contributed to her ending up in this hospital bed right now.

"Hello," Jack says. "I'll leave you to chat."

"Don't go on my account," Henry says, forcing a smile out now.

"No, no." Jack runs a hand through his hair. "I have to see to the kids anyway."

"They're okay?"

"They're fine," Lucy says brightly. "And so am I. A touch of whiplash and a knock to the head, so they're keeping me in for observation, that's all. Really, it's a big fuss about nothing."

"You fell asleep at the wheel with our kids in the back," Jack mutters, his tone low but hard. "It's not nothing."

Lucy, for once, doesn't speak, but her eyes fill and she blinks hard.

"I'll come back later," Jack says, softer now. He nods to Henry and then leaves, closing the door behind him.

"Lucy?" Henry says. "Are you really all right?"

She nods, as much as the neck brace allows, and smiles, the action squeezing a tear from her left eye, which she quickly rubs away. "Really, I am. It was a shock, that's all, but I've been so lucky: everyone's okay, I didn't hit another car or anyone on the street, I just went into a hedge, which could take the knock, frankly. But when I think about what could have happened, I just . . . I mean, God, I could have killed them, and I just . . ." The tears slide freely down her cheeks now, and she doesn't wipe them away.

Henry hands her a tissue from the box beside the bed and sits down on the chair Jack has vacated. "It didn't happen," he says. "There's no point brooding over what might have been." He hears his own words and swallows the irony—*he* would offer such advice when he clearly can't take it himself?

"Yes, I suppose." Lucy sniffs. "But now Jack hates me even more."

"Hates you? Of course he doesn't. He's upset, and in shock, I expect. People say things they don't mean when they're upset."

"You don't." Lucy smiles. "You're a good person, Henry. Much better than me."

Her words take him aback, and his response flies out before he can think about it. "Yes, I do, and no, I'm not," he blurts.

"What?"

He hesitates. *Oh, what the hell.* "I misjudged you when we met, Lucy. I thought you were this silly young woman with verbal diarrhoea. And I was mean to you, the other week, after we found out the necklace wasn't Greta's and you wanted to continue looking anyway. Also, I never called a woman back whom my sister forced me to go on a date with, and she was a very nice woman who didn't deserve to be ignored. So you see, I'm not always a good person."

There is a moment of silence, and he flushes to see her face; it's not often Lucy is rendered speechless.

"Thanks, Henry, that's made me feel so much better!" She bursts out laughing. "So now we've established we're both terrible people," she continues, wiping tears of mirth from her eyes. "Update me, please. What's the latest? What did Lena say? Did you email the shop?"

"You don't want to hear about all that now."

"No, I do. I really do! It would be a good distraction from all this." She waves her hand around the hospital room.

So he tells her about Lena's bravery, her time in prison, how she'd forged a new life in West Germany. He relays her attempts to write to Greta and her family, and her strange encounter with Friedrich Schmidt years later. As he speaks, Lucy sits gripped, her eyes boggling a little more with every revelation.

"I googled him but nothing came up—at least, lots came up but nothing that would give me an idea of which one he is. Schmidt is an extremely common name." He shrugs. "So we're at a dead end, I think. The shop in Canada confirmed that the jewellery designer is German, but that hardly means anything, and it was always going to be a long shot."

Lucy glares at him. "Henry Henderson," she says, a brusqueness in her tone. "I am not done yet. I have plenty of ideas for what to do next. I want to do more work to track down Angelika. We could email all the Friedrich Schmidts and ask them if he's *our* Friedrich Schmidt—though that might take a while, to be fair. And you must tell me if there's anyone else that you remember. Who were her friends in Britain? Who did she work with?"

Henry smiles. She's a dog with a bone, this woman. "Well, she wasn't close to anyone at the café she worked in, nor the translation company, since she mostly worked from home. She did have one good friend she met at Amnesty International. She used to go to meetings there. Sarah, her name was, but I have no idea of a surname, and anyway I contacted her after Greta left and she was as clueless as I was. Oh, and then there was Olaf—this friend of Friedrich's father whom she visited occasionally. But he was just some old man who lived alone in London. She used to go there to make sure he was okay. I think she felt sorry for him."

"Ooh, but he might know something, if he was somehow connected to Friedrich? He might even know where Friedrich is now."

Henry shrugs. "Perhaps. But he's surely dead by now—he must have been in his sixties back then."

"You never know. Do you remember his surname?"

Henry shakes his head, but then a glimmer of a memory comes to him. "Long—or Lange, perhaps?"

"Well," Lucy says, "that's a start. Leave it with me."

He leaves her to sleep and slips out the door. As he does so, a woman looks up from the row of seats against the wall opposite. The first thing he notices is the mass of curls falling around her shoulders, grey in colour yet abundant in volume and as striking as her prominent cheekbones and large hazel eyes—though her eyeshadow seems unnecessarily heavy-handed. She's wearing a dark green jumper and slim black jeans, a colourful scarf loose around her neck. She looks both his age and not, as though youth simmers beneath the skin of a body that's growing old gracefully.

"You must be Henry," the woman says. "Lucy's told me all about you. I'm her mother."

Henry's eyebrows shoot up. "Yes, that's me."

"Rosalind." She sticks out her hand. "Ros, to most." Her cheekbones seem to protrude even more when she smiles. "It's good of you to stop by."

"Nice to meet you, Ros. Though I'm sorry it's in these circumstances. You must be very worried."

"It was a shock to get the phone call, but she's going to be absolutely fine, physically. It's her mental health I'm more concerned about. It's been a tough time for her recently, and now this. But perhaps it's a wake-up call for both of them. Maybe they can sort things out now." She cocks her head, as though assessing him. "Anyway, Henry, I think I'm going to leave Lucy to get some much-needed rest and go for a coffee. Would you like to join me? Jack's taken the kids home, and I'd love some adult company after minding the little terrors for hours."

Henry looks at his watch. He needs to get back to the workshop to finish those chairs, but Ros's words have intrigued him. What do Jack and Lucy have to *sort out*? "Yes, okay, just a quick one."

They go to a café at the hospital entrance, and Henry takes a seat, brushing off a few crumbs first, while Ros goes to the counter. He doesn't remember this café being here when he'd visit his father all those years ago, fortifying himself against the inevitable bad news with vending machine coffee the colour of dishwater. So long ago, and yet the memories rise up now: another person he loved about to leave him, another relationship he cherished—his parents' marriage—about to end. At least he knew the reason that time: too many snacks and beers over too long a period had taken a toll on his father's arteries, and there was little the doctors could do but wait for the inevitable second heart attack that would kill him. Henry remembers his mother's face when it finally happened, the way it crumpled in on itself, as though his father's death had robbed her own body of something physical, too. *Love*, he thought; *that's what it does after a lifetime together*. It only made him yearn even more for Greta, for the marriage that could have emulated his parents' in length and strength, if only she hadn't left him.

"It wasn't the flawless thing you think it was, you know," Charlotte once said to him when he'd confessed how much he wanted to have a marriage like their parents had had, to re-create the family life he'd cherished as a child. "Mum almost left Dad in the sixties, only stayed because she didn't have independent financial means."

"I don't believe that for a second," Henry scoffed.

"Why would I say it otherwise? Mum and I talked about that stuff. Anyway, they worked it out in the end."

He brushed away her comments. His parents had never had anything to *work out*. Or so he thought then. Now he wonders if Charlotte was right, if something else was lurking under the surface of their parents' marriage, just as he's coming to wonder if something was lurking beneath his own.

"I hear you repair the most wonderful things." Ros's voice breaks into his thoughts. She sits down opposite him, coffee sloshing out of both cups as she places the tray on the table. "Lucy raves about what you do. And that vase—I couldn't believe it when I saw it, couldn't even tell where the break had been."

"Thank you." Henry takes a napkin from the tray and wipes up the spilled coffee, which Ros hasn't seemed to notice. "But I think Lucy mainly likes the peace and quiet of the workshop."

"Well, that, too, yes. She doesn't get a lot of quiet these days with those two little monkeys. Do you know the best thing about being a grandparent, Henry? You get all the joy of young children, coupled with the ability to give them back when it gets too much." She laughs, but doesn't ask the obvious next question. She already knows, he remembers. *Lucy's told me all about you.* She knows he doesn't have children or grandchildren. She knows he's been trying to find his vanished wife. He shifts in his seat, uncomfortable with her knowing but grateful she doesn't ask.

"Yes, my niece and nephew were a handful when they were younger," he offers by way of thanks. "I had to ban them from my workshop as they made such a mess of everything it took me hours to get it all back in its rightful place afterwards."

Ros takes a sip of coffee. "Making a mess of things is what kids are meant to do, though, wouldn't you say?" She picks up a packet of sugar and starts to fiddle with it. "And what most adults *still* do, come to think of it. My darling daughter certainly did." She rolls her eyes. "But I have faith Jack will forgive her in the end. It's tough, being a young mum and feeling like you've lost yourself a little under all the nappies, especially when your husband is at work all day and not able to share the burden in the same way. It's no wonder Lucy was so susceptible to an old friend's attentions. I've told Jack that, but otherwise I try to stay out of it—it's between them, in the end. But I do wish Jack would give a little leeway. It's not like he's entirely blameless; he was like a nervous hen when Millie was born, always needing Lucy to tell him what to do, as if she weren't completely new to parenthood, too! And then going back to work so quickly and using that as an excuse to never do any of the night feeds, so it was always Lucy with the broken sleep. I think, after repeating the experience with Oscar, she was simply grateful that someone was recognising her as a woman again, rather than just a mother and a milk machine. And in the end, she made a mistake, it was a one-off, and she's dreadfully sorry for it, so I think she deserves his forgiveness and understanding, don't you agree?"

Ros's packet of sugar has split and the contents are now all over the table. He wants to reach out and still her hand, to stop her making any more mess, but he is paralysed by her words—so many words, just like her daughter, yet the meaning stands out clear as day: *Lucy cheated on Jack.*

Everything he knew about his young almost-friend seems turned on its head. Jack isn't the uncaring, useless, absent husband and father Henry assumed he was. Jack has been hurt, badly hurt—badly enough to have moved out of the family home, perhaps. Yes, that must be it, Henry thinks as the jigsaw pieces in his head slot into place: he isn't simply never there; he doesn't actually live there anymore.

"I didn't know . . ." he says softly. Lucy, who spends so much of her life rushing around after her kids, had time to have an affair? Lucy, who seems so in thrall to his love story, has actually messed up her own? He thinks of her sudden emotion that day in his workshop when he returned her repaired vase, the vase Jack gave her. Her red, puffy eyes when Henry arrived unannounced at her house. The family trip to Legoland that she didn't go on.

"Oh, I assumed she told you. She tells most people most things, after all." Ros smiles. "But please, don't think badly of her; it wasn't a full-blown affair, just a silly kiss on a rare night out for a friend's birthday. I do understand how it's affected Jack, of course—and he's always been a sensitive soul—but in the end nobody's perfect. Everyone makes mistakes, and it was a small one in the grand scheme of things."

A kiss with an old friend. A small mistake, yes, yet a mistake none-theless. A breach of trust, a lie, an act of betrayal that he, too, would have found hard to forgive should Greta have done that to him. *Lucy*, he thinks. *How could you?* And yet, to his surprise, his heart clenches for her, for the young woman who talked her way into his workshop and his life and doesn't seem to want to leave, the woman who has treated his love for Greta seriously and done more to help him find her than anyone else has for many years.

Is that why? Has she has been so determined to fix his relationship because she can't fix her own? Does she need one of them, at least, to find their happily ever after? *It's not right*, she'd said to him about Greta's departure, *and I suppose I want to make things right.*

"Are you okay, Henry?" Ros is looking at him with concern, her brown eyes searching his face, and he realises he hasn't responded.

"Yes," he says, "I suppose that's true."

Nobody's perfect.

He's always thought that's one of those stock phrases people say, some-thing used as an excuse for below-par behaviour, for cheating spouses and selfish siblings and jealous friends. He's always thought you should *try*, at least, to be perfect, to treat people well, to love with all your heart, to make things—objects, relationships, lives—as perfect as they can be. He'd always thought he and Greta had it pretty perfect, that she was perfect for him and he was perfect for her, and they would have continued leading their perfect life for a long time to come, if she hadn't vanished.

I'm not surprised she disappeared, given what she did.

But maybe this image of perfection that's been lodged in his head for so many years has masked the truth.

That Greta *wasn't* perfect. And he wasn't, either. Then something happened—something that she failed to tell him about and he failed to see.

23

GRETA, 1983

We never did have a flat-warming party. You wanted one, but I put you off with excuses, saying it would be expensive to buy booze and food for lots of people, that we didn't have enough chairs, that the flat was too small and I didn't want to ruin the lovely carpets. In truth, I didn't want your friends—John and Ant, Mike from work, Charlotte, everyone who knew I was from the DDR—to meet and chat with my friends from Amnesty (the only guests I could contribute to a party, after all), who thought I was a *Westler* from Hamburg.

We did, however, have Sarah and Kevin around for dinner one night. You wanted to meet them, and they wanted to meet you, and so I told you what I'd said to them about my origins, and why.

"I understand why you said that at the beginning, but couldn't you tell them now?" you asked. "They're your friends; it's weird lying to them. They'll understand why you said it, won't they?"

You were right, they would. But something held me back. It was a big leap from my origins behind the Iron Curtain to suspecting me of having anything to do with getting that Amnesty contact arrested, but in my head it was as clear as day. I felt so guilty, Henry, I felt sure it was written all over my face.

"Please, *Schatz*. You don't have to lie. We just don't speak about it, or we change the subject if they bring it up."

I saw something unfamiliar flitter across your face—disapproval?—and then your usual equanimity returned and you smiled, shrugged. "Okay, my love. If that's what you want."

You all got on famously. Sarah and Kevin complimented us on the food, gushed about our little flat, brought us a bottle of wine and a potted plant for the windowsill, and the four of us got gradually drunker and more relaxed the longer the dinner went on.

"God, isn't it amazing to think how life can change just like that!" Sarah said over coffee and Mr Kipling French Fancies, which they'd also brought with them and you'd opened accordingly, not knowing that their association with Olaf's Battenberg made me feel faintly queasy. "If you hadn't gone to Hamburg, Henry, you'd still be there, I guess, Greta. Might be married to some German guy! Might never have known the joy of cheap plonk from Safeway and Mr Kipling's cakes!"

We all laughed, and your eyes slid to me.

"Yes, thank goodness," I said. "How did you two meet?"

"Oh, down the youth club in Witney. Known him forever."

Kevin's eyebrows shot up. "You say that like it's a bad thing."

Sarah shrugged. "Well, they do say familiarity breeds contempt." Then she leant into her husband with a smile. "Nah, you do my head in sometimes, but I wouldn't be without you."

He laughed. "Now that's true love." Then he gasped, holding up a finger, as the first strains of "Bohemian Rapsody" came from the radio.

"It's our song!" Sarah screeched, and then the two of them started singing, heads together, attempting to hit notes only Freddie Mercury really could. I turned to you and smiled, and you reached for my hand under the table, and I knew you were thinking the same as me: that perhaps that would be us one day, that our still-new marriage would evolve into the kind of relationship where we had a song, a shared history, and cultural touchstones that brought back happy memories.

Later, when we were all half cut, we turned the radio up and I pulled you reluctantly from the sofa to dance around the living room to "Red Red Wine" and "You Can't Hurry Love" and "Total Eclipse of the Heart."

We never called it our song. But whenever I hear that Bonnie Tyler track, I think of you, and that evening, and the happiness I felt belting out a power ballad in your arms in the front room of our little flat, pushing my guilt aside and looking only to the future, thinking that surely everything was going to be okay now.

But it turned out it was the calm before the storm, because a few days later a letter arrived from my mother. I remember that day so clearly. It was a Saturday. I'd wanted to go somewhere, to jump in the car and drive to a place I hadn't been—Bath, I think, to follow in the footsteps of Jane Austen, whose books I was currently devouring—but you said you were tired and could we have a quiet weekend at home instead, so I'd shrugged and swallowed down my disappointment.

We'd lingered late in bed, until you got up to make us a fry-up. The post was on the table when I came into the kitchen, wrapped in a dressing gown. I intended to go for a run later, while you would start stripping back that old wooden chest of drawers we'd found in a junk shop. You were excited to have a project, to do something with your hands that didn't involve industrial machinery, and you were talking about how you'd begin to tackle it when I sat down at the table and tore open the letter.

My face must have fallen because you asked me what was wrong immediately. So I told you: my father had been demoted, Mutti had written. My father—one of the most respected employees at his publishing house, the man who had managed his department for twenty years and trained countless apprentices.

We can't understand it, Greta. They say it's for "security reasons" but that makes no sense. He's devastated, of course. All these years of service and that's how they repay him! Please send him a note, to lift his spirits.

I sat with the letter as you served me breakfast. You shared my surprise—my shock—and told me it would be okay, there must have been a mistake, and why don't we send them something nice to cheer them all up? You had no idea why it could have happened, you said.

But I did.

My legs were shaking as I stood on the porch of the house in Stockwell the following Tuesday, waiting for Olaf to answer the intercom.

"Greta, dear. I wasn't expecting you." He ushered me up the stairs and into his flat.

"I wasn't expecting to come back." I didn't know how to play this, Henry, so in the end I decided to say it straight. "But my father's been demoted, and I think it's because of you, so here I am."

He closed the door and looked at me. "Please, sit."

"I don't want to sit. I don't want your *Kaffee und Kuchen*. I want you to acknowledge what you've done and reverse it."

He sighed. "I'm going to make myself a spot of coffee, and then we'll have a proper conversation."

So he made me wait, my insides ablaze with anger and fear, as he boiled the kettle, filled the cafetiere, and whistled to himself in the kitchenette.

"Well," he said finally, settling in his usual armchair. "Here we are."

I stood at the back of the room, arms folded over my chest. "I trusted you. I came here as a favour to a friend, and I trusted you were a decent person."

He spread his hands out. "And I am, Greta. I didn't want it to come to this."

"But you didn't stop it. I want you to get Vati reinstated."

"It's not up to me," he said calmly.

"That's rubbish. You can influence their decision."

He shook his head. "Listen, Greta. Believe it or not, I don't agree with all the actions taken by the Party and their . . . proxy. But sometimes the end justifies the means. This is a war—a cold one, yes, but if we don't do all we can to protect ourselves, it may end up becoming extremely hot. So we must fight—*now*. We must fight to preserve everything the GDR has achieved and stop those who only want to undermine it."

"I don't need to listen to this. I don't need your justifications. I want you to undo what's happened."

"I can't, my dear." He spread his hands, and the gesture infuriated me. "I can't change what they've done, and I can't stop what they might do."

What they might do?

"Your sister, you wouldn't want to hurt her chances of getting into university, would you?" he continued. "And your mother, she must miss her sister so much—how sad she'd be if Ilsa's visits were to be blocked. And then there's your father. If he doesn't like being demoted, how would he feel to lose his job altogether?"

His words, so gently spoken, landed like a series of punches to the stomach. My family would tolerate all those things if it meant I didn't have to entangle myself with the Stasi. But it didn't mean I wanted them to.

"Greta," Olaf said quietly. "You know how it works."

And I did. I knew that blocking people's careers, educational opportunities, and ability to travel was only the tip of the iceberg in the Party's struggle to force its citizens into line. I knew that if I didn't cooperate, the Stasi could haul my parents in for interrogation, make their lives a misery, force them to say things that weren't true, implicate themselves in a supposed crime against the state. They could easily end up like Lena's uncle Jürgen, languishing in prison, their lives ruined.

"You're an intelligent person, Greta," Olaf said when I didn't reply. "An asset to your country." He smiled, but there was sadness in it. Did he really want to do this? Was he being manipulated as much as I was? But I shook the thought away. He was good at that, at making me feel akin to him, but it didn't mean it was real. This wasn't my grandfather, my friend. "So I know you'll do the sensible, intelligent thing," he went on. "Go back to Amnesty meetings. Continue as before. Talk to your new friends. Find out as much as you can about the organisation's aims and campaigns and contacts. And then come back and tell me what they said."

"Simple." I laughed, but tears sprang to my eyes, and I looked down, blinked furiously. I'd come here seeking freedom. I'd arrived in Britain thinking everything would be different. And yet here I was, being controlled and manipulated just as before. "And if I do, you'll get Vati reinstated?" I needed him to say it out loud, to acknowledge the way he was blackmailing me.

He smiled amiably as he produced his trusty penknife and began cutting slices of Battenberg, and I genuinely think he believed what he was saying was reasonable. "My dear," he said in a gentle voice, as though pacifying an angry dog, "life's all about bargains. And this isn't a bad one. You get to help your father *and* your country. What's wrong with that?"

Back home, in the days before the next Amnesty meeting, I struggled to concentrate on my translation work. At the café, I made frequent mistakes—serving Earl Grey instead of English Breakfast, dropping a pot of coffee on the floor, breaking so many mugs that the manager docked my pay. And when I went out running, my mind ran, too. Could I do this? Should I refuse and sacrifice my family? I pounded the streets until I couldn't any longer, but the answer never came.

The only thing that calmed me a little was making jewellery. In the evenings, I sat for hours, twisting and bending and sculpting, making earrings and pendants and bracelets. It was a form of therapy. It was something to do with my restless hands. And it was filling my time as I waited impatiently for a reply to a letter I'd written, a letter of desperation to the one person I thought might be able to get me out of this situation.

I know you didn't approve of my marriage, Fred. But we were good friends, once, and I never wanted to lose that friendship. So I'm begging you, if you care for me at all, if you care for my family, please don't let Olaf do this to me. You know what I'm talking about.

I waited. I let myself hope. But I never got a reply.

24

GRETA, 2018

Novichok. That's the latest from the UK. A nerve agent of Russian origin, used in an ordinary British town on an ordinary Sunday afternoon. A policeman seriously ill in hospital, as well as the Russian double agent and his daughter.

Greta didn't sleep well last night, changing position every five minutes, hot and uncomfortable, until eventually getting up from Tomas's bed and going into the living room. She sat on the sofa with her bag of jewellery-making equipment and picked out a roll of wire, her hands working quickly with a pair of pliers, bending and shaping the metal into an intricate bracelet. Yet the act of making didn't still her mind as it often does. It didn't stop her imagining what could have happened back then: she and Henry out for lunch at a restaurant, returning home to the flat they shared, turning the door handle and being contaminated with something that could have killed them both.

She thinks about this as she lies in bed next to Tomas in the morning. It is Monday, his day off, and they usually spend it together: a lazy lie-in followed by blueberry pancakes for breakfast—his recipe; she cooks—and then some kind of activity. In summer they might swim or hire kayaks, or perhaps take a drive somewhere, discover a bit of this vast, wild island that she hasn't been to before. She likes the unconventionality of it—pretending Monday is Sunday, playing truant while most other people work—and the spontaneity of doing whatever takes their fancy on the day. Despite working hard, or perhaps because of it, Tomas isn't one for sitting around reading the paper. He'll clap his hands and say, "Right, let's go for a walk in the rain," or "There's a new ice cream supplier in Nanaimo I want check out, shall we go?," or "I feel like taking a boat out fishing, want to come?" She loves that about him, and it feeds the adventurous side of her, the side that can't sit still, that longs to see and do and experience.

But this morning she feels only the risk she represents to him throughout all that. She is a ticking time bomb, and he doesn't even know it.

"Hey, you're awake and staring at me—that's a little weird," Tomas says with a sleepy smile. He pulls her in to him and kisses her. "*Guten Morgen*, beautiful."

"Morning, *Schatz*," she whispers.

"Are you okay?"

She nods, thinking of that other morning, the day she left Henry. That was for his own safety, too. It was the right decision. It was the only decision she could make. And though the threat was more immediate back then, the headlines tell her that it's still there. "I had a bad night's sleep, that's all," she says.

"Was I snoring?"

She shakes her head. "Things on my mind."

"What things?"

She rolls over and gets out of bed. "I'll put the coffee on."

"Marianne, don't do that. You can talk to me, you know."

"It's nothing." She throws on Tomas's towelling robe and pads to the kitchen. She wonders if she could actually let her guard down and tell him everything. If, for the first time, she could confess all the shameful things she did and bear the inevitable disbelief and disappointment and disgust she would get in return. It is testament to his good nature that she, who has struggled to trust anyone for so long, believes he would keep her secrets to himself, whatever he thought of them. But what would it achieve? Even if, by some miracle, he forgave all her misdeeds, not to mention all the lies she's told him about herself, the risk remains. She is a danger to him. He will be better off without her—a liar, a liability—just as Henry was. Just as Sean was, in Ireland, and all the other lovers and would-be friends she has endangered with her presence over the years.

She pours the coffee, whips up some pancake batter, and turns on the hob. Each step fills her with dread, because it is a countdown to the moment that must come.

"That smells amazing." Tomas slides onto a stool at the breakfast bar.

"Here." She places a mug of coffee and a plate of pancakes in front of him, but she can't look at him, can't smile. *Just rip the plaster off.*

"Aren't you eating?" he says when she sits next to him, cups her hands around her coffee.

"I'm not hungry." She puts her hand on the bracelet on her left wrist, the one Tomas gave her at Christmas. It's a silver bangle with an engraved design depicting the Raven. She doesn't know if he chose the Raven for a particular reason or if he simply liked the design, but when she read the First Nations artist's card that came with it, it seemed apt: *Known as the "keeper of secrets," the Raven symbolizes the unknown and the idea that everyone sees the world in a different way.*

"Marianne?" Tomas puts down his fork. "What's up?"

She takes a breath and looks at him. How could she ever have thought she could stay with this man? How could she put him at risk like that? She doesn't deserve his love, and he deserves better.

"I'm sorry, Tomas," she says. "I've changed my mind. I can't move in with you. I can't . . . be with you anymore."

He looks at her, stunned. "Is this a joke?"

She shakes her head, mute. Isn't it better now rather than years later?

She's setting him free to find someone else, just as she did for Henry. Someone who can give her whole self to him, a whole self that is real and true and good. That's what he deserves.

"I don't understand," he says. "If you don't want to live with me yet, then I guess we can wait. It's not the end of the world. I mean, come on, Marianne, you can't mean this?"

She takes a breath, braces herself to speak the words she must. "I'm not the right one for you, Tomas. I'm no good for you."

He puts his hands on her arm and forces her to look at him. "You are absolutely right for me, my love. You are better than anyone's been for me for a very long time."

"You don't know what I'm like."

"Then tell me!" He throws his hands up in the air. "I want to know, Marianne. I want to know everything about you. I love you, and I'm listening."

She shakes her head and looks down, eliciting a snort of disgust in return.

"You know, I knew you were guarded, somehow. Private. Independent. Had your secrets. I mean, who doesn't, at our age? But I thought we were getting somewhere; I thought you actually loved me and wanted to be with me, but I guess I was wrong." He stands up.

"I'm sorry," she whispers.

"Yeah," he says, his voice breaking, "me, too."

Back in her van, Greta folds up the bed against the wall. She washes and dries a cup and a plate and puts them in the cupboard, making sure to lock it afterwards. She disconnects the van from the campsite's electricity and water supply. She cleans the windscreen and checks the pressure on the tyres. The van hasn't moved much in two years, because she and Tomas usually explore in his car—apart from that week's holiday last September, when they drove the van up the Campbell River. She fights the heat that rises behind her eyes as she thinks of the days of swimming and hiking, the evenings barbecuing fresh fish and lying out under the stars, huddled together against the cold, scouring the night sky for satellites.

She will miss him so much.

But she has done this before, and if there's one thing that going through the worst has taught her, it's that she can survive it—so she will survive again. Albeit alone. Always alone.

Over the years she has left behind everyone she cares about: her family, her best friend, her husband, all the people she's met over the years who have tried to get close to her. She's ripped them all off like the petals of a daisy, one by one. And now she's leaving Tomas, too.

What a pointless kind of freedom this is, she thinks as she readies herself for the journey ahead, *without anyone to share it with*.

She slides behind the wheel, turns the ignition, and drives away.

25

GRETA, 1983

The board was beautiful—two contrasting woods for the light and dark points, with a third, pale wood for the playing field, and mother-of-pearl inlay around the edges. Yet there was a collective groan in the pub when Rod produced the backgammon set from his rucksack.

"You know how to play?" he asked me, and I shook my head. "I can teach you if you like?"

Sarah drained her wineglass and nudged me. "Run, now, Greta, before it's too late!"

"That's definitely *my* cue to leave." Kevin pushed back his chair and put on his jacket. "Shall we?" he said to Sarah, who nodded.

"People, c'mon!" Rod said, mock-hurt, and I understood that this was a running joke, that Rod was a backgammon nerd and the others had endured game after game over drinks in the White Hart, the group's post-meeting pub of choice.

But I didn't mind. In fact, it was exactly what I needed: a chance to be alone with Rod, to do Olaf's bidding and find out if our esteemed leader might be sympathetic to the communist cause.

Ach, Henry, I'm imagining how you'd react if you read this, imagining how you'd feel when you realised what I was, what I did. Because I was now a Stasi informant. There, I've said it. A spy. A traitor to Britain. An awful, terrible person who didn't deserve these good people as friends.

Years later, after the Wall fell and the Stasi's files were opened to the public, stories emerged about the numerous *informelle Mitarbeiter* who had acted as eyes and ears in Berlin. And they were normal people, Henry. Husbands informing on wives. Friends on friends, colleagues on colleagues. All giving the Stasi information they could use to control and coerce people they knew and loved. But the newspaper articles didn't explain why they came to do what they did. Were they acting out of loyalty to their country? Did it make them feel secure or special or powerful? Were they denied something they needed, or promised something they yearned for? Did they consider it a necessary compromise? Did they perhaps not even realise what they were doing? Or were they being blackmailed and threatened—like me?

As I sat in the pub that night, waiting for the right moment to probe Rod's politics, I told myself that perhaps I could get through this with my morals more or less intact—or, at least, not compromised any more than they already had been. I didn't have to tell Olaf anything useful; perhaps I could even make things up. But I knew it was a fine balance. I had to give him something, and the information had to look genuine, or he'd soon suspect I wasn't playing ball and my family would suffer for it. Was I brave enough to deceive him? I thought I was, but now I see I was kidding myself. I was no better than all those eyes and ears in Berlin who deluded themselves that the information they were providing was harmless. All those who justified their actions by saying it was better they report innocuous titbits about their friends' or colleagues' lives than the Stasi recruit a less-friendly source to do a more thorough job.

People will tell themselves anything if it eases their conscience.

"I'd like to learn how to play," I said to Rod that evening, as the others prepared to leave.

"Oh, Greta, you can't say we didn't warn you." Sarah laughed and gave me a hug. "See you on Thursday?" I nodded. We'd planned a shopping trip, despite my growing guilt about our friendship. I wasn't who she thought I was. My small lie had morphed into something bigger, something this strong, justice-driven, liberal woman would have hated, and I despised myself for it. Yet I needed her friendship. I needed the easy camaraderie of browsing the shops, listening to her style advice, trying on things I'd never buy, laughing over cappuccinos and chocolate cake in a café afterwards. So I put my guilt aside and said yes to her invites, to her warm, open, honest smile, and tried not to think about what my best friend back home would think of my duplicity. Lena, whose family had already suffered at the hands of people like Olaf. Lena, who would have expected me to be stronger, to stand up to them and endure the consequences. I hadn't written to her lately; the guilt was too much to bear.

I bought the next round while Rod set up the backgammon board. He explained the rules and we played a couple of games; I even won the second, though I think he let me win, which told me, if I hadn't known already, that he liked me. And I remember thinking that if he did, it would be easier to manipulate him, to bring the conversation around to what I wanted. This is what Olaf had turned me into, Henry.

"My friend's father plays," I said after the second game. "He's won competitions in Germany."

"Huh, in Hamburg?"

I shook my head. "Actually, no." I paused. Would I really say it? "I'm not from Hamburg. I grew up in the DDR, in Berlin." I watched his jaw drop. "I didn't say before because I didn't want to be the centre of attention in the group, you know?"

Rod's eyes widened. "That's amazing! But how did you make it over here?"

I told him about meeting you, about getting married and applying to leave, and Rod listened so avidly I felt sure he'd be able to recite my exact words back to me afterwards. When I was done, he looked at me with more than a little awe.

"All we hear is how it's so difficult to leave, how people are risking their lives trying to smuggle themselves out, or being punished for applying through official channels, and yet you just . . . left."

I thought of the interminable paperwork, the money, the long wait, Friedrich and his contacts. "Yes," I said, "I suppose I was lucky."

"Incredible." Rod shook his head. "I want to know everything. Is it as bad as they say? Did you feel like a prisoner there, growing up?"

I recalled the complicated feelings I'd had when you'd said something similar, back in Berlin. How long ago that seemed! My response, back then, had been nuanced, but now it was straightforward. I had been rendered as cynical as Lena, all my positive experiences cancelled out by Olaf's blackmail.

But it wouldn't do to say that to Rod.

"No," I said instead. "Not at all. I had a happy childhood, a comfortable home. We had holidays and school camps and birthday parties and football games, same as here."

"And you didn't ever . . . I mean, you didn't feel your lives were curtailed in any way?"

I shrugged. "I always wanted to travel to the West, sure, but otherwise, no." I took a breath, prepared myself to say what I had to, the words Olaf would want me to say. "But I suppose I can understand that the government only wants to protect what it's created from outside influence while the country continues to develop. I'm not condoning some of the measures used, but what we have there—what I had—isn't all bad, as people here make it out to be." I paused. "I hope you don't think me awful to say that."

I waited, Rod wearing an expression I couldn't interpret, before he slowly shook his head. "No, I don't, Greta. I was actually heavily involved in socialist politics at university. I don't disagree with the principles. In fact, I'd say communism is a pretty good idea on paper. It's the way it's implemented that isn't right: the arrests, the closed borders, the oppression of free speech. But as you say, you can understand that to an extent. I wish . . ."

"What?"

"I wish the West would encourage reform, instead of wanting to crush communism completely. They're scared, of course—the capitalists, I mean. They're still harping on about bloody domino theory. And it's only because if communism became more widespread, there'd be fewer opportunities for fat cats like them to make money."

I nodded but said nothing. There were plenty of fat cats in the Hauptstadt, according to Lena's father.

"I think there's an opportunity, actually, to live in harmony with communist states while encouraging democratic reform within them," Rod continued. "We do what we can, us Amnesty foot soldiers, but I do get frustrated by all this bloody letter writing. I wish I could just go over there, engage in proper, constructive discourse with communist leaders. Perhaps I could make a difference, convince them their repression of human rights is only undermining the socialist project, you know?"

"Is there a way to try?"

He shrugged. "There are Amnesty missions, occasionally. People are sent to the GDR to observe trials, or to try and engage in dialogue with officials. But I'm not involved in all that, more's the pity."

"Shame," I said, knowing I'd got what I needed. I stayed for another drink all the same, letting Rod question me further about my life back home, and it was late when we parted ways outside the pub.

"Greta, this has been fascinating, thank you so much for telling me all that."

"You're welcome." I was due to see Olaf the following week. I would have to decide if I should tell the truth, if I would say, *Yes, Rod's sympathetic to communism; yes, I think he could be persuaded to help.*

"I'll see you at the next meeting?"

I nodded. "Please don't say anything to the others about my origins. I'd rather stay in the background, you understand?"

Rod smiled and tapped his nose. "Our secret." He bent forward, and for a half second I thought he was going to kiss me on the mouth, and I instinctively turned my head so he found my cheek instead.

"See you, then." I squeezed his arm, attempting to neutralise the hint of embarrassment on his face. But I felt his eyes on my back as I turned and walked towards the bus stop.

Your warm, handsome face soothed me when I got home that evening. You were sitting in front of the television watching that programme you loved—*The Good Life*—and I heard your laughter from the hallway as I shrugged off my coat and stepped out of my shoes.

"Hey, how was the meeting?"

"Fine."

Fine. One small word, but I still remember the guilt I felt in saying it—and in *not* saying so much more. Because I decided not to tell you what I was doing, Henry. You'd have been appalled, you'd have told me to break contact with Olaf immediately and have nothing to do with this, and I couldn't do that, for my family's sake.

"Come and watch, this is a good one." You reached for my hand and tugged me towards the sofa.

I sat next to you, leaning in to your familiar, comforting presence as you wrapped an arm around my shoulder. On the telly, Barbara and Tom were attempting to look after pigs, canned laughter testifying to the hilarity that ensued, but I couldn't laugh, couldn't even focus on it.

"Maybe we could do that someday," you said casually.

"What, keep pigs?"

"Well, maybe not pigs, but live in the countryside somewhere in the

Cotswolds. Grow veg, maybe have a few chickens. It'd be great for our kids. And I think you'd look pretty good in dungarees."

You just fancied that actress, and I told you so.

"Not as much as I fancy you," you said, and I smiled, fighting back emotion. Would you still have wanted me if you knew what I was doing? And with that thought came a second question, more unexpected yet just as clear in my head: Did I even want the kind of life you were proposing?

"Or maybe we could be a little more adventurous." I looked sideways at you as you watched the telly. "We could go travelling together, live somewhere else for a while, get to know another culture—somewhere completely different." Italy, or America, or Australia. Somewhere far away from everything I was getting myself into.

You laughed as Barbara slipped in pig shit. "Maybe," you said, as though you hadn't properly heard me, and in that moment I understood something I'd suspected for a while: that despite the stories you'd told me when we met of snorkelling in Italy and festival-going in Spain, you were a homebody, not an adventurer. You hadn't lied to me, but perhaps, heady with love and desire, you'd said what you knew I wanted to hear.

I didn't blame you, but oh *Schatz*, if only that maybe had been a yes!

Later, as you spooned me in bed, I imagined myself in dungarees, pottering about the garden of a rambling old farmhouse, a baby on my hip. I imagined myself in Olaf's flat, accepting whatever mission my Stasi handler wanted me to take on. And I imagined myself running alongside the Thames, all the way out of Oxford and beyond; running, running, running, away to some place where I could finally feel free.

26

He is expecting Lucy to answer the door, but instead it's her mother, holding Oscar.

"I'm so sorry," he says, "I should have called ahead. I was hoping to see Lucy."

"I've sent her for a mani-pedi. The poor girl deserved a treat. But she'll be back soon. Come in and wait, and I'll make us some coffee?"

Mani-pedi? He doesn't ask. He just smiles and follows Ros down the hallway. It is Wednesday afternoon; he should be working, but he had another email from the shop in Canada last night, an email that has set his mind ablaze, distracting him from his work all day, and he needs to discuss it with Lucy, to get her take on what it means (as well as see how she is, of course), so he's abandoned his workshop for the afternoon to come here.

"Millie's at school, and Jack's picking her up afterwards to take her out for pizza, so it's just me and Oscar here at the minute. Do you take milk?"

Henry shakes his head. "Black, no sugar, please."

The house is much tidier than last time. The Lego bricks are in a box,

231

Millie's books are stacked neatly on a side table rather than strewn across the floor, and there are no cloths of dubious cleanliness on the sofa. It is as though an expert gardener has pruned and chopped and trimmed, managing a place that would otherwise run wild.

"Jack hasn't returned, then?" he says when they are installed on the sofa and Oscar is crawling around the living room.

"No, sadly." Ros takes a sip of her coffee. "It's tough being young, isn't it? When you're not yet hardened to the ups and downs of relationships. It's been such a whirlwind for those two. They got engaged so quickly, and Millie came along nine months after the wedding, and I think they didn't really get the chance to enjoy the honeymoon period before everything changed. Perhaps they didn't have enough of a basis to weather these storms, I don't know. Not that I'm one to talk! Lucy's father and I didn't manage much better. I think that's why it's hit her so hard, all this. Lucy really wanted to do better than we did." Ros laughs, but there's sadness in it.

"You're divorced?"

She nods, waves her hand in the air. "Ages ago, but Si has always remained very much involved in Lucy's life—and mine, for that matter. I consider him one of my best friends."

"Gosh, that's very good of you. I don't know if I could be best friends with . . ." he trails off, shakes his head.

"You're looking for her, aren't you?" Ros asks, before adding, "The necklace . . . it's quite a story." She smiles, a touch apologetically, and Henry finds he doesn't mind as much as he thought he would that she knows about his defunct marriage.

"Yes, Lucy's been trying to help. I'm not entirely sure why, but it's good of her."

Ros laughs. "Because she's a hopeless romantic, that's why."

Henry raises his eyebrows. He was right, then.

"The whirlwind romance, the speedy engagement, the big white wedding with all the trimmings: Lucy is a massive romantic, always has been.

Always loved fairies and princesses, despite me never reading those sorts of stories to her. Pink is her favourite colour. It's funny, people say society pushes kids into traditional gender roles, and I think that's true, to an extent, yet I do believe some people naturally gravitate towards those tropes. I brought her up with feminist values; I never told her that her life's main aim should be to get married and have children, yet here she is. And that's perfectly fine, of course. Jack's a good man, and I love those kids to bits. But I do wish she'd stop thinking relationships are all Mills & Boon. She's always had such a rose-tinted view of marriage and kids that I think her little slipup has been as much a shock to herself as it was to Jack. She's rocked her own boat, so to speak, and now she's desperate to get things back on an even keel so she can forget all about it and pretend everything's smooth sailing again—I'm going overboard with the sailing metaphors, but you get my gist, Henry."

"I do," he says, adding almost to himself, "more than you know."

"Oh?"

He flushes. "I mean, she's not the only one with a rose-tinted view of marriage."

Ros considers him for a second or two, and he squirms a little under her gaze, as though she's looking right inside him. Then she smiles and says softly, "Well, it's hardly a crime, is it? But then you'll understand when I say that I think Lucy's mission to help you find your wife is as much about solving her own marital crisis as yours."

Henry nods. "I did wonder."

"Not that I'm saying it's all about her. I can see she'd genuinely love you to find your wife. My daughter has always been a very *helpful* soul. It so happens that it would also fit in with her idealistic notions about relationships." Ros sighs. "I blame all those musicals she saw as a child."

"I'm sorry?"

"Her father was in so many when she was growing up and we were both so proud of him, so I wasn't going to say she couldn't go and see him perform, but perhaps all those sugary storylines and heartwarming endings had more of an effect on our impressionable young daughter than I thought."

"You mean your ex-husband was an actor?"

"Still is! He'd have been here for Lucy right now if he weren't off on an international tour of *Mamma Mia!*" She smiles with something that looks like pride. "He plays one of the fathers."

"Gosh."

"And I'm one, too."

"A f—?"

"An ac*tor*," she says with sardonic emphasis on the second syllable. "Although parts have been thin on the ground in recent years. Honestly, it's as though the world doesn't believe older women have anything interesting to say." She rolls her eyes. "But don't let me get on my soapbox about *that*, Henry."

"Right."

"Because if you ask me, older people—and that most firmly includes older *women*—have a lot to offer the world, don't you think? We're wise old sages with a wealth of life experience behind us. Yet the only parts I ever get offered involve being someone's wife or mother or evil stepmother. Although, I will be playing Madame Arcati in *Blithe Spirit* in Nottingham next month."

"Who?"

"A crazy old medium who conducts a séance at a dinner party. It'll hardly require any acting at all!" She laughs and Henry smiles back. He doesn't think she's crazy. Garrulous. Lively. Loud. A touch exhausting. But not crazy at all.

When Henry hears the sound of a key turning in the door, he is neighing at Oscar as he bounces him on his lap in some approximation of a horse ride. Oscar is laughing riotously and the sound fills Henry with so much joy that he doesn't even mind the string of drool falling onto his trousers. He'll put them in the wash when he gets home.

"Henry!" Lucy greets him with a smile when she enters the room, then plucks Oscar from his lap and gives the baby a noisy kiss on his head. "What are you doing here?"

"I wanted to see how you were. Your mother kindly invited me in for coffee." He smiles at Ros, sitting in the armchair opposite. Time has sped by, talking to her. They've covered her colourful acting career, his path into woodworking, and their shared love of Oxford's architecture. And though he still doesn't quite know what to make of her, he finds he likes her. Her openness challenges the barriers he knows he puts up with women, and yet it is refreshing. Easy. Straightforward. Nothing like Greta. *In a good way*, his brain whispers. Greta, who could be infuriatingly private and bewilderingly selfish. Greta, who never seemed quite satisfied with her life here in Oxford. Greta, who never expressed any desire for the kind of child-filled home he is sitting in now. "There's plenty of time, *Schatz*," she'd say when he brought up the subject, and he believed her. But perhaps she never wanted that at all, he thinks now. And perhaps he should have read between the lines; he should have asked her what she *did* want, instead of assuming it was the same thing as him.

"I'm much better, thanks," Lucy says. "I have to keep this silly neck brace on for a few more days, though it seems like overkill to me, but Mum says I need to do what I'm told for once, so I'm trying!" She laughs and he's glad to hear it. She's wearing jogging bottoms and an oversized jumper, her hair up in a messy bun, but her cheeks are flushed and there's a light in her eyes that he hasn't much seen before: the light that comes with getting a good night's sleep.

"How was the mani-pedi, darling?" Ros asks.

"Heaven!" Lucy sticks out a hand and Henry sees her nails are painted in a glossy pink. Ah, a *mani*cure. "Thanks so much, Mum."

"You're very welcome. Now, you sit, and I'll get you a coffee." Ros goes into the kitchen, and Lucy sits beside Henry on the sofa, Oscar on her lap.

"Mum's been amazing," she says. "I don't want her to leave! Having someone to help cook for the kids and pick them up from school and nursery, and remembering to put a wash on occasionally and . . . I mean, since Jack isn't here." Her face flushes.

"He'll come back," Henry says, and his own face heats to acknowledge aloud the thing Lucy hasn't ever told him, the thing she clearly now knows he knows.

"Maybe." The sadness in her voice sears his heart. What can he do? Lucy has done so much to help him find Greta—what can he do in return to make Jack give her another chance? "Anyway," she adds, waving her hand in the air in a gesture of dismissal, "let's not talk about that. I have some news for you, actually, about Greta."

Henry cocks his head. "You're meant to be resting and recovering, not investigating the whereabouts of my ex-wife." He says it without thinking, but his chest jolts as he hears his own words. It's the first time he's said *ex*.

If Lucy notices, she doesn't acknowledge it. "I'm perfectly rested now. And anyway, it's quite exciting, actually—in fact, you might find it a bit of a shock." Henry waits through Lucy's dramatic pause. "I found Olaf Lang!"

"What?"

"Yes, I know! He's still alive—he's, like, ninety-eight or something—and *get this*," she says, pausing again, "he spent fifteen years in prison for *treason*!"

"*What?*"

"That's the only reason I found him really. I googled the variations of his name that you remembered—I can't believe you've never done that before, Henry!—and I found an article online from ten years or so ago by a journalist investigating what happened to three people convicted in the 1980s for spying for the communists! Olaf Lang was one of the names; it says he was jailed at the end of 1984 along with a young couple who were living under false names and turned out to be KGB illegals! I mean, this must have been huge back then, Henry—don't you remember it?"

Henry frowns. Nineteen eighty-four, the year Greta left him. All he remembers from that period is spending too much time trying to block out his thoughts by watching inane films like *Police Academy* and *Ghostbusters*. He wasn't following the news back then. He was too submerged in self-pity to be concerned about the world around him.

"Anyway," Lucy continues when he doesn't respond. "This article, which was published in 2007 or something, said Olaf had been living a quiet life in Lymington ever since getting out of jail. I couldn't find him in the phone book—I mean, would a former spy be in the phone book?—but given I knew he'd be pretty ancient by now, I took a punt and rang around a few nursing homes in the area pretending to be his long-lost great-niece—and I found him! I spoke to someone there, and visiting hours are every afternoon from two till five, so all you need to do is go down there sometime—I mean, I'd go *soon*, he's ninety-eight—and ask what he knows about what happened back then. I bet he knows why Greta left. He might even know where she is now."

She hands him a piece of paper, an address and telephone number scribbled across it.

Treason. Spying. Jail time. Was Greta somehow connected to all this? Was that what Friedrich meant? But how—and *why*? She wouldn't have had anything to do with Olaf if she'd known he was a spy, surely. His chest hurts to think that such things may have been hiding beneath the surface of their marriage. That something huge could have been happening to Greta and he didn't even see it. Did she lie to him, or just neglect to tell him? He never thought of her as a liar, but actually she *did* lie, at least once that he knows of. She lied to her Amnesty friends about her origins, and she asked him to lie to them, too, or at least not to tell the truth. "Thank you," he says when he is able. "I can't believe you found him."

"It wasn't that difficult." Lucy shrugs, and he smiles at her nonchalance. Lucy Kenny, PI, never to be underestimated.

"I have something to say, too, actually." He tells her about the shop in Canada, and about the owner's reply to his last email. Yes, the German jewellery maker Marianne Kerber is often seen running around the area. Yes, she's in her late fifties and has blond-grey hair. Could it be Greta? He's spent all morning telling himself not to get excited, that surely, out of the three million Germans in Canada (he googled it), it's not unlikely that there's another late-middle-aged woman who enjoys running and makes jewellery of a particular style. But when he sees Lucy's reaction now, he thinks, well, maybe it *is* unlikely.

"Oh my God, Henry, it must be her!" Lucy's eyes are saucers. "Why don't you ask the shop woman for Marianne's email address? She must have one."

"She doesn't have a website, so maybe she doesn't use email, either."

Lucy arches one eyebrow. "Well, that's pretty strange, for someone who makes stuff to sell." She nudges him. "Go on, ask anyway. It's got to be her!"

He smiles at Lucy's enthusiasm, but for the first time he feels a flicker of apprehension about this mission. He's spent so long viewing Greta through rose-tinted glasses that now they're sliding off, he's afraid he won't like what he sees.

"Or not," he says, glancing up to see Ros watching them from the doorway, wearing an expression he can't read. "I mean, why would Greta change her name?"

"No idea," Lucy concedes. "But I have a feeling Olaf Lang might."

27

Greta, 2018

She drives inland. She doesn't really know where to; she just drives and drives, and will stop when she's had enough, when she can drive no more. The windscreen wipers swing back and forth across the glass and the sky outside is grey, mirroring her mood. She's allowed herself a flash of colour, these last months with Tomas, but now that chapter is closed and she must move on again. It is for the best. She is doing the right thing, to protect him, to protect herself.

So why does it feel like she's made a huge mistake?

She drives for several hours, until she sees the signs for the Comox-Powell River ferry. She didn't know where she was going when she set off, but now it seems like the right thing to do. She will leave this island, cross to the mainland, and lose herself somewhere remote for a while. Canada is a huge country. There are plenty of places in which to lose yourself.

She stands on deck watching the shore recede as the ferry leaves Vancouver Island. She imagines Tomas in his restaurant, prepping for the evening's service. Does he know yet? Would someone have seen her camper driving out of town and told him? Would he care to know in any case?

When the ferry docks a couple of hours later, she heads north, not entirely sure where she's going. It doesn't matter much, after all, as long as it's not where she's been. But perhaps she should have actually looked at a map, because she's only been driving for half an hour when the road runs out.

It comes to an abrupt stop in Lund, a small coastal town that clearly enjoys its remote status. There is a sign declaring the end of the highway, which has run up the coast for 177 kilometres before finishing right here, and another proclaiming the town GATEWAY TO DESOLATION SOUND, a name that depresses her, all the while feeling quite appropriate for someone looking to hide themselves away from the world. To her right is a smaller road, a track really, with another sign indicating THE END OF THE ROAD REGIONAL PARK up ahead. Greta laughs. She has literally reached the end of the road. After so many years of moving on, running away, perhaps this is the universe telling her there is nowhere left for her to go.

The next day, she sets out to explore her new surroundings. She heads to a sports rental place in town, thinking that hiring a sea kayak would be the best way to discover the local area on a day like today, which is cold but beautifully sunny, the sky illuminated by the uniquely bright light of early spring. She would kayak sometimes with Tomas, sticking close to the shore as he showed her how to gather kelp that he could use in the restaurant, but she won't think about that now.

"You new here?" the man in the hire shop asks, and she supposes it's inevitable, in such a small place, that a new face would be quickly noticed, particularly outside of tourist season.

"Just arrived. Staying in the campground for a little while."

"Welcome." His smile is warm, genuine. "I'm Kyle. I sure hope you like it here—it's a friendly place, Lund, you'll get to know folks pretty quickly."

As she leaves with her kayak, she wonders if this isn't the best place to have come, after all. It may be in the middle of nowhere—literally at the end of the road—but perhaps it will be too hard to keep a low profile. Maybe she'd be better off in a large city, where she can lose herself in a crowd, where no one remarks on her presence or notices her absence. But for a long time now she has naturally gravitated away from big cities. Apart from those early years in the life of Marianne, when she attempted to both lose herself and find her new identity in Kuala Lumpur, Singapore, Bangkok, she has preferred to be in smaller communities, close to the countryside: the coastline around Calella, north of Barcelona; the fjords near Bergen in Norway; the wild, lush countryside of Ireland's County Wicklow; the wide-open spaces and endless horizons of this country she now calls home. The space brings her relief somehow; it allows her to breathe, to feel free, unlike the skyscrapers and traffic-clogged streets of big cities, which only make her feel hemmed in, pinned down.

She paddles all day in calm water, stopping from time to time on secluded beaches and rocky coves to refuel on snacks and contemplate the start of this new phase of her life. Another new phase, after so many before. The sun is low in the sky, skimming its light over the water, when she arrives back in Lund. She returns the kayak to the hire shop and heads back towards her van, which is parked up in a campground not far from the sea, much like the one she left behind in Tofino. There is an electricity hookup, hot water in the shower block, and a firepit near the van. But there are no other people this early in the spring. Hers is the only camper, and the single tent she saw over the other side of the campground appears to be abandoned, the fly sheet flapping in the breeze. Her van stands alone, silhouetted against the fading light, exposed, vulnerable.

She walks closer and then abruptly stops.

The door is open.

Her heart jumps into double-time. Could she have left it open? But she knows she didn't; she never does. She waits, stock-still, hackles raised. Is this when they finally come for her, after all these years? Is this when she meets the person sent to exact revenge for what she did so long ago?

But to her surprise, after those initial seconds, her instinct to flee deserts her. Instead, a vast weariness descends, like liquid concrete pouring into her limbs. She is so, so tired of running. She has run so far, over the years, has kept herself constantly on high alert, continually anticipating a moment like this, bracing herself for some kind of attack, like the one on Litvinenko, on Skripal, and she can't do it anymore. She is so tired of running that it outweighs the risks of standing still, she realises suddenly. If this is it, then so be it. She will face whoever it is. She will fight, and she will live or die. So be it.

She hears nothing from inside, but as she gets closer, she sees a shadow filling the doorway, a dark shape she can't quite make out—until a figure emerges into the low, pink light of a Pacific Coast dusk, and she sees exactly who it is.

28

GRETA, 1983

In the days following my tête-a-tête in the pub with Rod, I debated what I would tell Olaf, and what he might do with the truth, if I relayed it. Would Rod be "recruited" like me, as a higher calibre source whose information could endanger more dissidents, more of those who risked everything to speak out against the system? Could he, as a group leader, much closer to the heart of AI than I was, be persuaded to offer up information about Amnesty that could be useful to the Stasi in some way? I didn't know, but whatever it was, it couldn't be good, and Rod, for all his idealistic notions about constructive discourse and democratic reform, didn't deserve to be entangled in Olaf's world. So I resolved to lie. I would tell the old man, *No, Rod is left-wing but not a communist; he doesn't think it's a workable system, doesn't believe there's a future for a country that has to control and restrict its citizens in order to achieve its aims.*

But if there was one thing that living in such a country had given me, it was the ability to know when I was being observed. Little things in the days preceding my next visit to Olaf made me think I was being followed. A fellow jogger in Port Meadow who almost pointedly refused to acknowledge my presence. A figure feigning sleep in a car parked on the street outside our house. A woman in the supermarket whom I could have sworn I'd also seen in the pub sitting a few tables away from Rod and me.

Perhaps it was simply paranoia, but I wouldn't have put it past Olaf to send others to spy on his reluctant spy. Maybe it was a test. Maybe he already knew all about Rod's politics and this was an exercise to see if I'd tell him the truth.

So I was feeling jittery when I got home from a run one Sunday afternoon and saw your beaming face.

"Come in here." You beckoned me into the front room with an excited grin.

"I really need some water and a bath," I grumbled, as I kicked off my shoes.

"It won't take long." You ushered me into the room and gestured to the junk shop chest of drawers, the one you'd been renovating so avidly in the past weeks. "What do you think?"

My slight irritation dissolved instantly. "Oh, *Schatz*, it's beautiful." I stepped forward and ran my hand along its smooth surface. I'd witnessed its gradual transformation, but it was still quite something to see the finished object: the polished handles you'd picked up from the DIY shop now installed on the drawers, the damaged right-hand corner so perfectly repaired that I could hardly see where the crack had been.

"Henry, this is amazing. You've done such a brilliant job."

You glowed under my praise, your eyes shining in a way they never did when you returned from the engineering firm. "I loved doing it."

To my surprise, I welled up.

"Hey, what's the matter?"

I didn't know, really. You and the beauty you had created, next to me and the hole I was digging myself; perhaps that's what it was. "This is the job you should be doing," I said instead. "Not stuck installing dull machines."

You laughed. "Maybe one day. But I'm happy for it to be a hobby for now. I've got a lot to learn." You put an arm around my shoulder and pulled me to you, then recoiled almost instantly. "Wow, you really do need a bath."

I smiled and left you there, gazing at your handiwork, as I headed to the bathroom.

I meant what I said, Henry—it was beautiful, that chest of drawers— but as I sat in the tub that afternoon, washing off my sweat and dirt, I couldn't stop my eyes filling again, because your restoration project had unnerved me a little, too. Part of me wished you'd retained some of that chest's dents and scratches and watermarks. It seemed to me that you'd erased its history, and though we knew nothing of that history, though its backstory wasn't important to us, it might have been important to whoever had owned it before us. It said something about them, just as this renovated version said something about you. I expect you'd think that ridiculous of me, Henry. It was only a chest of drawers, abandoned in a secondhand store. Perhaps it hadn't been important to anyone at all. But your act of sanding and polishing its flaws away felt like a metaphor for our relationship. You were the saviour who had rescued me from a flawed country and brought me to the West to live happily ever after. But you could sand and polish me as much as you liked, Henry—I would still be flawed underneath.

I thought about that when I went back to Olaf and told him exactly what Rod had said.

"I think we need more wine, Greta."

It was a cold, rainy October evening. Oxford's streets were slick with sodden leaves blown from the trees by the gale-force wind. You were out with your former housemates, and I was in the Turf Tavern with Rod, whom I was about to ask to steal information for the Stasi.

"I think you're right." I gave him a broad smile as he stood up to go to the bar. Nausea swelled in my stomach. I couldn't drink any more, but I would, to get what I needed. The wine had the added benefit of numbing my self-disgust.

It hadn't been difficult to get him here. Ever since I'd told Rod about my East German background, I'd become his pet project. His eyes lit up when he saw me, and we'd taken to going to the pub without the Amnesty crew, once a week or so, under the guise of playing backgammon, while he let forth his opinions about East-West relations—and those of everyone else he knew, too. Rod loved the sound of his own voice, and he was a voracious gossip, so I soon knew all about the Oxford University professor who was a member of the British National Front, and the ardent socialist Rod studied with who was now a high-ranking, Thatcher-hating civil servant in Whitehall, and the student son of a Labour-supporting schoolteacher friend of his who would next year embark on a semester studying in Leipzig, behind the Iron Curtain.

I reported everything Rod said to Olaf when I saw him, fearing he'd be able to tell if I didn't, thanks to whoever he'd sent to keep tabs on me. What he would do with all this information I still didn't know. "That's not for you to worry about, my dear," Olaf said the one time I tentatively asked. "It's better you know as little as possible. For your own good." I didn't press him. I didn't really want to know—that way I could pretend I wasn't complicit, wasn't getting the people I spoke about mixed up in things they didn't want to be. Was the teacher's son ever approached by Stasi agents during his time in Leipzig and coerced into helping the regime on his return to Britain? Was the Thatcher-hating civil servant ever flattered and cajoled into supplying confidential information about UK government foreign policy? Not knowing was the only way to live with myself.

But one day, when I told Olaf that Rod had mentioned he was going to Amnesty's British headquarters in London for its annual conference, the old German's ears pricked up more than usual. "See if you can find out if he'd be willing to snoop for us," he said as he sliced the Battenberg.

I didn't reply at first. The word *us* seemed to ring in my ears. I thought of my parents, who'd brought me up with ethics and a moral code. Would they want me to compromise myself like this, whatever the consequences for them if I didn't?

"I don't think so," I said. "Rod's not the sort to do anything illegal."

Olaf smiled as he leaned forward and passed me a plate of cake. "Men will do anything for the love of a good woman."

What? A prickle walked up my spine, and something inside me panicked. Was he suggesting what I thought he was? No, no, I wouldn't do that. I wouldn't seduce Rod, betray you with another man, in order to get Olaf what he wanted. But then I thought of my family, of why I was doing all this, and wondered how far I would actually go, if he pushed me enough.

"And if I can't persuade him?" There was more defiance in my voice than I should have allowed myself to show.

"Then you can't persuade him," Olaf said, hands spread wide, a picture of innocence. He sat back in his chair and cocked his head, those shrewd blue eyes on mine. "But I believe in you, Greta, and so does the HVA."

The initials hung in the air. I knew what he meant—the Hauptverwaltung Aufklärung, the foreign intelligence service within the Ministry for State Security. I thought of that vast building on Normannenstraße, a place we dubbed the house of one thousand eyes, and imagined the Stasi officers within, discussing me, discussing my family.

"They appreciate your assistance, Greta," Olaf continued in a gentle voice, as though he, too, was aware that this was the first time he'd openly acknowledged that he—no, *we*—were working for them. "And so do our KGB comrades."

A chill expanded in my chest. It wasn't new to me that the Stasi and the KGB worked together, but I hadn't thought about it until now. Was the information I was providing helping the Soviets, too?

I exhaled, and perhaps Olaf saw the fear in my eyes.

"Your father has been reinstated, hasn't he?" he asked lightly, as though I'd imagined the threat in his words. "You're doing the right thing."

"Don't pretend this is a choice," I shot back.

He pursed his lips. "Just do your best with our friend Rod. Just do your best. Isn't that what your parents always told you to do?"

So there I was, in the Turf Tavern, with Rod and a second bottle of warm Chardonnay.

"What's going to happen at this conference, then?" I asked as he poured me another glass. The wine tasted sharp in my throat.

"It's a chance for AI members around the country to get together. I think there'll be various talks by HQ, setting out the organisation's priorities for the next year and so forth."

"The DDR among them?"

"*Natürlich*," Rod said with a smile, and the word, though spoken in an English accent, turned me cold as it reminded me of someone else. Friedrich. He'd never responded to my pleading letter, and I hadn't contacted him again. What was the point? His silence was as knowing as mine.

"I suppose you'll be meeting people high up in the organisation. Could it be an opportunity for you to put yourself forward for a mission to the DDR?"

Rod laughed. "You give me more credit than I'm due, Greta." He grinned at me, clearly flattered. "I'm only a small fish—they won't be sending me anywhere."

I hesitated and took another sip of wine as an idea formed in my head, an idea inspired by the childhood friend who had got me embroiled in all this. "What if I could help you?"

There was a moment of silence, and I feared he could hear the rapid beat of my heart.

"How do you mean?"

"I . . . I know someone—an old friend—who knows people . . . high up, I think."

"You *think*?"

"He's never said, but I'm pretty sure."

Rod's gaze was so intense that I had to force myself to meet his eyes. "These people, they'll want to talk?"

"I think it's worth a try." I shrugged, feigning nonchalance. "Like you said, dialogue is the best way forward. The UK and the DDR have to try to understand each other, and I think you'd be the perfect go-between." I moved a little closer to him. "I mean, you're a good talker, Rod—I expect you can be pretty persuasive when you want to be." I hated myself with every word, Henry, but the look in his eyes told me my flirting was working.

"Oh yeah?" He put his hand on my leg. "I'll bear that in mind."

"No promises, but perhaps I could see if my friend could set something up for you, if you want." I had no intention of doing any such thing, but he only had to believe I did. "I mean, wouldn't Amnesty HQ agree to send you, if so?"

Rod blew out a short, sharp breath. "God, maybe! I really think I can make a difference, Greta, given the chance."

"I think so, too." I forced a smile. "And perhaps in exchange you could do a favour for me?"

"Anything." He squeezed my leg.

"I'd love to know a little more about Amnesty. This conference of yours, would it give you the chance to dig a little deeper, do you think? Could you find out what their long-term strategy is towards the DDR, and maybe who they're in contact with back home? I wonder if I might know any of them, and if so, perhaps I could help in some way." I smiled, but my chest was tight. Would he bite?

He grinned and leaned so close I could smell the wine on his breath when he spoke. "Let me see what I can do."

I went to see Olaf the following Tuesday, and he clapped his hands when I told him about my conversation with Rod. "Wonderful," he said. "The Firm will be delighted with their little Ingrid."

"Ingrid?"

"Your code name, my dear. I named you myself. If I'd had a daughter, I'd have called her Ingrid."

His words struck me momentarily mute. Was that his way of telling me he cared about me? Did this Stasi old-timer think of himself as my surrogate father? I should have felt angry, yet I didn't. I think, if anything, it underlined how out of touch with reality he was. This old man, who had no relatives and seemingly no friends in the UK, who lived alone in a tired and slightly grubby one-bedroom flat, who was in thrall to a country he'd never lived in, whose deluded views had him working for an organisation of oppression . . . despite all he'd made me do, I felt sorry for him, Henry.

"I expect you'll be starting a family of your own soon?" he asked me then, to which I frowned and shook my head. "Don't you want to have children?"

"Of course. But not yet." I was still saying the same to you, when you asked me, as you often did. *Not yet, there's plenty of time.* I didn't quite know why I felt like that, besides the fact we were young and there was no rush, but I knew something else was holding me back.

"That's a shame."

Anger flared inside me. "Why do you care?"

"Because I care about your well-being, my dear. And I'm sure you'd be a marvellous mother." He paused. "Not to mention, it's perfect cover."

"Excuse me?"

"Well," Olaf laughed, "no one expects a doting wife and mother to be a spy."

I left soon after, any sympathy I'd had for him now gone. I speed-walked to Stockwell station, flushed and shaking. I wanted to lose myself in the anonymity of central London's busy streets. I wanted to sit on the Tube and let it take me somewhere I had never been, somewhere no one knew me. *Ingrid*, the unwilling Stasi informer. *Ingrid*, the surrogate daughter of a deluded old communist. *No one expects a doting wife and mother to be a spy.* He'd got me, Henry; I saw that now. This wasn't a one-off mission. He'd caught me in his net and would keep me there forever, dictating my life—our lives—as he saw fit.

I was on the train back towards Oxford when I realised what was stopping me saying yes to having children with you. A baby would be another tie to this life. And I couldn't have ties. Because I had to get out of this perilous, increasingly compromised life I'd created. I had to get out—somehow.

That's no excuse for what I started to do to you as a result. I can only tell you that my unpleasant actions were a form of self-flagellation. The more you tried to create our perfect life together, the guiltier I felt, and the more I wanted you to punish me for it.

I started doing little things that I thought would annoy you—selfish things, hurtful things, subconsciously designed to provoke you. I'd leave half-full mugs of coffee around our flat, the cold liquid scummy on the surface. I'd "forget" to put a wash on when you were at work, despite telling you I would, so you ended up having no clean work shirts a couple of times. I wouldn't tell you when I was going out to meet Sarah or Rod, so you'd arrive home from work hungry with nothing in the fridge. I think I wanted you to shout at me, or at least to grumble a little. I wanted you to berate me for these small things since you couldn't for the big thing you didn't know about. But you never shouted, never even mentioned these day-to-day irritations. Was it that you hated confrontation? Was it that you couldn't see past your idealised view of me? Or was it simply that you were a kind, forgiving person whom I didn't deserve? Whatever the reason, you'd clear up my half-drunk mugs, put a wash on yourself, and ask me if I had a nice time with Sarah. And the more you did that, the guiltier I felt.

Only once did I push you into a reaction, but even then, even then . . .

I'd been in our bedroom one afternoon, giving myself a break from a translation I was struggling with by changing the sheets on our bed. I'd taken a glass of water in there and put it, unthinkingly, on the chest of drawers you'd so carefully renovated. When I came to leave again, I picked it up and noticed a wet ring on the wood. I went to wipe it off—you'd hate that, and it wasn't too late to stop it staining—but then I stopped myself. I stared at it for a few seconds, railing inside, furious at myself, furious at you for not seeing what a terrible person I was, and then I walked off and left that watermark right where it was.

That evening, I found you in the bedroom with a cloth and some cleaning spray.

"It won't come off," you muttered, unable to look at me. But still, you didn't get angry, didn't call out my selfishness.

"I'm sorry," I said quietly, and you finally looked up, hurt so plainly worn on your face.

"Never mind. I can redo it." And the small smile you forced yourself to give nearly broke me with its generosity.

Why didn't I tell you? If I'd wanted you to shout at me, if I'd wanted to smack you over the head with my imperfection, I could have just come out with it. Surely even you couldn't have ignored me telling you I was aiding and abetting the Stasi.

It wasn't only because you would have told me to stop. It wasn't just because I couldn't leave my family to suffer whatever consequences would have come their way if I had.

It was because it was too big a flaw, too far from perfect for you to cope with, surely. It was unforgiveable, even for a forgiving person like you. I wanted you to know what I'd done and love me anyway—but I didn't think you would.

29

HENRY, 2018

Henry finds the nursing home easily enough and parks up in the visitors' car park. He sits for a minute, staring at the pale pink building, its pastel shade clearly a popular choice in this coastal town. It reminds him of that last weekend trip he and Greta took to St. Ives, of the quaint B&B they stayed in, where they ate a fry-up in the old-fashioned dining room each morning, prepared with love and extra grease by the grey-haired land-lady, before going out to walk along the wind-whipped beach. *You've made me so happy*, she said to him then. *Always remember that.* Is it possible the man in this building can tell him why those halcyon days couldn't continue?

In the last few days he's read the article Lucy told him about, along with many others. He accessed a digital newspaper archive and read story after story about the arrest and trial of Stasi spy Olaf Lang and his KGB as-sociates. He read about Lang's background: his staunchly communist par-ents, their views fuelled by the poverty and unemployment that emerged in the Weimar Republic and the rise of hate and persecution under Hitler in the thirties; his flight to the UK as a young man shortly before the war and the disappearance of his parents into the camps; and his defiance in court, as he continued to advocate for communism as the only way to prevent the rise of fascism once again.

As he read the articles Henry couldn't help but feel some sympathy for the man, yet he was also struck by his tunnel vision. How could he be so blind to the tyranny perpetuated by one authoritarian regime in the name of protecting people from another? How could he think that the oppression within the GDR was the answer to the oppression of the past? Why couldn't he see they were two sides of the same coin? Was it that he hadn't actually lived there and seen the reality with his own eyes? Did he live in an idealised past fuelled by the example of his lost parents, still striving for a perfect utopia that could never exist?

It takes one to know one, thought Henry.

He gets out of the car and walks to the entrance. As he steps through the automatic glass doors into the lobby, a peculiar smell hits him—flowers, overlaid with disinfectant.

"Henry Henderson, here to see Olaf Lang," he tells the receptionist. "I'm expected." He called earlier, telling whoever answered the phone—this woman?—that he was a family friend. "Oh, that's wonderful," she said. "Mr. Lang never gets visitors; he'll be delighted."

"Room three, down the hall to the right," she says now. "He's having a good day, I'm told, so you should find him lucid."

"He isn't always?"

"He has dementia. Some days are better than others."

"Right." Henry's hope for answers about Greta deflates as he walks down the corridor to room three. He knocks softly, takes a deep breath, and pushes the door open.

Henry never met Olaf, back then, so he has little idea what to expect, but somehow the man he encounters sitting in an armchair by the window doesn't match the picture he'd created in his head from Greta's descriptions. He is clean-shaven, for starters, and what hair remains on his head is grey and thin, the pale pink pate of his scalp visible beneath a fine comb-over. His body slumps in on itself, like a deflated balloon left up too long after a party. He is hardly the hirsute, corpulent man he remembers his wife telling him about.

"Hello, there," Henry says.

Olaf turns to him, eyes bright. "Do I know you?"

"No. But you knew my wife, a long time ago. I've come to ask you about her, if that's all right by you."

The old man says nothing, but his eyes are fixed on him like a headmaster peering at an errant schoolboy.

"Do you mind if I sit?" Henry gestures to a second chair opposite Olaf's and receives a shrug in reply. "It seems very pleasant here."

"Bunch of amateurs. I tell them I don't eat beef and yet they serve it to me every day."

"Every day?" Henry half laughs.

Olaf leans forward. "That's what I said, young man." He sighs and turns his head to the window.

"Okay. Well, er . . . I'm Henry. Henry Henderson. My wife was Greta Henderson. Schneider, before she married me. She was from East Germany, from Berlin—like you."

For a few seconds Henry thinks the name hasn't registered, but then Olaf fixes his eyes on Henry once again.

"Greta, dear."

Hope swells in Henry's chest. "You remember her?"

Olaf mutters something in German that Henry doesn't catch—despite marrying a German woman, he never got to grips with the language, beyond *Ich liebe dich* and a few phrases learned to impress his new in-laws at the wedding.

"I'm sorry, I don't—"

"I want the window open."

"All right." Henry gets up and turns the handle on the window, pushing it open. The cool spring air is a welcome relief after the stale heat of the room. "So, my wife. Do you—"

"She was a pretty thing," Olaf interrupts. "Pretty and clever." He taps his temple.

Henry's heart lurches into a sprint. "Yes." He feels like he must tread carefully, lest he disturb the man's delicate thought patterns and remove him from whatever fleeting memories he has. "She left me. Less than a year after she came to England. I don't know where she went, and I haven't seen her since. I wondered if you might know. I wondered if she might have been involved with . . . your situation." Henry scrutinises his face, alert to any reaction his words might provoke. "Do you know, Mr. Lang? Do you know where Greta went, or why she left? It was the same year you . . . went to prison."

Olaf eyes him a few seconds more, and then picks up a packet on the side table next to him. "Fudge?" he says. "It's rather good."

Henry takes one. "Thank you. So is there anything you can tell me? Anything you remember about my wife?" But Olaf doesn't respond, doesn't even seem to register the question, and Henry's hope drifts out the window. This is useless. The man knows nothing—or, at least, he's pretending to know nothing, because something tells Henry that there's more going on behind those bright eyes than he's making out. "Well, I should leave you to it, then," he says after a few moments of silence. "It was nice to meet you, Mr. Lang."

He is nearly at the door when the old man mumbles something.

"I'm sorry, what was that?"

"She betrayed you." Olaf's gaze is fixed on some point outside the window. "And then she betrayed me. Didn't know what was good for her."

"Betrayed, how?"

Olaf takes another piece of fudge and pops it in his mouth, chews slowly.

"What do you mean, Mr. Lang?" Frustration knots in Henry's chest.

"What do you mean she betrayed us? Did she have something to do with whatever you were wrapped up in? The . . . spying?"

Olaf looks at him, and Henry feels himself holding his breath, as though by keeping as still as possible he might aid the flow of the man's memories. "It's really quite ridiculous," Olaf says finally. "I don't eat beef, but these stupid people serve it to me every single day. They say it's pork but it's beef! Do they think I can't tell?"

Henry sighs. "I'm sorry to hear that," he says. "I'll tell them you don't want it anymore."

On the way home, Henry's eyes are on the road, but his mind is elsewhere. On Greta's laughter during their first date at the ice rink. On their swaying drunkenly around their living room, singing badly to "Total Eclipse of the Heart." On her emotion when he showed her the chest of drawers he'd renovated. On the feeling of pure contentment he'd feel when they lay in bed together, her smooth limbs entangled with his.

She betrayed you.

How? With another man, as that policeman so casually suggested at the time? With *Olaf*?! No, he has never believed she would have cheated on him. It never rang true for him. They were newlyweds. She had come to Britain on a wave of positivity, ready to forge a future with him. She loved him—her best friend said so. Anyway, that's not what Olaf meant—he knows that in the churn of his stomach and the throb of his head. None of the possible explanations he considered back then have ever rung true. It is only now, when faced with the idea that it could have been something bigger, something involving whatever spying ring Olaf was mixed up in, that Henry feels like he has finally stumbled across a grain of truth.

Yet it is the most outlandish possibility of all. It is incomprehensible.

At home, Henry parks the car outside his house, but he suddenly doesn't want to go in. Doesn't want to go through his usual solo evening—

a frozen quiche in front of the telly, a bottle of wine for one. He could go to Charlotte's—a text from his sister invites him to join her and Ian for dinner—but he doesn't want to do that, either. She will only ask him once again why he never called Samira, and he can't tell her about his search for Greta without getting another lecture.

Instead, he walks down the road and enters his local pub, an "old man's pub," according to Charlotte, but he likes it. He *is* an old man, after all (although sitting opposite Olaf Lang today showed him that there is old and then there is *old*, and he isn't there yet).

He orders a whisky from the bartender and takes it to a seat near the fire. The Siberian cold from weeks ago has given way to the usual damp, grey, spring weather Britain does so well, but he is still grateful for the fire, and for the cosy familiarity of the pub.

After Greta left him, he spent many evenings in the pub—not this one, but his local at the time, in Summertown. He'd slide onto a barstool and order pint after pint, with the occasional whisky chaser, staying until he was turfed out at closing time.

He brings the whisky glass to his lips, feels the familiar burn as the honey-hued liquid slips down his throat. Another.

He stands up, and it is then that he sees him. Jack. Lucy's husband is sitting at the bar by himself, a half-full pint on the counter, his phone in his hands. You can always tell a person's age by the way they act when alone in a pub, Henry thinks. Someone of his age might read the paper or do the crossword, or perhaps engage in conversation with a stranger. But someone of Jack's age will always be on their phone.

"Same again?" Henry gestures to Jack's pint as he looks up.

"Oh, hi." Jack puts down his phone. "Okay, thank you."

Henry orders for both of them and sits on the adjacent stool. "You mind?"

Jack shakes his head. "It's Henry, right? The woodwork guy?"

"That's me." Henry smiles, nods to the younger man's pint. "Drowning your sorrows?"

"Something like that." Jack picks up the glass, drains the liquid, and pushes the empty towards the bartender just as he places the new one in front of him.

"I know the feeling."

Jack half laughs but says nothing. He is a shy man, Henry understands suddenly. A man who is more comfortable playing with his phone than talking to a stranger. He's nothing like Lucy, who clearly would talk to—or at—any stranger who gives her the opportunity. How on earth did these two get together? He knows the story, of course—the two bars called Giraffe and the Giraffe's Neck, the laughing all evening, the whirl-wind romance followed by the big traditional wedding—but what was it about this quiet man and that talkative, heart-on-her-sleeve woman that forged a connection so strong, so right, that it would lead them to declare they'd stay together *until death do us part*?

Henry hesitates. He wants to know. He wants to know what brought them together and what has pushed them apart, what lurks below the waterline of Lucy's extramarital encounter.

"Good game?" he nods to Jack's phone, now lying on the bar top, its screen still alight and animated by colourful moving figures.

"Oh." Jack places his hand on the phone and the screen goes dark. "Yeah, it's just a silly game I play to destress after work."

"What is it you do?"

"Sales for a computer game company. Not *this* game, though."

"Do you like it? Lucy said . . ." Henry pauses, unsure if he should have mentioned her name. "She said you work really hard."

"It's busy, yeah. And I like the company, which is why I took the job, but it's not really what I want to be doing." He takes a sip of his pint.

"And what's that?"

Jack glances at him, a flush rising to his cheeks. "Designing, I suppose." He gives a short laugh, as though the notion is ridiculous.

"Designing games?"

"Yeah."

"Well, why don't you?"

Jack shrugs. "I've been in sales for fourteen years, since I left university, and it's not easy to shift to a creative role. I'd need training, which would mean going back to college and then starting again at the bottom, with an entry-level salary. I've got two kids."

Henry nods. "There must be a way, though. Evening classes? A weekend course?" He thinks of the courses he did years ago, the joy of discovering something he could be passionate about, the satisfaction of using his hands to create. It was only then that his depression lifted, only then that he stopped spending evenings in the pub drinking and brooding.

"Yeah, but evenings and weekends are the only time I get to see the kids as it is. And Lucy . . ." Jack shakes his head, raises his pint to his mouth, and silence hangs heavy between them.

Henry hesitates. He and Greta never got to the kids stage, so what does he know? But he can understand the strain it puts on relationships, the sacrifices parents must make for the sake of their children. He's seen it with Charlotte and Ian. Seen it with his friends.

"It seemed like . . ." Henry considers how to phrase it. "Lucy seems regretful to have given up work herself. Perhaps there's a way she could go back and you could reduce hours and do a training course instead?"

Jack blows out a long breath. "Yeah, maybe, but being a vet's assistant doesn't bring in much, and we'd have to pay for full-time nursery for Oscar if we were both occupied during the day. And anyway, who knows what's going to happen. Lucy and I . . ."

"I'm sorry."

"Yeah, well."

"Listen, I want to apologise . . ." Henry starts. "At the hospital, I know I was a little frosty with you. I'd got the wrong end of the stick, you see. I didn't know why you two weren't together, and I—"

"Ah, you thought I'd walked out on her and the kids for no reason."

"I didn't know you'd left at all. I simply thought you weren't around much. Lucy always seems so stressed and tired and a little lonely, and I put the blame at your feet. I shouldn't have."

"I *wasn't* around much, and she *is* stressed and tired—and maybe lonely, too, sometimes. I do get that. I do get that perhaps I didn't acknowledge how hard it's been for her lately. But still, that's no excuse for what she . . ." He shakes his head, looks into his pint, embarrassment emanating off him. "And now I'm stuck in some shitty Airbnb that's costing us a fortune we don't have."

"Can't you forgive her?" Henry says quietly.

"Maybe." Jack casts a glance at Henry and then back at his pint. "It was only a bloody snog with an old mate, and she told me about it straightaway. It wasn't like she . . . But it was still a betrayal, wasn't it?" He shrugs, gives a half smile, continues talking into his pint. "You know, I couldn't believe my luck when we got together. She's so outgoing, so . . . *lively*. I didn't know what she saw in me, but she told me she wanted to be with me and I believed her. And I guess all this has . . . I don't know, made me doubt that belief a bit. I don't know if I can trust her anymore."

Henry watches the younger man's cheeks redden, sees him take a large gulp of beer to mask his embarrassment at revealing this vulnerability about himself, and a pang hits him in the chest. Henry knows exactly how Jack is feeling, because it's like he's sitting with himself thirty years earlier.

He trusted Greta implicitly. He told her his biggest hopes and darkest fears, he made himself vulnerable to her like he'd never done with anyone before. She knew him inside out and back to front. And he thought he knew her in the same way. But he didn't. Clearly, she held so much back from him, for reasons he still can't quite grasp.

Can you ever really know a person? His sister's words come back to him. He thought he could. He thought he *did*. And perhaps that's the true reason why he hasn't been able to love anyone else since Greta left him. Not because she was so perfect that no one lives up, but because he can't let himself trust anyone like that again, lest it be thrown back in his face.

Yet right now, sitting here with Lucy's husband, he wants nothing more than for Jack to forgive his wife, to trust her again, for them to put their family back together, as it should be.

"I understand," Henry says. "But for what it's worth, I think Lucy adores you. And everyone deserves a second chance, don't they?" As he looks at the younger man, staring into his beer as though the answer lies within, he knows that he would have given Greta a second chance if she'd let him. Whatever she did—however she betrayed him, whatever flaw would have sullied the perfect image he had of her—he'd have tried his hardest to forgive her.

But did Greta know that?

30

Greta, 2018

Tomas. It is Tomas, standing in the doorway to her van. Her whole body seems to collapse inwards with relief—relief and love and happiness and worry. He is here. He shouldn't be here. But she is so glad to see him.

"I thought you were an intruder," she says, her voice cracking on the last word. "A burglar or something."

"I still have a key."

Yes, so he does. She gave it to him many months ago in an attempt to meet him halfway, to allow him to access her life in the same way he wanted her to access his.

"I shouldn't have used it, though," he adds, coming towards her. "I should have waited for you. Sorry. I was worried."

"What are you doing here? How did you find me?"

"My buddy Logan is a cop," Tomas says. "He plugged your reg into the system and you were caught on camera driving up the Sunshine Coast Highway. And since this is the end of the road, I figured you couldn't have gone much past here."

The idea of him wanting to find her so much that he would ask a friendly police officer to do something illegal . . .

"I heard you'd left town, and I couldn't just let you disappear like that," Tomas continues, his voice soft. "It takes more to fob me off than some half-hearted bullshit about not being able to move in with me. I know you like to keep a part of yourself back from everyone, Marianne, but I also know there's more to this runaway act than not wanting to be with me. Are you going to tell me what it is?"

She longs to take him into her arms and breathe him in, to fold herself into him like she has so many times before, but instead she turns away. Nothing has changed. She can't be with him, not when her presence puts him at risk. But *Scheiße*, why does he have to make it so hard?

"No means no, Tomas," she says, trying to keep her tone cold. "We broke up. I can leave Tofino if I want to. I can do whatever I want. I don't need your permission."

She looks back and sees the hurt in his face.

"That's true," he says quietly. "But I think I deserve more of an explanation, don't I? A proper one?"

He's right, he does. Just like Henry did. She messed up with that note, she has always known that. He needed to believe she'd left him, but she knows her note was inadequate. *All my love.* Despite all the lies she'd already told him, she couldn't bring herself to say she no longer loved him. That would have been the kinder thing, but she was too selfish. What would he have thought, reading it? Would he simply have accepted she'd gone, without any real explanation? No, she doesn't think so. He'd have tried to find her, just like Tomas has. How long would it have taken him to let go of her? How long till he moved on with someone else?

"It was for your own good," she says now. "Really. You don't want to be involved with me. I've messed up my life, and I don't want to mess up yours, too. You're better off without me."

"But how do I know that?" Tomas says simply. "Look, just explain to me what's going on. How exactly you've messed up your life. And then, if you still want me to, I'll leave again. I'll leave you be." He looks out to the sea, dark now as the last of the day's light sinks under the horizon. "I just want to understand," he adds. "Please, Marianne."

She looks at him, at the hurt in his kind face, at the lips she's kissed so many times and the hair she's run her hand through. How exhausted she is from lying all the time! He would never in a million years suspect the truth, would never believe her capable of the things she's done—she can see it in his face, just as she could see it in Henry's, back then. She remembers the way her husband ignored the minor irritations she purposely inflicted on him. Remembers how he'd sanded and polished that battered old chest of drawers until it was nothing less than flawless. Remembers how she couldn't tell him what she'd done as she feared he wouldn't love her anymore.

Perhaps, she thinks suddenly, the truth—or a partial truth, at least—will kill two birds with one stone. It will end her cycle of lies, and it will make Tomas let go of her for good.

She exhales and steels herself.

"Well, for starters," she says, "that's not my name."

31

GRETA, 1983

I hoped Rod would have failed in his snooping mission. I hoped he wouldn't have had the guts. I even hoped he'd have seen through me and suspected the intentions behind my request weren't entirely honest. I doubted he'd think I was a Stasi spy—it seemed so outlandish I almost failed to believe it myself—but surely instinct would have told him not to give out confidential information.

And yet, there he was, back in the Turf Tavern one evening in early December, sliding a thick brown A4 envelope over the table towards me.

"I have a mate at HQ who left me alone in his office for a few minutes," he said, a flash of pride on his face. "So I did a bit of photocopying."

I stared at the envelope without opening it, tried not to show my shock. "Right, well thanks, I'm sure it'll be an interesting read." Perhaps it was just some boring report, nothing of any use to the Stasi. *Please let it be that*.

"It goes without saying that this is only for you, Greta. This isn't the sort of stuff that should be spread around—I wouldn't want it to get into the wrong hands, if you know what I mean."

Or maybe not.

"Of course." My heart was thudding so hard I felt dizzy.

"So will you contact your friend?"

"Sorry, what?" I couldn't take my eyes off the folder.

"Your friend back home. The one you said had contacts."

I looked at him and saw his thinly disguised hope, his forced nonchalance, and I understood why he'd done this for me. He was ambitious; he thought his place in the world was bigger than leading a small group of Amnesty do-gooders in a shabby community centre in an Oxford suburb. "Oh yes," I said. "I'll write to him as soon as I'm home tonight."

I didn't, of course. Instead, after an anxious bus journey, the envelope stashed under my coat, my chest battering at the slightest glance from a fellow passenger or the merest hint of a footstep on the pavement behind me, I entered the thankfully empty flat, went to the bathroom, and locked the door. There, I slit open the envelope and flicked through the contents.

Confidential internal strategy documents.

Minutes from private meetings with British politicians.

Names of major Amnesty donors.

Transcripts of interviews with named ex-prisoners talking about prison conditions in the DDR.

Lists of contacts in the DDR, the Soviet Union, Poland, Czechoslovakia.

It was almost unbelievable, Henry. Rod been trying to impress me, and he had, he really had. He'd also struck fear into me, because this was a gold mine for the Stasi, for the KGB, for the intelligence services of any government behind the Iron Curtain that could use it to manipulate and blackmail and coerce.

And it was in my hands.

I knew, right then, with a clarity I hadn't felt until now, that I was finished feeding information to Olaf. I couldn't give this to him; it was too damaging. I had done much that I wasn't proud of until then, but it turned out there was a limit to what I would do, even for my family.

The next day I wrote to Olaf saying I was busy and couldn't get away but would visit in the new year. I hoped this would buy me a bit of time to decide what to do with the files. Could I give him some of them, but keep back the most damaging? Could I pretend Rod had changed his mind, or simply hadn't been able to get hold of anything? But I feared Olaf would know that he had. I feared someone would have told him, that my instincts about being watched weren't paranoia, and doing nothing at all wasn't an option.

In the meantime, I slid the files under the mattress of our bed. They were there, like an undiscovered land mine, when we made love, Henry, and when you curled into me as you slept, snoring softly as I lay there with my eyes wide open, wondering how the hell I was going to get myself out of this.

A few days later, I met Sarah to go Christmas shopping. My heart was hardly in it, but I couldn't think of a good reason to say no, and anyway, I figured it was best to carry on as usual, to do whatever regular people did, people who weren't Stasi spies with a stash of illegally obtained documents under the bed.

The city centre was packed, and I felt harried immediately. Every shop had a Christmas-themed window display, from the tasteful to the gaudy. Everywhere I went, I heard the same few jolly tunes, which soon lodged themselves in my head and played on a loop until I felt sure they were driving me mad. I trudged around after Sarah without my usual fondness for her company. I didn't want to be there. I wanted to be with my family for the *Jahresendfeier*, as our atheist leaders would have preferred us to call the celebrations. I wanted to bake Stollen with my mother, using the dried fruit Ilsa always sent us from the West; I wanted to drink *Glühwein* with Lena at the fair on Alexanderplatz, and decorate a small tree with candles and the wooden figurines from Erzgebirge that had been handed down through my mother's family.

But instead, we were staying in Britain and spending Christmas with your family, so I was shopping for presents to send to mine, Western presents that I knew would make their eyes pop. For Lena, I bought the most beautiful scarf and mittens, made from the softest wool in a rich blue. I hoped they'd bring a smile to her face, after the recent letter I'd received, in which she'd seemed so down. For Angelika, I'd chosen a delicate silver bracelet, and for my mother a knitted jumper that I would tell her to wear as often as she liked, rather than saving it for best, as I knew she'd be tempted to do. I was still looking for something for my father. Something he'd love so much he'd be unable to dismiss it as unnecessary Western excess, as he was wont to do.

However, wandering around Oxford with Sarah, I had to admit that a part of me saw my father's point.

"Look, isn't that bag gorgeous?" Sarah nudged me, pointing to a display on the ground floor of Boswells department store, where we'd come to look for something for her sister-in-law.

"It's beautiful." I touched the rich burgundy leather of the bag, before glancing at the price tag. *Scheiße.*

"I've been dropping not-so-subtle hints to Kev, but he never seems to take them," Sarah said. "Maybe I should just tell him what I want and be done with it."

I smiled at her, but I didn't really understand. It felt like Christmas in England was all about the presents. At home, it was mostly about spending time together as a family, cooking and playing games. Gifts were modest and often handmade. Never would I have received or given an Italian leather bag with an astronomical price tag like the one Sarah was looking at now.

"Isn't it nicer to have a surprise?"

"God, if I left it completely to him, I'd be lucky to get a pair of socks." Sarah rolled her eyes. "One year, he gave me a vacuum cleaner. I mean, bloody hell, that's grounds for divorce!"

I laughed and left her to browse as I headed to Blackwell's to pick up a book for you. The bookshop had quickly become my favourite place in Oxford, not only because of the sheer variety of books I could find there, but because of the relative quiet and the warm atmosphere within its low-ceilinged rooms. Even today, on a Saturday in December, there was a natural hush in the building as customers browsed the shelves in near-silence, the only audible voices those of the sales assistants at the tills. Being there calmed me, made me almost forget what I'd done and the dilemma I was now grappling with.

Until . . .

"Good choices."

I turned to see a man in his thirties, wearing a brown overcoat and hat, a grey scarf around his neck. Smart, professional, with a warm smile.

"Oh, have you read them?" I asked, gesturing to the books in my hand. One for you, and one I was considering for myself.

"*The Color Purple*, yes. Fantastic book."

"That's good to hear. I think I'll get it, then."

He nodded at the second novel in my hand, *The Running Man*, a dystopian thriller about a game-show contestant trying to evade a team of hit men sent to kill him. "That one's brilliant, too. I'm sure Henry will enjoy it."

My mind did a backflip. "I'm sorry, how do you know my husband?"

He smiled. "I know *of* him. In fact, I know most things about you, Greta."

His words paralysed me for a moment. "Who are you?" I whispered when I was able.

"That doesn't matter," the man said in a mild tone. To anyone watching it would have seemed as if we were friends catching up. "What *does* matter are your regular journeys to London, and your monthly attendance at Amnesty meetings."

A chill ran through me. I'd been right, then. It wasn't paranoia.

I instinctively turned away from him, needing to flee this man—this Stasi agent?—but he caught my arm. "Stay calm, Greta," he said. "There's nothing to worry about."

"What do you want?"

"We just want to have a little chat with you. It's very much for your own good. And Henry's."

I put my hand on a pile of books to steady myself. Was he threatening me? And worse—*you*? "Who's *we*?"

"All will be explained in due course. What I'd like you to do is head down the road to the café on the other side of Broad Street. There will be a woman there waiting for you. I suggest you let her buy you *Kaffee und Kuchen* and hear what she has to say. I thoroughly recommend the chocolate slice."

A few heartbeats passed. "How will I know her?"

The man's mouth twitched. "She'll be reading a copy of *Nineteen Eighty-Four*."

32

HENRY, 2018

"Look, Oscar!" Ros bends down over the pushchair and looks at her grandson while pointing at the zebra. "It's a horse with stripes!"

Oscar shrieks and waves his fists in the air, and his expression of pure, innocent delight brings a smile to Henry's own face. They are maddening at times, these kids; they can be exhausting and too loud and overly energetic and ruled by their raw emotions, but he must admit they are also quite fun, and there is something about their childish enthusiasm that is infectious. He probably hasn't been to a wildlife park since he was a child himself.

"Will you come with me?" Ros asked when she called him a few days previously. Lucy and Jack were going away together for the weekend, she told him—news that made Henry's heart soar; maybe his chat with Jack in the pub had done some good—and Ros was looking after the kids, or in her words, tasked with making sure they wouldn't come to any harm for forty-eight hours. She'd feel happier if she had someone with her, and she'd thought of him, so would Henry come with her on Saturday?

So here he is at the wildlife park on a brisk but thankfully sunny spring day, playing grandparents with Ros. His main tasks so far have been picking up Oscar's glove when he drops it from the pushchair approximately every two minutes, and ensuring Millie doesn't run too far ahead, eager as she is to see the penguins, and then the giraffes, and then the lemurs. He can't say it doesn't make him a little antsy that Ros didn't seem to care when Millie spilled chocolate ice cream all down her pale blue jacket, or that Oscar's nose appears to be permanently running, or that Ros couldn't remember which of the sandwiches she'd brought for their picnic lunch were jam and which were ham. "Pot luck," she said with a laugh when she passed Henry a foil-wrapped package, and he smiled uncertainly while inspecting the contents to find a slick of raspberry preserve. But it was actually quite nice to have a change from his daily ham and pickle. And Oscar's running nose and Millie's chocolate-smeared coat don't seem to bother them, so he is trying hard to not let those things bother him, either. "Don't sweat the small stuff," Ros told him when they set off. "If they're still alive at the end of the day, then that's a win."

To his surprise, he finds there is something quite refreshing about lowering one's standards.

"Lucy loved going to places like this as a kid," Ros says as they stroll towards the elephants, Millie leading the way. "She always loved animals, right from when she was a baby, so it was no surprise when she announced she wanted to become a vet. Si was over the moon—I think if he hadn't been an actor, he'd have been a vet, too."

"That's your ex-husband?"

She nods. "They were joined at the hip when she was little. They'd come to places like this nearly every weekend and spend hours cavorting around together. Sometimes I'd come, too, but it felt like their special time, you know? Lucy and I bonded over different things—shopping, I suppose, and movies—oh, and baking. Si couldn't bake for toffee—he tried to make Lucy's birthday cake once and after using what seemed like every utensil and piece of equipment in the kitchen, he produced a cake that was horribly burnt around the edges and yet undercooked in the middle. Extraordinary, really—I don't know how he did it!" She laughs. "He went to the bakery and bought something in the end."

"It sounds like you . . ." Henry tails off. "I mean, he sounds like a decent husband, a good father."

"The best," Ros says, and then throws him a wry smile. "You're wondering why we split up? Turns out the best ones bat for the other side."

Henry stops on the path. "Hang on. He married you, but he was gay?"

"Well, yes." Ros smiles. "But, of course, it wasn't always easy, in those days, for gay people to be open and proud of who they were, and he'd tried to hide it from himself for so long, I could hardly blame him for hiding it from me, too."

"How long were you married?"

"Five years." Ros laughs. "I must have been blind as a bat. But I'd married my best friend and had two lovely children with him. If the sex was a bit lacklustre after a while, I suppose I put that down to the demands of parenthood and the natural waning of lust in a long relationship."

Henry looks at the ground. He supposes actors like Ros don't get embarrassed easily. "Weren't you hurt he'd kept such a secret from you all that time?" he says to his shoes.

"Of course. But not enough to lose my best friend over it." Ros shrugs. "Millie, slow down, darling; it's not a race, the elephants aren't going anywhere! And anyway," she turns to Henry. "I couldn't regret it. We had Lucy and her brother, we'd had a happy marriage on the whole, and at least he told me in the end."

"Gosh. I'm not sure I could have forgiven such a big deception so easily."

Ros raises her eyebrows. "You never know until it happens, Henry. You never know."

They visit the elephants, and Millie laughs a deep, throaty cackle when one of them defecates in front of her. They go into the dark tunnels of the insect house, where Millie's screams at the tarantulas and scorpions reverberate off the walls. They visit two rescue bears splashing about in a swimming hole in their large enclosure, and Oscar giggles as the ursine siblings tussle with each other, batting a ball back and forth and dunking each other in the water.

"Shall we try and talk to them, kids?" Ros proceeds to let out a low, roaring noise that makes other visitors look at her and laugh.

"My turn, my turn!" Millie puts her hands on the rails, and with concentration on her face, lets out a higher-pitched roar. The bears glance at her. "Look! Look! They're looking!"

"Let's do it together." Ros puts her arm around her granddaughter and they roar in unison. Millie giggles as the bears look at her, nonplussed.

"Come on, Henry!" Millie says. "We're roaring."

"Oh no, no." Henry glances around him and sees the smiles on the faces of the other people standing nearby. "People are staring."

"So what?" Ros says. "ROAR!"

Henry laughs but looks down at his shoes. "Roar," he says, half-heartedly.

"You can do better than that! Just open your chest and ROOOAAAR! I'd forgotten how much fun this is—I haven't done it since drama school!"

"I'll leave you to it." He walks a little way off and gets out his phone, pretending to be engrossed in whatever messages he's received, though there are none. The Canadian shop owner still hasn't replied to his request for Marianne Kerber's email address, he notes, surprised to realise that's the first time today he's thought of his search for Greta. He supposes spending the day with two young children and an embarrassingly uninhibited actress who enjoys roaring at bears has been a little distracting. He shifts from foot to foot, sneaking glances at the three of them while scrolling aimlessly, and he can't help but smile. Happily distracting, it seems.

When they're all roared out, they walk back down the gravel path in the direction of the car park.

"This has been such fun!" Ros says. "Thank you for coming with us, Henry."

"Thanks, Henry!" Millie looks up at him, a wide smile on her face, and slips her hand into his.

"You're welcome." Henry squeezes Millie's hand.

Ros launches into the chorus of "Oh, What a Beautiful Mornin' ", her voice rich and full and actually rather lovely.

"It's the afternoon," Henry says.

Ros laughs and slaps him gently on the arm. "Spoilsport! It's from *Oklahoma!*, my favourite musical. I played Laurey at Bristol Old Vic back in seventy-five. You like this one, too, don't you, Millie?"

She repeats the line with even more gusto, and the young girl joins in. Henry smiles as their voices fill the air, the sonorous alto of Ros complemented by her granddaughter's high, childishly sweet tone.

He looks around him, but no one is nearby. And then something comes over him that he can't quite explain. An abandon. A recklessness. A release of all the pent-up emotion that he is coming to realise, in spending time with Ros, he keeps inside him. He opens his mouth, and his off-key, rarely used voice joins the others for the final line.

He's still humming the tune when Lucy's windswept face appears at the door to his workshop the Tuesday after her weekend away with Jack. He turns the key in the lock and in she clatters, as much of an interruption to the peace of his pine forest as ever, yet he is glad to see her.

"Henry! It's so good to see you. I just had to come over, even though I've got a million and one things to do since I wasn't here at the weekend, although Mum was a total star so at least the house isn't in a state and there's a bit of food in the fridge. Honestly, I don't know what I'd do without her right now, and I hear you had a brilliant time at the wildlife park—thank you so much for keeping Mum company and helping her with the kids. I know she finds it a bit much having them both together all day."

Don't mention it, Henry opens his mouth to say, but she is still talking, so he doesn't.

"And it was *soooo* worth it," she continues, unwinding the scarf from her neck, "because Jack and I had the loveliest weekend; it was exactly what we needed and we talked so much and laughed and drank lots of wine and had the best dinners, and it felt like it did before, you know, when we first got together, and the best thing of all is that Jack said he's willing to try again. He's going to move back in and we're going to try and make it work, and I'm *so* relieved. And I have to thank you, because Jack mentioned he'd seen you in the pub and you'd had a chat and talked about second chances, and I think it really helped, Henry, it really did. So I can't thank you enough, but can I start by making you a cup of tea?"

Henry laughs. "You can."

She puts the kettle on and he goes back to his workbench, where a wooden train set is sitting, waiting to be repaired. A train called Terrence, according to the name handwritten in faded red letters on the engine. There's a large crack down the side of one carriage and scratches and dents on all the others, with wheels missing here and there. The owner told him it was hand-made by her father, and was played with and loved by her and her siblings, and then their own children, for many years. Now she wants it repaired so she can give it to her daughter and son-in-law, who are finally having a baby after many years of fertility problems. Henry has agreed to fill the cracks, replace the missing wheels and repaint the scuffed and faded paintwork, but he thinks he might leave some of the rough chisel marks created in the making of it, and perhaps even some of the traces of wear and tear it has gathered over the years. They are evidence of an object made and used with love, of the rough-and-tumble of family life, of the squabbles and laughter that will no doubt continue into the future as its newest member grows up.

"I'm so glad you and Jack are going to make a go of things," Henry says over the boil of the kettle. "He seems like a nice lad, your husband."

Lucy beams. "Oh, he is. He really is. We just stopped talking, really *talking*, you know? We forgot to appreciate each other, and then I did an awful thing, but it wasn't because I didn't want to be with Jack. I felt un-noticed, I guess—unheard. He says he understands, and he'll try to listen more and help more, now. And I've promised to listen to him more, too, because perhaps I didn't, always, you know? He's told me he's stressed and miserable at work, and I knew that, but perhaps I didn't really *hear* that, and so we talked about how we could make a change, maybe he could go back to study . . . I forget what course he said but something exciting that could lead to a new career."

"Computer game design?"

She laughs. "That's right. See, you listen better than me."

But he hasn't always. He thinks of all the memories of Greta that have come back to him during these last weeks. The frown on her face as she pored over travel brochures, yearning for destinations they couldn't afford. Her tired, taciturn demeanour when she got home from that low-paid, un-fulfilling café job. The fixed smile and restrained politeness she adopted when listening to the unfortunate attitudes of his parents over a Sunday roast. The way she batted away comments he made about starting a family. And the look in her eyes, he remembers now, after she so carelessly water-marked the surface of his chest of drawers, as though she'd done it to hurt him. She wasn't happy, he sees now. And she should have told him that more openly. But he should have listened harder, too. Should have made her feel it was okay that things weren't perfect, instead of convincing himself they were. Perhaps then, she would have told him what was happening to her.

Lucy puts a steaming mug down on Henry's workbench. "That's a lovely train. Are you going to redo the name? Terrence is a bit wonky."

"Do you know, I might not," he says. "I think it's rather charming as it is."

Lucy cocks her head, smiles. "Yeah, maybe you're right." She takes her place in the armchair. "So, enough about me. I haven't seen you since you met with Olaf. Tell me what happened."

He gives her a summary of his visit: the old man's dementia, his comments about Greta's betrayal. "But he couldn't tell me anything about her whereabouts."

"Okay, but that doesn't matter because we still have the shop in Canada! Have you heard back yet?"

Henry shakes his head. "Maybe they think I'm some weird stalker."

She throws him a stern look. "Or maybe they can't give out an email address for data protection reasons or something. But never mind, we can try something else; there might be another way."

"No." Henry shakes his head. "It's time to give it up, Lucy."

"But—"

"Really, I mean it this time." He smiles as he realises he actually does. "I'll always be sad about what happened to Greta and me. I'll always have unanswered questions. But that's life. I'm glad *you've* got your marriage back on track, at least."

"Are you sure? I mean, from what you said about your visit to Olaf, she was involved in something pretty fishy, don't you think? Maybe she was forced to leave you, for some reason. Maybe she'd come back, if only you could meet with her again, talk with her."

He catches the emotion in her eyes, and a rush of affection floods through him. This young woman. A romantic like him, still yearning for this happy ending for him and Greta, just like her and Jack. For so long, he wanted that, too. But to his surprise, he's not so sure he does anymore.

He can't picture Greta as she is now. His image of her is thirty-four years out of date, a faded historical document of a time long passed. And now, after everything they've discovered, it's a historical document he can't even trust—an unreliable source, a memory muddied by all the secrets it's become obvious his wife must have held tight to her chest. He's had his rose-tinted glasses removed, but the image he's left with is anything but clear.

Instead, he can picture the face of an actress roaring at a bear, and muddling jam with ham, and singing loudly in public places, and embarrassing him with intimate details of her life, and doing so many other things that are nothing like Greta would have done, things that could be annoying and frustrating and unappealing and yet somehow, oddly, make him smile more than he has done in years.

33

GRETA, 2018

Greta and Tomas are on the harbour wall in Lund, at the end of the road. It is dark and bone-cold; Greta has taken a blanket from her van and wrapped it around them both as they sit side by side for warmth. So far, they haven't spoken. Tomas is waiting for her to start, and she knows he will wait forever, because that's the sort of man he is. And she *will* start, soon—but first she wants to revel in the simple pleasure of being with him again, the presence of his body next to hers, the familiar scent of his aftershave, the velvety brown of the eyes she knows so well.

It will likely be for the last time.

It is a clear night and the stars glow bright in the thick darkness above. It is comforting that she is a mere speck of dust in this universe, that her mistakes, lies, and betrayals are nothing in the scheme of things and will someday be forgotten forever. But they matter now, that's the thing. It matters to Tomas that he didn't know her real name, that he has known practically nothing true about her life before she met him. And it matters to her that she is about to hurt him again, to change his opinion of her with a story that she still, after all these years, can't quite believe is hers.

"It's true that I'm German," she begins, "but I'm not Marianne Kerber from Hamburg, as I told you. I'm Greta Schneider from Berlin. East Berlin, as you would have called it. Die Hauptstadt der Deutschen Demokratischen Republik."

Tomas looks at her, eyebrows raised, but says nothing. He has asked, and now he will allow her to tell him, in her own time.

And so she does—at least, a version of it.

I was a young woman who dreamed of seeing the world, she says.

I met a man who could fulfil my dreams, so I married him.

But when I left my country, the people who had let me leave asked me to work for them in return, and I said yes.

I did terrible things for them and didn't tell my husband about any of it.

I fled the country to get away from it all, and I've been running ever since.

"You spied for the Stasi?" The words are propelled out of Tomas by incredulity, as though he can't believe them until he's said them aloud.

"I did."

Tomas gets up from the wall, and their shared heat leaves with him as the blanket slips from Greta's shoulders. She waits as he looks out at the boats in the harbour, their dark masts swaying gently in the breeze, knowing he is withdrawing from her, and that it's for the best.

"You know what, Marianne?" He shakes his head. "I mean *Greta*. I came here ready to hear your story, to understand. But *this*? I mean, Christ!"

"I know. I still find it unbelievable that this happened to me." It slips out before she can stop it, this sliver of self-pity, and it sounds hollow in the wake of the half-truths she has told him.

Tomas gives a short, sharp laugh. "It didn't happen *to* you. You chose to do it. You chose to work for an organisation of oppression, a tool of a police state. You chose to use your husband to get to Britain and then walk out on him. I assume you didn't tell him why?"

282

She shakes her head.

"What reason did you give him, then, for the divorce?"

"I . . ." She looks out to sea, can't meet his gaze. She's always presumed Henry would have divorced her in absentia, but she's never known for sure.

"You're still married?" Tomas laughs again. "Well, I guess nothing would surprise me now."

I didn't want to work for them, she wants to say, *but I needed to protect my family. I didn't want to walk out on the husband I loved, but I knew he'd be safer without me. I always tried to do the right thing, but somehow I never did—and I've paid for that. I've suffered for it, Tomas. I'm alone and lonely and tired, so tired of this thing I used to call freedom.*

He takes a step forward towards her, his eyes dark and shining. "I don't know who you are anymore," he says, a catch in his voice. "Other than a liar and a commitment-phobe."

His words sting like he's slapped her. She looks down, face burning, heat pulsing behind her eyes. She longs to tell him the story properly. But it's better for him if she doesn't, better for him if he walks away from her right now. In any case, she deserves his anger, his disgust. She deserves this punishment, for all that she's done.

"You're right," she says. "I am. So you should go now, Tomas. Please go."

He turns towards the sea for a second, and then nods and starts to walk away.

She stays on the harbour wall, reeling in the aftermath. Her breathing comes in shallow, rapid gasps as her eyes fill up, and she shivers in the cold, or perhaps with the shock of what she said to drive him away. She is alone again, as it has to be.

Until she hears a sound behind her and she turns and he's standing there, Tomas, his cheeks wet, his face full of hurt, of bewilderment, and of something else she can't quite identify. "I was wrong," he says softly. "I *do* know you. What you've said . . . it doesn't fit with what I know about you, and I refuse to believe that after all the time we've spent together over the past year or so I don't know you at all. You're a good person, Greta. And I'm a good judge of character. So I know there must be more to this story." He shakes his head. "I'm not going anywhere until you tell me what it is."

PART THREE

34

GRETA, 1983

I'd been to that little café on Broad Street several times before. It was run by Italians and served great coffee. I hesitated outside the door and looked around me. The street was busy with Christmas shoppers, readying themselves for a season of joy, but all I could see in their faces was a threat. Was I about to become even more trapped in something I desperately wanted to escape?

I saw her as soon as I opened the door. Older than the man in the bookshop, probably in her late forties or early fifties, but with similar gravitas. She was slim and well put together, wearing a pressed green shirt tucked into a black pencil skirt, with neatly coiffed wavy brown hair and large tortoiseshell glasses. She was sitting at a table for two in the back corner, a pot of tea in front of her along with a newspaper and a copy of *Nineteen Eighty-Four*. My brain paused on the novel in a way it hadn't when the man mentioned it in Blackwell's. Surely the Stasi wouldn't use a book that was forbidden in the DDR as a signal? They weren't exactly known for their ironic sense of humour.

As I approached, the woman stood, stepped forward, and grasped my hand in both of hers, as though we were old friends. "Greta, good to see you."

I took in the upper-class tone of her voice, the musky scent of her perfume, the heat of her hands on mine, but my voice failed me.

"It's all right," she said more quietly, when we were both sitting down. "You have nothing to fear from me. Can I get you a tea or coffee? And maybe a pastry? They're ever so good here."

I thought of Olaf, his delicious coffee and carefully cut cake and clipped English, and I shook my head. "Who are you?"

"You can call me Judith."

"And the other man, in the bookshop?"

"That's Rupert. I hope he didn't scare you. He does have a tendency to over-egg the cloak-and-dagger stuff."

I looked her in the eye. "Not at all," I said evenly. I was sick of people trying to scare me. "I simply thought he had very good taste in books."

Judith laughed. "I can see we're going to get along, Greta, so I'll cut to the chase. I wanted to meet you today because I think you could be useful to us—and us to you."

"Who is 'us'?"

"The other side of the coin. The *right* side."

It was as though she'd cracked me open like a can of cola and released the pressure within. Not the Stasi, come to demand those files. Not some agent of Olaf's, here to bring me into line.

I exhaled. "The one with the Queen's face on it."

"Exactly." Judith took a sip of tea. "You like living as one of the Queen's subjects, don't you? You enjoy your life here?"

"It has its good points and bad points, like anywhere."

"But you don't like working for the people who put your friend's uncle in prison, do you? The people who demoted your father."

I didn't reply. I was aware of the in-out of my breathing as the waitress arrived to clear a table nearby and we fell silent. I glanced around the café, scanning faces—a mother and young son eating pastries, an elderly woman sitting on her own, a man reading a newspaper—until the waitress left and Judith spoke again.

"I've been watching you for a while, Greta." Her tone was so light and warm that she could have been saying *We had such a lovely holiday this summer* or *We'd love to invite you to dinner sometime*. "To be honest, it took quite a bit of effort on my part to persuade my superiors you were worth watching. They dismissed you, you see, being a woman and a newlywed—they didn't think it would be money or time well spent. Thought your head would be filled with fashion and babies." She took a sip of tea, her eyes meeting mine over the rim. "But I knew better, so I put you under surveillance, and now I know everything about you. Your preferred brand of orange juice. Where you go to get your contraceptive pill. How many miles you like to run each morning. What you like to watch at the cinema—*Flashdance* is jolly good fun, isn't it?"

"What's your point?" I shifted in my seat. My relief that she wasn't Stasi was tempered by anger. It was British intelligence, then, who had followed me. MI5 agents who had put me so on edge that I'd done Olaf's bidding, that I hadn't lied to him or watered down the information I gave him because I feared he'd sent people to keep tabs on me. And now this woman wanted something from me?

"I know you've been coerced into doing what you're doing, Greta. I'm sure it's been very difficult for you."

"You have no proof I'm *doing* anything." It sounded more defiant than I felt.

"That used to be true, until Rod Kendall gave you an envelope of stolen documents and we photographed you carrying them home."

I waited, rendered mute, heart racing.

"But don't worry, Greta. It's not you we want—or Mr. Kendall, for that matter. So rather than simply arresting you, which I could, of course, I'd like to offer you a way out. A way to do the right thing."

"And what's that?" I managed to say.

"Use those documents to help us trap your hirsute friend and his associates and stop them from working against the country that has given them a jolly decent home for decades."

I glanced around me, but no one was looking at us. "To betray Olaf, you mean. To put myself and my husband in danger by double-crossing the—" I couldn't say the word. I couldn't contemplate what she was suggesting. Even being here, with this woman, this British spy, was risky.

"We'd protect you. The safety of our agents is very important to us," she said. "I want to make it clear, Greta, that I won't force you to do this. We are not like them. But I think you would agree that you find yourself in an unfortunate situation. This would be a way to help yourself, to put your life back on track, while also helping the country as a whole."

Her voice was polite, kind, measured, so very British. *We are not like them.* Maybe not, but if arrest was the alternative, it wasn't much of a choice. Although perhaps arrest would be the better option of the two, it occurred to me then. Olaf couldn't continue to use me after that. And he wouldn't punish my family if I refused to give MI5 anything on him. I'd lose you, though. I'd surely lose you when you discovered what I'd done. "Why didn't you just have me followed the next time I went to visit Olaf?" I asked. "You could have arrested us both when I gave him the documents."

Judith cocked her head. "I would have. But you weren't going to hand them over, were you?" she replied. "That's why I knew you would help us—and why I want to help you."

I met her gaze and something like mutual respect passed between us. I thought of those files under the mattress. I thought of Lena and my family and all the other people back home who were being used and abused by people like Olaf, and I knew I would do this, I would try to atone for what I'd done.

"How exactly will you protect Henry and me?" I asked. "And my family need protection, too. I'm only in this situation because I didn't want them to suffer."

"I can't go into details right now. For the moment, I need you to trust me."

A bitter laugh shot out of me. "I don't trust anyone anymore, except my husband."

I saw pity on her face as she replied, "I'm terribly sorry to hear that, Greta."

I stared at my hands for a moment and then looked her right in the eyes. "And what then? Are you saying if I do this, it would be over?" It was all I could hope for, whether it was true or not.

Judith nodded. "It would be over."

I gave you *The Running Man* on Christmas Day at your parents' house. It was a modest gift by your family's standards, but you seemed happy with it. "The best gift is that you're here with me," you whispered to me, and I knew you meant it.

We'd given your mother a bottle of Anaïs Anaïs—the same gift she requested every year, apparently, which I found a little strange. For your father you'd selected a new fishing rod, while Charlotte received vouchers for Topshop, another odd present in my opinion, but you said if you picked out something specific for her, she'd only take it back, so it was best she chose what she wanted herself.

Christmas dinner was at three o'clock, and the amount of food on the table was astounding, yet your mother had struck again: the turkey was dry and bland, the sprouts were watery, the carrots verged on mush and the less said about the potatoes, the better.

"Have you spoken to your family today?" your father asked me as we ate.

"Not yet." I didn't intend to, fearing I wouldn't be able to keep my voice steady and they'd guess something was seriously wrong. I'd written instead, enclosing a letter with the gifts I'd chosen. *I miss you so much. I wish I could see you, but maybe I can come for a visit next year, if we can afford it.* I hoped it was true. Hoped we'd be free of all this by then.

Your mother leaned forward, her voice quiet, conspiratorial. "And will they . . . have enough to eat?"

"God, Mum," Charlotte rolled her eyes. "They don't eat pigeons from the streets and scavenge in bins for scraps." She smiled at me. Your big sister's attitude towards me had thawed in the months since our marriage, yet there remained something that I didn't quite trust about her. Perhaps, in hindsight, it was that I suspected she saw through me in a way you didn't. While you persisted in only seeing the good in me, I feared Charlotte glimpsed what lay beneath, the tangle of untruths and bad decisions that had created a mess of my new life.

"Well, I don't know, darling," your mother said. "That's why I'm asking Greta."

I smiled. "Oh yes. They'll probably be eating pheasant or goose with sauerkraut and potatoes. Mutti is an excellent cook."

Your mother seemed surprised, and I stifled my annoyance. I'd been coming here for months, now. I had told her many times what it was like in Berlin, had said that we had supermarkets and clothes shops and televisions and washing machines, that we had plenty to eat, even if we couldn't always get hold of the products we wanted. Yet she insisted on clinging to her Stalinesque vision of the place. Still, they tried, I suppose, in their own way. Your father proposed a toast to my family as well as his own, and after we'd waded through the main course, followed by a too-large portion of Susan's plum pudding (dry, again, though edible with lashings of brandy butter), your mother ushered me onto the sofa as you helped her clear up, before you both joined us to watch a film as a family. I leant into you, your arm around my shoulder, and half watched Peter Ustinov try to solve a murder in *Death on the Nile*.

No one in the room with me then, on Christmas Day 1983, would have thought they were sitting with a Stasi informant and newly anointed double agent. But I couldn't forget. My thoughts drifted often to Judith. There was sweet relief in now working for the British, for a country that allowed free speech and fair elections and didn't imprison people on charges that infringed international human rights. I was still lying to you—by omission, at least—but I could look you in the eye and know I wasn't betraying your country. I could sleep next to you at night and know I was atoning for what I'd done; I was making things right.

Yet to do so, I would have to go through something that terrified me: betray Olaf.

I'd met with Judith again in a corner of Port Meadow while out for a run. She'd told me how we could contact each other through a complicated system of chalk marks and dead drops that made me feel like a character in one of those Le Carré books you liked. My instructions would come in the new year, she said, and I should sit tight until then, carry on as normal.

But this was anything but normal. My head ran scenarios on repeat: Olaf, somehow knowing what I was going to do and punishing my family for it; my father going mad in solitary confinement; my mother arrested and interrogated until she signed a false confession implicating her in my treachery. I clung to Judith's promise of protection, told myself I had to trust her, but I couldn't quite quell my worries. When I couldn't sleep, I started thinking of ways to escape it all—Olaf, Judith, everything. Maybe you and I could run away together, make a life in a new place, where they couldn't find us. Maybe I could persuade you to ditch your plan for chickens in the Cotswolds and start again somewhere else, somewhere no one knew us. At times, I nearly told you. I nearly opened my mouth and confessed everything, told you how I'd messed up this life you'd given me and begged you to forgive me.

Nearly.

"What do you wish for next year?" I asked you that night, in bed at your parents' house in the early hours of Boxing Day.

You hugged me to you as I lay on your chest. "Just to be with you, *meine liebe Frau.*"

I smiled at your accented German. "Here in Oxford? Or maybe we could move somewhere else, somewhere far-flung, away from everything."

You laughed. "You've haven't been here very long!"

I sat up, turned to face you. It was worth one more shot. "I know, but don't you dream of escaping sometimes? Having an adventure?"

"Berlin was adventure enough for me," you said with a wry grin. "I'd love to take you on holiday to Italy, like I promised, and other places when we can, but I don't want to *move* abroad. I love it here, and I love that you're getting to know my family. I mean, don't you?"

"Yes." I lay down again, felt the rise and fall of your chest against my cheek. "Of course."

"Anyway, I think they need me nearby right now." Your voice wavered as you related how your mother, tipsy with drink in the kitchen after dinner, had tearfully confided that your father had high blood pressure and angina but was too stubborn to do anything about it. "He drinks too much and refuses to cut down on snacks," you told me. "I'm worried about him."

I reassured you, told you we'd try to do what we could to encourage him to look after himself a bit better, and you squeezed me tight, kissed my hair. "I love you so much, Greta. I've got everything I need, right here."

And I couldn't do it. *Oh, Henry, by the way, I've been a Stasi informant these past few months, and now I'm double-crossing them for MI5, but I'm worried it's going to go wrong, so will you leave the life you love and the family you adore and run away with me?*

I couldn't say it. Couldn't admit that I'd been lying to you for months. And even if I managed it, even if you forgave me for the things I'd done, I couldn't take you from your home, your beloved family and friends, and force you into a life you didn't want. There would be no new start far away from everything, you and me on an adventure. There was only this life—together—or a new one for me, alone.

35

GRETA, 2018

Greta untangles herself from Tomas's limbs and slips out of the fold-down bed in her van. She puts the coffee burner on her stove and switches it on, before turning back to look at him lying there, snoring lightly.

She tried; she really did. But she's no longer strong enough to push him away. She wants to be with him so badly, and there he is, this infuriating man who insisted on knowing every bit of her story, who insisted on her explaining why she did the things she did, who insisted—after his initial shock had gone—in seeing the good in her.

"So you ended up working against the Stasi for the British intelligence services?" Tomas asked, pacing about in front of her in the dark last night. "The whole thing must have been fucking terrifying!" He stood in front of her, one hand on his hip, the other on his head. "And your husband, you didn't marry him to get to Britain. You loved him, and you left him to protect him?"

She nodded.

"*Greta.*" He came to her then, took her hand in his. "You are the bravest person I know."

"No," she said with a vehemence that had him visibly recoiling. "I'm a terrible person. I've done awful things. I've hurt everyone I ever loved. I don't deserve to have them in my life." Her voice broke then and she fell into him, and he held her as sobs juddered through her, repeating that she was a good person, a person deserving of love, and she wondered if there would ever be a point in her life when she could believe that.

"Hey." Tomas opens his eyes as she drinks her coffee at the stove. "You're staring at me in my sleep again."

She can't bring herself to smile. "I was thinking."

He props himself up on one elbow. "That sounds ominous."

"I'm so glad I told you everything, Tomas. You can't know what a relief it is to tell the truth and to know you don't hate me for it. But now you must understand that by being with you I'm putting you in danger."

He sighs. "Are you sure about that? From what you've said, it seems to me that in the grand scheme of things, there were much bigger betrayals than what you did to Olaf Lang. Are you sure all this running hasn't just been an . . . excuse?"

"What do you mean?"

He sits up in the bed and looks at her. "You feel awful about everything you did—spying for that Stasi guy, leaving your husband—that's clear from what you told me last night. You've been carrying around this burden of guilt for thirty years. So my take is that you use the potential risk you face as a reason to run away from anyone who gets close. You're punishing yourself. But you can't outrun guilt, can you? You have to forgive yourself, don't you think?"

She flushes and looks away. She can't forgive herself. Not unless Henry has forgiven her.

"I have never known how much risk I face," she says, ignoring his question. "They may have forgotten about me, or they may not have. I could stop running—and God, how I want to stop running!—and I can hope they won't track me down one day and put Novichok on the door handle of my van or slip polonium in my coffee. But I can't let you take the risk with me, Tomas, however small. I *won't* let you. So we can't be together. I'm not worth the risk."

He shakes his head. "Isn't that for me to decide?"

She hesitates—*is it*? She has never considered that before. Should she have allowed her parents to decide if they would accept the consequences of her refusing to work for Olaf? Should she have allowed Henry to decide if he wanted to come with her when Judith's plan went wrong and she had to leave?

"I don't know, Tomas," she says. "I don't know if it is."

She watches him drive away as she sits on the harbour wall. "I have to get back to the restaurant," he said as he left her, "but I'm not letting this go, so promise me you won't disappear again, okay?" She only nodded and said nothing.

Spring is blooming properly now, she can feel it in the air, see it in the changes around her: the first bees and bugs, the dawn chorus rising to a cacophony, the trees budding with new life. It reminds her of those first weeks with Henry, so long ago, when the harsh February chill of the night they met gradually gave way to milder temperatures, and the days lengthened as their relationship progressed, as though their burgeoning romance was working a little magic on the world.

What will she do now? Where will she go? She won't run anymore; she knows that. Perhaps she will simply stay here, at the end of the road, living this solo life and bearing whatever risk still exists until it finishes with a bang or a whimper or something in between. There are worse ways to live.

Her phone throws a message alert into the silence, startling her out of her thoughts. She reaches into her coat pocket and takes it out.

An envelope symbol tells her she has mail.

From: ashley.tremblay@Tofinoartgifts.ca
To: Marianne.Kerber23@gmail.com

Hey, Marianne,

I've had several emails from this guy in England who seems to think he might know you. He wants your email address, but his questions seemed a little strange to me, so I thought I shouldn't pass it on, just in case! Anyway, I'm forwarding his message, below, so you can get in touch if you want to. And sorry for the delay—I've been off sick for a while, so I haven't kept up with emails!

Come into the shop soon, won't you? I need some more stock!

Have a nice day.
Ash

Greta scrolls down and reads the message underneath. She reads it twice, three times, unable to take in what she sees.

After all this time, someone has finally found her.

Henry.

36

GRETA, 1984

I met Judith behind a withered old tree on the banks of the Thames in Port Meadow to go through the final details of her plan.

It was an ice-clear January morning. A Wednesday. My skin was clammy from the miles I'd already run, and I was cooling rapidly as we stood there together, a twenty-four-year-old East German double agent and her British intelligence handler.

"Did he bite?" she asked.

I nodded. I'd been back to see Olaf the previous day and, on Judith's instructions, had told him about the wealth of information Rod had given me. "But I didn't feel comfortable travelling here with stolen documents, so I didn't bring them today. What should I do?"

Olaf had eyed me with something verging on respect. "Sensible to be cautious, my dear," he'd said, as though I were a protégé who had passed a test with top grades. "You'll leave the files in a dead drop, then. There's a place in Oxford, a tree with a hollow at the base, next to a children's playground in South Park. Wrap the files in something waterproof and leave them in the tree. Don't be hasty, though. Wait for a time that feels right, when you're sure no one is watching you. When it's done, put a line of Sellotape at head height on the nearest lamppost to your home. I'll send a courier to look out for the signal and collect the documents."

"All right." I'd tried to keep my voice steady, despite the gallop of my pulse.

"Well done, Greta. I knew I could rely on you."

"You give me no choice but to be reliable," I said, and I forced myself to look in those all-seeing eyes and believe I'd played my part well and he didn't suspect I was now working for the other side.

"Excellent," Judith said now, on that muddy riverbank. "You won't be the only one in his network. We want to see who else is working for him, and this might draw them out. We can tail whoever picks up the documents and it will be them who lead us to Olaf."

"But he'll know I was compromised, surely."

"He may suspect you were under surveillance, yes, but he'll have no proof you were working with us, and we intend to plant a trail of bird-seed, so to speak, that will suggest an alternative explanation."

"How?"

She put her hand on my arm. "I'm sorry, I really can't say more. You really do have to trust me. I'll do everything I can to protect you."

I shook my head. "If they find out it's me, then I'm in trouble—and therefore my family's in trouble. I need you to promise that isn't going to happen."

"I can't make promises, Greta. It's not in the nature of the work. But in the unlikely event that the worst happens, I'll do what I can to help your family. We have people there, of course. There are ways to help, to get people out."

"You mean that?"

Judith looked me in the eyes. "You have my word I'll do what I can."

A few seconds passed. *Trust me.* "I'll drop the documents off on Friday morning," I said finally. "Henry and I are going to St. Ives that weekend."

"Perfect. Best you aren't around during the operation, just in case."

In case anything went wrong, she didn't say. In case Olaf somehow knew this was a setup. In case nothing she'd said was true and I was about to make the worst mistake of my already error-strewn life.

It felt like both the beginning and the end of us, that trip to St. Ives. It was mid-January, a funny time for a romantic break by the sea, but you'd found us some cheap accommodation and presented the idea to me right after Christmas, perhaps as some unconscious reward for spending the festive season with your family, or to placate my Boxing Day plea to get away from it all. Thankfully, it didn't feel like January; it was cold, but the sky was clear and a rich blue, and I felt a sense of hope as we approached the coast and I glimpsed the sea. I was so tired, nerves so frayed; hope was all I had to cling to.

We spent that first morning in bed at the guesthouse, where the walls were so thin, I felt a blush spread across my cheeks when we later saw the landlady, a petite woman in her sixties who served us a late fry-up brunch without looking us in the eyes. By lunchtime, we were out and about, strolling down the sand, shoes in hand, yelping when the frigid seawater crept over our naked feet. When the wind dipped, we lay on the beach, you snoozing with your head in my lap, while I tried and failed to concentrate on a book. Later, we went to a café and ordered a cream tea, and you watched me in horror as I spread jam on my scone, spooning a dollop of clotted cream on top. "Don't I know you at *all*?" you said in mock outrage, as you proceeded to apply your toppings the opposite way round (I'd never had one before; I didn't know). I shook my head and laughed, fighting a lump in my throat. *No*, I thought. *No, you don't, and it's all my fault.*

But maybe this was a turning point. Once Olaf was arrested, it would be over. I could put everything behind me, stop lying to you, forget about

this extraordinary episode and focus on our life together. No wonder I
was jumpy that weekend. No wonder I barely slept, making my metal
jewellery obsessively while you snored beside me. If you noticed, you
didn't say. Perhaps you were used to my insomnia by then, another flaw
you accepted without mention.

Do you remember our final night? You'd booked a fish restaurant for
a special meal. It was pricey, a cut above the takeaway pizzas and pub
roasts we sometimes had back home, but you said we deserved it, that
we should splash out a bit after months of scrimping and saving. We de-
molished a seafood platter and a bottle of wine. We laughed and talked
and held hands over the table. We were the picture of a young couple in
love, so much so that the woman on the table next to us asked if we were
newlyweds.

"More or less," you said. "Delayed honeymoon."

"I wish you all the best," the woman said, and I swear I saw tears in
her eyes. "It's so lovely to see a young couple just starting out, with their
lives in front of them. Make the most of it, won't you?"

"I intend to," you said, squeezing my hand. "I can't believe my luck
that this amazing woman wanted to be my wife."

We walked back to the guesthouse along the beach, arm in arm. The
tide was in but the wind had dropped and the sea was calm, its gentle in-
out a lullaby. I wanted to stay there all night, fall asleep to the sound and
metaphorically bury my head in that beautiful sand, but all I could think
about was what might have happened back in Oxford in our absence. Had
MI5 arrested Olaf? Was I finally free? I shook the thought away. It was
too soon to be thinking like that.

"Don't do that, Henry," I said instead. "Don't put yourself down like
you did back there. Why wouldn't any woman in her right mind choose
you? You are kind and generous and lovely and would be a catch for
anyone."

You laughed. "I'm glad you think so. But honestly, Greta, you've
made me the happiest man alive."

"I mean it," I said without smiling back. "If ever . . ." I shook my head, the words stuck in my throat. *If ever something happened to me, you'd find someone else—someone better . . .* But nothing was going to happen. Everything was going to be all right. I couldn't contemplate the alternative.

When I think back, writing this now, I wonder what would have happened to us if I hadn't left. Because no relationship is perfect, is it? Yet you thought ours was. So what would have happened, years down the line, after the extraordinary way we met had segued into an ordinary life? Would we have emerged from that honeymoon period intact? Would my many flaws have finally broken whatever spell I held over you and we'd have moved forward with a more realistic, balanced love: a love where you acknowledged that I was as lucky to have you as you were to have me; a love which enabled me to admit that perhaps I didn't want the same kind of life that you did, with 2.4 children and a flock of chickens in the countryside, but I wanted us to figure out a way we could both be happy. A love that was messy and imperfect but real.

I hope so. But I guess we'll never know.

"You've made me so happy, too, Henry," I said, placing my hand on the lovely, trusting face of the man I'd married. "*Ich liebe dich.* Always remember that."

I thought you were going to ask me what was wrong, since I felt sure you'd noticed the emotion I was struggling to contain, but you gave only a brief, almost imperceptible shake of your head and then kissed me, slowly and softly. "I love you, too, Greta."

I let myself remain cocooned in the bubble we had created for the rest of the holiday, until we parked up outside our flat after the long drive home and that bubble abruptly burst. There was a chalk mark on the wall beside our gate. A small diagonal mark, unnoticeable to anyone not looking for it, but a signal to the person who was. To me.

37

HENRY, 2018

Henry feels surprisingly chipper as he tucks into his sister's sticky toffee pudding. The sunny, springlike weather he enjoyed on his outing with Ros has persisted, and with it his good mood. So when Charlotte said Ian was away for a golf tournament and she fancied some company so would he come round for dinner and a film, Henry didn't hesitate. It's been a while since they've had one of their Wednesday evening dinners, and he's missed her, despite her digs about his sad old life and her frustration over his failure to call Samira. He was also keen to counter those frustrations by telling her about Ros. He has met someone he likes, he said after she'd opened the wine. He doesn't know if she likes him back, or if it will lead to anything, but for the first time in a long while he feels there is potential for new love in his life. He even said the words "You were right, Charlotte, I *have* been living too much in the past," and he thought that would please her no end, because Charlotte always likes to be right, and yet all she said was "That's great, Henry, I'm so pleased for you" in a slightly sad voice that seemed totally out of character. Something feels off.

"The new kitchen looks fantastic, by the way," he says now, as he scrapes the last of the sauce from his bowl. "Is Ian happy?"

"Oh, he moaned about the cost, but yes, he likes it."

"And I see you got a new coffee machine."

"The old one was all clogged up." She shrugs but doesn't look at him.

"Charlotte." Henry puts down his spoon and stares at his sister, willing her to meet his eyes. "Are you still angry with me about Samira? I am sorry, but you can't force these things. She seemed like a wonderful woman, and I'm sure she'll meet someone else who's far more worthy of her. You know, she mentioned a Venezuelan salsa dancer—I mean, that would be a much better bet than this old codger with two left feet." He smiles, hoping his words will make her laugh, but she only shakes her head and puts her spoon down with a clatter.

"Oh, Henry, you still haven't learned your own worth, have you?" She sighs. "My little brother. I have only ever tried to support you and be there for you—you do know that, don't you?" Her voice is soft now, verging on cracking.

"Of course I do." He watches in shock as a tear slips down her face.

"And I'm sorry if I've been too harsh, too blunt, over the years. If I've said and done the wrong thing. It may not have always felt like it, but I do love you. Very much."

His stomach plunges. "Charlotte, are you ill?"

She wipes her eyes and laughs. "No, Henry. I'm not ill."

He waits, seeing there is something else she wants to tell him, and then she gets up from the table and walks to the kitchen, where an envelope lies on the new marble surface.

"Yesterday, this came for me at work—well, you, actually. Special delivery. I debated not giving it to you, but then I realised I simply couldn't do that to you." She holds it out to him. "But please, Henry, think carefully about what you do with it. Remember what you've told me tonight. Remember Ros, and your positive future, won't you?"

He stares at the envelope. "What is it?"

"What you've always wanted."

Dear Charlotte,

I know it will be a huge surprise to hear from me after all these years. Before you crumple this letter up and throw it in the bin, I beg you to read to the end.

We both know we were never the best of friends. Though we didn't ever speak about it, I understood that you thought I had used Henry to leave East Germany, and my departure from Oxford would have been confirmation in your eyes. I also understand that you loved your brother deeply and wanted to protect him. You had his best interests at heart.

Well, I want you to know that I did, too. I left because I thought it was the best thing for him, despite how much it hurt me to do so. And I have stayed away all these years because, like you, I believed that continued to be true. But now I've learned that Henry is trying to find me, and I can't ignore that. So please, I'm asking you to put aside your dislike of me and allow us to communicate.

I have posted this letter to you and not directly to him because our communication cannot be straightforward, for reasons I will explain to Henry. I have created a new email account. If Henry wishes to speak to me, he can log in and write an email in draft. It is very important that he does not send it. We must only ever communicate through drafts. The email address is HUG_82@gmail.com and the password (all lower case) is a song that got us both singing our hearts out in the living room of our Summertown apartment one evening a long time ago, when our friends Sarah and Kevin were with us. Our song, it could have been.

Thank you, Charlotte.

With my very best wishes,
Greta

38

2018

HUG_82@gmail.com
Drafts folder
Subject: You found me

Dear Henry,
　　You are the only person who has ever tracked me down, and I'm so glad it's you. I don't know how you did it. I don't know what to say. But I'm here. I'm listening.
Greta

―――――――

Greta,
　　A couple of months ago a young woman walked into my workshop wearing one of your necklaces. I can't quite believe it's led me to you. I've wanted to talk to you for so long but now

I don't know what to say, either. There's too much. This doesn't even feel real. Am I writing to a ghost?
Henry

———

No ghost. I want to say I'm sorry, but that feels incredibly inadequate. What is it you want, Henry? I only want to do what you want. Nothing else would be fair.
G

———

I suppose what I want—what I have always wanted—is to know why you left me. Can you tell me that, please, Greta?
H

39

GRETA, 1984

We met at Long Hanborough train station, a location conveyed to me by a note placed under a brick on top of a wall near the community centre at the end of our street—the place Judith had instructed me to check if ever I saw that chalk mark.

Urgent meeting Monday, 11am, Hbr. Take all precautions. J

Long Hanborough was only an eleven-minute train ride from Oxford, yet it took me several hours to get there, as per my instructed "precautions." Instead of taking the direct route, I caught a train to London, getting off at Didcot and catching a taxi to Witney, from where I took a bus back to Long Hanborough. I was hyper-alert the whole way, constantly checking for familiar faces, so by the time I turned up to see Judith waiting for me at the station café, I was tight with nerves.

"Did you catch them?" I asked, dispensing with a greeting.

"Let's walk," she replied.

We were strolling down a rough track, the hedgerows bare, the sun a hazy glow beneath thick cloud cover, when she told me the news that would change my life once again.

"In answer to your question, yes, we did. The man who picked up your documents is an Oxford University administrator who, it transpires, is also a Soviet illegal we frankly had no idea about. We suspect his wife of being the same—turns out she works in the bloody Home Office. After tracking the man to London, we were able to arrest Olaf Lang, too. So it's been quite a coup. Three for the price of one, so to speak. Stasi *and* KGB: the double whammy. My superiors are delighted, and so am I, Greta."

I could have been filled with helium for how I felt at that moment. I laughed with the relief of it. I saw our lives spread out before us, free from the threat and worry and fear that had hung over my first months in Britain. It would take some time to get over my guilt at working for Olaf, but at least I'd atoned for it.

"What will happen to Rod?" I asked, needing to ease my conscience about the Amnesty leader.

"Ah." Judith looked a little sheepish. "I suppose it doesn't hurt to tell you now. Rod Kendall was actually working for us."

"*What?*"

"We approached him after you'd been to a couple of Amnesty meetings and their contact in Berlin was arrested. We suspected that was down to you, that you'd become an informant of some kind, so we asked him to work you, to do whatever you wanted." She shrugged. "It was necessary, to get to Mr. Lang. We'd suspected him for some time but needed proof."

I flushed. Of course. Of course Rod hadn't freely offered me confidential Amnesty documents. He'd played me, just as I'd played him—and I'd fallen for it. Unease washed over me, dissolving my relief. Judith had asked me to trust her, and I had, but she hadn't been honest with me. I looked at her and I saw it, then. I saw it on her face that I still hadn't paid for my actions, that there was more to come. "It's not over, is it?" I whispered.

Judith looked down at her feet. "No, I'm sorry to say it isn't."

I remember this so clearly, Henry. There was a crow cawing in the tree in front of us. Puddles on the path from last night's rain. Spots of mud on Judith's elegant, lace-up black boots.

"I'm afraid our carefully laid plans to deflect from your involvement did not pay off. Frankly, right now we don't know why." She paused. "It's possible we have a . . . leak."

My breath hitched in my throat. "You're saying they know what I did?"

"We believe so."

I bent over, dizzy with her words. "So I'm in danger?"

"We can't say for sure. You're really a rather minor player in a vast game"—and that phrase stung, because the risks I'd been taking hadn't felt minor to me—"but Soviet involvement changes things, too. They're attack dogs, Greta, with the memory of an elephant. You've outed two of their deep-cover illegals, and I doubt they'll take kindly to it."

I exhaled a long breath. This couldn't be happening. "You'll protect me, then—put security on me." It wasn't a question.

"We don't have the budget or resources to put surveillance on you twenty-four-seven for the foreseeable future, Greta. At least, not where you are now."

"You already did! You tailed me when it was in your interests."

Judith pursed her lips. "That was short-term. This is . . ."

"For life, is that what you're saying?"

"Potentially. The KGB don't forget easily." She hesitated. "So it would be better—*safer*—if you disappeared. We could put you in a safe house, but that would be somewhat . . . limiting for you. Or we can give you a new identity and a decent amount of money to tide you over. You can start again, somewhere new, where no one knows you. You'll be free, then."

I repeated her words to myself, as though by doing so they might actually sink in, but I couldn't fathom her proposal just yet. "What about my family back home? You said you'd help them, if things went wrong."

"I'm certain your family will come to no physical harm as a consequence of your exposure," she said, to which I could only utter a bitter laugh. *Come to no physical harm.* There were other ways to *harm*, as my family well knew. "I can probably get a message to them to say you're all right, but it's best we don't tell them what you've been doing. If they don't know anything, they have nothing to say to the interrogators. And if they were to be jailed on spurious charges, I'd make sure they were a priority for buying-out."

I was shaking now. "And Henry? Is he in danger, too?"

"Even the KGB refrain from targeting innocent civilians in foreign countries, but there's always a risk he could inadvertently be caught up in whatever actions they may decide to take against you. So if you want to tell him, we can offer him a new identity, too. He can go with you."

I knew then that our life together, here in Oxford, was over. My presence was putting you at risk. I was in this situation because I'd been desperate to protect my family—and I'd failed on that score, it seemed. But I could still protect you.

I pictured your face in the moonlight as we walked along the beach in St. Ives. So kind, so loving. I could tell you what I'd done and perhaps you would forgive me now, because you'd see I'd tried to atone, to make things right. You might actually say, *Yes, I'll come with you. I'll leave my home, my family, my job, my whole life.* But as I thought it, I knew I couldn't ask that of you. Give up everything to either fester in a safe house or go on the run? Always be looking over your shoulder, wondering if someone was watching, following? You'd still be at risk, by my side. And you'd be living a life you didn't want, an unstable, unpredictable life far away from here. You'd have hated it. You'd have ended up hating me. No, it would be fairer to you, and safer for you, if I left, if I disappeared from your life as abruptly as I'd entered it, if I freed you to find someone else, someone much more deserving of you than the lying wife I'd turned out to be.

But *how* could I? How could I leave the man I loved?

"I can't do this. I can't just leave!" Surely she would understand. She must have loved ones, a husband, maybe children . . . but when I scoured her face, I realised I didn't know the first thing about her. I didn't even know if Judith was her real name.

"I believe you can, Greta," she said. "You've already shown such courage. You've been of great service to us, and we are extremely grateful. You can hold your head up high knowing you've done an incredible thing. And we would like you to be safe from any potential consequences. But the decision is yours. You can stay in Oxford, take that risk, or you can start again in a new location. I would advise you to do the latter."

I looked at her and felt something inside me crumple. "I trusted you," I said, my voice cracking.

"I know." She paused, her face creased in sympathy. "For what it's worth, I'm so very sorry."

I couldn't do it. For two days I dithered, unable to do anything but stay inside and think. Perhaps Judith was being overly cautious. Perhaps the risk was minimal. Nevertheless, I jumped at every sudden noise: the sharp slap of the letter box when the postman delivered the mail, the shriek of a fox in the dead of night, the clatter of a metal bin lid buffeted by the wind in the street outside.

I couldn't live like that. But I couldn't leave.

Until the phone rang one afternoon while you were at work, and on the other end of the line was Olaf.

"I need you to know something," he said in German. He was in custody. He'd been granted one phone call, and he'd chosen to call me. "You have made a huge mistake, Greta. You have betrayed your country. You have betrayed me. And you should be on your guard for the rest of your life, because we will not forget."

I said nothing. I hung up and went to pack a bag.

40

Greta, 1984

This is what I did the day I left you, Henry.

You'd already gone to work when I closed the front door behind me. I pulled your scarf around me as I walked down the street and shifted the rucksack on my shoulders. That modest bag contained everything I'd taken with me from our shared life together, which wasn't much, really—a few essentials, a few precious items. I didn't want to look like I was leaving for good, just in case anyone was watching, so this would be all I would have with me in a new, unknown life far away from you.

I put one foot in front of the other, farther and farther away from the flat I would never return to. My feet moved, but my head couldn't take it in, Henry. I was numb to the enormity of what I was doing. I thought of you standing in the cinema foyer later that evening, waiting for me, wondering where I was, your puzzlement gradually turning to worry and bewilderment. I thought of you reading my note, of not understanding—because how could you?—and I considered if I'd done the right thing by not explaining properly, by leaving you clueless in an attempt to keep us both safer, should anyone turn up asking for me. And then I shut my mind down again, focused on putting one foot in front of the other.

I didn't go directly to London. I followed Judith's instructions and went to Oxford train station, where I bought a ticket to Birmingham. I ducked into the platform toilets while that train left and then jumped on another to Reading, where I picked up a bus heading into London. There, I lost myself in the Tube network for a while before making my way to Victoria. I bought a green anorak and a baseball cap in a nearby shop and went to a café toilet, where I threw my coat in a bin and hacked at my hair with our kitchen scissors, which I'd brought with me for this very purpose. I fought hard not to cry as I did it, not because I cared about my hair, but because you'd always loved it, and it was another small step away from you, another cut to the ties that had bound us together. I looked at myself in the mirror as I washed my hands and saw someone else staring back at me: someone I never thought I'd become. A person who leaves her husband a pathetically brief note and disappears; a person who abandons her job, her home, her friends; a person who has no idea when she will be able to see her family again, the family she has likely brought nothing but trouble, the very opposite of what she wanted.

A large brown envelope was waiting for me in a left luggage facility. I shoved it into my backpack without looking at the contents, which Judith had told me would comprise a passport, a birth certificate, a driving licence, employer references, and a bundle of cash. Then I bought a train ticket to Gatwick and spent the whole journey in the toilet. I wondered then if that's how my life would be from now on: always looking behind me, never sure who to trust, hiding away from other people.

At the airport, I scanned the departure screen. *Pick wherever you like,* Judith had instructed, *somewhere you won't stand out too much, somewhere you could likely be a tourist or an expat. But buy tickets to two destinations, and choose at the last minute, lest anyone be watching.*

I walked up to one counter and asked for a one-way ticket to Bologna. *Italy.* I think I knew, as I bought it, that I couldn't possibly go to the country we'd dreamed of visiting together without you by my side. No, I would use the second ticket, to somewhere picked on a whim, somewhere that had no relevance or link to you and me. Somewhere I would go alone.

In fact, all the places I lived after I left you were reached alone. It is a sad fact of my life that I have never sat on a plane next to a loved one. I have always travelled solo, moving on from place to place when my fear of the past made me opt for a new future. And in all that time, I have never been to Italy. Never seen Rome or the Amalfi Coast or Tuscany or Venice or any of the places we talked about going together. I just couldn't.

Back then, on the day I left you, I didn't know any of that was to come. The world was my oyster. I had money in my pocket and no ties whatsoever. I could go anywhere I pleased. I had the freedom I had craved for so long, though I'd sacrificed so much to have it. My heart hammered as I bought my second ticket, the one I knew I would have to use.

I slid my new passport across the counter without looking at it, and it was only when the customer service assistant handed it back, a ticket to Kuala Lumpur sandwiched between its pages, that the enormity of what I was doing fully registered.

"Have a nice trip, Ms. Kerber," the woman said, a benign smile on her face.

I nodded but couldn't say anything in return. I turned away from the desk and opened my new West German passport to the photo page, reading the unfamiliar name and birth date below the photo of me, identical to the one in my real passport, which still lay in a drawer in our flat.

Greta Henderson was gone.

My future belonged to Marianne Kerber.

41

Henry, 2018

It is Wednesday but Henry is at home, on the sofa in his living room, his laptop in front of him, Lucy's necklace—*Greta's* necklace—in his hand. He is finding it hard to compute what he's just read, and who has written it.

Greta. Not dead. Not vanished. *Alive. Found.*

Greta, the Stasi spy turned double agent.

Greta, the woman he loved—and who loved him.

He sees that now. He sees he was right to believe in their love. She didn't simply use him to leave the GDR. She loved him and wanted to be with him, and she loved her family, too; and all that love was used against her in such a way that she ended up with none of them—not her husband, not her best friend, not her sister or parents.

Greta. My God.

He feels many things—shock, relief, and an odd euphoria to finally know, after all this time, what happened—but overlaid across it all is a profound sadness. For those two young people, so in love, who maybe never stood a chance to be together. For the mistakes they both made—her, in not confiding in him, not letting him help her; him for putting her on a pedestal and being blind to the truth. Because it has also confirmed what he's come to realise during this whole search: how different they were; and how quickly their love affair played out, so quickly that neither of them had fully understood those differences. Would they have made it, if politics hadn't got in their way? Would they have found a way to acknowledge their differences and forge a life together—a third way between his dreams and hers? He hopes so. He thinks so. Charlotte was right. They were forced apart when they were still in the honeymoon period. They never had the chance to figure out what compromises each of them had to make, to learn what a complex, imperfect ride love can be.

HUG_82@gmail.com
Draft
Subject: Thank you

Greta,

I've spent the whole day reading what you wrote. Thank you. After you left, everyone told me that you'd used me to leave Berlin, that you didn't really love me. For thirty-four years I've struggled to believe that. I'd look at that wooden bear key chain you gave me and fail to see how our marriage could have been about anything other than love. But without any explanation, it's been difficult. So you can't know how much it means to me to hear that you loved me and didn't want to leave.

I'm so incredibly sorry you went through all that and didn't feel you could confide in me. I'm sorry you lost everything because we met. But I can't be sorry that we did, Greta, and I hope you aren't, either.

Do you think we'd have made it, if all this hadn't happened?

H

———

Henry,

If I could have my time over, I'd do things differently. I'd tell you everything from the start. I have never forgiven myself for all the pain I've caused. It's not my right to ask, but I'm going to anyway: Can you forgive me?

I'm glad you kept that key chain and that it reminds you of love, because that's how I felt when I gave it to you. I loved you from the first days we spent together. I will never regret meeting you, or marrying you. Yes, I think we'd have made it.

G

He puts down his laptop, wipes his eyes. What time is it in West Coast Canada? The early hours of the morning, he guesses, and yet she is there, responding near instantly. His wife, at the other end of a wireless connection that didn't even exist when they last saw each other. His wife, whom he now knows he won't ever see again, because she is a woman on the run, still living with the consequences of what she was forced into all those years ago. Can those she betrayed really still be after her? It feels far-fetched to him, but then he considers the poisoned spy in Salisbury, and all the other, similar stories that simmer under the surface of this strange, murky world humans have created, and he thinks perhaps it's not so far-fetched after all. Either way, she will never know for sure, and so she remains trapped in the life of Marianne Kerber, still running, running, running, just in case.

She saved him from all that, he sees. By removing herself from his life, she allowed him to keep his. And it's been a good life. Though he may have spent the last few decades using the memory of her to stop himself from finding romantic love again, he has had so much that she hasn't. He's seen his relationship with Charlotte develop from bickering siblings to firm friends, and been around to watch his niece and nephew grow up.

He had his parents in his life and was able to be there for them when they died. He's developed his passion for woodworking into his own business in a city he adores, with his own house to go home to. And if he'd gone with Greta instead? Because she's right, he would have, if she'd asked. He'd have followed her anywhere she needed, keeping her safe through a nomadic existence that wasn't of his making, a life without his family and friends, without a stable home, a life that wouldn't have made him any happier than he has been these last decades without her.

> I don't think there's anything to forgive. Please don't punish yourself for what happened. I imagine you've been punished enough. I hope you still have love in your life, Greta. You deserve it.
> H

> You always were the kindest man. I hope there's someone in your life, too, Henry. I wish you all the love in the world.
> G

He closes the laptop and sobs, then. He sobs until he's spent, and then he takes a deep breath, stands up. His body feels lighter, somehow. Freer. He walks to the window and looks out. There is a figure approaching. A young woman with a baby strapped to her chest. She opens his front gate and smiles when she sees him standing there. She puts a hand up in greeting, and he waves back, the past draining out of him and the present rushing in.

42

GRETA, 2018

Greta sits in her van in the campground in Lund, reading and rereading Henry's emails. The sea still washes in and out. The sun still rises and sets. Nothing changed in the world around her when she communicated with her husband for the first time in thirty-four years.

She can hardly believe he found her—because of a necklace, the result of a habit she formed all those years ago during her short time with him. Her jewellery has been the only thing linking her to all the places she's lived since leaving Britain, a trail of metal left behind like the tail of a comet, visible to anyone who would take the trouble to look for it. But she has never considered it a risk to sell it locally, because nobody from her former life knew she was making it.

Except Henry.

Her first love.

The man she has been writing to for months with a confession she never thought he'd read.

But now he has. It was a leap of faith to contact Charlotte, whose workplace she tracked down fairly easily during an hour in an internet café, but it paid off, and now Henry has read every single word of her explanation, the raw, honest truth about what happened back then, and yet he doesn't hate her.

I don't think there's anything to forgive. Please don't punish yourself for what happened.

Tomas was right: she has carried so much guilt with her as she's run from place to place. So much pain and regret, so many things she has wished she could change. So much fallout from what she did—for her and for everyone she loved.

At first, in those early days after she left Henry, she was desperate for information. How was he dealing with it? What might he do to try to find her? And then there was her family. She knew Judith was right: she shouldn't try to contact them, shouldn't tell them what she'd done, both for their sake and her own. She debated trying to get a message to her aunt in West Berlin, but it wasn't out of the question that she, too, could be monitored by the Stasi sympathisers who roamed the West, just as they did in the East. So she let her heart bleed as she walked the streets of Kuala Lumpur, feeling like the wound would never heal.

It was five years before she dared to believe she might be able to see any of them again. She was living in Bergen, Norway, when the Wall fell, and she watched the events unfold on television like everyone else there—just another outsider looking in. She'd never thought she'd see the day, and yet on 9 November 1989, there it was, happening in front of her eyes: people swarming the checkpoints, standing on the top of the Wall, Easterners mingling with Westerners like they'd never lived apart all this time. A bloodless revolution had ended the division that had run through her city, her country, for her entire life. Soviet president Mikhail Gorbachev's reformist policies of glasnost and perestroika had paved the way for change in the DDR, for *Die Wende*, as the commentators called it, and the day the people finally stood up and said no more. Her parents and sister were likely there in the crowd, bringing their own mix of emotions to the momentous day: elation, joy, incomprehension, and perhaps a little apprehension, too, about what might come next. As for Greta, she sat in a bar, tears streaming down her face, watching those scenes with incredulity, and for a second or two she dared to think that her life on the run could be over, dared to imagine that any threat against her would disappear along with the Stasi itself.

Yet she knew she wasn't out of danger. Because she hadn't only betrayed her country, had she? She'd betrayed the Soviet Union, too, and despite Gorbachev's reforms, the KGB still existed.

Another year or so passed, the DDR was swallowed by a reunified Germany, and at the end of 1991 the Soviet Union was dissolved. While she was under no illusion that she was now safe, perhaps she was safer, and the temptation was too great. She travelled to Copenhagen, posted a letter to Ilsa, and waited. *There's a place Angelika and I always said we'd go together, if we ever could,* she wrote. *She'll know what I mean. I'll be there at two p.m. on the anniversary of the day Vati and Mutti met. Please come.*

They were so different, as sisters. Angelika had never yearned to travel in the West. Except for one particular place. A place she was now free to visit.

It was a cold, winter's day in February 1992, yet Greta was sweating like it was forty degrees as she stood under the Eiffel Tower in the heart of Paris. She was a skittish kitten venturing outside for the first time, brimming with excitement for what was to come but alert to the slightest danger.

She was early. She wondered if they might not come. If she'd hurt them too much. If they wouldn't understand when she explained what happened seven years previously. If they would want nothing more to do with her.

But then there they were, walking towards her: older, changed, yet so familiar the sight near burst her heart.

"Is it really you?" Ilsa was the first to speak.

Greta nodded, hardly able to see for the tears flooding her eyes, and then her knees buckled as Angelika flung herself at her sister, and the three of them hugged and cried and laughed and clung to each other for the longest time.

When they were able, they sat on a bench and Greta told them everything—Friedrich, Olaf, Judith—and she almost saw the pieces of the jigsaw puzzle fall into place in their heads. They hadn't known much. They'd spent seven years in the semi-dark, knowing only that whatever she'd done had incurred the wrath of the Stasi.

Because, just as she'd feared, her parents had been interrogated a few days after she fled Oxford. Her mother was released quickly, but her father had spent several weeks in jail, questioned repeatedly in Hohenschön-hausen, pressured to say he knew his daughter was a traitor all along, but he never did, and in the end they gave up trying.

"He got out in the end, but he'd lost his job at the publishing house for good," Angelika said in a matter-of-fact tone. "They gave him a position at the Narva lightbulb factory instead, but he hated it, said it was mind-numbingly dull, and he became quite down after that."

"And not only because of the job," Ilsa added, with a glance at Angelika. "He'd lost his idealism, I think; his hope that with reform, the country could succeed."

"And Mutti?"

"She kept her job—I suppose nurses were too important to sack—but it was never the same. Her colleagues shunned her socially, and she often came home crying."

"They didn't want to associate with a family who'd been in trouble with the Stasi," Greta whispered.

Angelika nodded, and she saw, then, how much her sister had changed; how carefree, innocent, happy-with-her-lot Angelika was no longer in thrall to the country she grew up in, the country that no longer existed; that like their father, she'd finally seen it with new eyes.

Greta squeezed her sister's hand, and then ventured the question she'd feared to ask ever since she saw her aunt and sister walking towards her. "Why aren't Mutti and Vati here, too?"

Ilsa and Angelika shared a glance, and then they told her. Rainer Schneider, her wise, proud, thoughtful father, had died of a stroke a few months before the Wall fell, after years of depression. *Because of the stress you caused him*, her aunt and sister didn't say, but they didn't have to. Her mother was still in Berlin, ill at ease and financially worse off in a capitalist country she didn't understand, and so nervous of the wider world that she wouldn't make the journey to Paris, not even for the daughter she hadn't seen in more than seven years.

"I'm so sorry," Greta said as her body shook in their arms, "so sorry, so sorry, so sorry."

"What will you do now?" her sister asked when their sobs subsided. "Can you be yourself again? Can you be Greta?"

"I don't know," she said. "I really don't know." Later, after she'd returned to Norway, hopeful that this reunion could be the first of many, she would contact Judith on the emergency line she'd been given seven years previously and be told, *It's up to you, Greta, but we can't tell you it's safe now.* The KGB may have been dissolved, but the people who worked for it had simply been absorbed into a new organisation, and the Russian Ministry of Security was a name that had far too many connotations for Greta's liking. So much had changed in the world, but so much hadn't.

"I want to try and see Henry in the same way," she said to her aunt and sister that day in Paris. "And Lena, too."

"I don't know where Lena is anymore," Angelika said, before relaying more news that tore at Greta's heart: shortly before Greta fled, Lena had been arrested and jailed. "She ended up in the West, but I don't know where she is now. We lost touch."

Greta blew out a shaky breath, trying not to think about what her best friend must have endured in jail, and how desperate she must have felt to have got herself arrested on purpose. She hadn't written to Lena in the last weeks of her time in Oxford, she remembered with a pang of guilt. She'd been too wrapped up in her own horror story. "And Henry?" she asked. "I still can't be with him, but I could explain now, if he'll let me."

Angelika had told her what she'd said to him on the phone that first day, when she didn't yet know where her sister had gone or why. *What did you do to make her leave, Henry?* She'd recounted how, once the Stasi arrested their parents and the family realised Greta must have done something serious, they were too scared to communicate with her husband in the enemy West; they didn't want to make things any worse for themselves than they already were. So they left his letters unanswered, and eventually they stopped coming.

"Greta, there's something else we should tell you," Ilsa said gently, glancing at Angelika. "I tried to contact Henry. It was some months after you left Oxford. I didn't know for quite a while that you had. I only knew that I hadn't heard from your parents for some time, and when I tried to visit I was denied entry to East Berlin. Eventually, I was allowed back in and your parents told me you'd disappeared and they'd been interrogated by the Stasi as a result. I read the letters Henry had sent them, saw that he didn't know anything, and so I decided to call him, to tell him what little I knew."

"You spoke to him?" Greta said in a whisper.

Ilsa shook her head. "No. He'd moved out of your flat, and the people living there gave me a number for his sister."

"Charlotte. He was staying with her?"

"I think so. When I called, she answered. I asked for Henry but he wasn't there, and when I told her who I was she just flipped. She was so angry with you, Greta. She said Henry was devastated, that you'd broken his heart. I wanted to explain about the Stasi, to say you'd probably had no choice but to leave, but it was hard for me, with my limited English, and she wouldn't let me speak, she just . . . ranted. I didn't understand everything, but I know she called you selfish, said she wished he'd never met you. She asked if I knew where you were, and I said no, that we were very worried, and then she got mad again and I started crying and . . ." Ilsa paused and shook her head before looking at Greta with creased eyes. "Before she hung up on me she said the best thing for Henry would be if you"—she switched to English—"stayed the hell away."

The words winded her. Wounded her. Henry, her wonderful, kind, gentle husband. She had hurt him so much. It was only right that she do what Charlotte said.

But it was the wrong decision, she sees now. *You can't know how much it means to me to hear that you loved me and didn't want to leave.*

She has made so many wrong decisions over the years. So many things she has hated herself for. For creating a situation that killed her father. For being unable to be a proper part of her sister's life, the two of them having met only sporadically over the years, when Greta deemed it safe enough. For not being there for her best friend, who resorted to such desperate measures. For failing her husband so badly, and then leaving him in stasis for thirty-four years, when all he needed was to hear that her love for him had been genuine.

Yet Henry has forgiven her anyway, just like that.

I hope you still have love in your life, Greta. You deserve it.

Until now she has only heard those last three words in German, in Friedrich's voice. She thought she "deserved" the life in hiding that his actions precipitated, thought the loneliness and isolation were her punishment to bear. But now she hears the phrase in Henry's voice and it means something so totally different.

Perhaps she can stop punishing herself now. Perhaps she can finally stop running from the guilt that has pursued her more than any external threat.

Now the man she loved back then has said she deserves to be with the man she loves today.

43

HENRY, 2018

The mess. The noise. Oscar is banging his spoon on the wooden surface—the lesser of two evils, Lucy said, since if she took it away, he would only cry. Millie knocked over a glass of water at the beginning of the meal, and a small hill of sodden paper napkins now lies in the centre of the table, a half-hearted attempt by Jack to clean it up. There is more food around Millie's plate than actually on it, and Oscar has half a banana split smeared over his face. But Jack, Lucy, and Ros don't seem to care about these things, so Henry is trying not to care, either.

It is Saturday, and they are in the Head of the River, a pub in central Oxford chosen for its family-friendly approach and good beer. "I wanted to thank you, Henry," Lucy said the other day, when she turned up at his house. "For helping Mum with the kids the other weekend, and for . . . well, you know, everything with Jack." He brushed away her words, said there was no need to thank him, yet Lucy insisted in that persuasive way she has, and so here he is, sitting at a table with a family that is not his own but is starting to feel just as important to him. He looks sideways at

Ros, at the mass of grey curls framing her face, the interesting hazel of her eyes. Charlotte would like Ros, he thinks, though he can never be entirely sure with his sister. He recalls her uncharacteristic tears when she gave him Greta's letter, and the surprising confession that tumbled out when he queried his wife's words: *I left because I thought it was the best thing for him . . . I have stayed away all these years because, like you, I believed that continued to be true.*

Like you.

Charlotte had spoken to Ilsa back then and never said, he now knows. And in her usual forthright style, Charlotte had told Ilsa exactly what she thought her missing niece should do. "You were slowly healing, Henry, and I didn't think it would do you any good to speak to Greta's aunt. She didn't know where Greta was, anyway. And I couldn't help myself, all my anger at what she'd done to you just fell out of me. It was a knee-jerk reaction and I meant well, I really did, but I'm so sorry."

He should have been angry, but it felt pointless, so instead he hugged her hard and they both cried a little and he felt once again how flawed people are, and how easily they can do the wrong things for the right reasons.

"Another pint, Henry?" Jack pushes back his chair.

"Don't mind if I do."

"We've made a plan." Lucy leans over the table when Jack goes to the bar. "I've seen a job to apply for at a local vet's, so if I get that, and Jack's boss lets him reduce his hours, he'll do a part-time degree in computer game development at Oxford Brookes."

"That's great, Lucy. But what about the kids?"

"That'll be down to muggins here," Ros says. "I've decided to move down to Oxford."

"Oh?" Henry says lightly, but his chest skips at her words.

"It's such a beautiful city, and it'll be lovely to be closer to this lot. I'll look after Oscar while his poor hardworking parents are at work, and we'll pick up Millie after school. Oscar will keep his current nursery hours, so it won't be all the time, and anyway, I do love spending my days with these two monsters, they make me feel like a child again." She turns to Millie, sitting next to her, and brushes a strand of hair behind her granddaughter's ear. "We're going to have all sorts of fun, aren't we, sweetie?"

"Yeah!" Millie shrieks. "Can we make a play?"

"We certainly can. We'll rehearse a musical and sing all the songs."

"Henry, did you know I can sing 'A Spoonful of Sugar'? Granny taught me."

"Did she?"

Millie starts to sing, her voice high and sweet and surprisingly loud.

Ros joins in, and Henry laughs, shakes his head. He glances around him and sees people looking, but they're smiling, enjoying the spontaneous spectacle.

"'Just a . . .'" Lucy launches in, so it's the three of them together now, child, mother, and grandmother, their voices full of joy and couldn't-careless abandon. By the time they get to the final line their arms are flung out wide, their smiles are broad and their elongated "waaaaaay!" seems to fill the whole pub.

They collapse into laughter and a smattering of applause from fellow diners. Jack, returning from the bar, claps a hand on Henry's shoulder. "Do you need rescuing, Henry?"

He laughs. "No, it's okay. I'm coping—just about."

"Oh, Henry, you know us well enough by now," Lucy says with a smile, touching the twisted metal pendant around her neck.

He nods. It is true, he does. He feels like he's been adopted into this family like a pet dog, and he's made himself right at home. All these years he thought he needed the perfect, wonderful wife he'd painted in his head, when actually what he needed was this: the mess and embarrassment and unruliness of life.

"Are you disappointed?" he asked Lucy when he told her about finding Greta, about the email exchange and the catharsis it brought him. "I'm sorry I can't give you the big romantic ending you wanted." But Lucy simply patted him on the hand, a mother consoling a child, a friend there for a friend. "Did it bring you what you needed, though?" she asked. "Because it was clear you needed something. I saw that right when I first met you." He nodded, swallowing down the tightness in his throat. "I think so." And she simply shrugged, smiled. "Then I got my happily ever after."

"God, what's that smell?" Jack says now, sniffing the air.

"Shit," Millie says, putting her hand to her mouth to stifle a giggle, and four pairs of eyes turn to her.

"How did you know that word, young lady?" Lucy's voice is faux-stern.

"Daddy says it."

"Thanks, Mills, dump me in it, why don't you." Jack rolls his eyes, but a smile twitches at his mouth. "But she's right, you know, I think Oscar's nappy's exploded."

"God, not again!" Lucy says as the baby starts to wail. "Right, that's it—time to go before he throws a complete wobbly." She stands up from the table and starts gathering together their belongings.

"Do you need some help back home, darling?" Ros says.

"No, no, you're all right, Ros, we've got it covered," Jack replies, throwing a glance at Lucy that warms Henry's insides. They have been through some tough times, but they will be okay. They have acknowledged and accepted each other's failings; they have worked through the tough stuff instead of running away or pretending everything's perfect. He thinks they will be absolutely fine.

"In that case, I think I might go for a stroll on Christchurch Meadow, along the river. It's such a beautiful day." Ros turns to him. "Would you like to join me, Henry?"

He looks at her, this woman who wears too much eyeshadow and is sometimes too loud for his liking and embarrasses him with her singing in public even though he actually quite likes her voice and admires her confidence. This woman who has been through a hard breakup and survived—no, flourished—on her own. This woman who has had an interesting life and, to his surprise, seems to enjoy spending time in his company. Is it possible she likes, admires, and finds him interesting, too, despite his many flaws?

I wish you all the love in the world. He pictures her face as he knew it—Greta, the woman he used to think was the only romantic lead in the movie of his life—and then he blinks and it is gone.

"Yes," he says, ignoring the knowing smile on Lucy's face and the little excited glance she throws Jack, the glance that says perhaps there's another kind of happily ever after to his story after all. "I would like that very much."

44

Greta, 2018

She has never gone back. In all the years she has been running, she has never turned around and retraced her steps to a place she has left.

Now here she is, back in Tofino.

She parks in her old campground and walks slowly into town, past the taco van, past her favourite café, past Ashley's gift shop, towards the dock at the end of First Street, not far from Tomas's restaurant. It is early evening, his team will be deep in dinner prep, so he is unlikely to be out here among the modest crowd waiting to watch the sun burn orange as it slips below the horizon. But that's okay. For now, she is simply content to be here again, refamiliarising herself with a place that has come to feel like home. If she stays—if he still wants her to—then they have all the time in the world.

She sits on the wooden boards, legs over the edge of the dock, and looks out to sea, thinking of the Russians, the old spy and his daughter, now out of hospital, according to the papers. What will happen to them now? Will they adopt new identities and disappear, or will they choose to stay in Salisbury and live with the risk?

"You came back."

She turns to see Tomas standing behind her. He's wearing his chef's whites, a striped apron, and a tentative smile.

"I did." She stands and walks towards him. "Something happened," she says. "I've been in touch with Henry. We've laid some ghosts to rest, I think." She smiles, but her lip trembles. It is so new, this feeling of peace.

"Wow, I . . ." Tomas reaches out and his hand grazes hers. "That's really great, Marianne—I mean . . ." He flushes at his mistake and glances at his feet. He is flustered, she sees, because he doesn't know what this means, this resolution she's found with her husband, her first love, the man who knew her by her real name. "How? You contacted him?"

"He found me. And it's possible that in doing so, he may have signposted the way for others to find me, too." She looks him in the eyes. "Or maybe you were right and no one is looking at all, and I've been simply running from myself all this time. And I could keep doing that. Keep pushing you away, keep running, keep punishing myself for all the bad things I've done, keep being a commitment-phobe and a liar, but I don't want to anymore. I want to be with you; to live with you, to trust you and commit to you and do all the things people do when they love someone, because I do love you, Tomas. So you were right; it's your decision. If you want to take the risk of being with me, then I'll stop running and stay here, with you."

There is a momentary silence between them, and then he takes a step forward. "The way I see it, every relationship is a risk," he says. "I want to be with you, too, more than anything in the world. So we'll risk it, together. And if you ever really need to leave, then I'll leave with you. I'll put the restaurant in Danny's capable hands and we'll take off in your van." He shrugs. "I've always wanted to go to the Yukon."

"You'd do that for me?" Just as Henry would have, but unlike him, Tomas would relish the adventure.

"I'd struggle with your two-ring hob and mini-fridge, but I'm up for the challenge." He smiles. "But let's not get ahead of ourselves. First, shall we start again? Get to know each other properly this time? For real? No more secrets and lies?"

She nods, and he beams back, his eyes crinkling at the corners, little lines of joy spreading across his temples. "Right, then." He holds his hand out for her to shake. "I'm Tomas. Nice to meet you."

She glances at the sea, the vast expanse of water where, deep down, orcas and humpbacks are swimming free, then she turns back to him and takes his hand in hers. "Nice to meet you, too, Tomas. I'm Greta."

Author's Note

NB: Please read this after you have read the book, as it contains spoilers.

I was twelve when the Berlin Wall came down in November 1989. I still remember quite vividly sitting with my family watching the television and seeing those extraordinary scenes. I'm sure I didn't understand the politics, but I did understand what a significant moment it was. For the whole of my life, the German Democratic Republic (East Germany) and the Federal Republic of Germany (West Germany) had been two countries, and now they were on the way to becoming one, and I could see from those scenes on the television what a historic and emotional thing that was. It was then that my interest in the Cold War was sparked, and when, many years later, I began writing novels, I knew that one day I would write a Cold War story. This is it.

Though my novel is entirely fictional, it is inspired by a number of real-life themes and events. I chose to write about a female spy after reading *Agent Sonya* by Ben Macintyre, the true story of a German Jew and committed communist who was a Soviet military intelligence officer before, during, and after World War II. For a time, Ursula Kuczynski (code name Sonya) lived in Oxfordshire in the UK (where I grew up) and was a handler for several important informants, extracting information that changed the course of history. She went undetected partly because she was a woman, a wife, and a mother; according to Macintyre, the only person to see through this happy housewife cover was another woman, MI5 officer Milicent Bagot, but her suspicions went unheard among her male colleagues.

My character Greta informs (albeit reluctantly) not for the Soviet Union's KGB but for East Germany's Stasi, which also carried out spying operations in Britain. In his book on the subject, *The Stasi Files*, historian Anthony Glees says the UK-focused aims of the HVA, the Stasi's foreign intelligence arm, were to obtain British political and military secrets, information it could use to repress dissidents in the GDR, and intelligence on British organisations that had an impact on GDR affairs, including Amnesty International. Glees notes the case of an East German woman who married a British citizen and moved to the UK in 1988, where she became a "talent spotter" for potential Stasi informants. It was the spark of truth I needed to create my own Stasi informer in Britain.

Though the KGB and Stasi were separate security agencies, they worked closely together. According to Glees, from the early 1970s onwards, around half of the intelligence gathered by the HVA went to the Soviet Union. It therefore seemed quite plausible to me that Greta's final mission, now as a double agent for British domestic counter-intelligence and security agency MI5, could unearth KGB illegals (deep-cover spies, as opposed to "official" spies with diplomatic cover) working in cahoots with the Stasi—with potential lifelong ramifications. In his autobiography *Man Without a Face* (written with Anne McElvoy), Markus Wolf, who headed the HVA, wrote: "It amazes me that otherwise intelligent Westerners believed they remained masters of their own destiny. No co-operation with an intelligence service is ever forgotten. It can be unearthed and used against you until your dying day."

Informers and the Stasi Files

Thanks to an estimated ninety-one thousand employees and some two hundred thousand unofficial collaborators (informers), the Ministry for

State Security, or Stasi, was able to keep tabs on the East German population, compiling files on around 5.5 million East Germans as well as half a
million Westerners during its forty years of existence. The aim was control: to understand the thoughts and actions of the population in order to
efficiently nip dissent in the bud. Informers weren't only encouraged to
report anti-state behaviour and opinions, but to relate details about people's everyday lives and habits—which parties and pubs they frequented,
who they were having an affair with, who their friends were, what their
weaknesses and desires were—that could potentially be used against
them if the need arose. The Stasi also bugged people's homes, read their
letters, tapped their phones, and even stole clothes from suspected trou-
blemakers, which they kept in jars, creating a sort of smell catalogue that
could be used if ever someone needed to be hunted down by sniffer dog.

After the Berlin Wall fell, Stasi employees in the Lichtenberg headquarters tried to destroy the millions of files they'd accumulated. They
were only partially successful—their poor-quality East German shred-
ders broke down so they turned to ripping up pages by hand, until brave
civilians stormed the building and put a stop to it. Nevertheless, millions
of pages had already been torn up, stuffed into around sixteen thousand
bags. Since the 1990s, first a dedicated agency and now a federal body
called the Stasi Records Archive—housed in the former Stasi HQ—has
been trying to reconstruct and index the hand-torn files with the help of
"puzzlers" who painstakingly piece together the scraps. So far, some 1.7
million pages from six hundred bags have been manually reconstructed.
Every individual has the right to view the file the Stasi held on them—if
it still exists—and find out who might have informed on them. Inciden-
tally, almost all the files relating to the HVA were destroyed.

Portland Spy Ring

The arrest of Olaf and two KGB illegals was very loosely inspired by the
Portland spy ring in 1961. For many years British couple Harry Hough-

ton and Ethel Gee, who had desk jobs at a naval base in Portland, UK, passed British naval secrets to the Soviets by travelling up to London on the weekends, ostensibly to take in a show, and handing over their stolen materials to their contact, a KGB illegal posing as a Canadian business-man called Gordon Lonsdale. Following a tip-off from a Polish defector, MI5 officers followed the couple on their regular trips to London and arrested them near the Old Vic theatre as they were passing documents to Lonsdale. The operation also uncovered two more Soviet illegals living in the London suburb of Ruislip, an American communist-sympathising couple with the cover names Peter and Helen Kroger, who would send the information they received from Lonsdale back to Russia. Houghton and Gee were sentenced to fifteen years in prison, while the others were later exchanged in prisoner swaps with Russia.

Amnesty International and "Prisoners of Conscience"

Amnesty International's principal concern regarding the GDR during the 1980s was the imprisonment of so-called prisoners of conscience—meaning political prisoners involved in nonviolent protest. That included people who had attempted to leave the country without permission; peo-ple who had persisted in applying to leave even after being denied per-mission; people who had helped others flee the country, including West German "escape helpers"; and those who criticised the government. Glees estimates that from 1949 to 1989, about 250,000 people were imprisoned for political offences. Around 25,000 of those died in prison, while some 33,755 were bought by the West under the scheme unofficially known as *Freikauf*, in which West Germany negotiated the release of political prisoners by essentially paying ransom money—which, by the 1980s, economically troubled East Germany badly needed.

Though the GDR tried to keep this human trade under wraps when *Freikauf* began in 1963, by the 1980s it was common knowledge, so much so that—like my character Lena—some East Germans got themselves arrested deliberately in the hope they might be deported. An Amnesty International country briefing from 1980 notes the case of a man who had tried repeatedly but unsuccessfully to obtain permission to emigrate to West Germany. In 1978, he walked up to the Berlin Wall and told the guards he was looking for a way through. As he hoped, he was duly arrested, sentenced to a year in jail, and after eight months was allowed to emigrate.

Amnesty didn't openly condone *Freikauf* because it feared it could incentivise the GDR authorities to arrest people simply to "sell" them to the West. However, neither did it condemn the scheme, since it did lead to the release of prisoners it was trying to help. The organisation's main focus was to put pressure on the GDR authorities to cease violations of human rights, hoping that would have a deterrent effect on future arrests.

Many political prisoners awaiting trial were sent to Hohenschönhausen Prison, which is now open to the public and which I visited when researching this book. According to my guide there, the authorities largely kept the prison a secret. Its location was scrubbed from city maps, the streets around it were restricted, and prisoners were taken there in a windowless van which travelled such a circuitous route that they wouldn't know if they were still in Berlin or many miles away. However, people I spoke to who grew up in the GDR in the period I've written about did know of the prison's existence at the time, so I decided to reflect that in my story.

The Salisbury Poisoning

Another true event that has provided context for this book is the poisoning in 2018 of former Russian spy turned British double agent Sergei Skripal and his daughter, Yulia, in Salisbury. They both survived, but the incident had tragic consequences for Salisbury resident Dawn Sturgess, who died when she encountered traces of the poison months later. At the time it seemed extraordinary to me that such a thing could happen on British soil nearly forty years after the end of the Cold War, and it only suggested, as the fatal poisoning of Alexander Litvinenko had in 2006, that perhaps it never really ended. As more recent events continue to show, today's world isn't so far removed from those Cold War days as we might have assumed.

Acknowledgments

This has been by far the most difficult book I've written (it doesn't seem to get easier!), and I'm grateful to all the people who have helped me get it to this point.

Firstly, thank you to those who shared their memories of growing up in the German Democratic Republic: Antje Kunert, Anna Petra George, Ines Bialas, and Christian Klaue. It was a privilege to hear your fascinating stories. While the experiences and viewpoints of GDR citizens obviously varied hugely and I couldn't possibly capture them all, I hope I have given some sense of life in East Berlin in the early 1980s. Antje, thank you for reading a draft and pointing out things I hadn't got right. Any remaining errors are my own.

Thank you to Ian Sanders for putting me in touch with Antje and for creating such a fascinating podcast series called Cold War Conversations—readers, I urge you to give it a listen! To my friends Sylvia Koller and Michaela Dignard for helping me set up interviews with Anna, Ines, and Christian, and for providing German language support. To historian Anthony Glees for answering my questions so speedily and willingly. To Malcolm Mathieson, archivist at Amnesty International, for being so generous with your time and providing me with a wealth of original documents detailing AI's actions towards East Germany. And to

Acknowledgments

longtime Amnesty member Heather Radmore for telling me what actually goes on in a meeting and for your valuable feedback.

Researching the period has been utterly fascinating, and, as well as the books mentioned in my Author's Note, I'd like to acknowledge and recommend the following: *Red Love* by Maxim Leo; *Born in the GDR* by Hester Vaizey; *Beyond the Wall, East Germany 1949–1990* by Katja Hoyer; *Stasiland* by Anna Funder; *Letters Over the Wall* by David Strack; *Tunnel 29* by Helena Merriman; *The Saddled Cow* by Anne McElvoy.

I also owe thanks to the cast of talented craftsmen and women in the BBC television show *The Repair Shop* for inspiring the character of Henry and sparking my desire to write about the way inanimate objects can embody incredible stories and evoke special memories.

As always, I want to thank my agent, Hayley Steed, who believed in this book from the beginning, who replies reassuringly quickly to my emails and is such a reliable, calm, and supportive person to have on my side in this crazy business. To my acquiring editor Sarah St. Pierre, thank you for seeing into the heart of this novel and providing such insightful comments and advice that helped me shape it into the story it has become. To Brittany Lavery, thank you for picking up the process so smoothly and helping me dig deep to find the final pieces of the puzzle to make this jigsaw of a book work. And to the rest of the team at S&S Canada, along with cover designer Jessica Boudreau and copy editor Nora Reichard, thank you so much for your dedication and hard work. I'd also like to thank the international publishers and translators who have brought my books to readers in different countries. It is a complete thrill to see my words in other languages and know that they are reaching new readers.

A huge thanks to my author friends who are always there to both commiserate and celebrate with, as the case may be, and all those who have read, endorsed, and shouted about my books. Being an author means enduring a maelstrom of emotions, and I'm so glad to be on this journey with others who understand.

Big thanks also to my friends and enthusiastic readers Sarah Green,

Acknowledgments

Rachel Bender, Mari Campbell, and Emma Hartwell; to my sister, Steph, and dad, Graham, for always wanting to read what I write; to my partner, Matt, for constant reassurance and for helping me brainstorm my way out of many a plot hole, as well as all the other friends and family members who have read my books and encouraged me along the way. Lastly, to all the readers and bloggers who supported my first two books. I write because I love it, but it's the cherry on the cake to know that others enjoy my stories. I hope you like this one, too!

About the Author

CAROLINE BISHOP is a freelance journalist, copywriter, and the author of three novels: *The Day I Left You*, *The Other Daughter*, and *The Lost Chapter*. For the past fifteen years, she has written on topics such as travel, food, and craft for many publications, including *The Guardian*, Lonely Planet, and *BBC Travel*. A British Canadian, she currently lives in Switzerland.